The Winds Of Revenge

The deadliest enemy may lurk in the least expected place

Julie McCullough

PROLOGUE

Bitterness of the coffee paled in comparison to the bitterness in his heart. *Someone must pay.* The man sat at his table, fresh steaming mug in one hand. He brought it to his lips, opened the newspaper and took a noisy sip. It burnt his mouth and throat but satisfied his taste. Another slurpier sip and another page turned. The warm liquid hit his stomach and its rush of caffeinated energy sped throughout his tense body.

He grunted. As usual nothing much worth reading in the paper. *Why bother buying it?* He closed it up. *But it helped fill the long, lonely days.* He grabbed the bottom corner, flung it open at a random page and gulped in a sharp breath.

A large headline and accompanying photo leapt out at him. He swallowed hard and coughed. Droplets of hot coffee shot from his mouth and nose showering the newspaper. He put the cup down and coughed again. His eyes watered and stung. Wiping them with the back of his hand, everything in front of him blurred.

His breath came in gasps, forcing him to cough harder and burning his throat. He got up, grabbed a used glass from the sink and filled it, downed several mouthfuls, and sucked in a long, deep breath. Blinking the blurriness away, one more cough cleared his throat. He clunked the glass back onto the sink and stared at the open newspaper.

He needed to read the article, but his hands seemed glued to the bench edge. His heart rate galloped up several notches. *Just go and read it!*

Hands let go and with two strides he was on the chair once again, eyes never leaving the printed article that horrified him to the very core. What his mate, Graz, had told him *was* true. The larger headlines shimmered before his eyes but hit like a ramrod through his gut and turned his heart to cold black ice.

'GRAZIER'S SON BACK FROM THE DEAD AFTER FIVE YEARS'

His gaze flickering from the headline to the picture, he studied the scarred man who looked to be lying in a hospital bed. A grotesque, angry hulk of a man. Why the hell should the doctors save him? He deserved everything he got, and more. Another photo beside that one showed him before he disappeared. A good-looking man. *Too bloody good looking.*

The man reached over dirty mugs, condiments, newspapers and scattered mail, for his glasses. Once he slid them on, he focussed on the smaller print of the article. With coffee forgotten, icicles prickled up his spine and out to his trembling fingertips. He clenched his clammy hands and fingers into a fist either side of the opened newspaper, his stomach churning to thick soup.

'*After five heart-wrenching years, well known Anchor Bay district graziers, Bruce and Linda Atkinson, had all but given their missing son Steve up for dead, but he has been found alive and living as a recluse deep in the bush an hour's drive from Anchor Bay. He'd simply vanished from home, taking nothing and leaving no explanation. Extensive police searches and private investigations had continued to find nothing.*

Sadly, Steve now appears to have total amnesia of any previous life and severe head and facial scarring from a horrific acid attack he barely recalls. Police sources inform us that Steve (or Seth, as he believed his name was) had been forced to work for wanted criminal mastermind, James McTaggart, who was recently shot dead in his cattle duffing operation of Bruce's cattle.

Ironically, if Steve had not found his injured sister, Grace, wondering lost in the bush after a fiery car accident, he may still be considered gone forever. He took her to his secluded house and nursed her back to health, unaware she was his sister. Due to his amnesia, increased bulk and scarring Grace did not recognise him as her brother until she'd been there almost a week. By then the police were staking the cattle heist and, even though Steve absconded on horseback they were able to track him down from one of the other men in the rustling ring disclosing his exact address.

Steve, a former rodeo champion and excellent marksman, refused to go quietly with police and attempted taking his own life rather than being arrested. Ignoring the danger and unaware she was believed dead, Grace ran to Steve's aide, shielding him from a possible police bullet once he'd turned his pistol toward police.

In a touching scene, surrounded by police officers, Grace revealed he was really Steve and she welcomed the reunion of Steve, her father Bruce, herself and her long-time boyfriend, Kain Burrows, who'd also initially believed Grace had died, due to the mistaken identity and severe burns of the driver of Grace's car.

In a further twist to this bizarre story, Kain had doubts over the identity of the body and, with the help of friends, had searched in rugged bushland for days for the love of his life. In a happy twist, Grace and Kain are expecting a baby. The Atkinson family is-'

"Enough!" The man squeezed his eyes shut and swiped the newspaper off the table with such force the pages separated and scattered about the floor. His coffee mug fell on its side spilling the now lukewarm coffee across the tabletop. His huge fist slammed down. Empty cups jumped and rattled for a second.

He inhaled deeply, his large chest rising. An inferno of rage boiled in his stomach, bringing sour acid to his throat. Swallowing it back down, he shook his head, running his hand through his short, thinning hair. This mushy, happy story was just not right. He'd read enough of the utter bullshit.

Just! Not! Right!

CHAPTER 1

"Steve, did you hear me?"

"Huh? Oh, sorry Doc." Steve focused his eyes and mind on the tall, lanky doctor standing by his hospital bed. "Umm..." He shook his head. It was almost impossible to think straight anymore. So much had happened in the past days. The two biggest things, learning his true identity and that Grace, his only friend, was his sister.

The doctor removed his wire rimmed glasses with one hand and rubbed his tired-looking eyes with the other. "I was just explaining the test results that have come back and was about to tell you what will happen next." He put his glasses back on, sat on the chair next to Steve's bed, crossed his long legs and leaned forward a little. "Do you need to rest? I can come back later."

"No, I'm all right. Still trying to get my head around everything. The hardest part is getting used to being called 'Steve'." He shrugged one shoulder. "Just doesn't sound like me."

"I understand". The doctor leaned back in his chair. "This is a very unusual situation and from all accounts, you are a very lucky man."

"Ha! You think so? I have no idea of who I am or of my life, I have no friends and I don't know my family." His heart flitted a moment. "Oh, except Grace." That fleeting pleasurable few seconds disappeared, replaced by a heavy weight in his chest and a gut full of dread. "My father hates me, the cops will put me in jail and throw away the key and," he sucked in a deep breath, hoping to ease the vice gripping his chest, "if that's not bad enough, I have no doubt one of Scott's men will come after me." He swallowed the lump of fear wedged in his throat. "Wish they'd just shot me that day."

The doctor scratched his chin, and his forehead creased. He seemed unsure what to say.

Steve covered his face with his hands for a moment, wishing he wasn't so angry toward someone trying to help him. "Sorry".

"We'll have a hospital counsellor and psychotherapist work with you. I can really only help you with the physical side of things."

To his credit, the doctor's patience remained intact and calm. Seth tried to tell himself to do the same. He intertwined his hands and fingers on his belly and looked at the doctor. "I know, and again, I'm sorry. Please tell me everything. I'm listening."

The doctor cleared his throat and glanced at the clipboard he held. "Okay. Well, so far the blood tests and x-rays have come back clear. We'll need to do some more extensive tests on your brain though, to determine why you have the blackouts or fainting spells. Can you tell me what emotional state you're usually in when you fall unconscious?"

Steve frowned. "How should I know? I don't realise it's happened until afterwards."

"Yes, I understand, but can you just think about it for a minute." He glanced at his watch and back to Steve with a warm smile. "No rush."

The last time he'd collapsed was when the police had him surrounded with all guns pointed toward him. He'd just wanted to die. They should have put him out of his misery there and then. A shudder swept through his body. If only he could forget everything since that morning. Steve closed his eyes. It was easier to concentrate.

The doctor's steady breathing combined with the whirring of a trolley being wheeled past his hospital room. Voices came from the nurses' station just down the hall. A buzzer sounded. A phone rang. A slight hint of disinfectant smell wafted into his sterile room. A world away from the wonderful fresh air in the bush.

His parents had insisted on him being admitted to the private hospital, at their expense. He liked the privacy of his own room, but it was nothing compared to the peace and quiet of his home beyond the mountain range. These foreign hospital sounds kept him on edge. They hurt his ears and seemed so loud. He just wanted to go home. Dingo howls, insects chirping, but mostly bird songs were the most common sounds back home. Home...

"Steve."

He jolted and opened his eyes, having forgotten for a moment what the doctor had asked him.

"I thought you'd fallen asleep." The doctor chuckled.

"Umm, almost." Steve breathed in deep and sat himself up a bit higher in the bed. "The last time was when the police were going to shoot me and I wished they would, so I was pretty stressed and scared."

"Fair enough. Can you remember other times?"

"Yes, the time before that was after – ." He stopped himself just in time before blurting out about burying the man the horse had killed at Scott's cattle yards. Phew. Nothing had been said about that yet. Hopefully it never will. A familiar sick feeling settled in his stomach. "After a conversation with Scott...I mean *James McTaggart*, about the cattle duffing job he forced me to do." Steve's heart *ba-boomped* louder in his chest. He sucked in a slow, long breath, hoping to calm it and hoping the doctor couldn't hear it. If so, he'd probably know he'd just lied. "So, I suppose I was pretty stressed and scared then, too." He reached for his glass of water on the bedside table and drank the lot, hoping it'd help his dry mouth.

The doctor watched him, without so much as a twitch or a blink.

"Why are you staring at me so hard, Doc?" It was hot, but a sudden chill washed over his body, leaving him with an uneasy feeling, like he was on display. He pulled the white blanket up to his chin.

The doctor smiled and shook his head. "Sorry, I didn't mean to. It's just that you must have an amazing story to tell, if only you could remember it all."

"If only I could *forget* it all." He would love to completely forget the pain of his beating and the acid burning his skin. He would love to forget the taunts and abuse from people in the streets. He would love to forget the lonely aching need for a friend or a lover. Most of all, he'd love to forget ever meeting Scott and the horrible jobs Scott forced on him. Those evil eyes. He'd never forget those cold, murderous eyes.

Steve swallowed the sour that had ascended from his stomach at the horrific memories flooding his brain. The drink of water hadn't helped his bitter, dry mouth. Maybe it was coming from his heart. His heart that had pounded in fear and dread more times than he could count but had found warmth and goodness when Grace had unexpectedly come into his life.

When she was at his home, his heart had skipped and jumped in ways he'd never known since losing all past memory from the beating. It had swelled with love and pride when she'd smiled at him or thanked him for some little thing he'd done for her.

But then, his heart shattered and ripped apart when she revealed he was her brother and that nothing could ever be between them. *It never would have anyway, you idiot. She was too good for the likes of you!* That annoying inner voice continued to haunt him. How he'd love that gone from his pathetic life for good.

To top it all, his father, Bruce, revealed he'd hated him for years, blaming him for the death of Steve's twin brother, Jon, when they were little. If his father had hated him this long nothing would change that now. Or would it? Could it?

His father's hard and disbelieving eyes had stared at him when Grace revealed his true identity. Stared at him with nothing but disgust and shock, not one little flicker of love or relief.

And Grace. She pitied him more than anything. The past days spent lying in this hospital bed had given him plenty of time to think. For sure, she loved him. After all, he was her brother, but it was so dammed hard thinking of her as a sister. He didn't know what that felt like anyway. She loved Kain, that was clear. Kain, who'd stood up for him when a slob had abused him while fuelling up at the servo. And now they're having a baby. It's Kain's arms she lies in at night and Kain's lips she kisses. *Stop!*

"Argh". Steve clenched his teeth and slammed the heels of his hands into his temples.

The doctor jumped up and leaned forward. "Are you in pain?"

"No." Steve wiped an escaping tear and swallowed back more threatening to flow. "Not physical, anyway." His tense shoulders sagged down into the pillows. "I don't want to talk about this anymore, Doc."

"That's fine. We'll leave that for now." He returned to the chair, crossing his legs again. "There is something else I want to discuss with you. It's about your facial surgery."

Steve jerked his gaze toward the doctor and his heart lightened. The possibility, no matter how remote, of being able to look normal again eased the tension in his mind and body. *Don't get your hopes up too high.* "Yep. I'm all ears."

What a *stupid* thing to say. He brought his hand to his left ear a moment, or what remained of his left ear, and scolded himself in silence.

"We've been working with your parents to secure a top plastic surgeon to work on your scarring. Your father insisted on only the best surgeon for the job."

"Hmph, probably his guilty conscious." Steve sucked in a deep breath and blew it out between his lips.

"Regardless." The doctor shrugged. "Don't knock it."

"You're right and I *am* grateful. I just don't understand why he's bothering if he hates me so much."

"I'm sure deep down your father loves you. Maybe he just can't express it. Some people show love in actions rather than words." The doctor stared at him again.

Steve wished his hat was on so he could pull it down over his head and face. Lying in the hospital bed left him too exposed. Too many curious medical staff, looking, touching and asking so many bloody questions, but most of all, *staring.* "Why do you keep staring at me?" His anger and frustration rose, but he remained calm. No point causing a scene.

"This may be a little unorthodox, but my sister has recently completed her journalism degree and is looking for stories of human interest to submit to magazines and newspapers. Any chance you'd be interested in being her subject?"

"What? No!" The thought of yet another stranger probing his confused and unsettled mind horrified him to the core. He turned away and stared at the blank wall on the opposite side of the room, afraid he'd explode if he continued looking at the doctor.

"Okay, I'm sorry about that. I should have realised it was too much too soon."

Steve turned back but couldn't think of a reply so just grunted.

"Back to the surgery, then." The doctor lifted the top page on the clipboard and read the page beneath for moment. "Basically, to cut a long story short, a leading Brisbane plastic surgeon, Doctor Thebo, has agreed to cut his annual holiday a bit short to operate on you later this week."

Steve nodded, unsure what to say. He hadn't expected anything to happen so soon. "Umm, that's good. Will he do it here in Anchor Bay?"

"No, you'll have to go down to Brisbane, I'm afraid. That was one of his conditions because he'd prefer to work in his own practice with his own staff. From all accounts you'll be in the best hands."

"How will I get to Brisbane?" A terrible thought of him spending a God-knows-how-many-hours trip in a car with his father, festered in his stomach and threatened to dislodge his breakfast. *Please, no.*

"You'll be flown down in the aerial ambulance, I imagine."

"Why can't I just leave the hospital and go by normal plane? I feel all right. I'm sick of being cooped up in here." He glanced out his window. Two magpies played and flitted about in a tree, only some thirty metres or so away. Their beaks open, he assumed they were warbling their beautiful song but he couldn't hear it. The window glass must be too thick. Oh, how he missed that soothing sound.

Grace. His throat constricted in disgust at how he'd kept her locked in. Now he understood how she must have felt. And the fear. Her terrified face when she awoke and first saw his horrible, scarred face and huge bulk standing over her. Fear of what lay ahead. But it was for her own good at the time and she eventually realised he meant her no harm. Injured from the car accident, she'd needed nursing back to health, and, just maybe, become his friend. She needed to also get over the cold-hearted dumping by Kain. What an idiot he was to hurt her like that. Then he'd heard on the radio she was believed dead but kept that from her, otherwise she would have tried to escape for sure.

"No, Steve, we can't release you until the police investigation is done and they decide what, if any, charges will be laid against you. I'm sorry, I would have preferred the police tell you that themselves, but that's how things stand at the moment."

An elephant weight dropped on Steve's chest and stomach, squeezing life out of him. For a minute he'd forgotten about the police and his crimes, but hearing those words hit hard. It was just all too much. A dry stone wedged in his throat, forcing tears to his eyes. He wanted to cry. Wanted to curl up in a ball and howl his eyes and lungs out. Wanted to shout and throw things across the room. Instead, he clenched his fist, swallowed hard and wished Grace was here. She'd make him feel better.

His heart and soul ached to be back in the peaceful bush, surrounded by animals...and Grace. Grace who understood him. But he didn't deserve that. Didn't deserve to live in peace after the terrible crimes he carried out for Scott. Now he must lie here and wait for the medical reports, wait for the police, wait to see if his angry father will visit. The father who glared at him with contempt.

"Then there's your amnesia that has to be addressed, but you shouldn't need to be in hospital for the recovery part anyway. Familiar settings, familiar people and familiar things are the best for treating amnesia, depending on what initial tests show. Specialised personnel will work on that with you." The doctor hesitated a moment. "I'm sorry this is upsetting you."

"How long will I have to be in Brisbane for?" He tried to focus on one thing at a time, and the surgery seemed the main thing for now. The main thing he wanted, that was possible, anyway.

"I can't tell you that. It will depend on how the surgery goes." He nodded. "I'm sure some of your family will be there for support."

"I hope it's my mother." She didn't seem to have any problems with him. She looked at him with nothing but love in her eyes and would cry when she'd arrive to visit him and cry when she had to leave. He felt comfortable with her.

"And Sophie". His little sister. She cared too, that was obvious. During visits, she'd tell him stories of when they were younger and laugh at funny things he'd apparently done. It warmed him inside to be assured how much he'd been missed and how much they loved him, but it was all a blank. A total blank.

It was just all stories about some bloke called Steve, as far as he was concerned. Sometimes the stories bored him, but he'd nod or shake his head or ask the odd question to let Sophie think he was interested. Not one fleeting thought or speck of feeling connected him to those stories. Perhaps it was better that way.

Maybe he needed to distance himself from his family a bit. Forget about trying to get his memory back. Just move on and stay away from them. Seeing Grace only hurt him, but she was the only person that really knew him. Knew him as Seth. He preferred to remain as 'Seth'.

"I'm sure whoever you wish to have accompany you and be there for you, will be, Steve."

"What's your sister's name?"

The doctor took a second take, his brows creased as if he hadn't heard correctly.

"The journalist." Steve folded his arms across his chest. "I just decided I will meet her, but *after* the surgery."

"Oh, it's Jenna. And for what it's worth, I think she should meet you before your surgery. There's nothing to be afraid of, Steve. She won't judge you. She's level-headed and has a heart as big as Queensland."

"If you say so." He glanced at the doctor then straight ahead at nothing. It couldn't hurt to meet a new person and take his mind of Grace and his father and the police and...

"Good on you. I'll call her tonight and see if she can come in sometime in the next day or so."

"What's your name, Doc? You've probably told me, but I can't remember." He turned toward the doctor.

"Doctor Tim Leeson."

"Oh, that's right." Steve held out his right hand. The doctor returned the offer of the handshake, brief but warm. "I'll try to remember from now on."

"Okay, so, as it stands, the plastic surgeon will be calling me in the next couple of days to finalise things and he'll also be in touch with your parents. We'll be taking numerous photos of your scarring and sending them to him, so he knows what he's dealing with."

"Just as long as I don't have to see the photos. I never want to have to see this again." Steve pointed to his face. "Bad enough having to look at my fingers." He dropped his hand and expelled a long breath. "I just want the surgery done so I can start to look a bit normal."

"You will most likely need more than one surgery."

"*What!*" Steve's shoulders tensed.

Doctor Leeson held up his hands in a 'stop' mode and shook his head. "Woo back. I'm not an expert in this field, but until Dr Thebo has examined you or at least studied the photos we send, he won't know for sure what or how much surgery will be needed. Let's just wait until he checks it all out, shall we?"

Steve sunk back down into the pillows, groaned and stared at the ceiling. Was there not one bit of his pathetic life he had any control over?

"In the meantime, you can meet Jenna and chat to her. Who knows, she may even be able to help you regain some of your memories. Then once the surgery is done and you're feeling up to it, the psychotherapist can work with you to get your old life back."

The doctor smiled like he had all the answers in the world. Well, it just wasn't *that* simple. "What if I refuse to work with the psycho...psychotherapist? Is that how you say it?"

Dr Leeson's jaw dropped and his forehead furrowed deep. "Why...why would you *not* want to work at getting your memory and life back? I don't understand."

With heart pumping faster and his mouth drying to desert sand, Steve glared at him. "Of course you don't friggin' understand. *Nobody* does. And I'm just a nobody. Out there in the bush, I *was* someone. I was Seth Andrews. I just preferred to be left alone to live among the trees and animals. Here, I don't know *who* or *what* I am, and I have no control of anything at all. Yes, I want my ugly face fixed, but I don't want to get my memory back."

"Calm down, Steve. You're just upset at the moment. It's all been a bit much."

"Yes it has and I've had enough. You can tell your psycho-*whatever* not to bother. Once I get my face fixed I'm either going to jail or back to the bush. Either one, I *don't* need to remember a thing as Steve Atkinson. Nothing! Got it?"

CHAPTER 2

Grace gripped her phone. "Ok, thanks Doctor Leeson. Tell Steve I'll be up to see him later."

"Can do. He'll be pleased to see you, Grace. You seem to be the only one who can get through to him."

"Yes, well hopefully that *will* change. Thanks again for keeping me up to par with everything. Bye." Grace cut off the call and glanced at Kain watching the traffic light, waiting for it to turn green. His 'Adam's Apple' moved as he swallowed hard. His knuckles white on his hands clutching the steering wheel. Even though it was a cooler, cloudy day, beads of sweat coated his forehead, temples and top lip. No doubt his nerves were kicking in during the drive to his doctor.

Should she tell him what the doctor said about Steve's state of mind? It might help him get his mind off the cancer and what Doctor Burns may or may not be about to tell him.

"That was Steve's doctor."

No response.

Grace raised her voice a little. "*Kain.*" The light turned green and Kain planted his foot. With eyes focussed on the road ahead he roared the vehicle forward. Maybe it was just the extra noise of his ute with the windows down that left him unable to hear her.

Grace placed her hand on his thigh and watched his handsome face. She was still getting used to his extra short hair after he'd shaved it in preparation for it falling out from chemotherapy he expected to receive. She used to love running her fingers through his blond waves. Her love for this man swelled her heart, surged up her throat and out through her eyes. She blinked back the wetness and placed her other hand on her abdomen, protecting the new life growing within.

The last few weeks had certainly been a rollercoaster of emotions. For *both* of them. She'd been absolutely gutted when Kain had abruptly broken off their - what she'd thought was pretty much perfect - relationship with some ridiculous excuse of wanting to go out and *find himself.* He'd even told her he didn't love her anymore. That had hit her like a sledgehammer slung right into her heart.

While driving to get away for a break to recover from the shock and heartbreak, she'd let the hitchhiker she'd just picked up, drive so she could text Kain. But her car had veered off the Range Road and tumbled down, down until it exploded in a fireball. A fireball from which she'd been damned lucky to have been thrown clear.

The flames. The *smell.* The fear. Horrified and in pain, she'd miraculously scrambled away and run through the bush, hoping to find help but had been found, instead, by hungry wild dogs. Again, she'd feared her life was about to end.

She shivered, remembering the dogs chasing her during the storm, knowing she had no hope of outrunning them. Thank Goodness for Seth having seen her and shooting one dead. *I really must get used to thinking of him as Steve now.*

What had unfolded during the following week was more than she could have ever imagined. Or hoped for.

Injured and in pain, she'd been literally locked in Seth's house in the bush. Fear of him had slowly dissipated until she trusted him and, as much as the thought still horrifies her, even wondered if she felt something for him. They'd kissed. *Kissed!* No, she had to clear that from her mind. No-one must ever know *that*.

Shaking her head, her memory jogged over the days following, when discoveries in Seth's house made her wonder if he had murdered Steve. But more findings had her concluding he *was* Steve. How her head had whirled when that realisation hit.

She'd saved him from certain death when the police had arrived after the cattle duffing had been thwarted by the Stock Squad. But that wasn't the end of it. Oh no, more shocks were in store. When her dad, Bruce, had turned up, she'd proved to him that Seth was Steve. Instead of him being happy and relieved, he looked at Steve in absolute horror with his scarring and refused to believe he was his only son.

Only son. More shocks abounded. Bruce admitted Steve had had a twin brother, but he'd drowned when they were little and had never been acknowledged since. Bruce had also admitted that he blamed Steve for Jon's death, thus eventually driving Steve away. After extensive police and Private Investigator searches, the devastated family had to believe Steve was dead.

Grace's mind wouldn't slow down. The drive to Kain's doctor, with Kain barely speaking, gave her plenty of time to reflect.

And all the time she was in Seth's house, everyone thought she was dead, but not Kain. She squeezed his bare thigh gently. She wanted to undo her seatbelt and lean over to give him a hug and kiss but held back while he drove. No, Kain didn't give up on her, or *them*. While she was cursing him for dumping her and wishing him to hell, he, Joe and Anthony were out searching in the unforgiving and dangerous bush for her day and night, rain and sunshine.

When they'd turned up at Seth's house just after the police, she'd initially wanted to ignore Kain, too angry to deal with him. She recalled balling her fist and letting him have it. Her face flushed hot at that embarrassing memory. Luckily, Kain hadn't mentioned the incident, so hopefully he had forgotten all about it. *Wish I could.*

Then, of course, it was the shock of Kain admitting he broke it off because he had cancer and feared he'd die, leaving her alone and devastated. Silly bugger. As if she wouldn't want to be with him and help him through it. She *loved* and adored him with every speck of her body and soul.

She watched him driving, wishing she could read his mind. Wishing she could take away his worry and fear of the cancer and worse - his fear of the possible outcome. But he'd said Doctor Burns had assured him this sort of cancer can be cured if caught early, which he was confident of in Kain's case. *We'll soon find out.*

The most wonderful memory of all came to her mind. When the doctor in emergency had confirmed her suspicions – she was pregnant. Kain had nearly fallen over. He'd floated on cloud 99 afterwards. Stunned. Elated. Speechless.

That night, Grace's first night home since everything had happened, she and Kain had held each other and cried, laughed and then cried some more. An intense lovemaking reunion had later turned to a more relaxed and gentle time of holding and caressing.

Neither had wanted to let the other go. Neither had wanted to fall asleep, for fear sleep would take away the magic and fulfilment each felt. She'd cried when his gorgeous blue eyes had filled with tears, as he told her of his devastation of her presumed death, how he'd blamed himself and how he'd attempted to end his misery so he could be with her in heaven.

Yep, this bloke was a keeper, and never would she doubt his love for her again. She smiled, thinking how lucky she was to have him. But the smile died when a tear trickled down his cheek. She reached up, gently brushed it away with her thumb and stroked his cheek. "It's okay, honey, I don't blame you for being worried."

He glanced at her, gave a brief smile and turned back to the road. "I'm just so glad you're here with me, Grace." He shook his head several times. "What an idiot I was to think I was better off doing this alone and you'd be better off without me." He reached for her hand. Grace squeezed his clammy hand for a moment before he took it back, needing to change down gears to turn into the carpark of the doctor's surgery.

Kain found a park at the far end of the parking lot. He switched off the ignition, took a deep breath and rubbed both palms on the front of his shorts. Chewing his bottom lip, he turned to Grace. His lip trembled. His glassy eyes looked terrified.

Grace unclipped her seatbelt, leaned across and placed her hands on the sides of his face. "We're in this together now." She glanced down briefly at her stomach. "All three of us, okay. It will all be good. You'll see." Tears of love and fear stung her own eyes, but in the hope of Kain not seeing them, she leaned closer, closed her eyes, and brought her lips to his.

She kissed him gently, again marvelling at how amazing it was to be back with him. Drawing back only centimetres from his face, she opened her eyes. "I love you, Kain Burrows." The words came out in a raspy whisper, having forced their way past the wedge in her throat.

Kain's stared deep into her eyes. Deep into her soul. He seemed lost in thought. He grasped the back of her head, drew her to him again and kissed her long and deep before pulling back. Tears spilled from his eyes. "I love you too, Grace. More than you could ever know." He looked at her stomach and shook his head. "I still can't believe we're having a baby. A *baby.*" A short sob passed his lips as he laid his hand briefly on her abdomen.

Grace grabbed a tissue from her bag near her feet and wiped his eyes. He took it from her, blew his nose and breathed in long and deep, expelling the air through his mouth. Kain glanced over toward the entrance to the doctor's surgery. "Come on, then. Let's get this over and done with." He squeezed Grace's hand again.

She nodded and smiled a reassurance. "Yep, let's go. I'm sure Doctor Burns will have some good news for us."

"I wish I had your confidence." Kain pulled the keys from the ignition, opened his door and jumped out.

CHAPTER 3

"Kain Burrows."

Kain jolted back from where his mind had wandered while waiting to be called into Dr Burns' consulting room. Even with Grace by his side, her thigh touching his, her hand holding his, he had gone to a dark place of fear, dread, and death. The cancer had overtaken his body and he was imagining an array of coffins. Luckily, Dr Burns' deep voice had dispelled the depressing visions.

He and Grace jumped up and, still holding hands, followed the doctor into his room. Voices in the waiting area, a baby crying, a phone ringing in reception, all drowned out by the thumping of his heart, way up to his ears. He swallowed hard and squeezed Grace's hand tighter. Never in his life had he appreciated her love as much as now. No way in hell could he have gone through this alone. What an idiot he'd been for thinking he could and coldly driving Grace away with her heart shattered. He'd spend the rest of his life making it up to her. *The rest of my life? I hope that's a long time.*

Dr Burns indicated two chairs beside his desk. "Please have a seat." He held his right hand out to Grace. "I take it you are Grace?"

"Yes." Grace returned the firm handshake, feeling small beside the tall, bespectacled doctor. "Nice to meet you, Doctor Burns."

Kain and Grace sat. Kain took the chair closest to the doctor, loosened his tense shoulders up and down and blew a breath out his parched mouth, wishing he'd had a decent drink of water before coming in. "So, what's happening now, Doc?"

"Okay, I have your blood test results back from the other day." He sat on his chair and swivelled around to look at his desktop computer screen. "Oh, by the way, I wasn't impressed you ignored my advice recently to come in immediately then, but I saw on the news how you'd helped find Grace, so I don't blame you."

"Thanks." Kain took his trembling hand out of Grace's, wiped both palms on his shorts and replaced his hand in the comforting clasp of Grace's. "W-what did the tests show?" Stomach cramps grabbed his insides, threatening to send him to the toilet. He shifted in his seat, hoping they'd settle. Grace squeezed his hand tighter.

"Your tumour markers are slightly elevated. We-."

"What exactly does that mean?" A wave of fear and dread swept over Kain, like a swarm of bees. He tried swallowing it down, but the bees continued their swarming.

Dr Burns turned to him, intertwining his hands on his lap. "It wasn't unexpected. We know you have testicular cancer, but just not sure at what stage yet. Chances are it could still just be confined to your testicle, in which case, after surgery your prognosis will be very good."

Hearing those last three words slowed Kain's galloping heart to a steady canter. "A chance?"

"Yes, but we need to do further tests. I will refer you for a CT scan plus to the surgeon here at Anchor Bay hospital, but you will have to also see the oncologist at Mackay Cancer Centre." He turned back to his computer, mouse clicked a few things and silently read the screen for several seconds.

Kain watched the doctor and held his breath. Grace murmured several words, but he didn't comprehend what she'd said for the now returned thumping in his chest.

Dr Burns looked again at Kain. "Do you have any family history of testicular cancer?"

Kain shook his head. "No, none that I know of."

The doctor nodded and looked back at his screen. "The bloods showed slight levels of alpha-fetoprotein, beta human chorionic gonadotropin and lactate dehy-."

The big words jumbled Kain's brain. Big and *bloody* scary words. "Don't bullshit me with jargon, Doc." He threw his hands into the air. "It means nothing. Talk to me in plain English." Right then he could've punched the crap out of something. Grace laid a firm hand on his thigh.

Doctor Burns stared at Kain for a few seconds, his dark eyebrows conjoining in a deep frown. "Yes, I can do that. Sorry. You don't need further stress."

"I'm sorry too." Kain breathed deep and placed his arm around Grace's shoulders.

"Right, this is what will happen." He reached into a wall pigeonhole beside his desk for a form, placed it in his printer and began typing. "This is a referral for a CT scan you can have here, hopefully in the next day or so." The printer spat out the completed form. He circled a phone number on the left side in red pen. "Best I ring and make the appointment for you so they understand the urgency." He picked up his phone.

A lightning bolt of fear gushed through Kain's entire body at that word *urgency,* and he squeezed Grace's shoulder. She placed her hand on his thigh. He couldn't take his eyes off the doctor, but hundreds of thoughts sped through his mind. Some bloody terrifying.

Doctor Burns hung up, jotted something on the referral form and handed it to Kain. "Tomorrow morning, nine-thirty. Be there about ten minutes early."

"Thanks, Doc." Kain glanced down at the form. "Then what?"

"I'll send an e-mail through to the surgical department here in Anchor Bay. Just what surgery will be performed depends on your CT results." He pointed to the form in Kain's hand. "I've also asked for those results to be sent to the surgeon and also to the Mackay Cancer Centre along with a referral and your details. You'll be appointed an oncologist and someone will call you with an appointment time as soon as they have these results, okay?"

Kain nodded. No words came forth. His brain too swamped with questions and all sorts of scary jumble including the thought of losing a testicle. How is a man supposed to cope with that? He looked at Grace a moment, who wiped at her eyes. His eyes dampened as well, but no, he wouldn't let the fear make him cry. Blinking several times, he swallowed hard.

"Now," continued Dr Burns. "Do you have any questions?"

Kain shrugged. "Hundreds, but they're all swirling around in my brain too much right now."

"That's understandable. It can all be quite daunting." The doctor's voice had softened. "Lots of good, factual information can be found on the Queensland Cancer Council website. They can also post out or email information to you. I'm not going to go into further treatment options and possible side effects with you, until we know exactly what we're dealing with, but the oncologist will go over all that with you anyway, if necessary."

"Thank you, Doctor Burns," said Grace.

He acknowledged Grace's gratitude with a smile and nod and looked back at Kain. "There is something you need to think about and talk to the oncologist about."

Kain leaned toward the doctor. "I don't like the sound of this. Why are you singling one thing out? Must be extra serious."

"You two are only young." He glanced from Kain to Grace. "I'm guessing you will want children one day."

"Yes," said Grace, her face breaking in a huge grin. "Actually, I am pregnant now. We just found out last week."

Kain looked briefly at her stomach and his thudding heart flushed with love.

"Oh good." Dr Burns smiled. "If, and I stress *if*, you need to have chemo, it *can* make you infertile, but not in all cases. You may want to think about having your sperm frozen for later on, if you want more children."

"That's a good idea." Grace looked at Kain. "Don't you think, hon?"

"Definitely."

"Right," announced the doctor. "You go and have that scan. I probably won't see you now for a while, because you'll be in the hands of the surgeon." He rolled his eyes. "No pun intended. And also the oncologist. But, by all means, come see me anytime you feel the need, but I would like to see you anyway in about a month or so, when your surgery is over, okay?"

Kain jumped up. "Thanks Doc, will do. Come on, Grace." He held her elbow as she stood and they headed out of the consulting room. He needed to get out of there. Needed fresh air. Needed to wake up from this nightmare.

Putting the keys in the ignition, Kain licked his dry lips and looked at his beautiful Grace in the passenger seat. Yet again, he mentally scolded himself for hurting her and thinking he could do all this alone.

For the umpteenth time Kain wiped his sweaty palms, but on his shirt this time and tapped his fingers on the steering wheel as he watched a woman walk out of the clinic crying. Maybe she just received bad news. What sort of news would he receive after this bloody scan? Would he cry? How the hell would he handle it? *Why* is this happening? *I'm too young!*

"You okay, darl?" Grace's warm, gentle hand rubbed his thigh.

Kain's stomach cramps returned. He gripped the steering wheel with one hand, pushed in the clutch and turned on the ignition with the other trembling hand. "Yeah, but the *shit* is about to get very real, Grace."

CHAPTER 4

Linda stood in the doorway of Steve's hospital room. He seemed asleep and so peaceful lying there, hands clasped on his rising and falling chest. But what horrors had her beautiful son suffered since he'd disappeared five years earlier? She drew her lips in, tear ducts threatening to overflow, and placed one hand on her chest hoping to ease the aching sadness in her heart. A mother's heart that had suffered the loss of three children, only to have two literally return from the dead. Except, this one came back a virtual stranger.

Her boy was in that scarred, angry exterior shell, of that she was certain, and she *would* find him again.

"Excuse me".

The voice startled her. She jolted and turned around. A young man stood right behind her holding a large camera. "Yes?" Linda cleared her throat, wiped a stray tear from one eye and took a small step back.

"I'm sorry." His young, bearded face looked worried. "I didn't mean to give you a fright. I'm Ben. I'm here to take some photos of Steve to send to the plastic surgeon.

Apparently, he wants them ASAP so he can get the job done."

"Oh, ok." Linda forced a smile. Although elated Steve would have his face restored as much as possible, knowing what a long, rough road lay ahead for him she didn't feel much like smiling. "Do you mind if I am in there while you take them? He might get upset."

"No, that's fine."

Ben walked into the room followed by Linda. Steve's eyelids fluttered, a low moan and a few mumbled words escaped his lips.

Doctor Leeson appeared at the door. "Good, you're here already, Ben. Take as many as you can, from different angles and come see me as soon as you're done." He glanced at Linda. "Oh, hello Mrs Atkinson. Ben, don't forget his chest and hands. Mrs Atkinson, I need to speak with you privately." He beckoned her to follow him out the door.

Linda looked back at Steve then to Ben. "Could you please wait a minute before you start?" He nodded with an understanding smile. She found the doctor standing several metres along the corridor but had to stop a moment as a nurse rushed past to answer beeping coming from the next room. "What is it, Doctor?" His solemn face too serious for this to be something minor. A niggling coil of dread unfurled in her stomach.

"I had a long chat with Steve this morning, about his condition and what is likely to happen."

"Yes-s-s...go on." Her heart rate increased. Tightness gripped her whole body.

"He was fine for a while then become agitated and adamant he *doesn't* want to regain his memory." His eyes widened. "At all!"

This didn't make any sense. Since Steve came back last week, believing himself to be called Seth, he'd shown no sign of not wanting his memory back. "I don't understand." Linda blinked back fresh tears. "What's going on?"

With a half-hearted smile, Dr Leeson gave a slight shrug. "I'm not sure. I think he just became overwhelmed with everything, and I suppose with being stuck in here when he's used to being out in the bush. He just wants to go back there but thinks he might end up in jail. He just doesn't want to be Steve Atkinson again, by the sounds." He touched Linda's forearm. "Perhaps you can have a chat to him and see if you can find out more."

"I will. Thankyou." Linda breathed in deep and walked back into Steve's room.

This wasn't going to be easy at all. If only Bruce was here to support her and their son. But he'd wanted to stay home while recovering from the gunshot wound to his leg. At least that's what he said, but his undertone hinted at something more. The thought of the rift between Bruce and Steve weighed her shoulders and heart down. Her broken family needed a lot of mending.

Steve was getting himself into a semi sitting position when she reached his bedside. "Oh...Mum." His eyes glistened among the facial scarring.

She took hold of one trembling hand but longed to hold him in her arms. "Hello, Steve. How are you feeling today?" She couldn't help brushing some hair away from the right side of his forehead. The left side of his head almost bald from the acid attack. Hurt and sadness only a mother could feel, balled up inside her. Even after days of seeing him like this she still couldn't believe this was her son. Her flesh and blood. How he must have suffered. He may be a large, grown man but she ached to hold and hug him, taking away all his pain. The back of her fingers wiped away the tear sliding down his cheek.

He nodded and shrugged one shoulder. "Yeah, as well as can be expected, I suppose. How are you?"

She pulled the chair close to his bed, sat and reached for his hand. Breathing deep, she was determined to remain strong for her son. "I'm good." A grin she didn't need to fake broke forth and her tense body relaxed a little. "I still can't believe you're back with us." She shook her head, not sure if she wanted to laugh or cry, but her eyes dampened anyway. "After *all* this time."

He frowned at her then his face softened. "I know. All seems like a weird, crazy dream." His face hardened again and his narrow eyes squinted to mere slits. "How's..." He looked away.

"Your father?" She spoke softly, all too aware of the strain and hurt between Steve and Bruce. She'd need to tread softly on this subject if they were ever going to be reconciled as father and son. How she hoped and prayed that was possible, and soon.

Steve let out a slight grunt she took as a yes, he was referring to his father.

Linda's mind raced. She had to word this just right. Bruce was having a hell of a time accepting all what had happened in the past week or so. First hearing of Grace's supposed death in such a horrific way, blaming Kain for the situation that led to her 'death' then he and Kain coming to blows. Bruce had hit the booze – something he hadn't done in a long time and, God, how she wished he'd *never* do.

The duffing of his cattle and discovering Grace alive and that one of the cattle thieves was his long-lost son, Steve, now a scarred amnesiac was enough, but to top it off, Kain had not only shown him up and proved him wrong about Grace still being alive but had accidently shot him in the leg. "His leg is getting better, but he still has trouble walking far and the pain is bad at times. The bullet must have done more internal damage than first thought. He'll be up to see you as soon as he can." Hopefully, that sounded convincing enough. He found it difficult facing his son, but Steve didn't need to know that although she could tell he sensed it.

Steve nodded and remained quiet with no further expressions on his damaged face. If only Linda could read his mind. She wished he'd open up to her more. She remembered how close they used to be. He'd come and tell her anything and everything and always valued her advice and opinion. Pretty clearly, she was going to have to chisel away at his mind and get to know him all over again.

Each day since he was found and admitted to hospital she'd come up and sat here by his bed. He never talked much, mostly just answering her questions in one or two words, but always listening as she'd tell him about his childhood and his love of rodeo riding including the many events he'd won...and some of the injuries he'd sustained. She'd brought in photos of family members and of him with his horses and his favourite dog, but there was never any hint of recognition.

One thing she was sure of – he missed his home and life back in the bush. She wanted to see that home, see where he'd been living or was it merely existing, but preferred to wait and let him take her there...if he would.

"Ahem".

Linda jolted and turned toward the voice. "Oh, I forgot about you." She got up. "I'll get out of your way." She stood near the door. "Do you mind if I stay in the room?"

"Of course you can." Ben smiled briefly at her and walked closer to the bed, fiddling with his camera. "Are you ready, Steve? This won't hurt a bit." He giggled like a nervous boy, but neither Steve nor Linda laughed. Ben's pale facial skin blushed pink.

Steve glanced at his mother. He seemed to want to say something. His eyes asked a silent question. Was that a slight hint of her boy looking to her for comfort? She smiled, nodded and gave him the thumbs up sign. This was just another step in his long road to recovery and she would travel that road with him, even if it was without her husband.

Steve lay silent and starred at the ceiling as Ben clicked away. Working quickly, he took dozens of photos of the front and left side of his face, zoomed up close and further back. He also took pictures of Steve's hands and mis-shapen fingers.

"Can you open your shirt, please? I was told to get some of your chest too."

"No!" Steve placed his hands together on his chest. "I don't care about my chest. I only want my face and head fixed." He looked at his fingers and wriggled a couple. "Maybe them too if possible, but tell 'em to forget about my chest."

Ben's face reddened again and he raised one hand, stepping back. "No worries." He looked at Linda. "Umm...well, okay, I'll get these to the doc. Thank you." He rushed out of the room.

Linda walked over to the bed and took Steve's hand in hers. "I think you made him a bit nervous." She smiled and squeezed his hand.

Steve gripped her hand tight. "Do I make *you* nervous?" His dark eyes glistened again.

"Never. Where is this coming from?" She sat on the chair, still holding his hand.

He stared out the window, quiet for several seconds. "Scott made me do some horrible things for him. I felt like the monster I look like. But I saw what happened to the blokes who disobeyed him. I had no choice." His bottom lip trembled.

Linda brought his hand to her mouth, kissed the back of it and held it against her cheek. Tears threatened and her heart pained for her son and his lost soul. "I don't care. I still love you just as much as ever. We'll do everything possible to get you back and make sure you aren't prosecuted. We'll get the best lawyer."

She certainly would try, but whether Bruce would agree, or care enough for that matter, was another thing.

CHAPTER 5

Grace walked into Steve's room. "Oh, Mum, you're here too. Good." Her mother's long, strawberry-blonde ponytail looked like it had been slept in. Not like her at all. Grace's hand involuntarily brushed the back of her own long hair.

Linda turned toward Grace, a surprised look on her face, stood and hugged her daughter. "How are you going, sweetie?"

"I'm okay, but you look tired." Her mum didn't just look tired. Worry and sadness also shrouded her face but that didn't need to be pointed out. What else could be expected from a mum who's coming to grips with everything that had happened with her and Seth, especially Seth...*Steve.* She *had* to get used to him being Steve.

"Hey Grace." Steve had sat up. He held out his hand and a huge smile lit up his face.

Linda let go of her daughter and stepped back, allowing Grace closer to Steve.

"You're looking good, big brother." Grace ignored his hand, leant down, placed her arms around his neck and hugged him tight, not really wanting to let go. It was *so* amazing having him back.

Steve let go first. "Okay, okay." He laughed a little. What a wonderful sound. "I'm not going anywhere... just yet anyway."

Grace blinked back tears and stood back a little. "What does that mean?" Surely he doesn't mean the police are taking him away. Her mouth dried and a wave of dread washed through her belly.

Steve's face remained bright. "It means that I'm going to have my face fixed. And soon. A bloke was just here taking photos to send to a plastic surgeon in Brisbane. By the sounds of it he can fit me in pretty much straight away."

The wave of dread dissipated, and Grace glanced at her mum. "Is that the Doctor Thebo you found?"

"Yes. He's supposed to be the best in Australia, but I would have sent my son anywhere in the world, if necessary, to have his face restored. I need to talk some more to Doctor Jensen about it, so I'll leave you two alone for now." She headed out the door but stopped and turned back. "Oh Grace, sorry, I almost forgot. How's Kain?"

Steve sighed and let out a slight grunt.

What was that about? Grace glanced from Steve, now staring at the window, back to Linda. "Oh, well... he's okay, I guess. Very worried and a bit more scared than he's letting on, I think. Poor darlin'. We've just come from his doctor who's setting up appointments and referrals to specialists and the Cancer Centre in Mackay. He's having a CT scan tomorrow then we go from there. He's just gone to talk to his boss, Eddy, to fill him in on everything and let him know he'll be needing time off work."

"Oh good. Okay my loves, see you both soon." She kissed her fingers, blowing it toward both her children in turn and disappeared as Steve turned and waved.

Grace pulled the chair close by the bed, sat down and reached to brush a few stray long, greying hairs from the right side of Steve's face. He smiled and rolled his eyes, clearly enjoying her fuss and attention. She rested her hands on Steve's forearm he'd placed by his side. "What was that sigh and grunt about just then?"

"What?" Steve looked away.

"When I mentioned Kain's name. You didn't sound happy hearing it."

Steve shrugged and remained silent.

She lowered her voice. "Steve, you have to let go of those feelings you had for me back in the bush, before we realised we're brother and sister. I'm going to help you all I possibly can, but I also need to be there for and *with* Kain. He's got a rough and scary road ahead of him."

Steve's large chest rose high and lowered slowly. His gaze bore straight into her. "I know. It's okay, Grace. It's just all so ... I don't know...confusing and frustrating and...I don't know what's ahead in the future. I don't know my past and the future frightens the hell out of me, too." He raised his hands in the air in defeat. "And as for the present. Lying here in this hospital bed is driving me insane." He pointed to the window. "I can't even hear any birds singing! I can't handle being stuck in here!" His voiced rose to an angry pitch. "If they're sending me to jail I just wish they'd tell me."

"Shhh." She took hold of his hand. "Look, we'll just take one day at a time, hey? The fact that the police haven't been back is a good sign."

"You think so?" Steve shook his head. "I don't."

"Yes, I do." She squeezed his hand. "The most important thing is getting you better and your face fixed and your memory back."

Steve grunted, withdrew his hand and folded his arms on his chest.

"You don't want to get your memory back?" Doctor Leeson had told her that but she didn't want Steve to know they'd talked about him. He may clam up, just like he did so often when he'd kept her in his secluded house.

"Nope!"

"But why? I, *we*, have missed you like crazy these past five years, Steve." The heavy, dull ache of losing her brother returned. How she'd cried and prayed many times he'd come back home one day. "You had a good life. You have lots of friends." Tears she could no longer control stung her eyes and spilled down her cheeks with the memories. "When the police closed the case and the private investigators gave up we held a memorial for you. Hundreds of people came. Every single one of them missed you and loved you in some way."

"Grace." He stared at the stark white ceiling, his voice raw but emotionless in defeat. "I don't know anything about that, or where I was at first, but it must have been some horrible place."

"But, don't you *want* to know? I would if it were me. Why don't you want to come back to us, Steve?" With both hands she wiped the wet sadness from her cheeks, only to have more follow. "*Please.* What about Mum? She has been through hell and even more than I realised since finding out about Jon drowning when you were both little." A loud sob cut through the thick uneasiness in the air. "And Dad. Wouldn't you like to just be part of a family again?"

"Grace, *STOP!*"

Grace jolted in her chair and gulped in a breath. She hadn't heard that sharp abruptness in his voice since he'd been found. It had frightened her several times at his house. "I'm sorry. I should have remembered you don't like being pressured." She pulled a tissue from the box on his bedside drawers, wiped her eyes, blew her nose and put the tissue in her pocket.

Steve adjusted his pillows until he was sitting up straight and looked her in the eye. "I'm sorry, too. I just scared you didn't I? Typical of the monster I am."

Grace's mind raced back to the day she regained consciousness in his home with him standing over her bed. His image had terrified her and his gruff, monosyllabic voice even more so. She didn't know what to say. She stared down at her hands in her lap. Silence enveloped them. An uncomfortable silence she hadn't expected.

"Look, I..." He fidgeted with the blanket covering the lower half of his body.

His softened voice eased her nerves and she took his hand again "Go on...Seth. Please tell me what you're thinking."

He didn't even acknowledge she'd called him the only name he knew. "I've given it a lot of thought and I don't want to remember my old life."

"But why? It doesn't make sense."

"I'm scared." He wiped one eye and clenched his lips inwards a moment.

She wanted to grab him in her arms and hug away his pain, but that wasn't possible. "What scares you the most?"

"Remembering." The word a barely audible rasp. He choked back a sob which jerked his whole body.

With a gentle touch she rubbed his arm. "Go on."

"Remembering everything." He cleared his throat and stared at the ceiling. "Remembering how Bruce – my father – hated me so much. Remembering what drove me from home and what happened after that, the beating and acid. All that. I don't want to know any of it."

Grace couldn't think of anything to say. No words seemed appropriate at this time.

Steve continued. "Mostly, remembering you as my sister. Once I do that I'll have no one to feel close to. No one to love. No one to make me feel at ease. To feel like they care about me. Things will be different. Too different."

It wasn't what she expected him to say and she had to think for a moment for an appropriate response. "I will always love and care about you just like I have my whole life. Nothing will ever change that. Once you get over the surgery and get used to things again I'm sure you'll find that special lady out there who'll make your life complete." She placed her hand on her belly. "And you might be able to give this little one some cousins to play with."

Steve looked at her with a grin which quickly disappeared. "I know you're trying to cheer me up and I appreciate that, but something like that seems totally impossible."

"Nothing is impossible." She squeezed his arm. "Look, just get through the surgery and we'll deal with the amnesia later, hey?"

"Fair enough, but don't expect miracles."

A knock on Steve's door broke the silence. Grace spun around.

A muscular man with short, thin hair stood there staring at Steve. Dressed in faded jeans and black shirt, his clean-shaven face showed no emotion.

"Yes?" said Grace.

He certainly didn't look like a hospital employee, but rather very uncomfortable and out of place. His forehead creased to a frown, further outlining the age and weather lines already there. Dark eyes widened then turned cold and staring. Lips tightened.

An icicle prickled all the way up her spine. "Can we help you?" She glanced at the buzzer, ensuring exactly where to grab if they needed help.

He looked at Grace several seconds then to Steve who stared back. The stranger's face reddened and hardened even further. His lips moved, but no words came out. One of his large hands clenched into a fist and unclenched.

Then he was gone.

Grace jumped up, ran out the door and looked along the corridor, but no sign of the frightening visitor. Very strange. She returned to Steve. Her heart rate bumped up several notches. "Who the hell was that?"

Steve's face had paled. "I don't know." He swallowed hard. "But I have a feeling I *should* know." His voice trembled on the brink of breaking and he stared at Grace. "And it's not a good feeling."

CHAPTER 6

Kain held his breath as the CT scanner whirred and moved along above him. Closed his eyes. Opened his eyes. Sucked in a fresh breath and held it again. Nope, no difference. The fear clawing and gnawing at his mind and soul wouldn't abate. Not one iota. He licked his lips and swallowed sour, sticky saliva. The machine stopped and the dimmed lights brightened.

"All done, Mr Burrows." The exotic accent of the dark-skinned man doing the scan returned him from the frightening place his mind had drifted. Was this bloke a doctor or a nurse or what? He probably did tell him, but it hadn't registered in his jumbled brain.

"Thanks." Kain jumped up from the long table, slid off the blue crepe gown and grabbed his clothes from a chair. Behind the thick glass window the man clicked away at his computer. Kain threw his shirt on and pulled up his shorts. "Can I go?" He needed to see Grace. Needed her loving words and arms. Damn, he needed her right now. He'd insisted he'd be fine while she organised leave from school and a few other things, but his jelly legs and trembling hands proved otherwise.

"Yes, you may go. We'll get this report and images to the surgical team and to your doctor as soon as possible."

"Thank you." Numerous thoughts whirled in his brain, but at least this part of his fearful journey was over. Now to try and keep his mind off the cancer while waiting for the results. Kain rushed out of the Anchor Bay hospital. The bright sunlight hit him, stopping him on the spot. He squinted and looked down rubbing both eyes. Lack of sleep had them itchy and dry.

He'd slept little while Grace was missing and any sleep he did have was usually interrupted with crazy, scary dreams. Now she was back safe the sleep still either eluded him or taunted him with endless nightmares. *Why me? Why can't life just be normal again?*

Tears of anger and fear built up but he refused to let them free. He focussed his gaze on the spot he'd parked his ute and strode off, switching his mind to his fun-loving mate, Joe, who could always be relied upon when times were tough.

Joe. His fellow plasterer and mate of many years. Since way back in high school. He'd been his best support, apart from Grace of course, since this horrible diagnosis. Joe had listened, hugged, humoured him and taken time off work to help search for Grace. Yep, the best mate a bloke could wish for and always good for a laugh.

"Hey buddy, got a dollar?"

Kain stopped and looked down at the source of the croaky voice. A skinny, middle-aged man sat on the grassy verge near the footpath. Bare, dirty footed, his long arms draped on his raised knees. Wispy greying hair hung down the sides of his head, just touching the collar of his stained blue shirt. His black trousers may have once been part of a suit. Whiskers flecked with grey covered a thin face below tired, squinting eyes. Eyes full of hope.

Kain stared for several seconds. "I..." He was about to continue walking, thinking this bloke was probably just a hopeless drunk, but a glint in those desperate eyes triggered something in his heart. "What are you going to do with money if I give you some?"

"Get some tucker. I haven't et nothin' for two days." His eyes widened and a grin spread across his face, revealing stained, chipped teeth with one top front tooth completely missing.

Kain leaned down close to the stranger and breathed deep. The stench of unwashed clothes, foul breath and a stale sweaty body reeled him back a step, but there was no hint of alcohol or cigarette smell to him. A scar smudged with dirt ran along the width of one cheek and one eyelid drooped. Seemed like he'd been beaten up at some point.

Kain's phone *pinged*. He fished it out of his back pocket and read the message. *'Darl, all good for work leave. Just visiting my class now then need to do a few things in town. Meet u at mum & dad's half hour or so. Will get the rest of my stuff. Hope u r ok. Luv u lots xxx'*

Okay, no need to rush since Grace won't be there yet. He replaced the phone, took out his wallet from the opposite side and opened it. He almost pulled out a twenty dollar note, but some invisible force stopped his hand.

His own situation seemed the worst in the world, but, shit, this cancer may not be as bad as he expected. After all, it *was* only a small lump in his sac and from information he'd read, the odds were pretty good at beating it. He had Grace back and a baby on the way. Life wasn't all *that* bad. But this poor bloke. What did he have? Absolutely nothing by the looks and sounds. And something in those eyes showed genuine sadness and helplessness.

"Come with me." He beckoned the man to his feet.

"Where ya takin' me?" The man's voice hesitant, unsure.

"Don't worry, mate, I'm not going to hurt you." Kain held out his right hand. "I'm Kain."

Sceptical eyes looked at his face then to his outstretched hand and back to his face. The dirty hand slowly reached out and shook Kain's. "I'm Ron."

"Okay, Ron, come with me. My ute's just over here. I want to help you." Kain began to walk off but eased back for Ron to catch up. A limp slowed him. "What's wrong with your leg?"

"Dunno. Bloody sore knee."

Kain stopped. "Are you from Anchor Bay? Do you have any family?"

"Nope not from here but me brother lives here. I'm tryin' to find him. Last I heard he'd got into some trouble so I dunno if he's still around or not. I was married once, but my beautiful Pearl and our daughter was killed. Murdered...and raped." His voice hardened to ice. "I saw him in court. Scum never even said sorry."

"That's terrible. I'm sorry, Ron."

"But I made him sorry. He escaped and me and a mate came face to face with him. He couldn't do nothin' like that ever again."

Kain had no desire to know the details. "I'm glad he got what he deserved."

"Yep, but then I ended up in jail and got into more trouble in there." He shrugged, panting to keep up. "I didn't care. I had nothin' to live for anymore."

"This white one." Kain unlocked his door. "Hop in, Ron." Kain jumped in, reached across and unlocked the passenger side door.

"Where we goin'?" Ron clicked his seatbelt in place. "Ya know, ya don't haveta do this."

Kain glanced at him and nodded. "I know, but I want to." He started the motor, reversed out of the park and headed up the street. "I'm taking you to the motel opposite the shopping centre. I'll pay for a couple of nights for you and give you some money for food."

"Oh, geez... I don't know what to say. No one has ever done anything like that for me before. What's the catch?" His voice hardened again. He probably didn't trust anyone.

"No catch. I'm just trying to stop feeling sorry for myself, so it's for my benefit too."

"Fair enough. What's your problem?"

"Don't worry, it's a long story." Kain had no desire to rehash everything, or even think about it. He wound down his window to lessen the stale stench coming from Ron.

They drove in silence. Kain soon pulled into the motel's public parking bay and switched off the ignition. "Come on." He pulled the keys and jumped out, not bothering to lock the doors with motel reception only metres away.

Out of his wallet he took his credit card and stood at the reception window.

A man behind the desk smiled, got up and walked to the window. "G'day there. Would you like a room?"

"I want a room for two nights for this gentleman. He just needs a place to stay and get himself cleaned up."

The round-faced, jolly looking man looked at Ron. His smile disappeared for a few seconds.

Don't even think about turning him away...please. Kain held his breath.

The smile returned. "Certainly. Actually, we have a special on this week in our economy rooms, three nights for the price of two."

"I'll take it."

The man sat down and clicked away at the computer. "Can I see your license, please?" He reached over, took it from Kain's outstretched hand and clicked away some more, before getting up and returning to the window handing the license back. "Here you go." He pointed to the EFTPOS machine. "Insert your card, please."

As soon as the formalities were over, Kain handed the key he was given, to Ron who stood back a little. "Room nine, mate. Just down here." They walked past several closed up rooms. "This one."

Ron unlocked the door and stepped inside. "Geez, this is pretty flash for someone like me."

Kain poked his head in and glanced around the basic, but clean, room. "You'll cope." He opened his wallet adding up the amount in notes. "Here." He handed Ron a few fifties.

Ron's eyes widened to dinner plates and he shook his head. "Nah." He brushed Kain's hand away. "I can't take all that, Kain."

"I'm impressed with your integrity, Ron, but I want you to have it. Go on." He moved his hand closer to the homeless man.

Ron looked at him with glistening eyes and his shoulders sagged. "Okay, but I'd like to be able to pay you back when I get on me feet again." Ron took the cash in a shaky hand and stared at it. "You know, I used to do all right for meself and Pearl. Had our own business, we did." He gazed out the window with faraway eyes. A faint sob coincided with his Adam's apple moving up and down his weather-beaten neck. "But it all went bad..."

"I'm sorry, Ron." Kain wished he could stay and chat more to this mysterious stranger, who, under the rough, dirty exterior seemed to have a decent heart. "You can pay me back one day, but I have to go now." He patted Ron on the shoulder. "Now, have a shower and go over the road and get yourself some food and toiletries. And maybe a new tee shirt or something. Oh, and some thongs!"

Ron chuckled and lifted one dirty foot. "Yeah, need some, hey?"

Kain hesitated at the door. "Good luck finding your brother. What's his name?"

"John Allen. But he could have a nickname." Ron shrugged.

Kain scoured his mind for any recognition. "Nope, sorry, I don't know anyone by that name."

Ron shrugged. "Didn't expectcha to. This is a pretty big town." He offered his hand to Kain. "Thanks again."

"Just enjoy the hot shower, comfy bed and some tucker." Kain released his hand and headed to his ute.

By the time he'd reach Bruce and Linda's cattle property, Grace should be there. At least if she were, there was less risk of a confrontation with Bruce. He and Kain's relationship remained strained since their blow-ups over Grace's presumed death. Bruce blamed him, due to him breaking off their relationship having driven her away. Away and up that dangerous mountainous road. Hell, he'd blamed himself too, but he felt it absolutely necessary at the time. He loved her too much to bear her suffering along with him during his cancer treatment and possible early death. Having to lie about the reason for the breakup made him feel a thousand times worse, but he'd needed her to hate him and stay right away.

Bruce had snuck into the home he and Grace shared and took all her things back to his and Linda's place, Grace's former home, leaving Kain an accusing message written in lipstick on the bathroom mirror. The arrogant, rich grazier had also had what was believed to be Grace's burnt remains cremated without telling Kain.

The remains turned out to be a hitchhiker Grace had picked up and allowed to drive while she'd texted him. That text never made it into cyber space. The car veered, rolled and burst into flames with Grace and her phone being flung out into the dust and dirt. He'd stumbled upon the phone while visiting the crash site, trying to make some sense of the tragedy.

But the festered anger, frustration and hatred between the two grieving men left them wary of each other.

Grace's new car was parked near her parents' front steps. Glancing upwards he whispered a "Thankyou", and his pummelling heart settled. He pulled up behind it as she walked down the steps with a box. Jumping out, he ran and took the box from her. "You shouldn't be carrying that."

"Thanks, darl." She let him carry it the several metres to her car, striding ahead to open the back door. "It was the lightest one. You can get the rest, 'Mr Muscles'." A cheeky little laugh and she playfully squeezed his biceps.

He put the box on the back seat. No sooner had he straightened up and she placed her arms around his neck, kissed and hugged him tight.

Kain held her close. "That was a nice greeting." Some of his worries melted away with the intensity and warmth of the hug. Her heartbeat against his own. His lips brushed her hair, shining brighter red in the sunlight. "Ahh, Grace, it's *sooo* good to have you back." The familiar swelling in his chest of utter love for this woman hurt sometimes, but a 'good' hurt. A beautiful hurt.

"It's good to have *you* back." She kissed him again and let go. "Let's get everything and go back to the flat. I'd love to race you into my old bed right here and now, but Dad's here somewhere." She glanced about. "I'd also like to put all this away today, if possible. I thought you'd have beaten me here."

A fleeting surge of warmth and yearning rushed to his groin but the thought of Bruce cooled the flames. "I just helped a poor homeless bloke out. Put him in a motel for a couple of days and gave him a few bucks for food and whatever."

"Awww, how sweet of you." She kissed his cheek. Soft and caring.

"Oh well." Kain shrugged. "He seemed desperate, and it took me out of the depressing things I was thinking."

Hand in hand they reached the top of the stairs just as Bruce come out of the screen door, on to the verandah. Kain's chest full of love zapped to dread. Dread which speared its ugly tentacles throughout his body to his fingers and toes.

"Hello, Gracie." Bruce's smile retreated. His voice hardened to concrete. "Oh, g'day Kain."

"Hey Dad. Kain is here to help me get the rest of my stuff." Her friendly tone a little reserved.

Kain duly nodded. "Bruce." He'd have been happy to leave it at that, but he also wanted to keep things comfortable, especially for Grace and Linda's sake. "How you going?" He almost asked Bruce how his leg was but seeing Bruce still walking with a limp answered that question so probably best to leave it alone.

Grace glanced toward the large shed close by the house. "I see mum's not here and Sophie is probably still at work too, I suppose."

Bruce sat his tall frame at the large table on the verandah. "Your mother should be back soon." The lines on his tanned face seemed etched deeper than ever. He ran his fingers through his dark, but greying, hair and scratched the rarely seen stubble on his chin. Bloodshot eyes looked away from Grace, past Kain and off into the distant paddocks of his prime beef cattle.

Grace shot a look at Kain with a crease of her eyebrows and slight roll of her eyes, then to her father. "Can I get you anything, Dad? Cuppa or something to eat?"

"No, love, I'm right thanks. Might have a beer soon." He gazed at his watch. Gazed longer than necessary to read the time. Almost as if he had no focus.

Kain had never seen the great Bruce Atkinson, respected pillar of society in the Anchor Bay district and breeder of award-winning cattle, looking so dishevelled and lost. He hadn't expected to find Bruce happy, but this shell of a man before him was not the proud and strong Bruce he had known for almost five years.

He thought of Ron. Ron had been dealt a cruel hand, but Bruce... He brought his woes on all by himself. Kain had always felt he wasn't good enough for Bruce's daughter, but it was him that didn't give up on her when everyone else believed her dead. And Bruce scorned him, abused him and physically attacked him. *Karma, mate.*

"Bit early, isn't it, Dad? You don't normally crave beer. A cuppa would be better." Grace stepped closer to her father, placing her hand on his shoulder while giving Kain a worried I-don't-like-this look.

"A cuppa doesn't take away the pain, Gracie." He dropped his chin toward his chest which rose and fell with a heavy sigh. "Beer does." He got up and wandered inside.

Grace sighed. "I don't know what else to try with him. How to make him see what he's doing. Not just to himself but to Mum and the rest of us too."

Kain held her in his arms. "Babe, I wish I could make things better, but you know how he is with me. No point putting my two cents worth in. It'd probably only make him drink even more." They stood in silence, locked in an embrace, both needing the other's love and support.

Footsteps back along the hallway had them let each other go. Bruce came through the screen door drinking from a can and holding another unopened one in his other hand.

Grace glanced at Kain, her face now showing disgust instead of sadness and hopelessness. Kain had no words for her.

Grace sat opposite her father. "Dad, how about I make you a sandwich or something like that?"

He looked at her with a confused expression. "Why?"

Kain had trouble keeping his mouth shut. The ignorant man couldn't even see his beloved daughter was trying to help him. Nor could he see how much he was hurting her, but then again, maybe he could but with his arrogant attitude he probably doesn't give a rat's. Tension mounted in Kain's body. With Bruce sitting down he was the perfect level to lay a decent punch into, but he couldn't risk further upsetting Grace. He turned and walked away several metres, looking out over the countryside and taking a few slow deep breaths.

Silence surrounded them. Uninvited, uncomfortable, stomach-churning silence. A rooster's high-pitched crow cut short the oppressive lull. Bruce's body twitched. He looked toward the chook pen near the shed and mumbled beneath his breath.

"Kain, can you get those other boxes from my old room while I talk to dad a minute." She sat opposite Bruce.

Kain headed inside, glad to be away from Bruce and the discomfort thickening the warm afternoon air. He grabbed a box and bag headed back out to the car. Grace and Bruce sat in silence as he walked past.

Bruce stared into the distance again. Grace glanced up at Kain and wiped one of her watering eyes. The tears turning them an even deeper shade of green. How he wished for something useful to ease Grace's pain over her father, but with his short temper and bitter feeling toward Bruce, he would only make things worse.

He threw the stuff in the car boot and ran up the stairs and inside for more. From inside he heard Bruce's voice rise to an angry pitch, but he couldn't understand what he was saying. He'd better not be getting up Grace. *I'll kill him!* Grabbing another box and placing a duffel bag on top of it he rushed them to the car and ran back up the stairs three at a time.

"NO, Gracie, it's *not* that simple!" Bruce slammed his fist on the table. Grace jumped in her seat and leaned back.

"But why, Dad? All you have to do is go see him and tell him you love him." Her bottom lip quivered. "You seemed happy last week that Steve was back, after you got over the initial shock. I don't understand. What's changed now?"

Kain put his arm around Grace's shoulders. His heart thumped along with the rush of adrenaline preparing him for another physical confrontation with Bruce if necessary.

He wasn't having Grace stressed. "Are you okay? You shouldn't be getting yourself upset, Grace." He glared at Bruce and ached to add, *he's not worth it,* but he was her father.

"A lot has changed, Gracie." Bruce got up and headed toward the screen door, eyes downcast. "I'm getting a beer." With a grunt he pulled the screen door open and limped inside, the door shutting with a bang.

Grace clasped her hands to her chest and sunk into Kain's arms wrapping about her. "This is not like him, Kain." A sob hiccupped from her throat.

He held her against his chest. "I know, but he has to deal with everything in his own time and way." Kain stroked her hair. "He'll get there, Grace, but right now he doesn't seem to want anyone's help."

"I'm worried for Mum. I have an awful feeling..." A louder sob spasmed her body, choking off her sentence.

CHAPTER 7

Steve sat up on the side of his hospital bed. He needed to move. Stretch his legs. Lying around wasn't a pastime he enjoyed, especially feeling like a caged animal awaiting its fate. Doctor Leeson had come in earlier and informed him the plastic surgeon had received the photos of his disfigurements the day before plus pictures of Steve before his assault, that Linda had supplied, and had studied them. Dr Thebo had replied he could see Steve tomorrow for the initial consultation and most likely operate the following day. An aerial ambulance was on standby to take him down to Brisbane that afternoon. He needed to tell his mother and hoped she would come with him. Just as he stood and took one step toward the door Linda and Sophie walked in, their faces beaming with huge smiles.

"Oh, g'day mum. Sophie". Steve nodded and grinned, losing some of the heaviness from his shoulders. Their happy faces meant some good news, surely. He stepped back and sat down on the bed again.

"Hello son." Linda leaned in, kissed him on the cheek then hugged him tight. A hug full of love. One he easily returned, placing his arms around her tall, slender frame. She let go and stepped back. "Where were you off to?"

Before he had a chance to answer Sophie hugged him. "Hey, big brother."

"Hey there, Soph". He returned the embrace, wishing he could remember her, but still feeling the love in that warm hug. Not quite the same as his mum's hug, but just as sincere.

He let go of his sister and looked at his mum. "Ah, just wanting to stretch my legs." He shrugged but his heart longed for the bush. "I wasn't going anywhere in particular, just along the corridor I suppose. I doubt I could get far before I'd be stopped." The longing in his heart changed to sickly dread. "The cops *still* haven't come and talked to me. Seems like they want to torture me too. Wish they'd hurry up and decide what they are going to do with me."

Sophie sat on the chair while Linda sat on the bed beside him and placed her hand gently on his forearm. "Doctor Leeson rang earlier and told me it's all systems go to get you down to Brisbane this afternoon and to the plastic surgeon." She squeezed his arm. "And Sophie and I are coming with you."

Relieved, Steve exhaled the breath he'd been holding. "That's good. I was hoping you would." His father's angry face came to mind. "Just you two?" *Please say yes.*

His mum's smile disappeared. "Yep, just us two." She looked at Sophie and nodded. Sophie smiled but the sadness in her eyes was evident. Sadness at the state of her brother and father's relationship, or lack of it, no doubt.

Steve swallowed down the lump of frustration or regret and cleared his throat. He really had no idea what or how to feel about his father. "So..." He wasn't even sure what to call him. "Bruce...Dad doesn't want to come?" His head told him that was wrong, but his heart lightened. Dealing with his father could wait.

"No, he's got a bit on." His mother didn't sound at all convincing especially when her gaze diverted to the floor. "He's still getting over the gunshot to the leg and there's a big cattle sale coming up next week. He needs to work out which ones he's sending and supervise the workers getting them ready."

Steve glanced at Sophie who gave a slight roll of her eyes. Enough said.

Linda's grip moved from his arm and took hold of his hand. Her warm fingers tightened around his. "Steve, there's something else I have to tell you." She took a deep breath as if steeling herself.

This wasn't good. What else could go wrong?

"Don't worry, Steve, it's actually good." Sophie said. She must have seen his fear. Her short, soft laugh relaxed him again. "Go on Mum, tell him."

Steve looked at his mother, hoping it was confidence in her eyes and smile. He couldn't help a grin. "Yeah, go on Mum, tell me." He squeezed her hand, feeling totally at ease with her, even though he still couldn't remember being her son.

"Well..." Linda hesitated a moment as if trying to work out the best way to say whatever it was she needed to say. "Because of the police investigation into...into what you were involved in, I had to sign a statement declaring you are in my care and giving them an assurance you won't try to ..." She looked away from him. Her hand began to feel clammy against his skin. "Won't take off and disappear again." She turned back to him, took her hand from his and held both sides of his face, but he could only feel one of her hands on his scarred skin. Desperation showed in her eyes. "Please, Steve, I know you long to get back to the bush but *promise* me you'll see this through." Tears formed and slid down her cheeks, but she didn't let go of his face. "We can do this! Sophie and I will help you. And Grace too of course. All of us."

The mere mention of Grace's name triggered a flurry of mixed feelings in his soul. "Why isn't Grace coming with us?" That certainly would have made the whole ordeal so much easier.

Linda dropped her hands to her thighs. "She has a lot on with Kain and his cancer appointments, and she's also had a bit of morning sickness lately, so flying probably wouldn't be a good idea. Plus, she's still a bit sore from the car accident. But she did say she'd come by today and see you before we leave."

"That's good." Relief swept through his body. Grace hadn't forgotten him. Hearing the mention of Kain and his cancer threw his mind back a couple of weeks when Kain had stood up for him while fuelling up at the servo. Some random yobbo had started calling him ugly among other things. It took all his restraint not to just drop the idiot on his flabby bum, but two police officers happened to be nearby and settled the confrontation. Kain had told the police what he'd witnessed and added that Seth/Steve had done nothing to deserve it. Steve and Kain had never met but Kain briefly mentioned his cancer and losing the love of his life, totally unaware she was safe at Seth's home. And Seth totally unaware Kain was referring to Grace.

Doctor Leeson entered the room. "Good. You're all here." With a smile, he nodded toward Sophie then Linda. "So, Steve, are you ready to jump on the plane and head to Brissy? The first step in the long road of getting your life back."

"I suppose so, Doc," replied Steve. "Just hope it works. Would be nice to look like a human instead of a mon-"

"Shhh!" His mother silenced his words. One finger to her pursed lips and her other hand over his mouth. "Don't *ever* use that word around me again, do you hear?" Her eyes wide and glowing with anger. "You are *not* a monster. You are *my son!* A human being and a damned *good* human being at that!"

Steve's mind flooded with images of some of the crimes he'd been forced to commit for Scott. *James McTaggart.* He must remember his real name now. He only knew him as Scott, most likely a nickname after his Scottish heritage. He wanted to blurt out that he was *not* a good human being, but his mother's anxious look of love and determination stopped his words forming. "Sorry Mum." He hated himself even more now that he'd made her angry.

"Okay," the doctor continued. "Let's just go over a few details then I have a surprise for you, Steve."

Steve frowned, unsure he liked the type of surprises he'd received lately, especially while in hospital. "What is it?"

"First things first." Doctorr Leeson handed Linda a folded piece of paper. "Mrs Atkinson-"

Linda brushed her hand through the air. "Call me Linda, please".

"Err, okay Linda. Here is the address and phone number of Doctorr Thebo's private clinic. It's not all that far from the airport and there are a couple of motels nearby that you and your daughter can stay in."

"Sounds good," Sophie quipped. "Do you know the names of them?" She pulled out her phone from her shoulder bag on the floor beside her.

"It's all written on the paper, names and phone numbers of the motels. Whether you book over the phone or online is up to you." He pointed to the paper Linda had now opened out. "Get to the clinic as soon as you can once you've landed. Dr Thebo will tell you if he wants Steve to stay in his clinic ward that night or not. Probably depend how early he wants to start the next day. Once we've had word you are on the plane, I'll let him know you're on the way."

"Doc," said Steve, "this all seems so quick. So..." He tried to think of the appropriate word. "All too easy. How can this be happening so fast? Surely if this bloke who does the plastic surgery is so good he'd have a waiting list a mile long. I don't get it. I'm no one special."

The doctor opened his mouth to speak but Linda cut him off.

"Steve, we arranged it all. Your father knows he can't do much to help you, but he can make this happen for a start."

She placed her hand on his shoulder. "Please don't worry about the hows and whys, okay."

Her smile warmed and comforted his soul, but he still felt a little uneasy. He was about to ask how much it was costing his father and was it a guilty conscience when a stranger appeared in his doorway.

"Hi there, I guess I've come to the right room." The young woman stood there and smiled. Her blonde hair tied back, she wore smart looking black pants and white blouse. Very official looking, especially the glasses, but nothing like the hospital staff Steve saw all the time.

"Oh, Jenna." Doctor Leeson strode to her and placed his hand on her shoulder. "Come over and meet Steve." She walked over with a slight limp.

The doctor introduced them and Jenna reached out to shake Steve's hand, something he wasn't expecting. He returned the shake and even though she looked at his disfigured hand and back to his scarred face there was not one hint of hesitation, shock or disgust on her pretty face.

After introducing Sophie and Linda to Jenna, Doctor Leeson excused himself, stating he had other patients to see but would be back before Steve left. Linda disappeared briefly out the door, returning with a chair for Jenna, which she gratefully accepted.

Linda nodded to Steve and smiled. "Actually, Soph and I might go get a coffee while you two talk."

Sophie jumped up from her chair. "Yep, good idea." She patted Steve's shoulder. "See you soon."

Steve had no idea what to say to Jenna. He glanced about the room and back to her. She was still smiling at him. "The doc told me you want to write a story about me, but I don't know yet if I'm comfortable with that." Visions swam in his brain of how strangers in Karisdale stared at him in disgust or crossed the street to avoid him. Why would anyone want to read about him and his miserable life? He shrugged one shoulder. "Why?"

"Tim said he told you a bit about me and what I am doing journalistically. I thought I could write this story straight from the heart. From what I learned from Tim -," she raised one hand in a truce mode, "Don't worry, he didn't break doctor patient confidentiality. I read about you in the papers and asked him if I could come see you. He *did* say it totally depended on you."

Some of her words didn't sound to be pronounced correctly. Almost like a slur and a bit slow. Was she drunk? But her eyes were clear. A bright blue clear. "Umm, Jenna..." Geez, how could he ask her? This day was getting stranger and more confusing by the minute. Surely the doctor could tell if she, his own sister, was drunk. "You sound..." This was becoming too uncomfortable. He poured himself a cup of water from the bed side stand and took a sip, avoiding her eyes.

She laughed a little. "Did you notice my speech isn't quite as clear as most other peoples'?"

He looked back at her but had no idea what to say so just shrugged again.

"It's okay. I'm used to that reaction. I have Cerebral Palsy."

Now Steve was totally confused. He shook his head. "What's that?"

Jenna smiled, seeming totally at ease. "Just something I was born with. It's no big deal." She gave a slight shrug. "My case isn't as bad as some. I just walk with a limp and need strong glasses." She pointed to her spectacles. "Oh, and my hearing isn't great but not bad enough to need aids yet." She laughed. "It's all good, but don't be surprised if I have to ask you to repeat yourself sometimes." She scratched at the side of her neck a little then held out that hand. "Oh, and my left hand is a bit weak and floppy at times."

Steve had never met anyone with any sort of physical problem, that he could remember anyway. She amazed him. So bright and bubbly as if nothing was wrong at all. He simply couldn't imagine ever feeling like that. Was it possible? He dared hope so. "Did you ever get teased or bullied?"

"Oh yes." Some of her bubbliness faded and her gaze fell downwards.

Oh no. *You've upset her you great lump of uselessness.* "I'm sorry, Jenna. I didn't mean to make you sad." He wanted to reach out to her, hold her hand. *Anything* to try and undo his gaffe, but she might not be happy with that and get up and leave. No, he couldn't risk that. He liked having her here. "Are you okay? We can talk about something else?"

She looked back at him and a slight smile returned. "It's fine. That's a long time ago and things are better now. The teasing was mainly before I had surgeries on my legs and spine. I was much worse then. Kids can be cruel little buggers when they want to."

"Not only kids," Steve mumbled.

"Pardon?" Jenna leaned toward him a little and laughed. "See, I told you."

Steve's heart lightened and a laugh came easy. Jenna certainly had such a pleasant way about her. He shook his head, still smiling. "It doesn't matter. Anyway, what sort of things do you want to know from me to write in your article?" His mind returned to seriousness as he made mental notes of what *not* to tell her.

Before she could answer, Grace walked into the room. "Hey there Steve, how are you feeling today?" She placed her hands on his shoulders and leaned down to peck him on the cheek. For a moment all was right with the world – *his* world. Grace was here.

"Yeah, not bad, thanks Grace. Good to see you." He introduced her to Jenna and briefly explained what Jenna was wanting or hoping to do. The two ladies exchanged pleasantries before Grace sat on the edge of the bed beside Steve.

Jenna stood. "You know, I can see you want to catch up with your sister and you have to get going soon anyway. How about I come back when you return from Brisbane, and we can get into the story then?" She touched his forearm and smiled. "I'm looking forward to it." Just as she started to turn, she stopped and looked back. "Umm, would you mind if I took a couple of photos of you now. I might be able to use them for the article?" She shook her head, a sudden look of disgust on her face. "Sorry, that was insensitive of me. I understand if you prefer not to have your 'before' picture shown."

Steve thought for a moment. There would be a hell of a lot of people who would see his ugly, scarred face in Jenna's article. Maybe even those responsible for his scarring and certainly some of those who'd stared at him in the street or rushed their kids away in disgust when he walked nearby. Might do them good to see what suffering he has been through. Might make them think twice about their ignorant attitude. Hang on, what if he goes to jail? If that happens, *which it probably will*, those same people will probably laugh. No, he can't give them that pleasure. "You can take only one, but..." He glanced at Grace. Stuff it! He may as well be honest with Jenna. She'll find out anyway. "Jenna, I might go to jail. If that happens I don't want that photo included in your article, okay? No one needs to see that."

Jenna nodded. "That's totally acceptable with me. I understand. But let's hope that won't happen. I can't imagine you could have done anything that bad anyway." She dug around in her bag and fished out her phone.

Again, Steve glanced at Grace who squeezed his forearm in reassurance, then back at Jenna. "I hope not." *But you'd be surprised...or terribly shocked,* he wanted to say.

Jenna held her phone up and into position. Grace got up to move. "No," said Jenna. "You stay there beside your brother." In an instant the photo was done. Jenna turned the phone to show them. "It's a great one. Thanks." She put her phone back in her bag. "Okay, well, I'll head off and I'll check in with Tim later on how you're going and when you'll be back. All the very best, Steve." A cheery wave and she disappeared out the door.

"She's nice," said Grace.

"Yeah, she is," agreed Steve. *Very nice.* "How are you? Mum said you've been sick." For some strange reason he didn't feel comfortable discussing just how nice he thought Jenna was. It was just too...odd and different to the feelings and thoughts he'd become accustomed to.

"Just a bit of morning sickness." Grace sat in the chair Jenna had just vacated. "That strange bloke hasn't been back has he?" She looked worried. "Can you remember anything at all about his face?"

"No. But I have a gut feeling I have seen him before, sometime, somewhere, a long time ago." The all too familiar pit of fear in his stomach began to stir like a cauldron. Icicles prickled up his spine. "He scares me, Grace."

CHAPTER 8

Grace pulled up back at her place and jumped out of her car. Steve, her mum and Sophie were probably on their way to the airport by now. She would have loved to have gone with them and Steve certainly would have preferred she did too, but Kain's CT Scan results would be available any time and she wanted, no, *needed* to support him as much as possible. Torn in two directions. Two men she loved dearly. One has her heart and soul and facing a life-or-death situation. The other has her love and support as a sister and her wish for him to regain his past 'normal' life. But he has many obstacles to overcome before then, which worried and saddened her.

Kain's voice came from inside, but no responding voice and no other vehicles were close by so he must be on the phone. She walked in the door. He rushed toward her putting his phone in his back pocket. "Grace, so glad you're back." His hands wrapped about her waist in a hug that warmed her troubled soul. He kissed her but looked worried. "That was the oncologist in Mackay that Doctor Burns referred me to. They want to see me first thing in the morning… for the results." He let out a deep breath and wiped the sweat from his forehead.

"Okay." Grace inhaled slowly, determined to remain calm and positive. The dreaded moment of truth. "Any indication of what we can expect?"

"Not much. He just said it wasn't too bad and not to stress too much." Kain rolled his eyes and swallowed hard. "Easy for him to say."

Grace took hold of both his hands in hers and looked deep into his terrified eyes. "Did he say it was definitely cancer?" Her own fear clawed at her heart but she must not let it show.

Kain gave a half-hearted shrug. "Well, he referred to it as *your* cancer."

His eyes watered and Grace hugged him tight to her chest. His heart thumped hard against hers. A loud knock on the front door separated them.

"Hey, anyone home?"

Kain's face changed into a grin. "Joe." Before he could get to the door his best mate walked into their lounge room.

"Hope I didn't catch you two lovebirds doing the horizontal tango?" His infectious, loud laugh bounced his brown curls about. "So good to see you two back together." He hugged Grace briefly and turned to Kain. "*Told* you it was bullshit for yous to break up, didn't I?" He poked Kain in the chest. "Next time you'll listen, eh?"

Kain laughed and playfully punched his shoulder. "Yep, but there won't be a next time! Want a beer?"

"Silly question, mate." Joe flopped down on one of the single lounge chairs. Kain went to the fridge in the kitchen.

Grace couldn't help a smile. A smile that calmed the butterflies in her stomach. Joe had that effect on people. "You're timing couldn't have been better, Joe. He was starting to get a bit down. We get the CT results tomorrow morning, but by the sounds it isn't too far advanced yet." She held up crossed fingers.

Joe's grin widened and his eyes lit up hearing those words. He gave Grace the thumbs up as Kain re-entered the room dropping an icy cold can of beer into his lap. Joe jumped a little and grabbed the can from his bare thighs. "Thanks." He stood, pulled the ring tab from the can and held it toward Kain opening his. "Cheers to good health, good friends and the best outcome." They clinked cans before downing a mouthful. Joe sat back down. "Now, tell me all what's been happening in the last few days. How's the baby?" He pointed toward Grace's belly.

Grace and Kain sat close to each other on the larger chair. Grace looked at Kain and smiled. "Gee, where do we begin?"

Kain touched and rubbed Grace's stomach. "It's all good in there. First ultrasound tomorrow afternoon."

Laughter and light-hearted banter continued through the afternoon.

The next morning Grace and Kain rose early to attend the oncologist's appointment an hour's drive away in Mackay. Kain had had a restless night. Probably more from worry than anything else. It hurt Grace that she couldn't take his fear away, but he kept assuring her that her hugs and love were all he needed. She called her mum and spoke to Steve as well. All was good so far regarding their trip to Brisbane.

The drive was relatively quiet. Grace pulled into the parking lot of a large, modern building located near the hospital. A slight wave of nausea swept through her. Was it fear for Kain and the future or just plain old morning sickness? Whatever it was, *not now, please!*

Kain looked at his watch. "Good. Just in time."

Grace found a park not far from the front entrance. She turned off the ignition and looked at Kain, placing her left hand on his thigh. "You okay?" He seemed devoid of emotion. She'd expected him to be more nervous.

He patted her hand. "Yep. Let's just get this over and done with." In a second he was out the car and walking around to Grace's side. She had a drink of water from the plastic bottle in her bag, got out and locked the car. Taking his damp hand in hers together they entered the Cancer Care Centre.

After reporting in at the desk they found a seat. The large, pleasant waiting room held comfortable chairs, large healthy pot plants, beautiful nature pictures on the walls plus plenty of positivity posters. A pile of magazines sat neatly on a small table under one of the large windows. Beside that table was another with a range of colourful beanies and turbans for those who lose their hair during chemotherapy. Each of the several other people in the waiting room sat quietly either looking at their phone or the large television set high on the end wall, telecasting one of the morning shows. The sound was low but subtitles allowed anyone to read what was being said. One older lady smiled at Grace and Kain as they sat down, then returned her gaze to the TV.

Kain leaned closer to Grace, whispering, "I'm the youngest one here."

She squeezed his hand tight but before she could answer, a door to their left opened and Kain's name was called. They rose and walked to the waiting doctor.

"Hello Kain, I'm Doctor Marc Thompson." He gripped Kain's hand and shook it. "I'm your Oncologist."

Kain looked him up and down. "Umm, g'day Doc."

Grace nudged Kain with her elbow then held out her welcoming hand to the doctor. "I'm Grace, Kain's partner."

The doctor shook her hand then grinned at Kain who's face suddenly looked as bright red as the doctor's shirt. "It's all right Kain, I bet you're thinking I don't look anything like what you expected."

Kain glanced about the small consulting room then back to the doctor, who indicated for him and Grace to sit on the two chairs beside his desk. "Sorry Doc, I didn't mean to stare but you do look like you'd be more at home on a Harley than doing...what it is you do." His face reddened even more. "Ahh shit, I feel so embarrassed." He placed his hands over his eyes.

Dr Thompson sat down, folded his muscular, tattooed arms, leaned back in his chair and laughed. A deep, hearty laugh that brought a sparkle to his brown eyes. Perfect white teeth showed between his dark beard and moustache. A gold cross hung from one ear lobe. His brown hair tied neatly back. "I love the funny looks I get from new patients. One little old lady dropped her bag when she saw me and her chin wasn't far off it." He laughed again. "And please call me Marc."

Kain nodded. His face returned to its normal colour. "Okay, Marc, hit me with it. No sense prolonging the suspense." He took hold of Grace's hand. His cold, clammy hand gave away his high level of fear.

Marc clicked at his computer keyboard and turned the screen toward Kain and Grace. "So, here is your CT scan pictures. This is-"

"Geez." Kain shook his head, leaning in closer to the screen. "Can you explain them to me?"

"Yes, I was about to." Marc glanced at Grace and gave a knowing smile. Obviously he was used to nervous and impatient first-timers. Using the blunt end of a pen he pointed to the screen then circled an area. "Here is your groin area. And here," the pen stopped, "is the nasty little unwelcome guest. A carcinoma in your left testicle."

Kain shifted in his chair. Beads of sweat appeared on his forehead, regardless of being in an air-conditioned room.

"But we can't waste any time. Surgery is the next step. Are you aware that testicle will have to be removed? And possibly some lymph nodes from there too, but that's not certain until the surgeon goes in."

Confusion and fear shrouded Kain's face. "Just do whatever has to be done." His leg pressed against Grace's and began trembling. "Anything to keep me alive." He glanced at Grace then dropped his gaze to her belly. "I have two good reasons to beat this. Grace is pregnant."

Marc nodded. "I'm sure you have more than two good reasons, but a loving, supportive partner is very important when going through all this and a baby on the way..." His eyes lit up with his smile. "Well, that's even better." He glanced from Kain to Grace. "Congratulations. First one?"

"Yep," Kain and Grace answered in unison.

"Great! Okay, now for what comes next." He briefly read from a sheet of paper on his desk then turned to Kain again. "The best treatment for you is to have what is called an Inguinal Orchiectomy."

Kain's swallow echoed in the small room. "Sounds scary." His eyes narrowed with a deep frown. He gripped Grace's hand tighter.

"It's the removal of that testicle. The surgeon goes in through a small incision in the groin. You'll be in hospital overnight and will be a bit sore for a little while so I suggest you organise time off work, especially if you do physical work, which it looks like you do."

"I'm a plasterer," said Kain, not taking his eyes off the doctor.

Marc typed on his keypad and brought up something different on the screen. "Just looking at your earlier blood test results. Your tumour markers were elevated so there is little doubt it is cancer, but more tests will be done on it after removal and then we determine what treatment is best for you after surgery."

Grace took her hand from Kain's and placed it around his shoulders. She knew this was coming but hearing it spoken loud and clear was more confronting than she'd imagined. Her stomach rolled and turned, but poor Kain's was probably feeling worse than hers. She leaned closer and kissed him on the cheek. "You okay with this, hon?" Her other hand reached across and rested on his thigh. "I'm here with you all the way."

"Thanks Grace." He leaned his head on her shoulder for a moment before taking a deep breath, ready to ask more questions. "Is the surgery done here in Mackay?"

"You're from…" He briefly looked at his screen again. "Anchor Bay, that's right. Actually, lucky for you the op can be done at Anchor Bay hospital, but any further treatment will have to be done here, sorry."

"By 'further treatment' you mean chemo?" Kain wiped his eyes. His chin trembled.

The doctor nodded, but there was no hint of a smile. "Most likely. But, we'll know for sure after the surgery." He glanced at the sheet of paper again. "Which, by the way, is scheduled for this Friday morning."

"Geez, they don't muck around, do they?" Kain's leg began shaking again.

"That's great news, thanks Marc," said Grace. "Best to get it over as soon as possible."

"For sure." Marc nodded to Grace then looked at Kain again. "So, Kain, later today or tomorrow you'll receive a phone call or email about your pre-op appointment and details of what time you are to be there on Friday. During the pre-op appointment they'll take some particulars about you, talk to you about the operation and you'll also speak to the anaesthetist."

Kain shook his head. "My brain is spinning with all this."

"It's ok, I'll be here to help him," assured Grace, rubbing his upper back and leaning in for another peck on his cheek.

The doctor gathered up papers from his desk. "Here are some details and the report from your scan." He handed the papers to Kain. "And this," he took out a small booklet from his desk drawer, "is some really helpful information on testicular cancer." He flicked through some of the pages. "It tells you all about the surgery and treatments and also goes into the emotional side of it all, especially for afterwards." He handed the booklet to Kain, who took it in his now trembling hand. "Oh, and by the way," continued Marc, "We have an excellent male counsellor here if you need to talk about it. He has actually been through this cancer too, so he understands your pain and worries."

"That's good to know. Thanks Marc." Grace stood up and shook his hand. Her belly felt like she'd just got off a wild ride at a theme park and her saliva glands went into action. She swallowed the excess down. What little bit of breakfast she did have earlier now threatened to vacate her stomach the way it went in. "I really need to use the loo."

Kain stood and shook Marc's hand. "Thanks mate. Guess I'll be seeing you again soon."

"Yes, you will and good luck."

Grace ran from the room and headed for the toilet she'd noticed just inside the entry. *Please don't let anyone be in there.* Sour contents rose in her oesophagus. She placed her hand over her mouth and tried to swallow it back down. The door was shut. She grabbed the handle. Engaged! No! Her head spun just as much as her stomach. She looked about, as hot liquid continued to rise and spilled out her mouth. A few metres away was a water dispenser with a bin beside it. She raced over, grabbed the bin, bent over and heaved her stomach contents into it. Her long loose hair fell forward. She tried holding it back as she continued vomiting. Again and again she heaved and retched until nothing but saliva dribbled out.

A loving hand touched her back. The click of the toilet door. An 'ugh' of disgust from the person leaving the loo. She didn't even bother looking at them. Their footsteps faded.

Slowly she stood upright. One of the ladies from the reception desk was right beside her offering an open tissue box. Grace grabbed several. "Thankyou." Her throat burned and stung as she wiped her eyes and blew her nose.

Kain handed her a disposable cup of water. "Here, this might make you feel a bit better." He grabbed another tissue and wiped saliva from the ends of her hair.

"Thanks. Oh yuk, sorry about the hair." She had several sips and handed it back to Kain who drank the rest. Grace turned to the other lady, wishing the floor would swallow her up. "I'm so sorry. I'm pregnant and-"

"Don't worry about it, love." The middle-aged receptionist waved it away. "It's no big deal in this place." She patted Grace's shoulder. "Congratulations."

"Thankyou." Grace looked down at the small bin where her vomit mixed with a few empty cups and used tissues. "Umm, I'll take this." She bent to get the sides of the plastic bag lining the bin.

"No, don't worry, we'll take care of it. You be on your way." The receptionist grabbed the bag from the bin and tied the corners shut. "Best of luck to you two."

Grace waved, grabbed Kain's hand and strode out the door. The heat in her face subsided with the cool outdoor breeze. She groaned. "How embarrassing."

"Do you feel better now?" asked Kain as they approached her car. "Maybe I should drive?"

"Umm, not sure. Yes, you'd better drive." She took the keys from her bag and tossed them to him.

They drove back to Anchor Bay again with little conversation. She felt too drained to talk much and Kain seemed to be deep in thought.

Upon reaching the outskirts of their town she remembered the ultrasound appointment. "Sweetie, we have about an hour before the ultrasound. Oh shit! I just remembered I have to drink lots of water beforehand." She took the bottle from her bag and downed several mouthfuls. "Hope it stays there."

"Do you want to go home for awhile?" asked Kain.

"Yes please. I might have a shower and see if I can eat a couple of dry biscuits or something." She *really* wanted to lie down, but the anticipation of the ultrasound was too exciting. "And have the dreaded gallon of water."

An hour or so later they sat in the waiting room for the ultrasound. Grace squirmed as her bladder filled to the brim. "I hope they aren't too much longer. I really don't want to embarrass myself here too." She looked at the clock on the wall. Ten minutes past her appointment time. *Come on!*

"Grace Atkinson!"

Grace jumped up, squeezed her pelvic muscles tight and followed the young woman who'd called her. Kain was close on her heels, but he'd been very quiet since they got back from Mackay. No doubt so much on his mind.

They entered a small, darkened room and Grace was handed a crepe gown by the sonographer. "Hi, I'm Trish. I'll be doing your ultrasound. Put this on. You can keep your underwear on, then lie here on this bed." She turned to go out the door but stopped and looked back. "Oh, is your bladder nice and full?"

"Well, it's full, but it's not so nice," laughed Grace whipping off her top. "Wait! Where are you going? I'm ready to burst." No light heartedness this time. Peeing oneself in public was no laughing matter. She was reminded of when she'd found herself in Seth/Steve's home and he'd initially kept her locked in a bedroom. She'd been bursting for the loo but didn't make it in time. Anger and embarrassment had engulfed her, but he'd taken it all in his stride, not making a fuss. Bless him. Hard to imagine now how frightened of him she'd been at first.

She got on the bed and Kain sat on the chair the opposite side to the machine. Trish entered and sat down in front of the sonography machine. "Okay, are we ready to see this bub of yours?"

Grace opened her gown a little for Trish to place some paper towel in the top of her undies and gently pulled them down a little before putting a squirt of lubricant on the doppler.

"This is it, sweetie." Kain said, standing and taking hold of Graces hand, a smile at last on his handsome face. "Our little one."

"Yep." Grace blinked back tears. Tears of love for her man and for this beautiful baby growing inside her.

Grace flinched when the doppler touched her abdomen. Quickly forgetting the cold gel and doppler pressure on her full bladder, she turned to the screen. A higher screen toward the corner of the room was probably easier to watch but craning her neck to see it much closer seemed a better idea. Even though she carried the baby, she wanted to be as close to its image as possible. Grainy, black and white odd shapes appeared. She frowned, unable to make out a definite shape of their precious little one.

Just as Grace opened her mouth to ask, Trish gasped toward the screen. She placed the doppler in its holder and got up. "I'm just going to get one of the senior sonographers." And she was gone out the door.

CHAPTER 9

Linda sat by Steve's bed and held his hand. "Dr Thebo said he'll be in shortly to take off these bandages." Seeing her son lying there, tube in his forearm, faced wrapped like a mummy, her stomach swirled with nerves, but her heart danced with excitement. Even though he'd need more surgery, Dr Thebo had told her this one had gone well and there should be some noticeable improvement. The first step in getting her wonderful son back to normal.

"Good," said Steve. He touched his face with his other hand. "Hope it has worked. It's pretty sore. So are my ribs where he took the cartilage." He shifted a little in the bed.

Sophie stood up from the chair she'd been sitting on beside her mother. "Would you like me to call a nurse for some more painkillers?" She reached for his buzzer near the head of his bed.

Steve held up his hand. "No! Sorry, no thanks Soph. I don't want to be spaced out when the doc comes in."

"Fair enough." Sophie smiled and sat back down.

Dr Thebo walked into the sterile white room. "Afternoon, everyone." His shiny black hair, flecked with grey, and olive skin a stark contrast to his pale blue medical attire. "Right, let's see what we have under those bandages."

Linda got up and moved her chair out of his way. The creepy-crawlies playing with her nerves became even more active. But her trepidation would be nothing compared to Steve's. She couldn't even begin to comprehend what he was experiencing. All she could do was support and encourage him, be positive and, most of all, love him. That was all very easy. Seeing him in physical and mental pain was not.

Steve sat up a little to allow the doctor to remove the bandages but remained silent.

"Now, I must reiterate what I told you before the surgery." Dr Thebo stopped rolling. "This is only the start. We've basically glued some synthetic skin on to your face and scalp where it was damaged, and that will take a bit of time to heal and prepare for your real graft, so a type of pressure mask will have to be worn."

Steve groaned but nodded. "For how long?"

"Not sure yet. Depends how well it takes." He continued removing the bandages. "So, please don't be disheartened if you can't see any real improvement yet." He glanced at Sophie then Linda. "And that goes for you too, Mum." He smiled a warm, empathetic smile. "But you should be able to see what I did with the droopy eyelid and the start of the ear reconstruction."

"Thankyou so much, Doctor Thebo." Linda clutched Sophie's hand. "I can't tell you enough how much we appreciate you doing this at such short notice." Her breaths stopped and her heart rate rocketed as the last of the dressing carefully came off.

Sophie's empty hand flew to her mouth, catching a sob. Her other hand gripped Linda's tighter.

Linda's eyes washed with tears. She pulled a tissue from the pocket of her knee-length shorts and wiped them, keeping hold of the tissue. Probably will need it again. Steve's scalp and facial skin, where it had been badly scarred on one side, looked angry raw and very sore. Bruising surrounded his left eye but the drooped eyelid was now back in its correct place. The knobbly stump that had remained of his left ear, was now bigger and slightly resembled an ear, but red with quite a few tiny black stitches holding it together.

Steve's brown eyes, full of hope, darted from one face to another. "Well?"

As hard as she tried, Linda couldn't stop the outburst of tears. She let go of Sophie's hand and grabbed Steve's again, sitting back down on the chair beside his bed. "Ohh, son." She stroked his cheek on his non-scarred side, unable to think of what to say. It was a start but he still looked...*frightful.* Though she mustn't let him see her horror and mentally scolded herself for thinking, or hoping, he would look 'normal' by now. She forced a smile but remembering her happiness on discovering he was still alive, turned her smile into a huge grin of relief. "It's looking good." She nodded and turned to Sophie whose face had paled. "Don't you think so, Soph?"

"Yep, definitely." Sophie grinned and wiped her glistening eyes and looked at the doctor. "What's your opinion, Doctor Thebo?"

The surgeon had moved around to the other side of Steve's bed. He nodded and smiled, showing perfect white teeth. "I'm very happy with it. We'll have you looking more like your old self soon, Steve."

"Good." Steve reached toward his semi-repaired ear.

Dr Thebo grabbed his hand. "No, don't touch it yet. You're prone to infection. We have you on intravenous antibiotics to help prevent it, but you don't want to take any chances and also don't want to risk moving the new cartilage. It'll be a bit sore and itchy for a while but that's normal. Although you're on pain meds you'll still feel some pain and discomfort."

Steve lowered his hand. "Fair enough, Doc. So, what did you actually do to me?"

Doctor Thebo sat on the edge of the bed. "Well, even without knowing what sort of acid was used in the attack, or how much, we were able to remove some of the damaged scarring and ascertain the extent of the damage. It was deeper in places than others, so it won't be possible to completely remove all evidence of the scars. I also used some laser therapy and we've covered it with the synthetic skin. Won't be long until we can use some of your own skin to complete the graft."

"From my bum cheek?" Steve started to chuckle but stopped and grimaced. "Oh, shouldn't do that."

"No," continued the doctor. "Try really hard not to use any facial expressions for the time being. Apart from the pain it might undo this first graft."

Linda stifled her involuntary laugh, ecstatic to see her son so cheery, albeit briefly. For that single moment all was right with the world.

"Can anything be done about his missing eyebrow and hair?" asked Linda.

The doctor leaned forward and studied Steve's face for a few seconds then sat back. "Most likely a tattoo for the eyebrow. They can certainly make things look very real these days. There might have been too much damage to transplant hair, but there's always wigs, or shave the lot!" He stood up. "Well, it's all looking good. At this rate I think I'll send you back to Anchor Bay hospital tomorrow. I don't really have the facilities here to keep a patient for long." He headed to the door of the room. "I'll just get the nurse to come and dress that again and I'll be back to see you tonight before I knock off."

"Thankyou," all three said at once.

Linda's phone jingled in her bag by her feet. She reached and grabbed it out. "It's Grace." She put it on loudspeaker and held it out in front of her. "Hi darling, how's things up there?"

"Hi Mum, things are okay...umm, what about there? How's Steve today?"

A nurse entered with bits and pieces in her hands. Linda and Sophie got up and moved to the opposite side of Steve's bed. He looked from the nurse back to his mother and her phone. The nurse greeted Steve by name, opened dressing packets and began redressing his face and scalp.

"Oh, he's doing really well, love. I've got my phone on loudspeaker, so you are talking to all of us. You don't sound real good. Is Kain alright?"

"Oh, just morning sickness hitting me hard. Yep, he goes in early tomorrow morning for his surgery."

"Oh good. Give him our love. We might be bringing Steve back tomorrow to recuperate in hospital there. He's going well, but we'll know for sure later or early in the morning."

"Hey, big brother," Grace said louder. "Can't wait to see you. How do you feel?"

"Hey, Grace, same here," replied Steve. "But I can't really talk now. Getting my head bandaged up."

Grace laughed. "Okay. See you soon."

Linda's happiness dulled. "Grace, have you seen Dad, or talked to him in the past day or so? He hasn't answered my last two calls. I'm a bit worried. He's not in a good frame of mind lately."

"I rang him last night, but he said he was going to bed and didn't talk much."

"How did he sound? Was he...?"

"Drunk? His words were a bit slurry, but not too bad."

A mother's instinct kicked in. "Grace, you don't sound very convincing." The familiar pit of dread opened in Linda's stomach.

"Sorry mum, I didn't want to worry you even more. But really, he wasn't as bad as when I saw him earlier in the week."

"Okay, love, I'll try him again shortly. You rest up and give that man of yours a hug from us here. Hopefully see you tomorrow sometime. Love you." She tapped the screen but held on to her phone.

Steve's face and scalp were now dressed in surgical white. The nurse tidied up, thanked him, smiled at Linda and Sophie and left the room.

He lay back down on his pillow. "Can't wait to not have to be wrapped up like this." He opened his mouth but tried in vain to stop a yawn. "I might need a bit of a sleep."

"That's okay, mate, we'll go get a coffee from over the road and be back later." Sophie patted his arm and looked at Linda. "That alright with you, Mum?"

"Yep, sounds good." Linda leaned down and kissed her son on his bandaged cheek. "We won't be too long." She patted his shoulder. "You get some sleep."

"I'll just try your father again," said Linda once they were outside the building. "You go over and order for us and I'll be there in a tic. Just want to let him know we might be home tomorrow."

Sophie nodded and headed toward the road. "Give Dad my love."

Linda tapped her phone. The home phone rang and rang but no answer. She tried his mobile. Fluttering butterflies in her belly morphed into galloping horses. Crazy to be this nervous about speaking to her beloved husband of thirty-odd years. But he had changed lately, and not for the better.

He answered with a vague and groggy, "Hello." Not even a 'hello love' or 'hello Linda'. This wasn't good. Her galloping horses turned into bucking broncos. *Why did this have to be so hard?*

She took a deep breath. "Hi Darl, it's me, Linda." Silence. "I'm just ringing to say g'day and see how everything is at home." More silence. "Bruce?"

"Yeah, I'm here. Sorry, I was asleep."

"Oh ok, sorry to wake you." Linda had never known him to sleep at this time of the afternoon. "Are you okay?" She knew damned well by his voice he wasn't his normal self.

"Yeah, yeah, just tired." He yawned and mumbled something she couldn't understand then cleared his throat. "When are you coming home?"

Was that a hint of irritability in his voice? She couldn't be sure but at least he sounded like he missed her. She missed the strong, tall, broad-shouldered man she could always rely on and loved dearly, but not so much this new version of her husband. She did her best to remain cheery. "Good news. We should be home later tomorrow."

"What, you and Soph?"

"And Steve. The surgeon said all going well he can go back to Anchor Bay hospital tomorrow to recuperate. Oh, you should see him. It's looking good and he seems happy. He's-"

"I don't give a shit!" Bruce's tone turned nasty.

Linda swallowed down the dread and anger simmering in her stomach threatening to ascend her oesophagus. "Wh-what do you mean? When we first found him you were so eager to help him." She looked about and spotted a seat on the footpath, hurried to it before her now shaky legs collapsed beneath her. Tears burned her sinuses, stung her eyes, shattered her soul.

"I mean, don't bring him back here!" His angry words hurt her ear and stabbed into her heart, like he'd split it open.

"What do you mean, Bruce." The words choked out her dry throat and trembling lips.

"I don't want that...that *creature* anywhere near me, do you hear?"

CHAPTER 10

Steve shifted his large frame in the not-so-comfortable hospital bed. He couldn't lie on his left side due to the surgery on that ear and side of his face. Lying on his right side also hurt his face and ribs. He was glad to be back in Anchor Bay, even if he needed to wear a pressure mask, but had now had a gutful of hospital beds and rooms. And of people and noises. The locked-in feeling grated on him the most. *Yeah, get used to it,* that annoying little shit of an inner voice was never far away. *You'll be locked in a jail cell soon. Maybe for years.* The room spun at that thought. No! He had to think of something cheerier. The call of the bush tugged at his heavy heart. Just to be back in his secluded home, with an abundance of wildlife, and left alone was all he wanted right now, but realistically it was just a fantasy.

He closed his eyes, switching his mind on to some of the different bird sounds he'd enjoyed every day - kookaburras laughing at dawn, raucous lorikeets feasting on the gum blossoms, magpies searching for grubs on his lawn and brightening up his day with their melodious warbling. The lonely *woop woop woop* of the pheasant far off in the bush.

And the other sounds. The constant *quiiick-kick* of the little rain frogs before a good storm. The happy croaking of the green tree frogs during and after rain. Rain hammering on his tin roof. The mating calls of the cane toads in the creek after rain. Howling dingoes after dark or just on daylight. The chorus of cicadas in the thicker bush at the back. Even the screeching fruit bats fighting over the gum flowers and, at times, his fruit trees, never bothered him. He'd take those sounds over traffic and voices any day.

The beautiful Pretty-face wallabies and other roos nibbling grass in the small clearing by his house during the late afternoon. A shy echidna occasionally waddling across his driveway. The sun sinking over the mountains, turning them all shades of blue and mauve, and spilling stunning colours into the approaching evening sky. He inhaled deep, imagining smelling the bush instead of a squeaky-clean hospital room with crisp, white bed sheets. Those precious memories spilled from his heart, moved up his throat and leaked from his eyes. The call of the wild.

"Hey Steve."

His eyes jolted open. Blinking several times, he tried clearing his blurred vision. Grace stood by his bedside, a huge smile on her pretty face. "Grace!" He sat up, pushed the pillow up against the bed head and onto its side before sitting back against it. "This is a nice surprise." He quickly grabbed a tissue and dabbed his eyes, careful with the left eye after surgery.

She leaned down and kissed the top of his forehead, taking hold of his hand as she did so. "How could I not be here for you?" A frown creased her brow. "Where's mum and Sophie? Mum said they were coming back with you." She let go of his hand, pulled the visitor's chair over closer and sat down. "I have something to tell them. And you too, of course."

"They did but went home a little while ago." He glanced up at the clock on the wall. "Sophie had some things to do but mum should be back anytime now. What is it?"

"I'll wait for mum." She touched his forearm with both hands, gentle and warm. "You were crying when I came in."

He stared at her. Her voice so soft, so caring. Her long auburn hair hanging loose. A twinge of the love he felt for her before learning they were siblings flickered throughout his body. But no. Just *no!* He shook his head, clearing away thoughts and feelings no longer appropriate. *Rather sickeningly inappropriate, you big lump.* He had no memory of anyone ever treating him with such care and kindness as Grace did back at his house, once she'd realised he wasn't going to hurt her. He shrugged. "Just sick of being in here. Sick of not knowing what's going to happen. Sick of waiting...and waiting. I just want to go home."

She took hold of his hand again. "I understand and I'm sure you'll be able to return one of these days." She brightened up. "Hey, a friend of mine is a hairdresser and she is willing to come and cut your hair if you like."

Steve grabbed a handful of his hair hanging down the right side of his head, above the dressing. "What there is of it." He thought about it briefly and nodded. "Yep, that would be good, thanks Grace. The sooner I change my ugly appearance the better. I don't care if she shaves it all off. When?"

"Great! I'll text her now. She's on holidays at the moment." Grace grabbed her phone from her bag by her chair and tapped away.

Linda walked in carrying a bunch of native wildflowers. "Hello you two." She placed the flowers on the bed beside Steve, hugged Grace when she stood up then leaned over to hug Steve. "How are you feeling, son?"

"Ohhh, alright I suppose, considering." He picked up the flowers, brought them to his face and sniffed. The scent of the bush. His home. The different coloured Grevilleas, Bottlebrush, Waratah and Native Wattle cheered him up a little but also increased the yearning to return to where he was most comfortable. "These are nice."

Linda opened the cupboard in his room and took out a glass vase. "Thought you might appreciate something familiar." She went into his bathroom and returned with the vase full of water. Steve handed her the bunch and she placed them in water, leaving them on his bedside table.

Grace had gone into the hallway outside his room and returned with another chair for her mother. "Mum, before you sit down I want to tell you and Steve something." She placed her hand on her abdomen, her face giving nothing away.

"Sure, love. Is everything okay? Is Kain okay?" Linda looked from her daughter to her son. Steve gave an I-don't-know-anything shrug.

"Yes, Kain is okay." Grace's face changed from neutral to serious. "He's still in surgery. I stayed with him for as long as they'd let me beforehand. Shouldn't be too much longer now." She broke into a grin. "But it's not about Kain...well, sort of is, I suppose."

Linda laughed. "The suspense is killing us. Come on, spill, girl."

"Kain and I are expecting twins!" Grace's grin remained but now her eyes watered. "It's unreal! We're still trying to get our heads around it. One was exciting enough but *two!*" She pulled a tissue from her jeans pocket and wiped her eyes.

"Wow, love, that's wonderful news." Linda hugged Grace tight. "When did you find out?" She let go and sat down.

Grace sat on the other chair. "At the ultrasound the other day. The sonographer had us worried for a bit when she jumped up to go get a senior. We didn't know what to think."

"I bet Kain is thrilled," said Linda.

"He sure is. We both are. But just hope it won't mean the morning sickness will be twice as bad." Grace rolled her eyes. "Not fun."

Linda laughed and patted Grace's knee. "It's all worth it in the end." She turned to Steve. "Great news, don't you think, Steve? Things are finally looking up for this family."

"Yeah, sure is. Congratulations, Grace." A fleeting stab of... what, *jealousy,* sped through his heart. *Get over it, you idiot!* Then it was gone and he surprised himself by feeling genuinely happy for Grace and Kain. Hopefully his face will look much better when the babies arrive. He didn't want to terrify his nieces or nephews with his scarred face like the numerous kids who'd run away from him on the streets of Karisdale.

Grace's phone pinged. She looked at the screen. "Amy just gave the thumbs up sign about cutting your hair. She only lives around the corner from here."

Linda frowned. "Who's Amy?"

"My friend, the hairdresser, Mum. Pretty sure you've met her. She's offered to cut Steve's hair."

"You mean shave it," Steve said. "I want it all gone." Swarms of fear and regret gushed through his veins and into his stomach. "I want all trace of Seth Andrews *gone.*"

A knock on his door. Steve looked up. Jenna stood there, holding a small gift box tied with a black ribbon.

"Jenna!" Steve's heart lightened. A smile almost reached his lips. Then a twinge of fear that she may not want to see him with his face still covered in the mask and dressings. But, as before, she showed no hint of shock or disgust. Just a lovely smile. "Come in. Mum, you remember Jenna?"

"Yes, nice to see you again, Jenna." Linda smiled and shook her hand.

Steve pointed to Grace. "And this is my sister, Grace. Grace, Jenna is Dr Leeson's sister. She wants to write my story."

Grace and Jenna exchanged greeting then Grace looked at Steve with concern. "You're okay with this? Not long ago you wouldn't have wanted a bar of something like that."

"At first I wasn't keen, but I thought about it and..." He shrugged. "It might help me get past all the sh-, bad stuff."

Grace's phone pinged again. "This might be about Kain." She quickly looked at the screen. "Yep, coming out of surgery now." She jumped up. "I'll catch you two later on." She kissed her mother and brother. "Have my chair, Jenna and nice to meet you." And she was gone out the room.

"Give my love to Kain," Linda called after her.

Jenna sat down and held up the small, colourful box. "Umm, apparently this was delivered to the nurses' station just before I arrived. When I asked if I could see you they asked me to bring it in to you."

Steve took it from her. What the hell could it be? 'Steve Atkinson' was written on the lid. Basic handwriting in black ink. Nothing familiar and nothing odd about it. He undid the ribbon and opened the lid. He glanced at Linda and Jenna. Both sets of eyes glued to him, faces curious. Inside was a piece of folded paper. He took it out, dropping the box on the bed, and opened out the paper. Nothing but a pencil drawing of two open hands, each one splattered with red paint. Or was it blood? His breath stopped in his throat with a gasp. Lightning bolts of fear pierced his heart and turned his stomach to instant mush before exploding like fireworks up his spine and out to his fingers. He dropped the paper. The air suddenly felt arctic cold.

He leaned back and closed his eyes. Who the hell sent this? Had to be one of Scott's men. But *why?* He couldn't recall hurting any of his men. Unless it was a victim of one of the crimes he'd been forced to commit. Who knows. His mind raged in a torrent of thoughts and fragmented memories. Memories of the past five years. Memories he wished could be totally obliterated and replaced with ones of his life before the brutal attack.

Linda snatched the paper from his trembling hands, gasped as it then fluttered down and landed on his forearm. "What the heck does this mean?"

Steve didn't answer right away. No idea what to say, especially when he didn't have a clue what it meant. He slowly opened his eyes. His mother stood by his bed, her face a mix of horror and shock and now quite pale. Jenna had picked up the paper and was staring at it, shaking her head, her forehead creased.

Steve inhaled deep and let it out slow, trying to calm the upheaval in his belly and every other part of his body. Or maybe buying himself some time to come up with an answer to his mother's question. "I don't know. Honestly." What more could he say?

"Hands splattered in red can only mean one thing," said Jenna, folding the paper back up and placing it on the bedside table. "Blood on his hands". Then hastily added, "*Someone's* hands." Her face showed no emotion.

"Steve, do you think someone is after you?" Linda's voice now laced with panic and worry. "We can ask for a policeman to sit outside your room. I know you are in my care but I can't protect you all the time." She let out a sob and clenched her lips together for a moment as she grasped Steve's hand. "I can't bear the thought of losing you again." Her bottom lip trembled and eyes glistened.

"You won't lose me again, mum."

A knock on the door drew their gazes. A short, dark-skinned lady stood there, her hair several different colours, braided and tied around her head. "Umm, hello..." Her large brown eyes darted to and from each person in the room. A nervous smile showed perfect white teeth. "I'm Amy, Grace's friend. I came to cut her brother's hair." She focussed on Steve, then looked confused. "I guess that's you." She reached into her large shoulder bag and brought out a smaller calico bag. "But, I can't really do it properly unless that pressure mask and dressing can come off." She shook her head, looking even more confused. "Maybe I misunderstood Grace. I thought she meant today."

Steve really didn't need this right now anyway. The room was becoming too crowded. Too noisy. Too *everything* he didn't like. People, pressure, stress and fear. What should he say? He appreciated Grace organising this for him, but just *not now.* "No, sorry, I don't think it should come off yet."

Linda must have sensed his agitation. "Hi Amy, I'm Linda, Grace and Steve's mum." She shook Amy's hand, adorned with multiple rings and long red fingernails. "This really isn't a good time. Something has just come up and," she glanced at the folded piece of paper. "Is it possible to come back another time soon?"

A friendly smile lit up Amy's face. "Sure, no problems. I'll stay in touch with Grace and we'll organise another time. It...", she hesitated, maybe in embarrassment, the smile gone. "It probably would be best to do it after all his surgical stuff is finished anyway."

"Thanks Amy," said Steve. "Sorry."

"I'm happy to pay you for your services," said Linda.

"It's all good." A little wave, a big smile and Amy left the room.

Jenna stood up. "Look, maybe I should come back another day, too."

"No, you don't have to go." Steve lifted his hand, almost reaching out and taking hers. No, too forward. He dropped it back by his side, hoping the anonymous drawing hadn't put her off him or scared her. Probably did. Story of his pathetic life.

Much to his surprise Jenna took hold of his hand. His heart flipped a little cartwheel. "I really should get going. I have an appointment soon anyway. Don't worry, I *will* be back, and soon. I'm more intrigued than ever by you, Steve." A beautiful smile, a shake of his hand and she turned and left with a slight limp.

"She seems very nice," said Linda, a slight grin and a strange look on her face. "Very nice."

"Yeah, righto Mum, don't get any ideas." But in his heart he totally agreed.

A large, suited up man appeared in the doorway, beads of sweat running down the sides of his stern, red face. Steve's nerves spun into overdrive. Who the hell was this? And why so many people today?

"Steve Atkinson?"

He looked way too serious. This can't be good. "Yes," answered Steve. "Who are you?" Hopefully another doctor.

"I'm Senior Detective Bill Clements." He pulled a handkerchief from his top pocket, wiped his face and fished his official looking badge out of the same pocket, showed Steve then Linda and returned both to that pocket. "I'm here to update you on our investigation into the crimes of James McTaggart and his accomplices."

A silent, but sickly wave of fear swamped Steve, dragging him down to unbreathable depths. "Accomplices? As in me?" The words croaked out a throat suddenly dry and scratchy as desert sand. Pointless asking the question. Steve already knew the answer. The moment he'd been dreading the most now here.

Linda stood proud and tall and offered her hand. "Hello, Detective. I'm Linda, Steve's mother. I'd like to stay for this."

The detective returned her handshake. "Yes, of course you can. You are, after all, his guardian are you not?"

"Thankyou and yes I am." Linda sat back down and gestured to the chair vacated by Jenna. "Would you like a seat?"

"No, thank you. I've just travelled from Mackay. I'll be comfortable standing." He pulled some folded papers from the inner pocket of his suit jacket, opened them out, read under his breath while running a thumb and forefinger down each side of his thick, dark moustache.

Steve looked at his mum who watched the detective muttering to himself what he read but Steve couldn't understand a word of it. Was it another language or his own? The seconds ticked by. The *whirr* of the morning tea trolley going past his doorway briefly diverted his attention.

Food? Glad the tea lady didn't come in. No way could his stomach hold any food right now. And no way did he need yet another person crowding his room.

Detective Clements folded the pages and returned them to his inner pocket and looked at Steve. "Right, Mr Atkinson." He folded his arms and lifted his head a little, forcing his chin outwards, looking like he was enjoying every second of this. "As you know, James McTaggart was shot dead during the robbery of Bruce Atkinson's, *your* father I might add, cattle. The other accomplices of that theft were arrested except for you." He squinted a little, not taking his eyes from Steve, and shooting daggers into his soul. "You absconded on horseback. Luckily one of them, Jimmy, told us your address and we soon found you, didn't we?" A brief smirk.

"Yes," sighed Steve, glancing to Linda whose eyes, now watering, continued to watch the detective.

"Jimmy and one of the others also told us everything they knew. Really spilled their guts." He nodded with one raised eyebrow and a definite smirk this time.

"E-everything?" Worse than Steve feared. Jimmy gets scared too easily. Probably peed his pants in fear and might still get off light after blabbing all he knew. Steve wanted to ask if he'd told the police about the horse killing the man at Scott's cattle yards and them having to bury him then and there, but decided to keep that quiet, just in case. Afterall, it wasn't any fault of theirs. The horse was wild and brutal. He wasn't called The Black Tornado for nothing. Nope, best not to mention it. Just go along with it.

"Yes." Clements cleared his throat. "There have been some very serious crimes committed. Heinous crimes. Crimes that can have you locked up for the rest of your miserable life."

Linda swallowed noisily, wiping her eyes.

Steve had watched movies set in prisons. The loud *clang* of the heavy cell door banging shut behind him jerked his head back. Plain coloured prison uniform. A bare cell, not much bigger than his bathroom back home. No window. No birds, trees or animals. Violent inmates at every turn. No seeing his family except through thick glass. For. The. Rest. Of. His. Life. "I'd rather die." He closed his eyes.

"It seems you might be spared a long sentence, though, Mr Atkinson."

Steve's eyes shot open. Did he just hear correctly? "What do you mean?" Was there hope?

Linda wiped her eyes. "What are you saying, Detective? Is there a chance my son won't be going to prison?" She gulped in a big breath and seemed to hold it.

"It's not over yet, of course, but with similar testimony from more than one accomplice, it's clear you were forced into committing these crimes. Is that true?"

"Yes, we all were. I never wanted to do any of it. Hated every second! But Scott, I mean McTaggart, never gave me a choice. Not once." His mind flashed to just one of the crimes. Images of dying horses sickened him. The gunshots echoing through the surrounding bush, followed by a retch of vomit from the sheer horror of what he'd just done. Beautiful, innocent animals shot by his own hands, simply because Scott seemed to hold a grudge against the owner. He had no idea what the problem was, just did as he was told or threatened with becoming dingo bait or the likes. He knew it would happen too. He'd seen what had become of those who crossed Scott or disobeyed the muscular, short Scotchman. Stomach acid rose to his throat at the terrifying memories of not just what he'd witnessed happen to some of the unlucky ones, but also the tortured state of others' lifeless bodies. Steve shuddered and gazed out his window, too afraid to look at his mother lest she was able to somehow read his thoughts.

"And," continued the detective, "you will be formally interviewed. But don't get too excited." He leaned toward Steve shaking his finger. "Even with being forced to commit these crimes you won't be getting off scot-free, I can almost guarantee that!"

Scot-free? Steve almost laughed at the irony of those words. No way in hell would he ever be *free* of Scott the evil monster, even if he was now six feet under. He turned toward the detective. "I don't expect to."

"Then there's your alleged amnesia to be addressed as well." He pointed to Steve's face. "And I'm assuming this surgical dressing is to do with the scars from an acid attack. Do you know who did it?"

Steve shook his head. "Nope. No idea. I remember hearing a few voices. Did Jimmy or any of the others say anything about it?"

"It was mentioned, but no one knew who did it. Jimmy said he didn't think McTaggart ordered it. Thinks it was someone else's doing."

Linda gasped. "Steve, do you think that's possible? You thought that Scott bloke had someone do it."

"I don't know what to think anymore, Mum." Tiredness swept over Steve. His brain hurt. Too much to think about. All this time he'd thought Scott was responsible for his attack but he knew no reason why he would have done it. He was never game to ask him outright about the attack, but Scott hinted a few times that if he didn't do everything he was told the beating and acid attack would be like a 'Sunday School picnic' compared to what would happen to him.

"I'll leave you alone now," said Clements, his tone and facial expression softening. "Get some rest and get your strength back. You have a long, rough road ahead of you. We will be in touch." He turned to Linda. "Nice to meet you Mrs Atkinson."

"And you." Linda smiled and nodded.

The detective turned to leave.

"Wait!" called Steve.

Clements stopped and turned around. "What is it?"

"I was just wondering if I will be able to go back home. To my home in the bush."

"You mean the house where you were arrested?"

"Yes," replied Steve, images of that frightening confrontation between him, his father, the police, Kain and Grace flickered through his weary mind. Guns. Gunshot. His father going down. Wanting to shoot himself rather than be arrested. Learning Grace was his sister. Learning who he really was.

"That property, along with several others belonging to James McTaggart have been seized. They are classed as proceeds of crime. No, you won't be able to go back there. Ever!"

"Never?" A landslide of disappointment smashed Steve like a ramrod, slamming his shattered heart to the floor. "Then you may as well lock me up and throw away the key."

CHAPTER 11

Kain drank the last of his coffee, put the cup back on the tray and pushed the bed table away from his hospital bed. He pressed into the mattress with each hand and tried to pull his bum back to sit up straighter but a sudden twinge of pain in his groin area stopped him. "Ow!" He flopped back on to his pillow. Anaesthetic must be wearing off.

"Take is slow, Kain," said Grace, getting up from her chair. "What do you want to do?" She took hold of his hand.

He gazed at her. The look of love on her beautiful face drove deep into his heart. His mind still a bit hazy, but clear enough to silently scold himself yet again for ever doubting their love and commitment to each other. Doubted enough to stupidly push her away which began a string of events that no one could have foretold, especially Steve, her long-thought dead brother being found and returning to his relieved family. Except Bruce, his and Grace's father. What an arrogant arsehole he had been after Grace's presumed death and still an arsehole now to his son. A son he should be grateful to still have. Kain had no comprehension at all as to how a father could be like that. His own parents both so loving and supportive.

"Kain!" Grace squeezed his hand. "You're still off with the pixies aren't you? Your eyes are glazed over." She smiled and stroked the side of his face with the back of her fingers. "Do you want to sleep? I can come back later, darl."

His mind switched back to the here and now. His Grace. His world. He took hold of her hand with both of his. "Grace, have I told you how much I love you? I'm so sorry for breaking things off last month. What an idiot I was."

She gave a chuckle and her green eyes sparkled. "Honey, it's all good. Yes, you've told me those things over and over since you found me at Steve's house." She nodded proudly. "At least I only think of him as Steve now and not Seth anymore." Grace sat back down. "Hey, you've barely touched the sandwiches they brought. Are you feeling alright?"

"No, a bit queasy, but I should be right soon." He swallowed the oversupply of saliva in his foul-tasting mouth. "Just glad the surgery is over." He'd lost a testicle. Shit! *He'd lost a testicle!* Half of what made him a man. What in the hell did that make him now? Sure, the pamphlets and doctor explained the procedure and made a point of saying it would no way affect his manliness or the ability to 'perform' in bed. And definitely wouldn't give him a squeaky voice. So why did he feel like...*like what?* He couldn't even fathom it himself let alone explain to Grace. He didn't know one other man who'd been through this. Maybe he did and they were too embarrassed to ever tell anyone. Then he remembered the oncologist had mentioned the male counsellor at the Cancer Centre had been through it all. "Grace, remind me to see the counsellor."

"That's sudden. Do you mean the one Doctor Thompson mentioned?"

"Yes, him."

"Sure, but you need to get over this surgery first. How about in a few days? You should be allowed home tomorrow. We can call and make an appointment then."

She gently brushed her hand up his forehead and into his short hair. It was growing again after he'd had it practically shorn in preparation for losing it from chemo. Another stupid, thoughtless thing he did. Grace had always loved his blond waves and he adored her long auburn hair, especially how it shone in sunlight. "Grace, please don't ever get your hair cut."

She smiled and frowned at the same time while shaking her head. "Where did that come from? I told you ages ago I wouldn't."

Kain shrugged one shoulder. "I don't know. Crazy thoughts are flying around my brain at the moment. Must be from the anaesthetic."

"Knock, knock." Joe entered the room, a brown paper bag in his hand. "Hey you two." He shook Kain's hand followed by a slight punch to his shoulder then pecked Grace on the cheek.

"Hey, Joe," greeted Grace with a smile.

"Good to see you, mate." Kain tried to return the punch but wily Joe sprung back, bouncing his trademark brown curls about.

Joe laughed. "Ha! Too slow, Burrows."

Kain looked about his room. "I was going to say, pull up a stump, but you'll have to go find yourself one."

Grace stood up. "Here, Joe, have mine. I think I need to go for a bit of a walk outside. Not feeling too great all of a sudden." Her face paled.

"Grace, no you don't look good." Kain sat himself up, this time ignoring the pain. It wasn't as bad as seeing his Grace suffering. "What's wrong?"

Joe took hold of her arm. "You sit right back down, young lady."

Grace smiled and gently lifted his hand off her arm. "I'm okay, just this bloody morning sickness that comes in waves." She had a sip of water from the cup on Kain's bedside table. "I don't know why it was ever called 'morning' sickness when it can happen any time of the day." She took another sip. "I just need a bit of fresh air." She pointed to her vacated chair. "Joe, sit your bum here and catch up with your mate for a bit." She leaned and kissed Kain on the lips. "See you soon." As she stood to leave she turned to Joe again. "Watch out he doesn't profess his love for you." She smiled, winked at Kain and left.

Joe turned back to Kain with a huge grin. "What's she on about? Are you batting for the other team all of a sudden?"

Kain laughed and the sombre mood brightened, driving the crazy thoughts clear out of his mind. Joe could always make light of a serious situation. "Nah, don't be silly. Just a private joke."

"Good." said Joe in mock seriousness. "I don't have to watch me back then."

"You idiot." Kain laughed again. "And why aren't you at work? Eddie wouldn't be happy with both of us off."

Joe sat on the chair. "He's as happy as a pig in shit, mate. We all put in long hours this week and got this job finished yesterday, days ahead of schedule so he gave us all the day off today. The painters are rapt. Now they can start. So, how are you, really? I can't imagine what you're going through." He handed Kain the paper bag. "Oh, here's a present for you."

Kain took the bag, unsure what to expect to find inside. Knowing Joe it could be some sort of prank or joke. He unfolded the top of the bag to find an array of individually wrapped chocolates and some packets of mixed lollies. "Jeez Joe, you trying to fatten me up or something?" He laughed. "Thanks mate. I'll have some later. Still a bit queasy in the gut right now." Kain put the bag on the bedside table just as the same lady who'd brought his food came and picked up the tray.

"Not too hungry I see. Tsk, tsk." She frowned but a little glint in her eye showed she was joking.

"Not yet, but thanks," replied Kain.

"No worries, buddy." And she was gone.

Kain turned back to Joe. "How's Sue?"

"She's great. She sends her love and said to tell you to get your boof head out of here soon and come over for a barbie, a few beers and shoot some pool, with Grace of course."

"We will." But then Kain remembered he'll probably have to go through chemo and God only knows what else. Probably be sick as a dog. What bit of food and drink he did just consume stirred in his belly, threatening to dislodge. Hell, if just the thought of chemotherapy made him almost spew what will happen when he is actually having it? He'd seen his Auntie suffer through it with breast cancer. Her hair slowly falling out until she was completely bald, her fingernails breaking and dropping off. Skin off her cheeks from the continuous watering eyes, not to mention how terrible she *said* she felt. But... she made it through okay and he could too. Hopefully. But then there was his grandfather who died while having chemo, not long after he'd proposed to his newish, and very lovely, partner who'd already begun wedding plans. A swirl of fear swept over him like some roaring dust storm. He swallowed hard, determined to keep his stomach contents right where they should be.

"Kain, did you hear me?" Joe leaned a little closer. "I said you have to share those chocolates with Grace and the little ones." A grin lit up his face. "How good is that, hey? Twins! I was rapt when you rang and told me the other day."

"What? Oh sorry, mate. I was miles away." Kain flicked his head, trying to get rid of that dust storm of doom. "Yeah, bloody good. Can't wait to be a dad." What if he died while having chemo? Leaving Grace alone as a single mother. No, that won't do. He may not be able to control his lot in life or whether he lives or dies but there was *one* thing he could do. "Joe, I need you to help me with something."

"Anything, just name it."

"I want to propose to Grace."

"That's great, but what can I do? Yous can have a romantic dinner or outing when you get out of here and you can pop the question then." Joe's smile was gone, replaced by confusion. "What could I possibly do?" He shrugged.

Urgency now replaced Kain's fear and dread. "No, I want to do it now. Today!"

Joe still looked totally confused. "That's great but…"

"I don't have a ring and I can't just run out and buy one right now. What do you reckon I could do or give her until I can get the real thing? Mate, she deserves the best after everything she's been through lately."

Joe's face lit up like a Christmas tree. "I have an idea. Wait here." He jumped up and rushed out the door.

"Well, I can hardly go anywhere, can I?" Kain called after him, then smiled to himself. Joe was the best mate anyone could wish for, since back in high school. They not only worked together but Grace and Sue were also good friends and the four often socialised together and always had each other's backs.

Joe was the one that got him out of the frightening black hole after his diagnosis and learning that Grace had been killed in that fiery car accident up on the range. He almost swallowed the whole bottle of his mother's sleeping pills. Only way he could see out of the pain and torment. But Joe stopped him and Kain soon realised it may not have been Grace that was killed as the body was burnt beyond recognition. Bull-headed Bruce used his money and community standing to have 'Grace's' remains cremated immediately, solely to prevent Kain attending her funeral. It still stabbed into Kain's soul that Bruce blamed him for Grace's assumed death. As if he hadn't already felt shattered to breaking point. Punching Bruce that day sure felt good.

It had taken a bit of convincing Joe that Grace may still be alive and defy the police to go search for her in rugged bush. Joe lied to their boss, Eddie, to take time off work and, although sceptical, he went along with Kain and another friend, Anthony, traipsing through the bush for several days, rifle in hand, camping rough, almost being bitten by a brown snake but eventually discovering her at Steve's house. Of course, the police and Bruce had to arrive at almost the same time and Bruce tried to take all the glory. Kain shuddered, remembering accidently shooting Bruce in the leg. Amazingly, Bruce never had him charged for that. Hmph! He still might, knowing him. Then there was Grace's mighty *thwack* to his jaw when he first found her and tried to explain. The proverbial redhead temper had showed through, but luckily, not for long. But he certainly did deserve that. Yep, he'd been such an idiot. He closed his eyes and thought about the beautiful reunion he and Grace had when she finally understood and forgave him.

Joe rushed back in holding out his open hand. "Here mate, this is the best I could do at such short notice."

A small ring containing a red stone lay on his palm. Kain looked from it to Joe. "What...where did you get that?"

"One of those little vending machines down in the foyer. I noticed it when I came in. Didn't think they still existed." Joe held it up between his thumb and forefinger. "It'll do for now, won't it?" He slipped it on to his own little finger. "It should fit Grace's finger."

Kain laughed and shook his head. "Of all the things I wondered what you would bring back one of those was definitely not on the list. Trust you. Let me have a close look at it." Kain held out his hand. "Better be quick. Grace'll be back any minute."

Joe tried to pull the ring off. His eyes widened. "Oh shit! It's stuck!"

"Yeah right, mate." Kain laughed again. "Come on, stop mucking around."

"Fair dinkum, I'm not." Joe pulled harder while trying to turn the ring. "Fuck!" He reached over and held the back of his hand close to Kain's face. "Umm, you wanted a closer look. Here it is." He stifled a laugh.

"Joe, it's not bloody funny this time. Spit on it. No don't! We don't need your saliva on it too." Kain glanced at the door then back to Joe. "C'mon mate, do something. Get it off!"

"How?" Joe continued to pull and twist. "It just won't friggin' budge."

Grace walked in. She looked from Kain to Joe and frowned. "What's going on? You two have weird looks on your faces."

Joe quickly stepped back, put his hands behind his back and gazed up at the ceiling, keeping his face straight and emotionless.

"You're back," said Kain reaching for her hand. "Feeling better?"

She kissed him and sat on the chair. "Yep, much better, thanks. How about you?"

"Pretty good now." The loving thoughts of Grace and the muddling mishap caused by crazy Joe must have chased away the nausea. He glanced at Joe. What part of his upper arms Kain could see were moving a little. He must be *still* trying to get that bloody ring off. "Joe, as I was saying, your hands stink a bit mate. I don't know what you've been doing but you really need to go in there." He pointed to his private bathroom. "And give them a good wash. Use plenty of that liquid soap on the wall."

Joe's face lit up with a momentary glance of *hey, good idea*. He spun around and disappeared into the bathroom.

Grace laughed but continued to frown. "That was a bit strange."

"Don't worry about it." Kain grinned, more from what he was about to do, or more to the point, what he *hoped* to do once he had that ring in his hands. "You know Joe. Unpredictable." That wasn't entirely true. Joe was reliable and quite predictable, in a good way, but Kain couldn't think of what to say that wouldn't make Grace suspicious and ask more questions. Questions he didn't want himself or Joe to have to bumble their way through answering.

Joe returned from the bathroom, one hand slightly closed. "Well, that's better. Sorry about that. I was cleaning a clogged drain before I came in. Mustn't have washed me hands properly. Actually, I gotta get going." He walked around the opposite side of the bed to which Grace was sitting and took hold of Kain's hand lying by his side. "See ya later, mate."

The ring dropped into Kain's hand, hopefully out of Grace's sight. "Yeah, Joe, see ya later. Thanks for coming."

Joe walked around the bed and patted Grace's shoulder. "See you later too, Grace." Behind her back he grinned, winked at Kain and gave the thumbs up signal before leaving.

Kain sat himself up straighter and reached for Grace's hand. "Grace, I love you like crazy." He blinked several times to dry his dampening eyes. "And I want to spend the rest of my life with you."

"I love you too and I want to spend the rest of *my* life with you, too." Her eyes glistened.

He held out the toy ring with his other hand. "Grace Atkinson, will you marry me?"

A huge smile lit up Grace's face. Her teary eyes sparkled and a tear slid down one cheek. "Of course I will!" She let go of his hand, stood, wiped away the tear and leaned down for a soft, beautiful kiss. "But what is this?" She nodded toward the ring.

"It's the best I could do...for now. When I can I'll get you the real thing, or you can choose it." Kain took hold of her left hand and slid the ring on. It was tight but a little push saw it all the way on.

Grace opened her hand out and held it up closer to her face. "It's..." she laughed a little. "It's beautiful, sweetie."

Phew! Kain's built up tension flowed from his body. "You don't think it's too cheesy?"

Grace laughed. "Don't be silly. I think it's very romantic. Can't wait to show it off. Mum and dad will be thrilled."

Her smile disappeared like a light switched off. "Well, at least *mum* will be."

CHAPTER 12

Steve ran his hand over his now bald head. It sure felt strange but in a good way. Part of Seth Andrews fell away with his scraggly locks of brown and grey when Amy had done the job. The nurse had removed the temporary dressing from his face before she'd shaved his head. Amy had then taken a hand-held mirror from her bag and asked if he'd like to see himself. He'd hesitated. Something he hadn't done in years was look in a mirror. No reason or desire to see his grotesque self at his home so he'd taken all the mirrors down and thrown them out. But curiosity had gotten the better of him and he'd looked in Amy's mirror. What or who looked back terrified him. Bald head, odd shaped left ear, red demonic eyes with no feeling. Redness over his face, still full of scars. He opened his mouth. Broken, stained teeth turned into fangs which grew before his eyes and dripped saliva. His red eyes turned yellow like the wild dogs. His mouth opened. A howling scream echoed out.

"Steve, wake up."

Something was shaking him. Or was it an earthquake? Or thunder? Everything quietened. Steve opened his eyes. "Huh?" He looked about his hospital room.

Dr Leeson stood at his bedside. He looked at his watch. "Yep, still morning. You must have been having a bad dream. You were twitching and groaning."

"Yeah, sure was." Steve flicked his head to try and clear it and inhaled deeply, relief washing over him.

The doctor raised his eyebrows and nodded. "Glad it's over." Leaning in closer he touched several parts of Steve's face and head. "This is going well." He grabbed Steve's chart from its plastic pocket hanging on the end of his bed, read some, lifted a page and read some more. "Hmm, looks like you're going back to Doctor Thebo next week for another graft. This time using your own skin." He looked again at Steve. "You should see a much better result after that." He replaced the chart. "Best of all you are going home today. Who is picking you up?"

"Umm, Mum is I think." Home. *Home* is out in the bush away from all humans, but he wouldn't be able to go there. His nerves jittered and danced, sending his stomach into a sickly swirl. Where *would* he go? The thought of going to his parents' place, at least the thought of being around his father, did nothing but sicken him to the depths of his soul.

"Good. It's very obvious she loves you and will take good care of you, too. They're on a cattle property, right?"

"Yep, that's right."

"Just be careful with your face and ear. Even with the mask try not to get dust on it, especially farmyard dust. Or wet. But I believe you've been given written instructions about all that." He patted Steve's forearm. "Oh, I think Jenna is keen to catch up with you again soon too."

"No worries, doc. Yes, I have some info." He nodded toward some paper on his bedside table. "And I'll be careful. And tell Jenna that'll be good. I don't have a phone anymore. Can you give her mum's number, please? She won't mind."

"I'll just have to check with your mum first. We can't just give out peoples' phone numbers."

His mother walked into the room, her face beaming. "Hello Steve. Hi Doctor Leeson."

"Hello Mrs Atkinson. Good timing. We just mentioned you."

"Oh, all good I hope. But nothing can dampen my mood this morning." She put an overnight bag on the end of the bed and looked at Steve, love glowing from her glistening eyes. "My boy is coming home." She took hold of his hand and squeezed.

Steve squeezed back. Second to Grace, he felt completely at ease and safe with his mother although he still couldn't remember her as mum. Hopefully that will change. "Mum, is it alright for Doctor Leeson to give Jenna your number to contact me on? I don't know when I'll be able to get another phone."

"Jenna?" She flickered a brief look of confusion, then a knowing smile. "Ohh, Jenna. Yes, of course." She grabbed a pen and paper from her bag, wrote the number down and handed it to the doctor. "Now you make sure she gets this."

Steve was sure a wink followed the words and his face flushed warm. *Oh mum!* No doubt doctor Leeson, as Jenna's older brother, would be horrified at the thought of him being anything more than a subject for her article. *Of course he would be you idiot, and with good reason. You're a criminal and a frightful looking one at that!*

Doctor Leeson showed no emotion as he put it in his shirt pocket. "Thanks, I will. Right, so everything is done here. You're good to go. You have a flight booked to Brisbane next week, don't you, for the follow up surgery? Everything all organised there with doctor Thebo?"

Steve looked at his mother. Things had been discussed and mentioned but he couldn't remember if it was all organised or not. "Mum?"

"Yes, all organised. You and I are flying down on Tuesday and the surgery is the next day."

"Well, I guess I'll be seeing you again sometime soon. Best of luck, Steve." He shook Steve's hand and started to head out the door but stopped and turned. "There's one other thing..." He looked unsure of what to say or how to say it.

Oh no, is this where he plays the protective big brother? Steve's face flushed hot again. He really didn't know how to handle this sort of thing but hoped he sounded calm and unnerved. He cleared his throat. "What is it, Doc?"

Tim looked at Linda. "I believe Steve is in your legal care. I was just wondering if you've spoken to the police in the last day or so. We had to call them yesterday to inform them Steve could be released."

"Yes," replied Linda. "All good. They rang me last night and gave the okay for me to take him home."

"Right. Good!" Tim smiled, nodded and left the room.

"Okayyyy." Linda's beaming smile was back. "Let's get you packed up and out of this place and home...where you should be."

Steve stood by his hospital bed and looked around his room. "Not really anything much to pack. All my clothes and things are at your place, right?" No way could he call his parents' place *home*. He only knew one home. With no recollection at all of his past life on the family property he had no idea of where he was going or what it would be like. There was no excitement tingling his bones, only dread in the depths of his stomach. Dread of the unknown and of seeing his father.

"Yes, son, but I did bring you some clean clothes and some new thongs." She picked up the bag and handed it to Steve.

"Thanks." He took the bag and went into the bathroom to change.

Travelling along his parents' driveway, Steve looked from one side to the other and ahead, hoping some sort of lightbulb of recognition would flick on in his brain, but so far nothing looked even vaguely familiar. Linda had wanted to chat during the drive from the hospital, but his mind was a beehive of activity with too many different thoughts and, of course, fears. Fears mainly of how he will handle and cope with being here.

Cattle grazing in lush paddocks reminded him of helping Scott and his men try and steal some of Bruce's expensive cattle. He'd had no idea the cattle belonged to his father. That operation was the downfall of Scott and the men who worked for him, even those forced to, like himself. Steve couldn't have been happier to be told by police that Scott had been shot dead. At least he'd never have to deal with him again, and that was a huge relief. But he still had to deal with the consequences of his involvement, and of course his surgery and amnesia.

Linda stopped the car close by the house. "Well, here we are." She placed her left hand on his knee. "Are you okay?"

Steve stared at the house. A neat Queenslander with a set of stairs leading straight down from a wide verandah to the ground only metres away from him. Some large, leafy pot plants hung beneath the edge of the verandah. "What? Oh, yeah, alright." He gazed further around. Multi-coloured flowering shrubs and roses looked right at home around the house. Over to the right stood a large shed. As much as he could see in the open bays, parked there was a land cruiser not unlike his own white one - technically Scott's - and a cattle truck. Beyond the shed a large set of wooden cattle yards stood, with several shady trees in and around them.

"I don't suppose you remember any of this?" Linda asked, her voice full of hope.

Steve looked at his mother. Her eyes also full of hope and possibly a tear. How he wished he could tell her what she desperately wanted to hear, but no point lying. "No, sorry." He got out of Linda's SUV and grabbed his bag from the back seat, closing both doors.

She was right beside him. "Would you like me to carry your bag?"

Not something he expected from his mum, or any lady for that matter. "No, Mum, you don't have to do that."

Steve took a step toward the stairs. Any fluttering butterflies in his stomach along the way had now morphed into fighting fruit bats. He dropped the bag and wiped his palms on the front of his jeans before picking it up again. He swallowed and wished for a drink to moisten his dry mouth.

Two dogs came bounding around the corner of the house, barking and jumping with excitement. A black and tan one stopped and stared at Steve. An older looking, male blue heeler continued on to Steve. He held out his hand. "G'day there, boy". The dog sniffed the outstretched hand, gave a low, short growl and stepped backwards, staring at Steve. It then walked several paces to the side, lifted its head upwards and let out a howl, looked at Steve again and gave several shrill barks. "It's okay, boy", Steve said, hoping he sounded calmer than he felt. The dog sprang at him. Steve jumped back.

"Buddy, *NO!*" yelled Linda, moving closer.

Buddy's eyes lit up. He jumped up toward Steve's raised hand and rested his front paws on Steve's thighs. Steve's racing heart slowed and he lowered his hand to Buddy's nose and mouth. Buddy licked it with a warm, rough tongue. He then sat on his haunches and held up one front paw with the closest thing to a big doggie smile on his face.

"That's Buddy." She patted his head. "He was your dog, Steve."

"Hey, Buddy." Steve patted his head and rubbed under his chin. "He loves that." A fleeting spark zapped through his brain. A blue heeler jumping up in front of him on a motorbike. It was gone as fast as it had come. He crouched down beside Buddy who jumped up, ran around in circles, yapped and licked Steve's hands again with gusto.

"He remembers you, Steve." Linda choked the words out and her hand movement indicated she was wiping her eyes. "Even when you look different."

Steve's own eyes were fixed on Buddy. Rubbing and scratching the very excited and appreciative dog. "Did he ever get on a motorbike with me?"

"Yes! Lots of times. He loved going with you on the bike. Can you remember?" Linda's high-pitched words came out amidst laughter. "You can, can't you?" She knelt and hugged Steve. "I knew it would come back to you once you were here. He moped about for ages after you left, missing you like crazy. He's old now, but he sure has the energy today."

"It was only a split second of something that came into my head. I can't remember anything else about him." Steve stood and looked up the steps. His father stood at the top, watching him, no smile, no emotion. A bolt of lightning hit the fruit bats in Steve's stomach, sending them scattering in fear throughout his body. He hoped his breakfast would stay down.

Steve nodded toward Bruce. He couldn't think what to say or even what to call him. Bruce gave a slight nod in return.

"Hello, love," Linda waved to her husband. "We're finally home. Look at Buddy! He remembers Steve. And Steve just had a quick memory of him getting on his bike. Isn't that exciting?" She placed her hand on Steve's back as they walked up the stairs.

Bruce stepped aside when they reached the top. He looked tired or sad, or was that anger? No way of telling. His greying dark hair wasn't combed, and his dark blue work shirt was only buttoned halfway up. Steve had seen him the day he was arrested and briefly in the hospital a couple of times. He was a total stranger to Steve, and one he didn't feel one bit comfortable being around.

Realising he'd have to make the first move as Bruce continued to stare at him, Steve held out his right hand. "Hello..." He so wanted to say 'dad', but the word just wouldn't form. "Bruce."

Linda kissed Bruce on the cheek. "Love, aren't you going to welcome your son?" She nodded toward Steve's outstretched hand.

Bruce took Steve's hand and shook it very briefly. "G'day".

Steve dropped his hand by his side. His father couldn't even acknowledge him by name. Stuff this! It was way too much to cope with. He looked back down at Buddy, faithfully sitting at the bottom of the steps watching Steve with nothing but love in his eyes. He returned his gaze to his father, watching Steve with nothing but...what exactly? That was it, *nothing* in his eyes.

CHAPTER 13

Grace sighed in dismay, watching the family scene before her as she and Kain pulled up at her parents' home. "I have a bad feeling about this". She reached across and lightly squeezed Kain's thigh for her own comfort. "Looks like Dad didn't want to shake Steve's hand. And Mum looks worried."

Kain turned off the ignition and took hold of her hand. "Babe, did you really expect him to welcome Steve with open arms?"

Grace shook her head. "Well...no, but – "

"Sorry Grace, I shouldn't have said that." He leaned over and kissed her cheek. "C'mon let's see what we can do to calm things." He got out and strode around to open Grace's door, but she was already out and heading to the stairs.

Grace rushed up the stairs and placed her hand on her brother's back. "Hey, Steve." She almost added *how are you* but realised that would be pointless. It was obvious he wasn't happy. She glanced at Bruce's sullen face and nodded once. "Dad."

Her father gave a quick half smile then turned to the door. "I've got things to do out the back." He disappeared inside the house, footsteps quickly fading up the hallway. The screen door closed louder than usual, or did it just seem that way due to the sudden uncomfortable silence?

Grace looked at her mother's sad face. "Try not to worry too much, Mum. I'm sure he'll come around." She gave her mum a hug.

Mother and daughter let go. "I hope so," Linda said with a long sigh. "Anyway." Her face brightened up with a huge smile and she turned to Steve. "C'mon son, let's get your stuff into your old room and I'll put the kettle on and get some lunch going." She bent to pick up Steve's bag.

Steve grabbed it first. "I'll carry it in." He took a deep breath before entering the door Kain held open. Steve nodded toward Kain. "Thanks mate."

Grace walked ahead and opened the door into Steve's old bedroom, second on the left up the hallway. She stepped in and to the side to let Steve enter, not taking her eyes from his face, waiting, *hoping,* he'd show some sign of recognition. Steve put his bag on the floor and looked about the room. The double bed was made up, the room neat and tidy. Linda had insisted it remain the way he'd left it, with all his personal belongings – clothes hanging in the wardrobe, knick knacks, rodeo trophies and framed action pictures on a bookshelf beside the wardrobe, along with some novels and hard cover books he used to read. His hairbrush, comb, a can of deodorant and a few horse and dog themed ornaments sat on his dutchess. Linda had always insisted he'd come home *one day.*

A large, framed picture of mountains and bush hung on one wall, as it had done for many years. Steve moved closer to it, staring hard. His eyes blinked several times. Was he fighting back tears?

He glanced at Grace then back to the picture. "Where is this?"

Grace stood beside him, placing her hand on his back for comfort. "I'm not sure. It's been hanging on your wall for about ten years. You bought it yourself. Does it look familiar?" She knew all too well he was thinking of his home in the bush. "It makes you homesick for your other home, doesn't it?"

Steve turned to her. "My *other* home?" His voice rose as he emphasised the word. "My *only* home, Grace!" He glanced about the room, his gaze stopping on the mirror.

As far as Grace could tell he was on the wrong angle to see his reflection. Silence except for noises and voices from Linda and Kain in the kitchen and the radio going. Good they left her and Steve alone, but his short sharp tone reminded her of how he'd spoken to her the first few days she was in his home. Terrifying few days, when she was injured, frightened and confused with no idea this strange, hulk of a man who'd saved her from the wild dogs was actually her beloved brother.

"Can you cover the mirror, please?" His voice trembled.

"Sure." She'd half expected this but hoped he'd accept how he looked now, given that the plastic surgery work was in progress. Grace rushed out of the room and grabbed a large towel from the bathroom, brought it back and hung the top of it over the mirror, covering all the glass.

"Thanks." He looked back at the picture on the wall and took a long, slow breath.

"What are you thinking, Steve?" She suddenly felt like an intruder in his thoughts and maybe had no right to ask. "Would you rather be left alone here for a while?"

He turned to Grace and expelled a heavy sigh. "No, I don't want to be alone." He sat on the edge of the bed. "I don't know what I want, Grace." Another deep sigh. "Everything just seems so…" He shrugged. "So crazy."

Grace sat beside him and took hold of his hand. "It's okay, Steve. No one expects you to just 'get over it' with everything you've been through and not just lately."

He squeezed her hand. "You know, the only time I can ever remember feeling happy was when you realised you didn't have to be scared of me anymore and we'd talk about different things."

A happy feeling gushed through Grace and she couldn't help but smile. "Yes, I was so relieved when I realised you weren't going to hurt me."

"I'm so sorry I scared you at first." He shook his head. "I don't know why. I suppose I just wasn't used to talking to anyone. Anyone nice anyway. Or having anyone care about me like you did." He stared deep into her soul. "Then when we kissed it was like…heaven."

Grace let go of his hand, stood and faced him, unsure for several seconds what to say. "Steve…" Her stomach swirled a little. No, surely not more morning sickness. Or maybe the memory of kissing *her brother,* or *anyone* other than Kain was too much to think about. "Steve, we talked about that. We agreed to forget it, remember? No one, especially

Kain, must ever find out. Neither of us knew who the other was and I was in a bad state after Kain had broken off our relationship. You mustn't ever mention it again, even to me. Okay?"

Steve lowered his gaze and his large shoulders slumped. "I know. But I can't help remembering it. For that short time I felt like the luckiest bloke in the world and I'd forgotten for a few seconds that I was just an ugly, hopeless loser who made little kids run in fear just by looking at my face."

Grace sat back beside him and placed her hand on his upper back. "I'm sorry. I didn't mean to make you sad." A different attitude might be needed. "Hey, big brother." She playfully punched him in the shoulder, something they used to do to each other when in stirring 'fun' moods. "I'll always be here for you, but we have so much to look forward to now. How about after lunch I dig out some old photo albums and we can look at them together. There's lots of pictures of you and I together."

"No, I don't want to see them. Not yet anyway." Steve abruptly stood up but didn't look at Grace. Didn't or *couldn't?* "You know what I want to do the most right now?" Enthusiasm flowed with the words.

"What?" asked Grace, glad his outlook had suddenly brightened, and that he seemed to have forgotten the awkward subject of their spontaneous kiss back at his bush home.

He turned to her. "Go for a ride on a horse."

That was not what Grace expected to hear. "Oh, okay. But mum's getting lunch ready. Aren't you hungry?" She stood. "I'll go check how it's going and leave you alone in your room for a bit." She patted his arm. "You really should eat something, and I bet anything she's making some of your favourites."

Grace entered the kitchen. No sign of Kain. Linda was setting the table. Something smelt delicious. "Mmm, what's cooking mum? And where's Kain?" She grabbed a glass of water from the sink tap. "Another hot one today. Wonder if we'll get a storm."

Linda looked up. "Oh, hi love. Just whipped up an omelette the way Steve used to like them." She frowned and briefly gazed about before giving a slight shrug. "I don't know." She looked confused. "He was here a minute ago but headed toward the hallway." She shrugged again and grabbed two pieces of toast that had just popped up. "Maybe he went to the toilet." She began buttering the toast.

"Yeah, probably. Steve just said he wants to go for a horse ride. He doesn't seem like he wants to eat." She pulled a chair out from the table and sat down.

Linda stopped what she was doing and looked at Grace. "How did he seem in his room? Any sort of recognition and memory? I thought it best to leave you two alone for a bit since he is more comfortable with you."

Grace shook her head, trying not to think of Steve's mention of their kiss. Nobody would understand. "No, nothing at all, unfortunately. Didn't even want to look at a photo of himself." She jumped up. "But...it's early days yet. It's not going to happen overnight. I'm going to look for Kain." She turned to head toward the front door but bumped into Steve just walking into the kitchen. "Woops! Didn't hear you coming." Like back at his house when he'd just seem to appear at her door with no sound.

Steve laughed a little. "Sorry, didn't mean to frighten you, Grace."

"All good. Mum has some of your favourite food made. Just going to find Kain." She headed down the hallway, checking in all the rooms along the way. Linda and Steve's voices faded as she walked out on to the verandah.

Kain stood over in the corner of the verandah, where it wraps around one side of the house. His back to Grace, hands gripping the top rail, arms stiff. Something didn't seem right. "There you are, darl!" She walked toward him but tension thickened the air or maybe because there was so much tension in the atmosphere at this house now. Hopefully that was all. "Are you alright? Mum has food ready." She leaned on the rail beside him and gently took hold of his muscular arm. He stared straight ahead, jaw tight, face pale and beads of sweat on this forehead and temple. Grace kissed him on the cheek. "What's wrong? You look upset." Silence. A cow bellowed over in the paddock. A bit of hammering and some cursing from Bruce in the shed. More silence. Something was very wrong. "Kain, talk to me, please." This was so unlike him. An uneasy feeling of dread formed in her belly and her heartbeat grew louder and faster.

He turned to her, with a tear sliding down one cheek. Was he sad or just plain angry? She'd never seen this look on his face before.

Linda opened the screen door. "Are you two coming for some lunch?"

"Yeah, soon mum. But yous start without us if Steve wants to get going for that horse ride."

"No worries, love. Plenty left. Steve is tucking in right now." She closed the screen door and disappeared.

Finally, Kain spoke. "Go ahead Grace, go and eat with your brother and mum. You need to keep up your strength." He glanced at her belly then away into the distance again. "I'm not hungry." He wiped the sweat that had begun running down the sides of his face.

"You're worrying me, Kain. You were okay when we got here. What has happened since then? Surely mum didn't upset you in the kitchen. Or did Dad come in and hassle you? Wouldn't bloody surprise me!" Grace shook her head. "I'll go have a word to him." She turned to leave but Kain grabbed her arm.

"It wasn't your father."

He stared deep into her soul, but it wasn't the look of love she was used to. More like contempt. Confusion filled her mind. She threw her hands in the air. "Are you going to tell me, or do I have to guess? Have you had a phone call from someone? Something to do with your cancer?" She didn't like this one bit. He turned away, like he couldn't bear to look at her. "Kain, you're starting to scare me."

"Just exactly what *did* go on while you were in Steve's house, Grace?"

Grace's heart raced even faster and her mouth dried. "What do you mean? I've told you all about it." Her head spun and she hung on tight to the rail for a moment until the dizziness subsided.

"You told me *everything?*" Kain continued looking away from her. "You sure about that, Grace?"

That was definitely an accusation. Oh no. He must've heard Steve mention about the kiss. Steve does have a deep voice. "I told you everything that was important, Kain. Anything else doesn't matter. All that matters now is we're back together and having a baby. Two babies! And I love you more than anything in this world. Don't you know that by now?"

He looked at her again, with anger. "You've kept something from me, Grace. And it makes me absolutely sick."

"Did you overhear Steve and me talking in his room?" She choked out the words. Words she'd hope she'd never have to say or even think about ever again. "About..." She took a deep breath. No point feigning ignorance any longer. "About a kiss?"

"Yes! How could you?" Another tear dampened Kain's cheek. He didn't bother wiping it away. "I was coming into his room to see how things were."

She fought back her own tears. "Kain, it was just an on-the-spur-of-the-moment thing. Nothing else happened." She clutched his hands. "You have to believe me."

He yanked his hands from Grace's and looked away. "I don't know what to believe at the moment."

"Kain, *please.*" Panic enveloped her body and what breakfast remained in her stomach threatened to come up. She swallowed hard to keep it down. "How can you have these doubts now after how good things are between us again?"

"Maybe that's your guilty conscious, Grace." The words hard and cold as stone and he still refused to look at her.

Grace wanted to cry at the hurt and anger. Wanted to hug Kain and hear him say *sorry, I overreacted.* Wanted to laugh at the absurdity of what he was surmising or assuming and accusing her of doing. They'd never been in this situation before in their five-odd years together. Nothing but love, mutual respect and great mates as well. Millions of words and thoughts flicked through her brain, but she still had no idea what to say to appease him. "That's not true, Kain," was all she could manage before the lump in her throat threatened to choke off her voice completely. Yes, she had been feeling a bit guilty about the kiss since she and Kain reconciled, and also for Steve's sake. But it was not worth all this upset and tension, surely.

Kain turned to her. "Then tell me what is true, Grace? Are you saying he forced a kiss on you?" He shook his head, eyes still angry, his breathing now louder.

"No! Steve wouldn't do that!"

"Well, explain to me how it happened."

Grace's legs weakened. "I need to sit down first." She walked several steps and sat on a large cane chair that faced out of that eastern side of the veranda. She patted the seat beside her. "Please sit with me, Kain."

With a slight shake of his head and obvious reluctance on his face, Kain joined her on the chair, but at the opposite end of the three-seater, like he couldn't bear to be near her.

That stabbed into her heart. "You can't even sit beside me?" Tears blurred her vision and she wiped them away with her hand.

He moved slightly closer. "Just tell me what the hell happened."

She took a deep breath, determined she wouldn't cry but that wasn't so easy to control now with the pregnancy hormones kicking in. Even the littlest things would sometimes set her off. "I've told you about being in his house and how he used to say how lonely he was."

"So, you just felt sorry for him?"

"Yes. No. I don't know." She shrugged. "It was hard not to after I realised he wasn't going to hurt me and hearing what he'd been through."

"That's no excuse, Grace. How could you even *think* about kissing someone else when we've been together for so long?"

Grace's confusion and hurt morphed into anger. Anger that had to come out. Her face flushed warm. She dried her sweaty palms on her shorts. "That's the thing, Kain! We weren't together, were we?" Apart from punching him in the jaw outside Steve's house she hadn't let out all the anger and confusion of Kain suddenly dumping her with no viable explanation. *'He needed to FIND himself. Didn't love her anymore'.* She thought it ridiculous at the time. "And why was that, Kain?" She had enough to deal with right now without this unnecessary stress.

Kain's sullen look switched to shock.

"Do you think you're the only one that has the right to be angry?" Grace's voice rose, but she didn't want anyone hearing them, especially Steve. He certainly had more than enough to cope with now too. She lowered her voice and spoke through gritted teeth. "You dumped me, remember. No remorse or reason. Oh, that's right, you had to *find yourself.*"

"Grace, I've apologised for that over and over. I thought you understood."

"Yes, I forgave you for that, even though I'll never really understand why you just couldn't tell me about your cancer. Things would be so different now."

"But you wouldn't have found Steve. And *he* is the reason we are arguing now, not my cancer or the stupid reason I told you for ending our relationship."

"Yes, that's true." Her brain swam with a million wriggling fish. "Oh, I can't even think straight anymore. Just know there is nothing to get upset about." She reached for his hand, but he moved his away. "Seth and I were both vulnerable and thrown together in strange circumstances." His former name just came out before she realised. "I mean Steve."

"Did you enjoy the kiss?" Kain jumped up and went back to the rail, looking away. "On second thoughts, don't answer that."

"What?!" She got up and stood closer to him. "No. I don't even really remember it. It was just a quick kiss, not a long passionate one like you seem to be imagining."

"I can't get the image out of my mind, Grace." He turned to her. "You kissing Steve. *Your brother!* Makes me sick."

"You know damned well I had no idea – *we* had no idea - we were brother and sister."

Kain glanced at her stomach. "Are the twins his?"

Grace's stomach contents rose to her mouth at hearing those words. She leaned over the rail and vomited on the green lawn below.

"Grace, I'm sorry." Kain placed his hand on her back. "I didn't mean that. I shouldn't have said it."

Once her stomach settled and she wiped the dribbling saliva from her lips and chin she faced Kain, blurred through her tears. Not just tears from vomiting but tears of absolute shock and pain from the knife he'd just plunged through her heart. She had no words. This was the last thing she expected him to say. Silence for several seconds. "But you *did* say it." The words raspy from her irritated throat.

"I don't mean it. Of course I know they're mine." His voiced softened.

But his words continued to sting. She shook her head. "I don't really want to talk to you anymore at the moment. You had no need or right to say such a thing. I want you to go."

"Go?" Bewilderment shrouded his face. He shrugged and opened his palms upward. "Go where?"

"Anywhere. Just away from me. At least until I can get past these ridiculous accusations." Grace wiped her eyes and headed to the front door.

Footsteps followed and he grabbed her arm, spinning her around. "Grace, please. I'm sorry."

She jerked her arm away, went through the screen door and headed to the bathroom to wash her face and foul-tasting mouth. Even the sound of the running tap couldn't drown out Kain's vehicle starting up and roaring off along the driveway.

CHAPTER 14

Steve swallowed the last of his lunch. "That was really good, thanks Mum." He got up from the table, put his empty plate and cutlery by the sink then looked at Grace sitting at the table, pushing some food around on her plate. "Grace, do you want to tell us what's wrong yet? You've barely eaten or spoke since Kain left." Her face grimaced at the mention of his name. Certainly not like the Grace he'd come to know. Loved her food. And her man. Right now both seemed to disgust her.

"He's right, love." Linda got up and put her plate on top of Steve's then placed her arm around her daughter's shoulders, worry lining her face. "You were both good as gold before. What happened out on the verandah?"

Grace gave a slight shrug. Slid her chair back and stood. "Look, please don't worry about it. I really don't want-" A sob stopped her words. She blinked several times and swallowed loudly. "I really don't want to talk about it now. It'll be okay." She rushed out of the kitchen and down the hallway. A bedroom door slammed.

Steve looked at his mother and shook his head. "I don't like this." An all too familiar ball of dread formed in his stomach.

Linda touched his arm. "Hmm, I agree. But we have to leave her be for now. I'm sure she'll talk about it when she's ready." She picked up Grace's plate and scraped the uneaten food into a container on the bench that held other scraps.

"Is that for the chooks?" Steve missed his chooks. Just like he missed everything else about his former home.

Linda nodded. "Yep." She stacked the plate with the others. "Do you still want to go riding?"

"Sure do." Steve scratched at the side of his face. "This mask thing is getting a bit itchy in this hot weather. Can't wait to get it off."

Linda looked at him with tears welling. "I know, mate, but it'll be worth it later on. Just have to put up with it a while longer." She wiped her eyes then the sweat from her brow and temples. "I'll just check on Grace and then we'll head over to get the horses." She left the kitchen.

Steve listened hard. He could hear Linda's words but couldn't understand Grace's more muffled responses. Loud footsteps up the back steps jolted his attention toward the back door. Could only be one person. His ball of dread swelled to fill every part of his body and his heart pulsed louder. He wanted to rush away, out the front door. *Don't run like a scared rabbit. Face it like a man.* That annoying inner voice was back.

Bruce opened the screen door and entered the kitchen. He glanced briefly at his son then grabbed a glass from the sink, filled it with water and drank it all down. "Where's Linda?" he asked, turning away from Steve and putting the glass back on the sink.

Steve stepped further away from him. "She's just in there talking to Grace." He pointed toward the hallway with his thumb. His mouth suddenly dried so licked his lips and tried to generate saliva. "There's lunch left in the pan on the stove if you're hungry." An urge to visit the toilet hit him. Good reason to get away from Bruce, but he had no idea where the toilet was. Linda was still talking to Grace and he didn't want to interrupt them. Bruce had gone to the stove and was looking in the pan. "Umm, where's the toilet?" The word 'dad' just wouldn't form. It wasn't even in his heart so it could never come out his mouth.

Bruce never bothered to look up. "It's near the bathroom or there's another one downstairs beside the laundry." His words flat and unfeeling. He opened the cabinet as Steve headed out the back door to the downstairs loo. Descending the stairs he breathed in deep with relief. The need for the toilet was not as strong as his need to get out of that room. The tension so thick it almost choked him. Even with his father saying so few words and barely glancing at him the hatred was there, filling the room like a cloud of poisonous gas.

Voices could be heard above him as he came out of the loo. But again, not clear. Linda rushed down the back stairs just as Steve walked out from under the house. Her neutral face gave him no indication of the outcome of either conversation she'd just had.

"Is Grace okay?" It tore him up inside knowing she was unhappy.

"Yeah, I think so." Linda's face saddened. "She didn't say what the problem was but she's going to have a sleep. We'll go for a ride and hopefully she'll feel a bit better when we get back." Linda grabbed riding boots from a boot rack under the house and headed off toward the smaller shed by the cattle yards.

Steve looked down at the thongs on his feet and hesitated.

His mum stopped and turned back. "Come on." She beckoned him with her hand and her face lit up with a smile.

Steve held up one foot. "I probably need better boots".

Linda laughed, put hers on the ground and strode back, going straight past Steve and in under the house. He followed but she was soon back out with an old pair of riding boots in one hand and a pair of black socks in the other. She held them out to him. "Here you go. These are your old pair. And the socks are clean." She laughed again. So good to see. Her laugh and smile were so much like Grace's. In fact, they looked more like sisters than mother and daughter.

"Thanks." He took the offering and was about to sit on the steps to put them on but a noise in the kitchen reminded him who was just above him and could come down these stairs at any second. Nope, not a good idea. "I'll put them on over at the yards." Two magpies warbled on the lawn. Such a beautiful sound and one of his favourites. He stopped and stared at them. For a brief moment he was back home in the bush.

Once at the cattle yards and booted up Linda pointed to the shed adjoining the yards. "Saddles and bridles are in here." Buddy and the other dog trotted about them, eager for some action.

Steve followed her in and looked around. Several saddles and their rugs sat on a support rail, and bridles hung from hooks along the back wall. Ropes, halters and other tack equipment hung along a side wall. The aroma of leather polish hit his nostrils. Shelves along the opposite side wall held containers of horse and cattle veterinary-type products – worming, fly and tick sprays, antiseptic sprays and so on. Three large drums stood just inside the door to the right. Steve lifted the lid off one. Horse feed. He sniffed deep. The smell so familiar and so good. He replaced the lid securely - can't have rodents getting to it. Everything neat and clean, right down to the concrete floor.

He looked at the saddles as Linda lifted one from the rail. "Which one will I use?"

She nodded toward one at the far end of the rail. "That one. It was yours."

Lifting if off the rail he tried to remember using it. Nothing came to mind. He carried it out of the shed into the bright sunlight. The dark brown leather shone like new in the sunlight. A carved picture on each saddle flap caught his attention. He lifted one knee, sat the saddle over his raised thigh and ran his free hand over the picture. Even with limited feeling in some of his fingers from the acid attack, he could still appreciate the finely carved lines and intricacy of the pictures. One side showed a rodeo rider on a bucking bronco. The other side depicted a man on horseback, stock whip in his raised hand and looking at several head of cattle. A flash of familiarity flicked through his brain. He'd seen these pictures in lifelike mode before, but *where?* "These pictures are great. Did you get someone to do it or buy it like this?"

Linda grinned. "Yep, you could say that. *You* did them."

"No, I couldn't have." He shook his head. "I don't have an artistic bone in my body."

"You're wrong." Pride flowed in her words. "You actually copied these from photos of you. And you've done other drawings and carved a couple of leather belts too." She stepped closer to Steve, her eyes glistening. "You were very good at it."

He had no words. No memory of doing anything like this. Maybe his mum was just telling him all this to keep him happy. He gave a half shrug. He'd go along with it if it made *her* happy. A loud 'neigh' from down the paddock a little caught his attention. "Okay, let's get these horses in."

Once the horses were yarded, with little effort, Linda pointed to a large bay coloured gelding with a white stripe down his face. "You can ride Blaze. He's fairly new but beautiful to ride and a nice temperament. Let him have his head and he'll take you far and fast."

Perfect! *Race the wind.*

The dogs darted about, giving little yips of excitement, tongues hanging out as they panted. "I don't think the dogs should come, especially Buddy. He mightn't keep up in this heat." Steve clicked his fingers to Buddy who ran straight to him. "I think you should stay here, boy." Buddy lifted his head and stood still, enjoying the scratch and pat from Steve. The other dog come over to get some attention as well. "What's this one's name?" He gave the black and tan boy a good rub on this head and neck.

Linda looked over from saddling her horse, a light grey. "That's Dozer. We got him about two years ago. Great cattle dog." She buckled up the girth and led her horse closer to Steve. "Yes, probably best they stay here. I'll go tie them up while you saddle up." She tied her reins to the yard rail and walked to the gate, calling the dogs. Both scampered after her.

Steve watched them head toward the house. Yes, best the dogs don't follow. He turned back to the horses – his bay, a black and two palominos. All beautiful and in tip top condition. The black looked similar to the wild and vicious 'Tornado' that trampled the man to death at Scott's yards. But this one certainly didn't have that killer look in his eyes. A shudder swept over his body. How he wished he could forget some things.

He walked up to Blaze. The horse lifted his head and snorted as Steve reached out to stroke his face. "Easy, boy." The other three walked to the far corner of the yard. Blaze shook his head up and down a few times then lowered it for the welcoming hand. Steve rubbed Blaze's face and neck before slipping the bridle bit between his teeth. Blaze immediately crunched on it as Steve gently pulled the bridle on and did up the neck strap. "Good boy." He rubbed

Blaze's neck firmly several times before leading him over near the gate where the saddle sat.

Dropping the reins, he grabbed the saddle blanket and put it on Blaze's back then lifted the saddle up and over. Blaze never moved an inch. Steve reached below the horse's belly, grabbed the girth strap and lifted the saddle flap to do up the girth. Some writing carved into the underside of the flap caught his eye. Quickly doing up the strap he leaned a little closer to read it. *Steve Atkinson.* His mother was right! He did carve the saddle. But it still didn't bring on any sudden memories. He wasn't sure if that was a good thing or bad.

"Ready?" Linda had returned and was about to mount her horse.

He jolted. He hadn't heard or seen her coming back. "Ah, yep, let's go."

Linda opened the gate for him. "We'll leave the others in or they'll just want to follow us."

Once on his horse and out of the yards Steve breathed the humid, country air to the depths of his lungs. The sky was a deep blue with a bank of grey clouds on the western horizon. Could be a storm later. One place he was very comfortable was on the back of a horse. Heart banging against his rib cage, adrenaline surging through his body, he felt free again. A flock of screeching rainbow lorikeets burst out of the large tree by the yards. Right at this moment life was good.

They walked the horses through another gate and into a large open paddock. Steve dismounted to close the gate. Linda made small talk as they rode, but Steve was more interested in looking about, taking in as much as he could. A welcome breeze cooled his bare forearms, but his jeans, boots and tight mask kept the rest of him uncomfortably warm. He wished he'd have had a drink before leaving. Rolling, grassy hills fed numerous fat cattle, mainly blacks but various other colours too. The blacks reminded him of the mob he'd been forced to help steal from Bruce. Again he shuddered at a memory wished forgotten. Shady trees dotted the landscape here and there with a jagged line of trees over to the right. "Is that a creek over there?" He pointed toward the trees.

"Yes," replied his mum. "Want to go there?"

"You bet! C'mon, let's ride." Steve worked the reins one-handed to turn Blaze right, leaned forward and gave him a slight kick with his heels. Blaze needed no further prompting. He took off, galloping toward the creek. Steve looked back. Linda was right on his tail, leaning forward with a big smile. She obviously loved riding as much as he.

They pulled up under a large gum tree by the creek. Several startled quails flew out of the grass right beside Steve. Blaze leapt to the side in fright. Steve felt himself falling, shooting his heart rate to full throttle, but quickly righted himself in the saddle. "Woah, boy." He rubbed Blaze's neck, warm and moist from sweat. "Settle down." Breathing heavy and with pricked ears Blaze looked about, then dropped his head to eat grass as if the fright hadn't even happened.

"You right?" Linda was off her horse and holding the reins, concern on her face. "He's a bit of a bugger for that shying." She stepped forward and rubbed Blazes shoulder area. "But that's his only vice. Sorry, I should've warned you."

"Yeah, I'm good." Steve got off and lifted the reins over Blaze's neck and head while he continued to eat, loudly chomping on the bit along with the grass. "Did give me a bit of a fright though."

"But you hung on," said Linda, her words again flowing with pride. "I'd have been shocked if you fell from a horse, Steve. People used to talk about what a good rider you were." Her gaze moved slightly from him to thin air and her eyes now held a faraway look. "Even your father was proud of your horsemanship."

Hmph, I bet. Steve found it hard to believe his father would be proud of him for anything at all, but just smiled at his mum and shrugged a little. Without remembering any of that he simply didn't know what to say and didn't want to upset her by speaking negatively of his father. Nor did he want to even think about his father.

In silence they walked their horses over to the water. Sandy gravel crunched beneath their feet as they neared the water's edge. Blaze wanted a drink but Linda's grey wasn't interested, instead wanted to go back a few metres to the lush grass. She tied him to a nearby bush so he could graze. Steve held the reins while Blaze drank his fill. He watched the powerful neck muscles contract with each swallow then realised he should drink too. The clean, clear water flowed nicely, trickling over rocks only ten or so metres away. It would be safe to drink. He crouched close to the edge, upstream side of Blaze, scooped water in his hand, leaned forward a little so as not to the wet the surgical mask, and drank it down. So cooling and refreshing in his parched mouth and throat. The water had a slight 'dirt and leaves' taste – the taste of the bush. But he'd rather drink creek water any day than the foul, chemical-tasting water at the hospital.

After drinking his fill Steve stood, just as Blaze lifted his head with water dribbling from his mouth back into the creek. Steve led the horse over and tied him to a bush not far from the grey and walked back to Linda, standing by the water's edge, looking downstream. A tear slid down her cheek.

Gone was her beaming smile as they'd ridden. "Are you okay?" He hesitated a moment, then put his arm around his mum's shoulders.

She looked up at her son, gave a fake smile and wiped her tears. "Yes, I will be." She leaned her head against his shoulder. "Just over there past those rocks," she pointed downstream to a slightly wider part of the creek, "is where Jon drowned." Her body shuddered with a sob. "I know it's been almost thirty years, but it still hurts."

Steve looked at the stillness and serenity of that part of the creek. Birds twittered in the trees. It seemed like such a nice, peaceful spot. He closed his eyes and tried hard but couldn't remember, except for the small, torn photo in his house. "I'm sorry if I did cause his death, mum." Linda's sadness radiated into his body. He fought back his own tears. Tears for a brother he couldn't remember knowing and now never would. Tears for a family torn apart by death and circumstance. Tears for his shitty life that has caused his family so much pain.

She stepped in front of him, her face stern, eyes boring into his soul. "You did *not* cause his death, Steve. You hear me! Your father couldn't handle it, still can't, but it was *not* your fault like he claimed." She took hold of both his hands. "It was a terrible accident. I think about it and Jon every single day and wish things were different." Her bottom lip trembled, and she took a slow, deep breath. "Don't ever think you are to blame." She squeezed his hands.

"Where is Jon buried?" asked Steve.

"He's not. We had him cremated and buried his ashes in the front rose garden and some here in the creek. He loved the water." Another tear rolled down her cheeks but the sad memories were disturbed by the shrill ring of her phone. She pulled it out of her shirt pocket and looked at the screen. "It's Grace." She tapped and put it to her ear. "Hi love."

Steve walked downstream a little to the spot where his brother drowned. He saw a small boy swimming and splashing about. Laughter rang through the trees. Was he remembering or just imagining? He closed his eyes tight, silently begging the memories to return, but still nothing. Must have just been his imagination. He opened his eyes to an empty, silent creek. No laughter, no splashing fun. A cold breeze sprung up and whooshed among the trees, shooting icicles down his spine. Then the cool breeze was gone. Everything stilled. The birds stopped singing.

"Steve." Linda took hold of his arm above his elbow. His body twitched in fright. "Sorry, I didn't mean to startle you. Looks like you're deep in thought."

She seemed to be asking what he was thinking. "Ah yeah, I was. Just trying to remember."

"Anything?" She sounded hopeful.

He shook his head. "Nope. Is Grace alright?"

"She says she is but wants to go find Kain. She needs to take my car, or asked if I could drive her. I'll have to head back, sorry."

"Do you mind if I stay here a bit longer? I might ride along the creek a bit more. It might help me get my brain working properly again and remember things."

"Sure. Good idea." She hugged him briefly then headed to her horse. Once in the saddle she called out. "See you back at home later." A smile and wave and she turned her horse back the way they came.

As soon as she was cantering off in the distance Steve untied Blaze from the bush and mounted. He walked him out away from the trees, pulled up and looked at the sun then around him. His mum and her horse were now a small figure in the distance. The house, shed and yards were further in front of her. He turned Blaze in the opposite direction and urged him forward with a slight heel kick. "C'mon Blaze, you're taking me home."

CHAPTER 15

Kain held the screen open and banged louder on the wooden door. "Joe! You home?"

Joe pulled his front door open. "Geez mate, keep your shirt on. I was just on the dunny having a -"

"Too much information." Kain strode in. The screen door closed behind him. "Sorry, but I need to talk to you."

"What's up? Wanna beer?" Joe headed to his fridge.

"Ah, no thanks. Well, maybe one. I don't know." Kain paced the floor. He had no idea *what* he wanted or how he felt right now except that he didn't feel good in any way. "I've been driving around thinking about things and knew I had to come see you."

Joe took two cans of beer from his fridge and handed Kain one before pulling the tab on his and taking a mouthful. "What's happened? You look like shit. Sit down." Joe beckoned him to the lounge chairs.

"Gee thanks. Just what I needed to hear." Kain rolled his eyes, took the beer and popped it open. He sat on one of the single chairs, took a mouthful then jumped back up to his feet. A painful twinge hit his groin area and he leaned forward a moment. "Ow, shouldn't do that." He slowly sat back on the chair, but only on the edge. His gut churned, heart caned like an angry drummer and a million scurrying ants raced through his veins. He couldn't relax if he wanted to.

Joe relaxed into a lounge chair. "Righto Burrows, what the hell has happened, mate?" He swigged some more beer.

Kain stared at the floor, reliving the conversation he'd overheard between Steve and Grace.

"Well?" Joe urged. "Are you going to tell me?"

Kain sat upright, drew in a deep breath and had a mouthful of beer before expelling his breath. "I really don't know how to say it." He shook his head. "I don't *want* to have to say it." He shifted in his seat. He really didn't want Joe or *anyone* to know about it but couldn't keep it bottled up inside. The anger and frustration would drive him to do something silly like punch a wall. That he knew all too well.

"Try starting at the beginning," said Joe, this time with genuine care in his voice.

"We were just at Bruce and Linda's place. Linda has brought Steve home."

"That's good," Joe cut in.

"Hmph, yeah, well it should have been." Kain swallowed more beer.

Joe frowned and shrugged, clearly confused. "I thought you liked Steve."

Kain stood, noisily squeezing in the sides of his now almost empty can. "I do! I did. But..." He walked to a window and stared outside a moment. It was now or never.

He spun back to face his best mate. "When Grace was at Steve's house they kissed!" He swallowed hard, hoping to hold down his stomach contents that were threatening to come up. His mouth turned bitter. The beer suddenly became unappealing. He walked into the kitchen and poured the remainder down the sink, watching it disappear. "Is Sue here?" He hoped not.

"No mate, she's shopping." Joe got up and went to Kain. Silence engulfed the room for what seemed like ages. "I really don't know what to say," Joe finally said. "Did she tell you this herself?"

"No, of course not." Kain turned toward Joe and leaned on the sink. His neck and face flushed warm. "That pisses me off the most! I had to overhear their conversation in his room at their parents. She couldn't be honest with me earlier and tell me then. Things have been so bloody good in the past couple of weeks!" He grabbed the can and crumpled it up in his bare hands before hurling it toward the kitchen bin. It missed. *Shit!* "I just don't know what to think or what to do." His eyes moistened and stung but he blinked them dry. "I love Grace so much but the thought that she'd kiss anyone else just..." He gritted his teeth until they hurt. "He's her brother, for fuck's sake!" He threw his hands in the air.

"Geez Kain, I certainly didn't expect you to tell me something like this. I need a smoke." Joe grabbed his cigarettes and lighter from the kitchen bench and went outside the sliding door from the dining area before lighting up.

Kain followed him out. "I know. I couldn't believe what I was hearing at first. It knocked me for six."

"Did you talk to her about it?" asked Joe, a cloud of smoke wafting upwards from his mouth.

"Yeah, tried to, but it just all went to shit. She got defensive and angry with me. Told me to go." Kain paced the tiled patio.

"And I bet you got angry too." A brief hint of a knowing smile on Joe's face was quickly replaced with a look of worry. "How serious is this? It's not gunna break you two up is it?"

Break us up? The words hit Kain's gut and heart like a cannon ball. Fear gushed through his veins. The possibility was unbearable. He hadn't thought it would come to that, but would it? *Could it?* "No!" He sat on a patio chair, leaned forward and rested his head in his hands. "I can't let that happen."

Joe stubbed out his cigarette in a half-full ashtray on the back patio table. "Then you should be talking to her, mate." He sat back in his chair, exhaled the smoke and coughed. "Pardon me."

Kain sat upright. "She doesn't want to talk to me. I wish I hadn't bloody heard their conversation." He flicked his head. "I just keep hearing it over and over in my mind."

"How did Grace react? Who brought up the subject, her or Steve?" asked Joe.

"Steve did. Grace told him not to talk about it. That he had to forget all about it. And that nobody, especially me, was to ever find out." A flash of anger hit him. "That just..." He shuddered. "I don't know. That bit hurts the most, I think. Just seems so wrong! I feel like she might have been laughing at me."

"C'mon Kain, do you *really* think Grace would laugh at you about it? That woman hasn't got a mean bone in her body. Of course you're the last person she'd want to know. She'd know you'd go off your brain about it, being the hothead that you are." He playfully slapped Kain on the shoulder. "Think about it. From what I know of her time there, it's probably not as outrageous as it seems. As far as she knew you two were over." Joe raised his eyebrows and stared at Kain with a grin. "You dickhead!"

Kain couldn't help a smile. Joe always seemed to make a bad situation better. "Yeah, yeah, I know. I need to get over it. Just hope she forgives me." Dread dropped a huge weight on his shoulders. "I can't lose her, Joe."

Joe placed his hand on Kain's shoulder. "Mate, you won't. She worships the ground you walk on. I see it in her eyes every time she looks at you." He gave a short, sharp giggle. "Well, except when we found her at Steve's and she thumped ya." He laughed again. "You deserved that!"

"You don't have to remind me." Kain shook his head, trying to dispel the memory.

"Want another beer?" Joe stood up.

"No thanks. It's not helping. Maybe a coffee though."

"Righto." Joe went inside and was soon back out with two steaming mugs of coffee. He handed one to Kain and sat back down, taking a sip before lighting another cigarette. "So, what are you gunna do now? Go see her or wait until she comes to you?"

Kain shrugged one shoulder. "I don't know. What would you do?"

"Honestly? I'd give her until tomorrow then go see her when things have cooled off a bit. And I'd be on my hands and knees grovelling like there's no tomorrow!"

Kain laughed. "Yeah, I bet you would."

"Remember, you've got those precious twins to think about. Surely that overrides anything else."

"Yeah, the twins." Kain's heart swelled with love and pride, forming a lump in his throat. "I can't wait to hold them." The love in his heart morphed to disgust. "But, I..." He hesitated, remembering his cruel words to Grace. "I might've really stuffed things there."

"How?" Joe sipped his coffee, a frown creasing his forehead.

"I asked her if the twins were his." Kain groaned. "I can't believe I did that."

Coffee splattered forth from Joe's mouth. "You what!!?" His eyes widened. "You dickhead!"

"I know," replied Kain. "No need to tell me. I feel like the biggest arsehole on earth right now. I just hope she can forgive me."

A car pulled into Joe's driveway. "Probably Sue home." Joe got up. "I'd better go and help her bring in the groceries." He disappeared inside but was quickly back. "Umm, it's Grace and her mum. You go out there, I'll just stay here." He sat back down. "Where it's safer."

Kain swallowed dread with another mouthful of coffee and headed out to see Grace. His stomach swam in a whirlpool of apprehension and a thousand thoughts and scenarios raced through his mind. She must be coming to tell him something. Something bad, otherwise she wouldn't have bothered, surely. His sweaty fingers slipped off the screen door handle. He wiped both hands on his shorts and opened the door to see Grace walking toward him. Linda remained in her car. Phew, at least he only had to deal with one, but no doubt Linda would give him a piece of her mind, that is if Grace has told her of his stupid accusations. Her long, auburn hair glistened in the sunlight, but her beautiful face looked pale and sad. Or was it angry?

"Grace." The word came out raspy. He swallowed and cleared his dry throat. "Are you okay?" Pathetically trivial thing to say, but nothing better would come out. His knees weakened. Was he about to lose her? Forever this time.

"I'm alright...I suppose." She looked just as nervous as he felt. "Can we talk?" She indicated toward chairs and small table on Joe and Sue's front patio, then sat down and wiped sweat from her forehead.

"Um, yeah of course. Can I get you a drink of water?" Kain turned to go back inside.

"No, I'm fine. I just had one in the car."

Kain gave a quick wave to Linda, who waved back but without a smile, as far as he could tell. He focussed back on Grace and sat opposite her. How he wanted to take her in his arms and hug her but first he had to find out what she was thinking. He plunged in. "Grace, I'm so sorry for those things I said earlier. I'm an absolute idiot and I'm so ashamed of my stupid self. Can you *please* forgive me?" He reached over and took one of her hands. Such a relief when she didn't pull it away. "I love you so much and...I can't bear the thought of losing you, but I don't blame you if you hate me now."

Her hard look softened and her gorgeous green eyes watered. A faint hint of a smile. "Yes, you were an absolute idiot, but I've been thinking about it a lot and I do understand why you got angry." She laughed a little through her tears and rolled her eyes. "Apart from the fact that's *you* to a tee, I should have told you about it sooner." She squeezed his hands.

Kain's belly full of dread disappeared. His heavy shoulders lightened. He took a deep breath and a smile came naturally. "So, are we good? I promise never to jump to crazy conclusions again."

"Ha! Don't make promises you can't keep, Kain Burrows!" Grace laughed again. Such a beautiful sound. Her sad, angry look now gone.

Without a word, both stood at the same time and fell into each other's arms. How amazing it felt to hold her close again. All Kain's fears and worries of the past hour or so vanished. Life was good again.

They pulled apart at the sound of clapping at the front door. Joe stood there with a huge grin. "And how it should be." He gave the thumbs up before disappearing back inside.

"Well, you two, I'm glad you've sorted things out." Linda walked closer, now with a relieved and happy look.

"Me too," said Grace. She put one arm around Kain. "I think everything will be okay now."

"Good," said Linda. "I'll head back home then." She looked at her watch. "Steve'll be back soon from his ride."

She grimaced; her smile gone. "I really don't want him and his father there alone."

CHAPTER 16

Steve pulled Blaze up just outside the back fence of his former home. The home James 'Scott' McTaggart had given him to live in while being forced to do his dirty work. He knew this bush and the back roads well and hadn't taken as long as expected to ride 'as the crow flies' from his family property. He'd watered Blaze at the little creek only fifty-odd metres back and quenched his own thirst. Steve got off, scratched his face where the mask irritated him, opened the small gate he'd made long ago and led Blaze through before closing the gate. The green, overgrown house yard appealed to Blaze, who immediately dropped his head to graze. "Hang on, mate." Steve pulled on the reins and walked Blaze through the grass, heading toward the front of the house. He looked about and listened hard for a sign of anyone possibly being in the house, but Blaze's noisy chewing on the last mouthful of grass he'd grabbed and the *swishing* of the grass as six legs walked through it made that difficult.

Over that noise all Steve heard were birds singing, the breeze whispering through nearby trees and distant thunder, which now seemed further away than earlier. He closed his eyes a moment, savouring the sounds of 'home'. A faint buzzing caught his attention. He opened his eyes and focussed his gaze on where it came from. The mandarin tree at the back of the house blossomed with flowers and bees. The sickly-sweet smell of over ripe mangos reached his nostrils. Many lay on the ground beneath the large tree, half eaten by birds and fruit bats. Several rainbow lorikeets staggered and squawked among them, drunk on the delicious, fermenting nectar. A huge bunch of ripening bananas hung from one of the banana trees. His chook pen beneath the mango tree and extending into the back corner of the yard, stood quiet and abandoned. Grace had organised for his chooks to be collected and taken to their parents'. He breathed deep, enjoying the clean, fresh scent of the bush on a summer's afternoon.

Rustling in the grass in front of him stopped him mid stride. Blaze jerked his head back, giving a painful yank on Steve's arm and shoulder. He stepped back and turned to Blaze. "Easy, boy." He rolled that shoulder up and down and put his other hand up to Blaze's flared nostrils. "C'mon, it's only a snake. He won't hurt you." Blaze lowered his head a little, but his eyes remained alert, darting toward the moving grass. Steve rubbed Blaze's sweaty neck while watching the moving grass over to his right. By the shifting movement of the grass the snake was obviously slithering away from them. Steve let go of the reins and walked several steps the way the snake had gone. He caught a glimpse of a black tail disappearing through the mesh fence and into even thicker grass and bushes outside the yard.

Satisfied the threat was gone, he went back to Blaze, now happily munching on the grass again. "Righto, mate, I might let you have a feed." He walked alongside the high house and scanned the fence. All looked good and the front gate was shut. Blue and white police tape hung along the front fence. Not unexpected. He returned to Blaze and removed the saddle and cloth, sitting the saddle just under the edge of the house and draping the cloth over it. Picking up the reins before Blaze stood on one, he undid the neck strap, held the top of the bridle and lifted it slightly over the horse's head. Blaze dropped the bit from his mouth and Steve pulled the bridle back over his head, leaving the bit dangling under his chin, redid the neck strap and tied the reins around Blaze's neck so he could graze freely.

Steve walked under the house and reached up to the top of the meter box. Good, his spare key was still there. Curious if the power was still connected, he opened the meter box. None of the mechanism moved so no power. *Bugger.* He flicked the Mains switch but still nothing. Oh well, that was probably too much to hope for. His land cruiser ute wasn't here. Police must have taken that.

Heading to the front stairs, he smiled at the sight of three Pretty-Faced wallabies grazing just outside the front of his yard. "Hey, little fellas." All three darted off into the bush. His heart sunk. In the past they hadn't seemed nearly as scared of him. They must either be different ones or they'd been frightened by strangers. He scratched at the side of his head again, through the mask. The surgeon had said not to scratch but it was difficult to put up with the itching in the humid weather. Maybe it was his mask that frightened away the wallabies. He shrugged a little and went up the stairs two at a time.

Once on his front verandah he stopped and looked about. The beautiful mountains to the west stood just as majestic as ever. The sun now behind some clouds but the storm seemed to have petered out. Probably a good thing. A pair of magpies flew on to the rail only metres from him and began their sweet warbling. One of the sounds he missed the most since being taken from here.

He sniffed the air. A faint smell of smoke drifted on the breeze, reminding him of a campfire. He scanned the bush in the direction of the oncoming, cool breeze. A small, grey patch of smoke hung about the tree tops a hundred metres or so away in the National Park. Everything was lush and green, no way a bushfire could be a problem. Probably just campers. He gave a half-hearted shrug and put it out of his mind.

His small table and chair sat in the same spot, just outside the door. How he missed sitting there in the mornings drinking his coffee and enjoying the numerous sounds and sights of the bush. He loved it best when it was raining, even storming, watching the lightning streak across the sky and occasionally striking a tree in the distance which then exploded in a shower of sparks, just like fireworks.

Pulling open the screen door he pushed the key into the lock. His nerves fired up, sending his heart rate up. He took a deep breath and pushed open the wooden door, unsure of what he'd see. Stuffy, stale air hit his nostrils. He stood just inside the kitchen and looked about. *Home.* The only home he knew. Everything was just the way it had been the day he left, but neater and the fridge stood empty and open. Toaster and electric kettle on the bench beside the sink. Coffee, tea and sugar in containers near the kettle. No dirty crockery. All seemed in their place in the wall cabinet. Someone must have been inside and tidied up, but who? Grace may have done it when they came and got the chooks and some of his clothes and things, but she hadn't mentioned anything about cleaning up.

He walked from the kitchen/dining area into the lounge room. Chairs still there and TV in the corner on its stand. Nothing different. So many lonely nights spent sitting on one of these chairs with nothing but the television for company. The days spent alone he could handle but the nights were a different matter.

He headed down the hallway and stopped at the first bedroom door. The room he'd kept Grace in. He shook his head and sighed. "So sorry I locked you in here, Grace." He'd already apologised to her several times, but it still weighed heavy on his mind. She'd been so frightened of him the first few days. He certainly couldn't blame her. She'd been in such a mess – injuries from the car accident; terrorised by the wild dogs he'd shot as one was about to leap on her in the bush while a storm raged and distraught that Kain had dumped her. On top of all that she had to cope with being locked up by a big, grotesque monster. How amazing it felt when she'd realised he wasn't going to hurt her and they'd sit and talk over a cuppa or a meal.

He went to his bedroom, next to the one Grace had used. The curtains were drawn, making it almost as dark as night. The air hung thick as he parted the curtains behind the bed head, reached through the bars on the window, slid open the screen and pushed the window open a little. He leaned close and took in a deep breath of fresh, cool air. Still a slight hint of smoke in the air.

He looked at his bed and gasped. It was unmade, with the sheets showing dirty patches and bits of grass and leaves. He *always* made his bed of a morning and never let his sheets become this dirty. The hair on the back of his neck prickled to attention. Something wasn't right. A wave of anxiety washed over him and settled in the pit of his stomach. He listened for any sound but could only hear nature outside. He walked as quietly as possible to his wardrobe and pulled open the doors. Totally empty. His tense shoulders dropped with relief. He had no idea what he may have found in there but was glad it was nothing.

Steve stepped across the hallway into the third bedroom. Totally empty. Then out into the sleepout at the back of the house. A single bed on one side, as it used to be, and nothing else. He looked through the bars out one of the large windows. Blaze grazed contentedly only metres away. That was a good sign surely. Being a nervy horse, he'd most likely show it if someone was lurking about. Steve shuddered at those bars, hoping for the millionth time he wouldn't be sent to prison. They'd given him peace of mind though after he was attacked. He'd felt safe here. Heading back to the kitchen, he briefly poked his head into the bathroom and toilet, opposite Grace's room, checking they were empty. Nothing out of the ordinary there.

Now that he was finally here and had looked through the house he had no idea what to do next. Realistically he couldn't stay here no matter how much he wished he could. Maybe he should head back. His mum might be getting worried by now. He shouldn't have put her through more worry. Feeling like a right lump of shit he walked out on to the front verandah, shutting the door behind him and pulling the key out of the lock. Best he get back as quickly as he could. Would she call the cops on him? *Please don't, mum.* Surely, they'd all understand he *had* to come here. A last look around and he headed toward the stairs.

A sharp crack pierced the air, echoing through the bush. Searing pain tore through his arm. Blood splattered.

CHAPTER 17

Linda ran back to the house with a bad gut feeling. No Blaze with the other horses and Steve's saddle and bridle not in the tack room. The sun was sinking toward the western horizon. He should have been back by now. "Where *are* you, Steve?" She stopped and looked back again, scanning the paddock in the direction they'd ridden, hoping to see him coming but only saw cattle grazing. *"Shit."* She raced up the back stairs and into the kitchen. "Bruce!" No reply. She headed down the hallway toward the front verandah. *"Bruce!"*

"Yep." Bruce sat at the table on the verandah. Can of beer in one hand and several empties lying on the table in front of him. He looked up at his wife. "What's wrong? You sound frantic." With not a shred of concern showing in his slightly red eyes he took another swig of beer.

"Have you seen Steve in the past hour or so?" She spoke fast in between puffs and pants.

Bruce looked about then back to Linda, raised his eyebrows but with a downturned mouth he shook his head. "Not since lunch time. Where's he supposed to be?"

Linda swallowed down the gulp of dread her nerves had stirred up and took a deep breath, hoping to slow her racing heart. Was there any point even telling Bruce where Steve should or, God forbid, *could* be? "He went for a ride." Without waiting for a response – that she probably wouldn't like hearing anyway – she headed back inside and grabbed her phone from where it was charging on the kitchen bench.

She tapped Grace's number. It rang. *Come on. Answer, Grace.* It went to message bank. "Grace, it's mum. Have you heard from Steve? He's not back from his ride. I'm worried. I'm going to jump on the four-wheeler and ride out to where I last saw him, by the creek. Ring me as soon as you get this message." She slid the phone in her back pocket of her jeans and ran to the shed.

Linda roared the four-wheeler motorbike down the paddock toward the spot by the creek where she'd last seen her son. The closer she got the worse her fears grew. She hoped like crazy he was still there, maybe just sitting by the water's edge, but her gut feeling told her he was far away by now. *How could you do this, Steve?* The wind dried her tears as soon as they formed.

She pulled up by the creek, switched off the key and brought her hand to her forehead to shade the setting sun while scanning around. No sign of Steve or Blaze. "Steve, are you here?" Silence except for a distant plane in the sky and a pair of squabbling mud larks over in the grass to her right. She cupped her hands either side of her mouth and took a deep breath. *"STEVE."* The mud larks stopped their squawking and flew away. No response. Her shoulders dropped with a huge sigh of hopelessness.

She started the bike and rode a few hundred metres along the creek, stopping again and calling out, but still nothing. She licked her parched lips and swallowed sticky saliva down her dry throat. This was not good. Suddenly it hit her. *Home. Steve's home.* He'd wanted to get back there badly and had made a point of not wanting the dogs to follow earlier. It made sense. She started the bike and tore back to the house as fast as she dared through the long grass. Hitting a small log, the bike bounced to one side, almost throwing her off the other. A bolt of fear shot through her, as she imagined ending up on the ground with broken bones. She eased up on the throttle a little.

Just as she pulled up near the back steps Grace and Kain came rushing downstairs to meet her. Linda switched off the ignition and got off. "Oh, so glad you two are here." She gave Grace a quick hug.

Grace looked worried. "Any sign of him yet, mum? We thought it'd be best to just come rather than call you."

"No, nothing." Linda brushed some loose hairs back from her face. "But I reckon he's gone back to his old place. God, I hope so, anyway."

"Let's go there, then," said Kain. "But we're only in my ute."

Linda headed up the stairs. "We'll take my car. I'll just grab a drink and let Bruce know." She downed a full glass of water from the jug in the fridge and headed through the house to let Bruce know what was happening, even though he'd be sure to think she was mad or he just couldn't care less. *Why do you have to make this whole thing so much harder than it should be?* She wiped a sneaky tear away and opened the screen door. Bruce was still sitting there, staring off into space. There didn't seem to be any more beer cans in front of him than what was there before...hopefully.

"Bruce, we're going for a drive. We think Steve has gone back to his old house." No reply. He didn't even look around. It was as if he hadn't even heard her. "Bruce! Did you hear me?" Her fear morphed to anger. His ignorance and non-caring attitude now getting a bit too much. She grabbed his shoulder. "I *said* we are going to look for Steve. You know...your son. *Our* son!"

Slowly his head turned until his eyes met hers. His eyes looked lost and sad, but then narrowed as a crease furrowed deeper in his forehead. On the table his right hand clenched into a fist. His lips tightened and turned downwards. Beads of sweat broke out on his forehead even though a cool breeze blew.

Linda let go of his shoulder and took a step back. She was seeing that look more and more lately and less of the loving husband she adored. "Okay then, we'll be back as soon as we can. If Sophie gets back before we do just let her know, please." She waited a second for some sort of response. When none came she turned to go inside and grab her wallet. Bruce grunted and mumbled something as she went through the screen door, but at that point she really wasn't interested in any drunken thing he had to say.

Grace and Kain stood by her car in the large shed. "Do you want me to drive, mum?" asked Grace. "I know the way well and you look pretty stressed."

Linda smiled with gratitude. "Yes, that'd be good, love."

Kain opened the front passenger door for Linda and then got in the back seat.

"Thanks Kain." Linda jumped in, dropped her wallet in the console and did up her seatbelt. "Grace, you know the new Steve better than me. Do you think he's gone back to his old place?" She held her breath, hoping to hear a yes. If not, she had no idea what she'd do next. She'd have to inform the police and they'd go after him. Bruce would just love that. The thought sickened her.

"Yes, I bet he has. That's the one thing he talks about the most – going back there." Grace started the car and reversed out of the shed. Before heading off she grabbed her mother's clammy hand. "Try not to worry so much. We'll find him."

Linda squeezed Grace's hand and sighed. "I'll try." She wasn't convinced Grace was as optimistic as she tried to sound, and her eyes also showed worry. "I've just got him back. I can't lose him again." The tension of the past hour or so released in tears. She covered her face with her hands and let it out. Tears and sobbing shook her body.

Grace rubbed her knee. "We'll find him, mum."

Linda wiped her eyes and sniffed. "I hope so." She tightened her lips together to try and stop them trembling. Now was the time she needed her husband's love and support, but no, he cares more about his bloody beer!

Kain handed her an open box of tissues from beside him on the back seat. She grabbed two. "Thanks." Wiping her eyes with one she blew her nose with the other and dropped them at her feet.

The outburst must have released much of her built up tension. She took a deep, slow breath, leaned back on the head rest and closed her eyes, thinking back to Steve as a kid. His first day of school. He'd wanted to ride his horse to school. It took a lot of convincing to make him understand it was way too far. He'd loved school as a little fella, but lost interest once in high school, but he'd excelled in sport and had lots of friends, including girlfriends. His father used to tease him in fun about the girls and Steve's face would redden with embarrassment. Despite the sadness of losing Jon, there were so many wonderful memories...

"We're here." Grace switched off the ignition.

Linda's eyes opened with a jolt. She must have dozed off. They'd stopped outside the front gate of the house. She hadn't been here before, not feeling comfortable about it to come with Grace when she and Kain had collected the chooks and Steve's personal things.

She jumped out before Kain and Grace and looked about. It was nice enough. She could certainly see why Steve felt at peace here and had wanted to return. She strode several metres, unlatched and walked through the small front gate. Kain and Grace followed right behind.

Heading to the steps something on the ground caught her eye and nostrils. "Look, fresh horse poop!" Her dread turned to hope. "He's here." She wanted to cry and laugh at the same time. *"STEVE,"* she yelled as loudly as she could while darting her gaze about. "Look, there's his saddle." She ran through the grass to the spot where Steve had put the saddle. She looked about, able to see the whole yard. No Blaze. The small back gate stood open. "STEVE!"

Grace gasped loudly. "Mum, come here." Her voice frantic.

Linda spun around and headed back to the front stairs. Grace had just walked up and on to the verandah.

"Shit." Was all Kain said, standing halfway up the steps and looking downwards, his face pale.

"What is it?" Linda began to race up the steps but stopped dead in her tracks, heart thrumming up into her throat. Drops of blood were splattered on almost every step. It glistened wet so still fresh. She ran up the stairs. "Oh no". More blood on the floor and some on the small table near the door. She grabbed the door handle and tried to open it, but it was locked. Banging on the door with her fist she called out to Steve but got no response.

"I'll try around the back," said Kain, and disappeared down the stairs.

Grace grabbed hold of Linda's shaking shoulders. "Mum, sit down for a minute and let's try to work out what happened here." A scrape on the floor and Grace had the chair there for her mum. Linda collapsed into it, propped her elbows on her thighs and dropped her head into her hands. "What the hell do we do now, Grace?"

Grace placed her hand on Linda's back for comfort. "I don't know, mum, but let's try not to think the worst, hey."

Kain trudged up the stairs. "No sign of him or the horse. I can't get in the back door. I could just reach up and look through a window. The house looks empty." He walked along the verandah a little way. "Hang on, what's that?"

Linda looked up and got off her chair. "What?"

Kain stood facing the front wall near the corner of the verandah. He poked at something on the otherwise clean, unmarked wall.

Grace and Linda rushed over.

Kain scraped at a fresh-looking, rough but small, gouge in the wall. He leaned in for a closer look. "There's a scrape and a bit of a hole." He turned to Grace then to Linda. His face paled even more. "Looks like a bullet."

A gasp escaped Linda's throat. Everything went black.

CHAPTER 18

Grace shut off the motor of her mother's car, back home in the shed. "Are you *sure* you don't want to see a doctor, mum? You could've hit your head when you fainted back there." She knew very well her mum's priority was finding Steve, and they were alike in many things, especially stubbornness, but it didn't lessen her concerns. "Do you feel okay? Not seeing double or anything like that?"

Linda took hold of Grace's forearm. "No, love, I'm *fine.*" A slight smile appeared on her worried face. "But thank you." She briefly squeezed Grace's hand before the smile disappeared as she got out of the car and strode off toward the house.

Grace sighed as she watched her mum walk away. She took hold of Kain's hand. "I don't know what to do or suggest to mum. I can't see we have any other choice but to call the police." She looked toward the west. "It'll be dark soon. Steve'll have to be found...one way or another." A lump wedged in her throat, imagining him lying injured or even dead somewhere.

Kain put his arm about her shoulders. "Come on, let's not think the worst. It might not have even been his blood. He could be on his way back now." Kain didn't sound very convincing, but she thought it best not to say more. They walked toward the house in silence. Linda had disappeared under the house. Kain stopped and pointed toward the cattle yards. "Grace look!

Linda was running in that direction crying and yelling incoherently. Someone was standing outside of the tack shed. Steve. Grace gasped and took off, running past the house toward her mother and brother, laughing but unable to prevent tears streaming down her cheeks, a tonne weight suddenly gone from her shoulders.

Linda reached him first, giving him a tight hug and almost overbalancing him. "Where have you been? I've been worried sick." She let go of her son and wiped her eyes.

Steve held his left arm against his chest, his sleeve blood-stained. "I'm okay."

Grace reached for his left hand, covered in drying blood. "Have you been shot?"

"Let's get him inside." Linda's voice was frantic, not giving him a chance to reply. She took hold of his right arm and began walking quickly toward the house. "We've just been to your house and saw all the blood on the steps. What happened? Who did this?"

"I don't know," was all Grace heard him say before she rushed ahead to get the first aid box from the bathroom.

"Just let me sit here." Steve sat down on the back steps with a groan and heavy sigh. "Can I have a drink of water please?"

"I'll get it." Kain walked past him up the stairs.

Grace was soon back with the kit and a clean towel. She sat on the step beside her brother while their mother stood in front of Steve, leaning down toward him, her sweaty face pale with worry and fear. Grace took out a pair of surgical scissors.

"The wound must be just above your elbow, going by the hole in your sleeve," said Linda. "Is that the only one?" Her voice rose to panic level. "Did he shoot you anywhere else?"

"No, mum." Steve held up his dirty right hand. "It's all right. Don't panic. I don't think it's all that bad. I've had worse things happen to me than this."

Kain passed Steve a large glass of water. "Here you go, mate."

"Thanks." Steve drank it in one go and handed it back to Kain.

"More?" asked Kain.

"No thanks." Steve gave a shake of his head then turned toward Grace, cutting his sleeve above the wound. "What are you doing, Grace?" He moved his arm away a little.

"I have to get rid of the sleeve to see how bad the wound is," said Grace.

Linda pulled her phone from her pocket. "We need to get you to the hospital?"

"No!" Steve pushed her hand containing the phone downwards. "No hospital! I said I'll be alright."

Linda's worried face turned to hurt. "I was just-"

"I'm sorry, mum," Steve cut in. He held her forearm for a moment. "I didn't mean to upset you. Let's just see how bad it looks. It's really not all that sore."

Not very convincing words, thought Grace, but again, didn't reply. With the surgical mask on it was impossible to see by his face what he was thinking or feeling. Going to the hospital certainly could get him into trouble for leaving the property. Hopefully it wouldn't come to that. She dropped the dirty sleeve on the ground beside the stairs and gently lifted his arm for a closer look. "Looks like the bullet has gone straight through. Probably a good thing. Can you move your hand and elbow okay?"

"How the heck did you manage to ride all that way with that injury?" asked Linda. "Is Blaze okay?"

Steve looked at Grace while moving his hand and arm. "Yes." Then to Linda. "Yep, he's back in with the other horses. It wasn't easy but I had no choice." He groaned a little as Grace lowered his arm. "Sorry, I had to leave the saddle there. Didn't have time to put it on him."

"We brought it back," said Kain. "It's still in the car. Neither Grace or I could lift it. It'll be right there for now."

"This might sting a bit." Grace poured some antiseptic fluid over the wound.

Steve sucked in a sharp breath but said nothing.

Still clutching her phone, Linda brought her other hand to the side of his masked face. "Do you feel okay? Dizzy or anything like that?"

Steve just shook his head.

Grace wiped the wound area clean as possible with a sterile pad then bandaged it. "It's not a big hole but I'm no doctor. You might need something more for it than this for the pain and stop infection. What about if we call the home doctor?"

Again, Steve shook his head. "No doctor. They might tell the police."

Grace got up and took the first aid kit back inside and did a quick trip to the loo. When she got back her mum was sitting beside Steve, one arm around his shoulders.

"Yes, I *was* coming back," Steve said, obviously replying to his mother's worrying question. "And I'm sorry I couldn't tell you I was going there – *home*. I knew you'd try and stop me. I *had* to. I don't expect anyone to understand though. I'd locked the house back up and was walking across the verandah when..." His voice trailed off.

"It's all right." Linda's voice was soothing. "You don't need to explain. You're here now and safe. Thank God." Linda looked up at Grace. "Is your father still out the front...drinking?"

"I don't know, Mum. I didn't go looking for him." Grace glanced at Kain, but before she could say anything he shook his head with a, 'don't-ask-me-to-go-see-him' look.

Linda's phone rang, startling her. She looked at the screen. "Number unknown." With a frown she answered it. "Hello." A faint female voice could be heard on the other end. "Oh, yes, Jenna." She nodded toward Steve, who shook his head. Jenna talked for a minute or so. "Okay, no worries. He's a bit busy right now, but I'll let him know you called and he can call you back." More talking from

Jenna. "Yep, thanks Jenna. Lovely to chat to you. Bye." Linda ended the call.

Footsteps came along the hallway upstairs. Grace looked at Linda whose unhappy gaze was fixed on the back door at the top of the stairs. "Sounds like Dad's coming, Mum."

Linda glanced at Grace then, with a roll of her eyes, back to the door. "Yes. Just hope he doesn't carry on."

Bruce appeared on the landing at the top of the steps. "What's going on?" He frowned and swayed a little. "What's happened to him?" His words slightly slurred and he clumsily pointed toward Steve a moment before taking hold of the side rail of the landing.

"Don't worry about Steve, he's okay," said Linda, before looking away in disgust from her husband. She grabbed the towel Grace had brought out and folded it up.

Awkward silence for a few moments. Grace held her breath and glanced from Kain to Steve to her mum. Everyone looked uncomfortable. The late afternoon air thickened with tension.

Steve cleared his throat. "If you must know, I've been shot!" He didn't bother looking around and up at his father. "But I'll live."

Linda placed her hand on Steve's shoulder, leaned in closer to him and said a quiet, "Shhh."

Bruce mumbled and cursed a little before turning and going back inside. A bump came from the kitchen. Louder cursing, then footsteps heading back toward the front verandah.

Grace expelled her deep breath. "I just don't understand dad anymore." She sighed in hopelessness. "What are we going to do about him, Mum? He's like a total stranger these days. Any other parent would be thrilled to have their child back from the dead, so to speak."

"Two children," added Kain. He squeezed Grace's arm gently. "And grandkids on the way." His words turned bitter. "Someone needs to knock some sense into him!"

Linda looked at Kain, a stern motherly expression on her now-pale face. "Yep, I know the frustration, but that's not the answer, Kain. We don't need a repeat of that other time you punched him."

"He deserved that!" Kain's face reddened. "After he blamed me for Grace's accident and then had a funeral without telling me."

"What happened about that, Mum?" asked Grace before Linda could reply. "Dad had the other lady in my car cremated, believing it was my burnt body."

"The police sorted it out when they found out who she was and as far as I know, the ashes were given to her family."

Grace remembered the hitchhiker she'd picked up and then let drive while she tried to text Kain. It wasn't like her to do that but in her upset and confused state after Kain abruptly ended their long relationship, she hadn't been thinking straight. The car had veered off the road so suddenly she still has no idea what caused the accident. All she could remember was the screams, tree branches, crashing sound, being thrown about in the car and sharp pain in her head and shoulder, and the dirt in her mouth after she'd been thrown out of the rolling vehicle. The explosion and the *smell*. She'll never forget that burning flesh smell. She had vomited then painfully dragged herself away from the wreck before getting to her feet and wandering off into the bush looking for help.

Buddy appeared at the bottom of the stairs, looked up at Steve and whimpered a little, as if he sensed something was wrong. Steve reached out and patted his head. "It's okay, boy."

Linda stepped down beside Buddy. "I'll go feed them. Bruce used to always do it, but it seems to have fallen onto me these days." And in a slightly quieter voice, as if to herself, "Just like nearly everything else around here." She headed under the house. Metal dog bowls clanged and a fridge door opened as Linda spoke to the dogs.

Steve's large shoulders slumped. "All this shit because of me." He turned to Grace. "I don't want to be here, Grace." The words choked out. "Feels like I've just gone from one crappy mess to another. Shame that bullet didn't hit where it was meant to." He slapped the left side of his chest.

"Stop talking like that!" His words sickened Grace. She put her arm about his shoulders. "Look, how do you even know it was meant for you? Could've just been a stray bullet from some cowboy out shooting in the National Park. No one could have possibly known you were there."

"She's right, mate," added Kain. "You could've just been in the wrong place at the wrong time."

Steve shook his head. "No, I wasn't. He was out there waiting for me. I saw smoke from his campfire."

"A campfire, yes," said Grace, trying to convince herself as much as her brother. "Like I said-"

"All done," announced Linda returning from beneath the house. "How about we get you upstairs and get some tea happening and a shower."

Before anyone had a chance to respond or move, a siren wailed along their driveway, getting louder with an accompanying roar of a vehicle. The sun had just disappeared over the western horizon.

Steve sat upright and gasped, looking about.

"What the..." Linda ran to the side of the house and looked toward the driveway. "It's an ambulance." She headed toward the front of the house.

"Who called them?" asked Steve, fear and urgency in his voice.

"I certainly didn't," said Grace. She looked at Kain.

"Don't look at me!" He threw his hands in the air. "I've been here the whole time. Must've been your father."

"Ahh shit," muttered Steve.

Linda rushed back to them, followed closely by two male paramedics. "They said they got a callout to a gunshot victim."

Grace stood up. "Who called?"

One paramedic shrugged. "We don't get told who makes the calls, sorry. We were sent here to treat a gunshot wound."

Steven tumbled forward from the third step on which he'd been sitting and lay in a crumpled heap at his mother's feet.

"*Steve*!" Grace and Linda said in unison, before rushing to him.

"Let us treat him," said the other paramedic stepping forward.

Linda and Grace stood back. Grace placed her arm about her mother's waist as Kain took hold of her other hand.

The paramedics lay Steve out flat on his back and checked his vitals. His eyelids fluttered and his head moved a little. "What happened?"

"You must have fainted again," said Grace.

"Again?" One paramedic frowned at her. "Is this normal?"

"Well..." Grace was unsure what to say. She didn't want to say anything that would get Steve into trouble. "Yes, he has a few times lately. So far doctors haven't been able to find out why."

The paramedics helped Steve up to a sitting position and one lifted his bandaged arm. "Is this the gunshot?"

"Yep," replied Steve, resignation in his voice. "I stuffed up. I-" He looked at Linda, who frantically shook her head with a finger against her pursed lips. She pointed to herself, opened and closed her hand in front of her mouth then pointed to the paramedics, both busy with their job at hand. Steve nodded knowingly and remained quiet.

"I think it best we just get him to the hospital." The paramedics stood and helped Steve up. "Is that alright with you?"

Steve just shrugged. "Do whatever you have to."

Linda clutched Steve's right hand. "I'm coming with you." She turned to one paramedic. "Is that okay? *Please.* I'm his mother."

"Yep, sure." He turned to Steve. "I'll go get the stretcher for you."

"I can walk," snapped Steve.

"I'll just go grab my bag and meet you out the front," said Linda before running up the stairs and disappearing inside.

Grace and Kain walked along the side of the house just behind Steve with a paramedic on either side of him. She briefly imagined it was two prison wardens walking beside him. No!

Linda was standing beside Bruce, sitting back on the table on the verandah. She said something inaudible to him then wiped her eyes. "I'll see you when I get back, okay?" With not even a peck on his cheek which used to be such a common sight, she came down the stairs looking angry and got into the ambulance after they'd settled Steve in the vehicle.

"We'll be up soon, Mum," called Grace just before they shut the doors.

The ambulance sped off along the driveway but no siren this time, or flashing lights.

Bruce's chair scraped along the verandah floor. Grace looked up, expecting to hear the screen door open and close, but her father walked over and leant on the railing, watching the ambulance disappear in a fine cloud of dust. Even in the fading light he appeared to have a smug look on his face.

Grace's heart sank to the pits of her stomach, churning its contents. *Surely not.*

"Dad, did you call the ambulance?"

Bruce dragged his glassy gaze away from the driveway direction and toward Grace. "Yes, I did."

"Please tell me it was because you care about him." Her heart rate banged up as she awaited a positive answer.

Bruce's eyelids narrowed and his mouth upturned as he shook his head. "Nope. Just wanted to get rid of him." He turned away and went inside.

Grace dry retched then vomited, narrowly missing Kain's feet.

CHAPTER 19

Steve shifted uncomfortably in his hospital triage bed. Voices, clanging, trolleys whirring by, a siren outside, all invaded his ears and tired brain. What a bloody long day it had been. Only that morning he was let out to go 'home' to his parents. The last thing he'd expected, or wanted, then was to be back here by nightfall. A doctor had treated his injury and then gone off to talk to his colleagues about the next course of action. He sighed, knowing it was no use fighting it anymore. They could do whatever they wanted to him. He was past caring. Going back to his home in the bush earlier hadn't been near as satisfying as he'd expected, and that's without being shot. Obviously, his father hated his guts. Grace has an exciting future to look forward to with her new babies and a man she adores. What would it matter if he did end up in jail? He looked at his mother sitting by his bedside. The worry and sadness in her eyes turned his apathy and self-pity to regret. *She* clearly cared and she didn't deserve all this worry. He reached out for her hand. "I'm sorry, mum. I've put you in a bad situation. You really don't have to lie for me."

"Steve, don't worry about that now." She smiled but it seemed forced. "It'll be okay. I've just decided I'll tell the police I knew you were going to your old place and that I trusted you to come back, which you obviously did. No point trying to say you were accidentally shot on the farm. Your father would probably shoot that down in flames." She gave a slight eye roll. "Sorry, not the best way to say that."

"I don't know..." He really didn't like the idea of her lying for him. "What if they find out the truth. Then you'll be in trouble too."

She shrugged. "How could they? We could have talked about it while at the creek."

"But Grace and Kain know."

"True, but I really don't think - hang on." She grabbed her phone from her bag. "I'll call Grace and warn her. They're probably on their way here now." She tapped the screen and almost immediately began talking quietly to Grace, nodding and smiling as she spoke.

Steve watched her but also listened for any footsteps approaching, his nerves stirring throughout his body. He didn't want anyone overhearing his mother. Would it be too much to expect this to all go smoothly? Grace would surely agree but he wasn't so sure about Kain who certainly wouldn't want her getting into any trouble. And neither did he, for that matter.

Linda ended the call with a satisfied smile. "All good. Sophie got home just before they left and all three are on their way here but had stopped for a bite to eat. They won't be too much longer." She dropped her phone back into her bag.

"That's good." Steve relaxed back into the pillows, staring at the ceiling while letting out a pent-up breath. Everything seemed so crazy and confusing. Nothing felt right and now he knew for sure someone was out to get him. Not just *get* him but out to *kill* him. But who the hell was it? And why? *That's a stupid question, you idiot!* He shook his head, trying to dispel that annoying inner voice that kept coming back when he least needed it.

Footsteps approached and the doctor who'd treated him parted the curtains and stepped in by his bed. "Alright, Steve, we are going to admit you to keep an eye on that wound and since you fainted we need to monitor your vitals. An orderly will be here shortly to take you upstairs. I've contacted Doctor Leeson and he'll see you soon, okay." The doctor nodded, patted Steve on the leg and was gone.

Linda pulled the curtain back shut. "It's good that Doctor Leeson will see you. I like him." Her frown lines had smoothed out a little.

Steve nodded, some of the weight and worry gone from his mind and shoulders. "Yep, me too."

A young orderly arrived with a wheelchair. "Okay, I'm looking for Steve Atkinson." With a smile he nodded toward Steve. "I take it that's you."

"Yep." Steve pulled the sheet off and got himself in a sitting position on the edge of the bed. "What about all this?" He looked up at the drip hooked to the canula in his forearm, feeding him antibiotics.

"That comes too." The orderly moved the tall, drip contraption a little closer to the wheelchair.

Soon Steve was in the wheelchair and being pushed out of emergency toward the lifts, his injured arm in a sling. Linda walked alongside, holding the drip machine and wheeling it beside Steve. No words were spoken.

They entered a ward of four beds. Three were already occupied by other men. The bed closest to them sat empty. An uneasy feeling swept over Steve. "Wait. What's this?" The idea of being in a room with strangers horrified him. He grabbed the wheel of the chair with his right hand, bringing it to a sudden halt. "Can't I go back to my old room?"

"Sorry, mate, I was told to bring you to this ward." He stepped in front of Steve, his friendly smile now gone, replaced with a look of annoyance. "Please take your hand off the wheel."

Linda placed her hand on her son's shoulder. "It'll be okay, we can close the curtains around your bed."

Her voice sounded tired and strained, no doubt what she was feeling. Steve didn't want to add to her stress. "All right." He stood up and walked the last few steps to the bed and sat on the edge. He was tired...bloody tired. He sighed and looked at his dirty clothes. "But I can't get into the bed like this. I need a shower."

"Grace is bringing you some clothes," said Linda. "She shouldn't be long now."

At that moment a solidly built, stern faced nurse walked in carrying a light blue hospital gown and neatly folded white towel. "Right, Mr Atkinson, we need to get you showered." She beckoned him to stand up. "Come on, I don't have all day."

Steve looked at his mother who frowned at the nurse, then looked back to the nurse. He'd never had anyone shower him before, that he could remember. During his previous stay he was allowed to do it himself. "I'd prefer to shower myself, thanks." She looked sour and gruff, and he hated the thought of her seeing him naked, let alone touching him.

She shook her head, her stern look changing to anger. "Look, you're hooked up to the drip and you've got an injury. Plus, your head mask can't get wet. Let's just get this done. We're flat out tonight! I don't need anyone stuffing me around." She strode over and opened the bathroom door, which was closest to the bed opposite him. Holding the door open she glared at him.

The orderly disappeared quickly with the wheelchair. Steve heaved his exhausted body off the bed and trudged to the bathroom. Linda wheeled the drip as far as the door where the nurse took it from her. He shrugged in resignation. Surely being showered by the drill sergeant here can't be as bad as many other things he's had to endure.

After his shower Linda helped him get comfortable in the bed. The nurse had left the ward. "How did that go? She didn't give you a hard time, did she?"

Steve grunted, preferring to forget about her. "Nah, it was alright I suppose. What time is Grace coming?"

Linda helped him adjust his pillows. "Should be anytime now." She pulled the curtain partway around his bed so he couldn't be seen by the other patients and dragged the visitor's chair closer to the bed. Once seated she leaned in close to him. "Remember, if and when the police come tell them I said you could go for a ride to your house." Her voice a whisper. "And go along with what I say, okay." She smiled and patted his forearm. "It'll be all right."

"Maybe they won't come." Steve was hopeful, but not optimistic.

Linda lowered her voice again. "The doctor who treated you said they always have to report gunshot wounds. Plus, we need to find out who it is and if it's the same person who sent you that horrible note." She cringed and her face changed to a look of fear. "It scares me, son. They obviously mean business."

Male voices increased in volume and the curtain was pulled open. Two well-dressed men stood there looking at him.

"Are you Steve Atkinson?" asked the taller, older one.

Steve glanced at his mother briefly then back to the men. "Yes." His heart rate increased and his mouth dried. He grabbed the cup of water by his bed and had a mouthful, swishing it around before swallowing. "Are you the police?"

"Yes," replied the one who spoke first. "I'm Detective Jones and this is Detective Wallace." He nodded toward his colleague before they both showed their badges. Jones looked at Linda. "And you are?"

Linda held out her right hand. "Hi, I'm Linda, Steve's mother." She shook each hand in turn. "What can we do for you?"

Again, Jones spoke. "We have to investigate your son's shooting." He took a pen and notebook out of his top pocket, flipped it open and looked at Steve. "Can you tell us exactly what happened?"

Steve shifted uncomfortably in his bed and glanced at his mother who gave him a slight nod. He was glad they couldn't see his face properly. He felt a little safer behind the mask but hoped his eyes gave away nothing. "Mum and I went riding today and-"

"Riding?" Detective Wallace cut in. "What? Bike? Horse?"

Steve's patience began to waver. He wanted to tell the detective to just shut up for a bit. "Horse. Anyway, we were out in one of the back paddocks and..." *Keep it together.* "And I wanted to go for a ride to my old place." His heart now thumped against his rib cage. This could be make or break time. He couldn't risk looking at his mother for fear either of them will slip up so stared straight at Jones. "Mum couldn't go with me but she said it was okay for me to go as long as I was back before dark." Out the corner of his eye he saw his mother nod.

"That's right," said Linda. "My daughter rang and needed me, so I told Steve he could go. I knew he'd come back," she hastily added.

Jones nodded but also frowned. "Then what happened?"

"I rode to my old house, let the horse eat grass in the yard and went inside."

"Wasn't the door locked?" Jones asked, his brow still furrowed. "How did you get in? Did you break in?"

Steve shook his head and took a deep breath trying to stay calm. "No, of course not! The spare key was where I always used to keep it." He gritted his teeth for a second before continuing. "I went inside, had a look around for a few minutes, then came back out, locked the door and was just about to go down the stairs to head back." He briefly switched his gaze to his mum. She watched him, seemingly holding her breath. Steve looked at Wallace this time. "Then I heard a loud crack of the gunshot and felt the pain in my arm and there was lots of blood. I ran downstairs and put the bridle on Blaze properly, ran to the back gate, jumped on bareback and rode back here as fast as I could." He shuddered at the memory of the blood and the fear the shooter may have been following him. He shrugged. "That's all I can tell you."

"So, you didn't see anyone or anything unusual before you were shot?" Jones asked, writing madly in his notebook.

"Nope." Steve hoped that was the end of the questioning but remembered the smoke. As much as he wished the police would leave him alone, he wanted to know who was out to kill him. "Wait, there was some smoke over in the trees. Like it was coming from a campfire."

"Which direction and how far away?" asked Wallace.

"East and a hundred metres or so, I suppose."

Jones looked up from his notebook. "You didn't think that was strange?"

Again Steve shrugged. "Not really. It would've been in the national park, so..." He didn't know what else to add there. "I wasn't worried. There's no way anyone could have followed me."

"Then possibly it was an accidental shooting. Maybe someone was illegally shooting in the national park and didn't realise you were there," said Wallace. "But we will go and check the area to see if any evidence was left there."

Steve hoped it was accidental, but his gut told him otherwise. "Maybe."

"Do you know anyone who might want you dead?" asked Jones.

Steve wanted to laugh at the irony of those words, but he had to be careful. "Not really but probably one of Scott's - I mean James McTaggart's - men." He almost added that it could have been someone he'd been forced to commit one of the terrible deeds upon but preferred not to think of any of those sickening actions.

"Why would any of them want you dead? Besides we have arrested his accomplices." Jones sounded pleased with himself.

Steve shook his head. "He had men everywhere. You probably only got a fraction of them. I don't know why any of them would want me dead. I don't remember hurting any of his men, or him."

Jones continued. "Seems you haven't been told that McTaggart had several bullets in his body when he died."

Steve frowned. "So?" He remembered firing his pistol back toward Scott as he galloped away on the Black Tornado. *No, couldn't be.*

"The forensic report showed the bullet most likely to have killed him was fired from the pistol in your possession, that we took when we caught up with you. So, it seems *you* killed him."

Beauty! I finally got him. But the feeling of sweet revenge left him as quickly as it had swept through his body and soul. "Does that mean I'm up for murder?" Familiar waves of dread now washed over him. "Is that public knowledge?" If so, it would certainly explain why someone was out to kill him.

"No," replied Jones, shaking his head. "It's on record as inconclusive but it's believed to most likely have been your bullet. And no, nothing has been said about charging you with his murder...for that reason."

Linda cleared her throat. "Sounds like Steve did everyone a favour by killing that monster." She stood up, looked lovingly at Steve then glared at Jones. "Just look what he has done to my boy! And God only knows how many others have suffered at his hands." Her voice rose to frantic pitch.

"Mum, it's okay." He appreciated her love and concern but really didn't want this made into something much bigger than it need be. He took hold of her hand for a moment of reassurance. "Don't upset yourself." She sat back on the chair.

"Okay," said Jones, "we'll search that area you saw the smoke coming from. Hopefully we find some answers."

"Can you please let us know what you find?" asked Linda.

"Yes, we will but right now we have the other issue at hand."

Oh no. Steve's gut swirled with more dread. "What's that?"

"You leaving your parents' care and going all the way back to your former home...*alone.*" Jones's voice turned hard. "You realise you can be arrested for that. You were given strict instructions, were you not, to stay under the watchful eye of your parents."

Steve glanced at his mother who looked as worried as he felt. "I told you Mum said it was alright for me to go. I only wanted to see the place and was coming straight back, which I did." He swallowed loudly. *Far* too loudly for comfort. Hopefully they didn't notice.

"That is exactly true," Linda added, but her eyes averted the detectives. "I trusted my son to do the right thing."

"Can anyone else back up your claim?" asked Wallace.

"Steve and I were alone at the creek when he asked me if it was okay, so no, no one heard me say it." Linda's face flushed pink. "I did tell my daughter, Grace, about it when I saw her though."

"Well, until we speak to Grace, we'll have to place you under arrest for breaking the conditions of your release from the hospital." Jones took a step closer to Steve's bed.

Linda jumped up. "Oh for Goodness sake, hasn't he been punished enough?" Her eyes glistened and face changed from nervousness to anger. "If anyone has be arrested it should be *me!*" She held out her wrists to Jones. "Here! Cuff me!"

Graced walked into the ward. "*Mum!* What are you doing?"

Linda turned. "Grace! I'm...the detectives want to arrest Steve for going off alone but since I okayed it I told them they should be arresting me instead."

Steve couldn't see his mother's face but the sudden change in Grace's expression from shock to comprehension told him Linda had given her a look of 'back-me-up-here'.

Grace walked closer to her mother followed by Sophie, looking worried. "I'm Grace," she said, looking at each detective in turn. "And this is our sister, Sophie." Sophie nodded and smiled before standing beside her mother and placing an arm around her.

Jones introduced himself and his colleague. "So, Grace, can you verify that your mother allowed Steve to go off by himself."

Steve sucked in a breath and held it, waiting for the correct response. Not that he doubted Grace would let him down, but she or Sophie may accidently slip up and give their lies away. No, that can't happen now. He willed his hopes and desperation toward Grace.

Grace frowned. "Yes, she did let him go. And as you can see he paid dearly for it, but he came back as he'd said he would."

Steve let out the held breath and his whole body relaxed. "Thank you, Grace".

Wallace looked at Jones. "Now what? Seems like there's nothing more to do here."

"You're right," replied Jones, then turned to Steve. "We'll let it go this time, but -", his face toughened again and he glared, "You do anything like this again and we'll throw the book at you, got it?"

Steve nodded. "Got it." But deep down he knew that was a promise he may not be able to keep.

CHAPTER 20

Kain couldn't contain his grin, slipping his phone back into his back pocket just as Grace walked into their lounge room.

"You look like the proverbial cat who swallowed the canary on this beautiful morning," she said. "Who was that you were talking to?" She plonked down on the bigger lounge chair.

Kain sat beside her. "That was the oncologist, Marc."

Her face lit up. "Does that mean we have good news?"

"Well...yes and no." Kain shrugged. "Better than I hoped for, anyway."

"C'mon, tell me," urged Grace, grabbing his forearm.

"He has the results of the CT scan and pathology tests on the testicle and lymph nodes they removed. No cancer anywhere else but in that ball itself." He let out a huge sigh of relief, dropped his head onto the back of the chair and stared at the ceiling. "Grace, you have no idea how good that sounds right now. I really thought, no I *expected*, that it would be much worse." The dead weight on his shoulders lightened.

"Oh, honey that is great news." She hugged him tight.

He wrapped his arms around her and buried his face in her shoulder. The embrace warmed his heart and soul. Though not wanting to, he pulled back. "But…" His smile disappeared. "He does still recommend chemo and radiation."

"Oh." Grace's happy expression changed immediately. She stared at him, seemingly not knowing what to say. After a few silent moments she spoke. "When do you start?" Creased eyebrows had replaced her smile. "I'll also research some natural things to help fight it too. We'll fight this bloody thing!"

"He's given me an appointment to see him Friday, so that gives me a couple of days to get used to it." Kain got up and filled a glass of cold water from the fridge. His mouth had suddenly dried to dust. He swallowed it down slowly while numerous thoughts flew around his brain. "We should talk to him about natural alternatives. He looks like he might be into that as well. I want to throw anything and everything at it."

Grace nodded in agreement, got up and walked closer to him. "Did he give you any other details about the treatment or is he going to fill you in then?" She rubbed his upper arm in reassurance. "Fill *us* in. I'm coming with you."

He put the glass on the sink and turned to her. Briefly yet again silently scolding himself for pushing her away. "That's good." He took hold of both her hands. "I was such an idiot for thinking I could do this myself."

Grace beamed her gorgeous smile and squeezed his hands. "Forget about all that. We don't need to even think about that crazy time anymore. It's over! Done! We have more important things to think about now. Getting you through this...this horrible time and then welcoming our babies. Hey, we should start thinking of names soon, too." She led him back to the lounge chair and sat down. "Now, tell me what else he said."

"Not a lot, just that the chemo will be a tablet for a couple of weeks and when that course is finished then I have radiation every day." Kain stared into thin air, trying to remember all the details of his conversation with the oncologist from his whirling and spinning mind. "I can't remember how long he said the radiation will go for...so many weeks, I think." He stood up and took a deep breath. "Ahh, shit. My brain is a complete mess at the moment." He spun and faced Grace also now standing. "Do you feel like going for a walk somewhere. Like out in the bush, or on the beach? I just need to try and clear my head."

"Sounds like a good idea." Grace hugged him briefly. "But first I want to ring mum and see how things are today now that Steve has been home from hospital for a few days. Yesterday she said it hadn't been *too* bad so far, with Dad basically keeping right away from Steve and not grumbling too much." She shook her head. "But it's pretty stressful for her and it worries me."

"Yeah," Kain said, but his mind had drifted to his up-coming treatment. "Oh, another thing Marc said was the chemo might make me infertile and that we should consider freezing sperm in case we want more kids. And sick...and bald." He glanced at Grace's noticeable baby bump and felt both happy and sad at the same time. Happy for the arrival of his twins but sad chemo sickness could render him too ill to be able to support Grace as he'd like during her pregnancy and impending birth. "And we have to have protected sex while I'm on chemo as it could harm the baby or even you." As much as he hated that idea he realised it was the least of his worries. "But anyway, let's get the appointment done on Friday and then we'll know exactly what we're in for."

Grace hugged him again. "Good idea." She let go and grabbed her phone from the coffee table. "Just give me a few minutes to call mum."

Kain nodded and headed out the back door to wander about in the back garden, taking deep, slow breaths to calm his jittering nerves. So much to think about. Everything seemed to be happening so fast. *Too* fast. But better than dragging it all out. He wished he could just click his fingers and the treatment part be all over. He wished he could just wake up from this nightmare. He wished it wasn't happening to him. *Fuck! Why me?* He pushed a patio chair into the small table and kept walking, but the chair leg got caught on something and he almost fell over it. Frustration and anger building, he kicked the chair across the back lawn which hurt his big toe. *Shit!* His hands balled into fists and his teeth clenched until the pain subsided. He wanted to go grab that chair and smash it to pieces on the ground. He strode to it, brought one foot back, then stopped. Smashing this chair would not change anything. He inhaled deep and thought of Grace and their unborn babies. She had enough to deal with and didn't need him giving her even more worries. He picked up the chair and placed it back by the table, proud he hadn't let his temper get the better of him this time.

There was no way he could go through all this without the love and support of Grace, but no matter how often she told him she loved him, or how much she hugged him, deep in his soul he knew this was going to be one scary journey that, ultimately, he must take alone.

CHAPTER 21

Linda tapped her phone and put it on the kitchen bench before placing the steaming pot of tea on the table, along with cereal, freshly made toast and a deliciously aromatic plate of scrambled eggs, just as she had done the previous two mornings since Steve had been discharged from hospital. Enough food for herself, Steve and Bruce. But, like the other two mornings, she expected she and Steve would eat alone while Bruce was 'busy' outside. Neither of them mentioning the obvious fact Bruce couldn't stand being near his son. Sophie had eaten hers earlier before leaving for work.

She walked to the back door and called to her husband, unsure of where on the farm he'd be. After shouting his name several times, he walked out of the tack room by the cattle yards. "Breakfast is on the table." She knew what his response would be but wasn't yet ready to give up trying to get him and Steve back into some sort of amicable father/son relationship, but it was a stressful, uphill battle.

"I'll have mine a bit later," he called back. "I want to finish up what I'm doing here, first." With that he disappeared back into the tack shed. No emotion or care.

Linda's shoulders slumped and she rubbed her tired eyes. Tired from barely any sleep again last night. Bruce had hardly spoken to her since she brought Steve home again. He'd be in bed sound asleep – or *pretending* to be – when she'd go to bed, or out in the shed until all hours then she'd find him in the spare bed the next morning, mumbling that he hadn't wanted to wake her. Things just couldn't keep going like this.

"Mum?" Steve walked through the kitchen to the back door. "I take it he's not coming to eat with us...again?"

Linda turned to her beloved son and shook her head with a long sigh. She felt like crying but had wept so much lately that there didn't seem to be any tears left. "Don't worry about him, Steve. He'll come around soon." Even as she spoke those words she doubted them. He could be very stubborn when he wanted. And his drinking hadn't eased. Not at all like the man with whom she fell in love, married and raised children. She still loved that man but not this new Bruce. Her disappointment and frustration with him were fast turning to contempt.

Steve sat at the table and began filling two mugs with tea. "I heard you talking before. Was that Grace?" He placed the teapot back on its stand and added milk to both cups.

"Thanks. Oh, be careful with that arm. I could've poured the tea." Linda sat opposite her son. "Yes, she is wondering how you are. And how things are going here." She put some toast on her plate but really didn't feel like eating.

"It's okay, mum. It's actually feeling a bit better today. What did you tell her?" Steve shook his head. "As if I need to ask."

"Well, you still need to take it easy. I don't want you going back to hospital." She picked up her fork and scooped some of the egg on to her toast. "Pretty much the same as I told her yesterday – that you're doing okay, and your father isn't bothering you too much."

"Look," Steve stopped eating and looked at her, "if it's too much for you having me stay here surely the police would be alright with me staying somewhere else, under the circumstances."

"No way!" Linda's tension rose. "You aren't going anywhere. This is your home and it's *him* with the problem." She almost added that she also needed Steve here to distract her from her stress over her husband's drinking problem and change of attitude but realised that would probably only worry Steve more and he already had enough on his plate. She softened. "It's fine. He'll get over it." She sipped her tea then began eating her breakfast.

"I would've liked to say g'day to Grace." Disappointment evident in his voice.

"She apologised for having to rush. Kain wasn't coping too well with the cancer situation, and they were on their way out somewhere."

"Fair enough. Speaking of the police," said Steve between mouthfuls, "have they called again since the other day?"

"No, I think they told us all they knew then – that the only thing they found in the National Park was evidence of a campfire, nothing else unfortunately. Especially no proof whoever lit that fire was after you." But the fear of someone possibly wanting her son dead gnawed at her and she put her cutlery down. "I just wish we had some answers there." The threat of tears tightened her throat. She took a few sips of tea. "Any chance you've thought of who it could be? They have to be stopped! I can't lose you again." Those ominous words opened the flood gates. No longer able to hold back, she put her face in her hands and burst into tears.

Steve's chair scraped backwards on the floor and he walked around to Linda's side of the table, placing his hand on her back. Silence for several moments before he spoke. "I don't...I don't know what to say or do, mum. But you have to try and not worry about it. I'm safe here. Whoever it is wouldn't even know I'm here." More uncomfortable silence for a minute or so. "The police will find him." His words didn't sound very convincing.

Linda grabbed a paper serviette from the holder in the middle of the table and wiped her eyes. Steve was doing his best to keep things calm, but she still worried. "I know. And you're right, you are safe here at home. Another reason you must forget about going anywhere else to live or going *anywhere* off the property anytime soon." She squeezed his forearm briefly. "Don't worry, I'm just being a mum. I can't help it, but I'll be okay." She took up her cutlery and began eating again. "Come on, sit back down and eat up."

"Aren't we going back to Brisbane on Sunday ready for the next lot of surgery on my face?" He swallowed down the last of his breakfast. "How about we just look forward to that? Hopefully this trip he'll be able to fix me, and I can take this bloody mask thing off."

Linda's fears abated, replaced by excitement at the prospect he may look like his old self again, but more importantly, have some self-confidence back. "Yep, you're right, I have a good feeling about this next surgery." She reached over and patted his hand. "We have some good things to look forward to." Her phone rang. She jumped up, grabbed it from the bench and looked at the screen. "Speaking of good things, it's Jenna. Here you take it." She handed it to him.

Steve got up, took the phone and answered it with a cheery hello. He smiled back at his mother and walked out of the kitchen toward the front verandah, talking as he went. At least he enjoyed conversations with Jenna. Linda hoped they may become good friends, if not more. A good feeling tugged at her heart, bringing a smile to her lips as she imagined Steve living a happy, *normal* life with a wife and children. Surely that wasn't too much to hope for, given all he'd been through.

"*LINDA!*"

Her smile disappeared as Bruce's loud, and seemingly angry, voice wrenched her mind away from those wonderful thoughts. She rushed out the back door and down a couple of steps until she could see him striding over from the tack shed. "Yes. What's wrong?" His angry face agitated the breakfast in her stomach. Breakfast she didn't really have any appetite for to start with.

Bruce stopped at the bottom of the steps, his phone in hand and face red with obvious anger. "Did you book those steers into the sale like I asked you to the other day?"

Linda wracked her brain, trying to remember him asking her, but nothing. There was no way she'd have forgotten to do that. She'd have been only too happy to book a truck load in if it meant he was showing some interest in the property and cattle again. Knowing it would enrage him further she had to tell him he *hadn't asked* her. "Bruce." She did her best to remain calm. "You didn't ask me to do that. I would have done it gladly, like I usually do, you know that." Her heart rate sped up. She took a deep breath.

"Bullshit! The sale is tomorrow. I asked you days ago." He glanced at his phone. "The Stock and Station agent just rang me to see if I had any to go. There's nothing on their books. He thought that was unusual." His eyes narrowed. "You just made me look like a fucking idiot! I told him a load was booked in."

Linda's breakfast swirled in her stomach as the now-all-too-familiar wave of anxiety washed through her entire body. Her legs weakened, forcing her to sit down on the stairs. Should she try and convince him he hadn't mentioned it or just apologise for 'forgetting' and see if it blows over?

"Well?" Bruce stood only metres from her. His menacing look prickled needle-sharp icicles down her spine.

"I'm really sorry, love, but I don't think you did ask me to do that." Her voice cracked but she did her best to remain calm. "Can't we just book them in now?"

"Too friggin' late now!" His voice rose and spittle flew from his mouth. "They're fully booked." He took one step up, closer to her.

Linda jumped up, ready to run if necessary. She'd seen him angry a lot lately, but not as angry and menacing as this. His face had completely changed to some sort of deranged maniac. "Well, wh-what about the next sale?" She stepped backwards up one step and held the rail for support.

"I wanted them in *this* sale!" He stepped back to ground level, turned his back to her for a moment, shoulders heaving up and down, then spun back around. "Your bloody problem is you're too busy with that...*him* up there." He clenched his jaw and thrust his pointed finger at the window above the stairs. "He's all you friggin' think about lately! All you do! I've had a gutful!"

How dare he speak about their son like that! Her fear and anxiety immediately burned to rage. She clenched her teeth. "*You've* had a gutful?" She glared at him. No tears, no fear, just bloody angry. "What about what *you're* doing? Or should I say *not* doing!"

His eyebrows creased in a frown. "What the hell are you talking about, woman?"

"You and your bloody drinking! *Every* day. You don't want to talk to us, you won't eat with us. You can't share a bed with me anymore. I've had a gutful too, Bruce."

His anger changed to defiance. "Nothing wrong with a few beers. And I told you *not* to bring him back here. You ignored me so how the hell do you expect me to feel?"

"A *few* beers?" She couldn't believe her ears. "You drink more now in one day than you used to drink in a whole week…or even longer! I hate what it's doing to you. How it changes you!"

Bruce scowled and gave a short snigger. "Bullshit. I haven't changed. It's you and him that make me want to drink. Sophie hardly talks to me these days. You've even turned Gracie against me. She's not the same anymore." His face saddened.

"Grace isn't *against* you." Linda shook her head in disbelief. "None of us are. And this is Steve's home too. We just can't understand why you seem to hate him so much. Your own son! When he first came back to us you were happy to pay for his surgery and any other medical bills to get him back to normal. Why can't you be pleased he's back with us?"

"You know why!" His voice rose up again and his face reddened.

"If it's about Jon's drowning, I thought we settled that. It wasn't Steve's fault!" She wanted to wring Bruce's neck or bang his head against a wall to knock some sense into him. She certainly did enough of that herself lately, trying to get through to him. "Do you realise someone is out to get him? Maybe kill him! Do you even *care*?"

Bruce's face went blank, as if he was lost for words, but there was no care in his expression.

Steve ran through the house and to the back door. "What's going on here?" He looked from his father to his mother. "Are you alright, mum?" He stepped down beside her and placed a protective hand around her shoulders.

"Thanks Son. I will be." She leaned against his tall, solid frame before her shaking legs gave way. "Let's go inside." At that point she couldn't even stand looking at her husband.

Bruce turned and strode off back toward the tack shed, cursing and muttering incoherently as he walked.

Steve filled and flicked on the kettle. "What's his problem now? I heard the raised voices but couldn't really hear what yous were saying until I stopped talking to Jenna. I didn't want her to hear any of it so I cut the call short." He leaned against the bench, waiting for the heating kettle to boil.

Linda sat at the table. Frustration and anger gave way to defeat. She sighed heavily. "I really don't know what is going on in that grog-pickled brain of his these days. He's blaming me for the way *he* is." She shook her head. "I just don't know what to think anymore."

Silence for a few moments apart from a hen cackling over in the chook pen and a pee wee squawking out on the lawn. The boiling kettle clicked off. Steve made two fresh cups of tea, handed one to his mum and sat opposite her with his. He took a sip before placing it down on the table. "Maybe I should ask Grace if I can stay with them."

"No! Please, Steve, I don't want you going anywhere. Something will work out." Sipping her tea, she remembered Jenna's call and her heavy heart lightened. "Anyway, what did Jenna want?"

"She wants to come see me and start working on this article she's planning to write."

"That's great. When?"

"Tomorrow...if that's okay with you." Steve glanced toward the back door. "Or maybe not such a good idea. He might go off while she's here."

Linda imagined the scenario – Bruce making a scene in front of the lovely Jenna. Her breakfast swam about in her belly. She swallowed the foul taste now in her mouth. "That would be horrible." She shrugged in defeat. "Anything is possible with him now. Maybe I could take you to her place. On second thoughts, not a good idea."

"No, probably not. Anyway, she wants to see this place – where I grew up. She said it'll help the readers understand me better."

Linda nodded in agreement. "Good point." She sipped her tea and thought hard. "I know, how about you two go for a picnic down by the creek, or one of the dams. You and I could go for a drive in the ute later and find the perfect spot." She couldn't hide her smile. "While you two are busy doing that I could go see Grace and do a bit of shopping. At least I can have a break from Grizzle Guts over there." She turned her head a little on the side and flicked it in the direction of the tack shed.

Steve smiled. "Good idea. I'm sure Jenna would be okay with that, and it will do you good to get out too."

"Well, you'd better call her back and organise it then." Linda reached for her phone which Steve had left near the end of the table. Just as she picked it up it rang. She looked at it and frowned. "Oh, it says 'No caller ID'. Probably bloody scammers." She was about to hit 'End' but thought better of it. "It might be the police or the hospital." She swiped the screen and put it to her ear. "Hello."

"Is that *Steve Atkinson's* place?" a gruff male voice asked, the emphasis on his name more like a snarl.

She glanced at Steve. "Who's asking, please?"

The phone beeped and went silent.

CHAPTER 22

Steve stopped the farm utility under a large, shady fig tree by one of the dams on the property. He and Linda had driven around the previous afternoon looking for the perfect spot he and Jenna could talk while enjoying a picnic lunch. Linda had wanted to prepare the food herself for them, but Steve had politely insisted he do it himself. He'd felt a little bad for refusing his mum's offer, but he just wasn't used to having someone do things for him, even though he knew she only wanted the best for him.

Apart from a few twinges with certain movements, his injured arm was healing well, and that scary incident was now pushed to the back of his mind, but the phone call asking for him weighed on his mind even with other, more pleasant things to think about - namely Jenna sitting in the passenger seat. He still had no idea if her interest was purely professional and he certainly didn't want to make a fool of himself in front of her, like he did Grace when she was at his secluded home.

"Oh, this is nice," said Jenna gazing about. "Look, even ducks on the dam. Those water lilies are pretty." She seemed in awe.

Her beaming smile glowed and brought out a grin from Steve. He hadn't had much to smile about for ages. "Yep, lots of wildlife around here." A twinge of sadness and homesickness tugged at his heart. It wasn't the same as being in the bush where he lived, but it wasn't far behind. He jumped out, intending to walk around and open her door for her, but she was already stepping out when he reached her side. He quickly turned and lifted the esky out of the back of the ute with his good arm. The sun shone brightly with just a few wispy clouds floating about on a slight breeze.

Jenna swiped away a fly from her face, reached back in the cabin and grabbed the picnic rug and her rather large bag. "Now to find a nice place to sit."

Kicking aside a few dried cow pats, Steve walked several metres to a spot that had shorter, soft grass and no cow manure. It didn't bother him, but he wanted this to be a nice experience for Jenna. He put the esky down and went to take the rug from her, but she had already opened it and was spreading it out down on the ground in front of them. One thing he'd learned already – she was independent, even with her disability, which obviously didn't hinder her. He admired that but also felt a little disappointed he couldn't do more for her. *Idiot! She's only here for your story.* That niggly and very annoying inner voice had returned yet again. He shook his head fast to shake it out.

Jenna stared at him. "Are you okay?"

"What?" He laughed a little. "Oh, just getting rid of a fly. Sit down." He indicated to the large rug, before lowering his bulky frame onto it as well, being careful not to sit too close to her lest it scare her away. He was used to frightening people away, especially children once they saw his scarred face. Hopefully that will soon be a thing of the past.

Steve leaned over and dragged the esky closer before removing the lid. "Hmm, let's see...there's some salads and some chicken." He put several lidded containers on the rug between them. He was just about to reach into the esky again when he stopped and looked at her. "Oh, I hope you like that sort of thing. I suppose I should have asked."

She smiled and her blue eyes sparkled, even though her glasses. "Yep, I'm not too fussy. Sounds great."

"Good." Steve brought out bread rolls, a bottle of cold juice, two plastic cups and a container of home-made biscuits. "Hope you're hungry."

Jenna's eyes widened. "Wow, your mum did well. I'll have to be sure to thank her when we get back to the house."

Steve wasn't sure if he should be flattered or insulted. "Umm, I prepared all this. I even baked the biscuits. Mum wanted to but I'm used to doing things for myself."

"Really! I'm impressed. You really are full of surprises. Are they choc chip?"

"Yes, how did you guess?"

Jenna shrugged and laughed. "Wishful thinking." She took out a large notebook and pen from her bag, opened the book, folded back the cover and wrote 'STEVE' in large letters on the first page. Next, she took out her phone and tapped the screen a few times.

"Are you starting the questions straight away? I thought we would eat first." Up until now he'd been okay with this whole thing but seeing her ready to write sent a wave of apprehension through his stomach. Maybe this wasn't such a good idea after all.

She stopped what she was doing and looked at him. "Oh okay, good idea I suppose." She picked up a plate and started putting some food on it. "Save us talking with our mouths full." She laughed. A sweet, genuine laugh with no pretence.

There wasn't much laughter in the Atkinson household so hearing her had him chuckling as well. It felt so good. "No, we can't have that."

They ate in relative silence barring small talk about the weather, the flies and the cattle in the shade of a grove of Iron Barks not far from them, contentedly chewing their cuds but with an odd swish of their tales to chase the irritating flies.

Steve poured two cups of juice and handed her one. She took it with a smile, nod and mouthful of food, but still managed a, "Thanks".

After Jenna finished her food, she drank most of her juice. "Do you drink alcohol, Steve?"

It wasn't a question he expected. "No, why?"

She shrugged. "Just wondered. Most men do."

"I suppose I'm not like 'most men'." Images of his drunken father came to mind. The scowls. The looks of anger and disgust on his face. The hurt and worry weighing heavy on his mum at her husband's complete change of attitude. "Especially not like my father."

"Does he drink a lot?" She looked worried.

"Seems to. Mum said he drinks a lot more since I came back than before."

"That's a shame. Do you know why?"

Steve's appetite waned. He put down his plate and stared off into the distance. "He hates me." He waited for the 'Why', but only silence, which suited him fine. He turned back to Jenna. "You don't look anything like your brother."

Her concerned look softened. "Who? Tim? He looks like dad and I took after mum." She giggled briefly and rolled her eyes. "Luckily."

Even with her mocking her brother and father's looks, it was obvious they were close. He tried to imagine being in a close, loving family, but nothing came to mind. He'd watched movies and TV shows that featured happy families, but just couldn't see his father fitting into a similar scenario. "She must be a-" he stopped himself short of saying, 'very pretty lady'. *Idiot! You'll scare her away.*

"A what?" she urged, before sipping some more juice.

"A very proud mother. Her son being a doctor and you being a journalist. Have you always wanted to be one?"

"Hang on, I'm supposed to be the one asking questions. You don't really seem to want to talk about yourself. I thought that was what we came here for." Her disappointed face saddened him. "Or is it just your father you don't want to talk about?"

Sadness turned to bitterness. "Yep. Don't even want to think about him!"

She put up her open palm in a defence mode. "Okay, we won't. I just thought-"

"Well *don't!*" Steve reached over past the edge of the picnic rug, picked up a stone and pelted it with all his might toward the water. It splashed down way out in the middle of the large dam, scattering the ducks skywards amidst loud 'quacking'.

"Maybe this wasn't such a good idea." Her voice soft, Jenna began putting the picnic things back in the esky.

As satisfying as it felt hurling that stone, as if it contained all his frustration with his father, he immediately realised he'd overreacted. Taking a quick, deep breath he turned back to Jenna. Her sad and confused face tore at his soul. *You great, useless lump. Look what you did!* "Jenna, I'm so sorry. I didn't mean to snap at you." An ache washed through his chest. "Please forgive me." He lifted a hand to reach out to her, but quickly put it back by his side. "It's just that...that Bruce and me..." Hell, how to word this? "I'm not comfortable talking about him and what he's like around me. Can we just talk about me?" He wanted to add, 'and you', but thought better of that.

She stopped midway through putting more things in the esky and looked up at him. "It's alright, Steve, I understand. Sorry, I won't ask about him anymore." She placed the salad containers in the esky and looked about, puzzled. "I thought I saw you with a flask of coffee earlier." She frowned then laughed. "Or did I imagine that? I could really go a cuppa right now."

"No, you're right," said Steve, getting to his feet. "It's still in the ute." He got the flask out and walked back to

Jenna sitting there gazing out toward the dam. She looked so beautiful. He'd have to more careful *not* to upset her. "Here we go, but...stupid me forgot proper cups to drink it from." Not that he cared what he drank from, but he'd mentally scolded himself for not thinking of her. He sat back on the rug.

"Never mind." She downed the last of her juice and held out her plastic cup which he filled. "This is fine. I'm not fussed what I drink it out of." She took a few sips. "Ah, that's good." Holding the cup in one hand, she picked up the notebook, placed it on her leg and began writing. "I'm just jotting down a few things I've learned already and a few more questions I've thought of to ask you, then we can get down to business."

"Okay." Steve sipped his coffee and watched her write. It looked very neat writing, which didn't surprise him. Her hands dainty and small, nothing like his large, scarred hands with some misshapen fingers.

The short, abrupt phone call the previous day came to mind. Could it have been that stranger who appeared at his hospital room door? And sent that chilling note? And who tried to shoot him? If it is the same man then he certainly knows where Steve lives. Thorns chilled his spine. Perhaps he's somewhere near, spying on him and Jenna, waiting to take another shot. Steve shuddered and looked about. Apart from the patch of trees shading that mob of cattle, there were no more trees for quite a way, right over by the creek. He couldn't see anything suspicious so put it down to paranoia.

"Right, I think I'm ready." Jenna's words jolted him back to their little space on the picnic rug and the reason they were there. "Oh no!" Jenna jumped up.

"What?" Steve's nerves buzzed. He got to his feet. "What's wrong?" His gaze darted about, expecting the worst. Adrenaline sped through his veins.

Jenna crouched and began frantically swiping her hands on the rug, toward the edge. "Ants!"

Steve breathed a huge sigh of relief then laughed. "Is that all?" He moved the esky and what else was left on the rug. "Here, I'll shake them off." Jenna got off the rug and he picked it up before walking several metres and shaking it well. "I think they're all gone now." He spread the rug in a different spot, before retrieving his half-drank coffee and the flask." Jenna looked worried though. "It's okay. I got rid of them." He sat back down.

She walked slowly to the rug but seemed hesitant. "It's just that I'm allergic to some ants and bugs. I nearly died from a bee sting once." She turned back and grabbed her bag, notebook and cup. "I have to carry an epi pen with me in case I get bitten, but it's no fun."

"That's no good," said Steve. "I'll keep an eye out for more ants and bees." The thought of anything hurting her was too much to bear. How he wanted to ask her about herself, but reminded himself this wasn't the time or place. Hopefully there'll be more times and places. Many more.

"Thanks Steve, I really appreciate that." She tapped at her phone for several seconds then placed it on the rug between them. "Do you mind if I also tape our interview? Just so I don't forget anything."

"No, that's alright," replied Steve, a little disappointed that she sounded so business like. *That's what she's here for, so stop with the hopes of anything else.*

"Good. I have so much to ask you. Do you have to go anywhere or do anything else today?"

"Nope, we have all afternoon. But don't be surprised if mum calls sometime to check up on me. She'll probably be a bit worried I might try and go back to my place again."

"Your place?" Jenna's forehead creased and she tilted her head a little to the side. "But we are at – oh, you mean the house you lived in before Grace found you?"

"Yes, that's really the only home I know." A pang of longing ripped through him, but he needed to stop thinking like that. "And I found *her,* well, at the start, anyway."

"I'd like to hear all about that day you found her. It was a miracle you were there when those dogs attacked her. I read that in the paper." Before Steve had a chance to answer, she continued. "But I really would like to go to your old home and maybe take some photos. It would give me a better idea of your life there and probably make writing this article a bit easier. I want the readers to really *know* you, Steve. How far from here is it?"

"I'm not sure of the distance but it took me a couple of hours by horseback, going through paddocks most of the way."

"I can ride," she exclaimed with excitement. "Maybe we could do that tomorrow. It'd be fun and give me more time to get to know you."

To get to know you. She said those words like a friend, not an interviewer. Steve smiled to himself and imagined them riding together through the bush and being able to show her his peaceful home overlooking the mountains and bush. Then reality hit. No way. If the shooter was after him, he couldn't risk Jenna's life by taking her there. He already had a nagging gut feeling he was putting her in danger just by spending time with her. Hopefully that was just nothing but unnecessary worry but he wasn't prepared to take the chance. "No, we can't go there."

Her shoulders slumped and her beautiful smile disappeared. "But why? I don't understand."

He had to think quick. "The police have it blocked off...now – until all their investigations are done. And I'm under the care of mum so I'm not supposed to leave the property, especially without her." At least that part was true.

"Well, couldn't she take us there in the car?"

Irritation stirred his gut. He wanted to tell her to just leave it alone but risked upsetting her again. "They told me not to go there at all, but one day I'll take you there, when it's all over and done with." *Yeah, when you get out of jail, as an old man.*

"Okay, I'll hold you to that."

The smile that came with those encouraging words lightened his shoulders and heart. He couldn't help but smile back at her. "You're on."

"So, let's get back to the day you found Grace. I want to hear every single thing you remember about it...and anything else you can tell me about your life. Oh, and see some more photos of you before all this happened. I saw the one in the paper. You were...you *are* good looking. There must be a wife or girlfriend glad to have you back?"

Steve shook his head. That hadn't even occurred to him, and no one had mentioned it either. "Nope." He hoped the smile that flickered briefly on Jenna's face was one of relief. *Don't get too excited, idiot.*

CHAPTER 23

Grace handed her mum a cold glass of juice. "Here you go. Let's go sit out the back in the shade where it's cooler." Both women headed out to the back patio.

"Where's Kain?" Linda asked, sitting down on one of the comfy chairs, drinking some of her juice and wiping a thin layer of sweat from her forehead. "Stinker of a day today."

"Sure is," replied Grace, sitting on the other chair. "Oh, he's gone out to do a few things and go see Joe. He shouldn't be too long." She sipped her juice. "You look as worried as you sounded on the phone earlier, mum. Has something happened? Is it Steve? Or has dad done something stupid?" She realised that was the first time she'd thought of her father as 'stupid'. "Sorry, I didn't mean to say-" As much as she disliked how her father had changed since Steve returned, she still loved him. She just didn't understand his attitude toward Steve at all.

Linda brushed it off with a wave of her hand. "No need to apologise, love." She sighed. "Honestly, I'm just about at my wits end with him." Her bottom lip trembled a few seconds before she placed her hands over her face and burst into tears, shoulders shaking with each heart-wrenching sob.

Grace hadn't seen her mum so distraught since Steve disappeared. She moved her chair closer, wrapping her arms tightly around her beloved mum, but unable to think of appropriate soothing words.

Linda pulled out of the embrace, wiping her eyes. "Sorry, love. I didn't mean to lose it like that. You have enough on your plate already with Kain's chemo about to start and your pregnancy."

"It's okay. I'll get you a tissue." Grace got up and went inside, grabbed the open box of tissues from the coffee table and took them to her mum.

"Thanks." Linda pulled out several, wiped her eyes and blew her nose before stuffing the tissues in her shirt pocket. She shook her head. "I just don't know what to do or say to him anymore. I can't seem to do anything right. All I seem to be doing lately is bursting into tears...or fighting them back."

"You told me on the phone he had a go at you yesterday for not booking the cattle into the sale when he hadn't even asked you to, and says you spend too much time with Steve. What else has he done or said since then?" A rush of panic struck Grace. "Steve's not there alone with him now, is he?" She imagined them coming to blows, knowing each one wouldn't back down, and unsure who'd come out the victor. Tall Bruce with his heart full of anger, or tall, younger Steve with his heart full of frustration and confusion.

"No, no. Steve's okay." Her face suddenly brightened. "He's on a picnic lunch with Jenna, you know, the journalist sister of Doctor Tim's. She's lovely."

"A picnic? Wow, that's great. But where?"

Her mum must have sensed the apprehension in Grace's voice. Linda laughed a little. "Far away from the house, don't worry. By one of the dams. Steve and I drove around yesterday looking for the perfect spot. Jenna wants to interview him for this article she's writing. They'll probably be gone for hours."

More concerns niggled at Grace. "You don't think he'd try to go back to his house again, do you?"

"Definitely not. Not after the shooting. He's assured me he won't leave the property. I can see you're worried, but I believe him this time." Linda finished her juice. "Especially after..." Her voice trailed off and she averted her gaze away from Grace.

This didn't sound good. "After *what*, mum?" Grace's nerves livened up, sending her stomach into a spin. She sipped some more juice, hoping she wouldn't need to rush to the toilet. The morning sickness still hit her any time of the day, and fearing bad news certainly didn't help.

Linda sighed again and that worried look returned to her pale face. "Yesterday, after your father went off at me, Steve and I were talking and I got a strange phone call. No ID and the man just asked if this was Steve Atkinson's place."

"Is that all he said? What did you tell him?"

"Nothing. I just asked who was calling, but he hung up."

"Did you tell the police?"

"No, I didn't really think of that." Linda shrugged in hopelessness. "With no Caller ID, I can't prove anything, especially that it was anyone bad." Her brow creased deeper. "But it probably was. Someone really wants Steve dead." She pulled out the used tissues and wiped her watering eyes. "I can't lose him again." Her lips clenched together as if trying to stem the tears. "You know, he even offered to move out of home so your father wouldn't keep giving me a hard time. Of course I told him he couldn't, but I also couldn't bear to be without him around now anyway, especially with your father barely talking to me. If he does it's usually with a grunt or just to complain about something."

Grace wracked her brain, trying to come up with useful advice. "So, do you think the man who is after him now knows where he is living?"

Linda nodded. "Yes, I do. It wouldn't have been hard to find out, especially after that newspaper article when Steve was found. And lots of people know Bruce. But I don't understand how he got my mobile number."

"I guess that doesn't really matter now. What's worrying is that he knows. I really think you should tell the police. Maybe they have a way to trace the call, or at least patrol the area near the property and see if anyone is acting suspicious." Grace stood up. "Do you want me to call them now and tell them? Does Steve have his own phone yet?"

"Thanks Grace, but it'd probably be better if I went to see them in person. I'll go there when I leave here. No, he doesn't. The police said he couldn't yet. Something to do with the investigation. Just a shame it isn't tomorrow that we go back to Brisbane for his follow up surgery, instead of Sunday. At least down there he'd be safer. Oh, I'd better tell them when we are going."

"Well," Grace grinned with a sudden idea. "Why not change your flight and go tomorrow. Find a nice place to stay for a couple of days beforehand. Just you and Steve. Somewhere by the ocean. Stay even longer after the surgery. Sophie and I will keep an eye on dad and make sure the chooks and dogs are being fed and watered. It'd do you both good, especially to get you both away from dad for longer." But a dismal thought hit her. "Dad hasn't stopped your access to the bank accounts or anything like that, has he?"

Linda's face turned to a look of surprise. "What? Oh no, nothing like that. I don't think he'd do that. Everything is in both names. And yes, that's a great idea about going down early. I'll have to check with Steve of course, but I'm sure he won't say no. Then I'll organise it." Linda chuckled happily. "He might ask Jenna to come too."

Relief washed over Grace. "That's good." She shrugged. "That wouldn't be a bad idea, would it? Jenna going? If she wants to, of course. Give her more time to get to know him better. So, what do you think about her writing an article on Steve?"

"I think it's good. She assured me when she arrived earlier and we'd chatted a bit that she wants to show Steve in positive way. She knows a bit about what he's been through and wants the readers to see that he's not some barbaric ogre who does horrible things for fun."

"So, obviously Steve is okay with it? He wasn't too keen at first."

Linda chuckled. "No, but now that he's got to know her a bit, he has a little crush on her, so no doubt hopes she feels the same way. I'm sure he'd love the idea of her coming along."

Alarm bells sounded in Grace's head. "But if she doesn't feel the same he'll be in for a big letdown. I worry what that could do to him." In one way it was a good thing as he can get over the feeling he had for Grace, before they knew they were siblings, and Kain wouldn't ever have to worry about that again, but she knew Steve's vulnerability and his apparent desperation to find acceptance and love. "Wish there was a way we could find out her feelings and thoughts on him. And she seems so young. Much younger than Steve. He has a lot of baggage. And worst of all, he might still go to jail."

Her mum winced, as if those words stung. "I know, darl. He has a hell of a lot to contend with, but it would be nice for him to have someone else helping him through it all. And we are one stuffed up family at the moment so a friend like her would be wonderful." She gazed into thin air for a few seconds. "It might be wishful thinking, or call it a mother's intuition, but I really feel he won't go to jail."

"I like your optimism." Grace wanted to agree with her mother's gut feeling, but her intuition said otherwise.

CHAPTER 24

Kain grabbed Grace's hand and jumped up as soon as his name was called. He still had some mild discomfort at the surgery site but little enough to ignore. Even though the Cancer Care Centre was a bright, cheery place with happy staff and nice, positive pictures on the walls, he didn't want to spend a second longer here than necessary. Every moment was a stark reminder of what he was facing – cancer. *Cancer!* At only twenty-eight years of age.

Doctor Marc smiled warmly while waiting for Kain and Grace to come through his office door. "Hi Kain." He shook Kain's hand and nodded toward Grace. "Hello Grace." He gestured toward the two chairs for them, sat behind his desk and looked directly at Kain. "So, how are you feeling today?"

Kain involuntarily shuddered. "Nervous." He took hold of Grace's warm hand. "I can't wait to get all this over and done." His left knee began slightly bouncing. He crossed his legs at the ankles to stop it, and wiped his dampening, empty palm on his shorts. "What happens today?" Grace squeezed his hand and gave him a loving smile.

Marc clasped his hands together on his desk. "Firstly, have you read through all the information I gave you?"

"Yep."

"I did too," added Grace. "I want to keep up with everything he goes through."

Marc nodded with a smile. "Good. Oh, by the way, how is your pregnancy going?"

"Good, thanks. Although I'm a bit over this so-called *morning* sickness. It hits me any time of the day." She screwed up her face.

Kain's mouth dried at the thought. "I suppose I'll soon find out how poor Grace has been suffering...once I have this chemo and get sick." He grabbed the water bottle from Grace's bag on the floor at her feet and took a mouthful, swishing it around before swallowing.

"Yes, unfortunately," said Marc, "you probably will but we can also give you some steroid tablets that lessens the nausea. But as with all medications, some people are lucky enough not to suffer too much while others do. I understand it's difficult under the circumstances, but you must try and stay positive. One patient told me once they seemed to suffer a bit less once they realised and told themselves chemo was helping them and *not* the enemy."

Kain let out a light-hearted *hmph*. "I'll try to remember that, but I've seen some people really suffer bad while on it."

Marc nodded sympathetically. "I know, it can be cruel on our bodies, but luckily your cancer was caught early enough before it spread anywhere else out of your testicle. But the chemo is recommended to 'mop up' any loose cancer cells that may have gone astray. You are only going to need one strong oral dose and then we'll assess you again in three weeks to see how you are coping. *But-*" he held up one hand to emphasize the word, "during that time, especially the first two weeks, after you've taken it, you *must* contact me or go straight to the hospital if you have any major problems, especially a high temp, okay?"

Kain swallowed a hard lump of apprehension and had another mouthful of water. "I will. But what happens if I do get a high temp and what does that mean?"

"It means you have an infection and may need antibiotics. As you would have read, chemotherapy suppresses your immune system and leaves you vulnerable to catching viruses and other germs, so it's really important you stay home for those two weeks or more, and not allow any visitors. And that goes for you too, Grace. Stock up on essentials, including bottled water, and stay home with Kain. You don't have any medical appointments in that time do you?"

Grace frowned. "No, I don't think so. I'll change them if I do." She looked worried. "But I promised mum I'd help Sophie with Dad and the animals at their place while she is in Brisbane with my brother for a week or so. They left yesterday."

Marc shook his head. "Definitely not! Stay away from animals, and," he looked at Kain, "especially you, Kain, also don't go scratching around in garden soils or potting mixes, okay? They can be toxic if your immune system has been compromised."

Kain's stomach agitated. "Geez, what *can* we do for those two weeks." He grinned and winked at Grace. "I can think of one thing I suppose."

Marc laughed briefly. "Sorry to burst that bubble, mate, but you need to remember the dangers of unprotected sex during chemo, especially with Grace being pregnant. That also brings us to the subject of possibly freezing your sperm. You haven't let us know you want that, so have you decided not to, or just not sure yet?"

Still unsure about this choice, Kain looked at Grace. "What do you think, darl?" He turned back to Marc. "We hadn't really made a decision with other things going on, especially with Grace's family." He shrugged. "I'm all for it if Grace wants me to."

Grace looked unsure as well. "In the info it says that not all men who have this chemo will become infertile."

"That is true," said Marc. "I've known a few that have conceived more children afterwards." He grinned with a roll of his eyes. "One poor bloke already had four kids and just assumed he would become infertile, but his wife got pregnant again...with *twins!*" His face turned serious again. "But quite a few do become infertile, so the choice is yours."

"It's probably mostly up to Kain," said Grace, "but I'm happy to just focus on these two." She patted her stomach. "I believe in what is meant to be will be, so if we are meant to have more kids we will."

Kain placed his hand around Grace's shoulders. "Yeah, I agree. I think we have enough to focus on and deal with for now. And for months to come."

Marc looked at his computer screen for a moment, then back to Kain. "Righto, the next thing is we do some tests on you."

Kain frowned, not liking that word. "Tests? Haven't I already had enough?"

Marc smiled. "Don't panic, these are just routine – for everyone who undergoes chemo. We run blood tests and also some heart tests. But I'm sure a young, fit looking bloke like you is in good health."

Grace laughed. "I've done my best to make sure he eats healthily."

"She sure has," chuckled Kain, "but I draw the line at kale smoothies!"

"And what's wrong with kale smoothies?" Marc looked insulted, then broke out in a grin, leaned toward Kain and whispered, "Don't blame you."

"Gee thanks," said Grace in mock seriousness. "Actually, that brings me to something I need to ask."

Marc nodded. "Go ahead. Anything."

"I like to use natural remedies whenever I can and have been doing some research on anti-cancer foods and supplements. Can I get some of these things into Kain to help keep the cancer away? I know some doctors don't approve of natural things."

Marc pursed his lips and raised his eyebrows as if he was thinking of an appropriate response. "Just as well I'm not like 'some' doctors, *but*... I do highly recommend you don't start doing that until after he has completed the chemo. You must give it time to work and some superfoods that are high in antioxidants can also protect cancer cells as well as normal healthy cells. Also, some things, especially some herbs, can interact with the chemo making it less effective."

"Fair enough," replied Grace. "I certainly don't want to hinder the treatment."

"I tell you what," encouraged Marc. "Do the research. Keep note of the best things you found. Might also be a good idea to join a likeminded support group on social media. When you come back in a few weeks, we can talk over what you found and then go for it. I don't think it hurts to throw everything possible at this bloody disease. Meanwhile, eat lots of fruit and veggies, stay off alcohol, rest and drink plenty of water. Oh, remember too, chemo can give you diarrhoea, or the other way, constipation. Maybe have something there beforehand for each."

Kain groaned. He had read that but had forgotten it. "Will do." He ran his hand through his hair, now grown a little since he shaved it. "Will my hair fall out?"

"May do, or it may just thin out. But don't stress about that. It will grow back. That's probably the least of your worries."

Kain exhaled a long breath out of his mouth as his shoulders sagged. "Okay Marc, what now?"

Marc tapped on his laptop keyboard for a minute or so then closed it up. "Right. You can go back to the waiting room and one of the nurses will call you shortly and do these tests. It'll take a couple of hours for the results, so maybe go have some lunch and stock up on things you need for your isolation. I'll call you as soon as I have the results and if they're all okay we'll give you the chemo dose.

We do need you to stay here for a couple of hours afterwards though, so we can monitor you and any reactions you might have."

The reality of it all slammed into Kain. *Cancer. Tests. Sick. Bald. Kids. No kids. Hospitals. Death. Why me? Why the fuck ME?* The room spun. Luckily he hadn't eaten much breakfast. Stomach acid rose from his convulsing stomach. His bowel gurgled and rolled. His mouth watered but he swallowed it down. "Thanks Doc." He jumped up and grabbed the door handle, but it slipped from his sweaty palms. He grabbed it again, pushed instead of pulled. *Shit!* Finally, it opened. With vision blurred he ran blindly out of Marc's office to the toilet, hoping like hell to make it on time.

CHAPTER 25

Linda enjoyed the peaceful view as she sat on the verandah of the holiday cottage and spoke to Sophie on the phone. Trees, gardens and a few wallabies grazing on the lawn merely fifty metres away, combined with the sound of birds, helped lower the stress levels. "Yeah, Soph, it's going well down here. Steve is more relaxed and he and Jenna are getting on really well. But I am so sorry to leave you in the lurch with your father and the farm, especially now that Grace is in isolation with Kain."

"It's all good, Mum," replied Sophie. "Dad seems more relaxed too and we haven't had any problems. I even heard him on the phone this morning to Max, asking him to come back to work here. Yes, Grace rang me yesterday and told me what's happening with Kain. I'll text her later and see how he is today. I'm so glad Steve is coping better, but I suppose he's a bit nervous about the surgery on Monday. You did the right thing going down there early."

"I don't think we had much choice. I just wish the police would have taken my concerns more seriously. They don't seem to think anyone really is after Steve. It worries me.

Oh, that's good he's getting back into some farm and cattle work. About time."

"Is Steve there with you now?" asked Sophie. "I'd love to say g'day."

"No, sorry, love. He and Jenna went for a walk along one of the bush tracks. He just wants to be outside all the time. Sounds like she's almost got enough info for her article. Oh, you should have seen him when we got here and he realised how remote and quiet the place is. He didn't say much at first, just stood outside looking around at the bush and breathing in the clean air. It must seem like his old place. He's smiled more in the past day than I have seen him smile since he came back to us."

"That's great, Mum. Any sign of romance there yet? Give him my love when they get back. I'll catch up with him next time I ring."

"Hmm, no, not really. Not obvious anyway. I'll ring you when he's here, tomorrow sometime. Oh, I almost forgot to ask – have you noticed anything odd happening or *anyone* strange hanging about?"

"No, can't say I have...which is good, isn't it?"

"Definitely, love. Okay, I'll give your father a ring a bit later. I tried early this morning but he didn't answer so I left a message. Can you please ask him if he got it? I'm just not sure if he doesn't want to talk to me or just hasn't got round to replying. He wasn't too happy about me going earlier than planned. I take it he hasn't mentioned Steve at all?"

"No, sorry," Sophie replied sadly.

"Oh well, maybe this will give him some time to think about things and especially his son...we can only hope." Linda could even hear the doubt in her own voice, but she lived in hope. Hope was about all she had to cling to these days. Hope that Bruce would change his attitude toward Steve also toward her and their marriage. Hope that Steve's surgery will be successful. Hope that whoever was after him will be stopped before he hurt Steve, or, God forbid, worse. Hope that Steve can regain his memory and not be punished for the crimes he was forced to commit. Hope that Kain will be okay. She breathed deep, barely hearing Sophie's reply.

"I'm sure it all will be. Let's just focus on the next few days anyway, hey Mum. I love you."

"I love you too, sweetie. Bye for now." She tapped the screen, placed the phone on the table in front of her and tied back her long hair with the colourful scrunchie she'd brought with her. It was a hot summer day and her hair annoyed her in the heat, but the cool breeze in the mountains outside Brisbane diminished the need to wipe away the sweat she was so used to back home up north.

Just as she was about to get up and go inside for a cool drink, her phone rang. She picked it up and looked at the screen with a frown – 'Private Number'. "Hello." She refrained from saying 'Linda speaking' just in case it was from that stranger again.

"Mrs Linda Atkinson?" a male voice asked.

"Wh-who's asking, please?"

"It's Senior Detective Clements. I met you in your son's hospital room."

"Oh yes, I remember," said Linda, recognising the deep, pompous voice. "What can I do for you?" Silently, she prayed he was calling to tell her Steve was a free man, or something equally as wonderful.

"I'm sorry to bother you with this right now. I believe Steve is undergoing more surgery in a couple of days, correct?"

"Yes, we're down here near Brisbane now. I did call into the police station to tell them we were going early… and *try* to keep my son safe from whoever the hell is after him." She couldn't help emphasizing that bit to show her frustration at their apparent lack of interest in his safety, or lack of belief he was in any danger.

"Yes, yes, I know that. You also said then that you and Steve may stay away longer after his surgery has been done. Is that still the plan?"

"Probably." An uneasy feeling started in her belly and crept up to her throat. "It depends on how he is afterwards and if I feel the need to keep him away from up there for longer."

"While I do appreciate your maternal desire to protect your son, we do need to speak to him as soon as possible."

"Can I pass on a message? What's it about?" That worsening uneasy feeling dried her mouth. She swallowed.

"We have just received some compelling information anonymously, regarding your son's criminal activities. It appears that he may not be as innocent as he claims. We need to interview him as soon as he is up to it and possibly begin court proceedings against him."

The words hit Linda like a mountain rockslide. Each stone smashing her with shocking pain. She gulped back tears. "Wh-what information?" This just can't be happening.

"I'm not at liberty to divulge that, but you will find out when you get back up here. I apologise for doing this over the phone, but we needed to let you know. Please ensure Steve does not abscond when he finds out...if he does, we *will* find him and then he will be in even more trouble."

Linda opened her mouth, but only a hoarse "Okay" whispered out. She dropped the phone on the table and stood up, but her trembling legs and knees threatened to give way. She sat back down and clasped her shaking hands together. This must be some cruel joke. It just *can't* be real. Things were finally starting to look up for Steve. There is no way he could handle this news and no way was she going to tell him, at least not before the surgery. How the hell would she tell him? Pent up tears burst forth and she covered her face until she'd cried them all out and her body stopped shuddering.

Oh God, she couldn't let Steve see her like this. She looked about for any sign of him and Jenna returning, but thankfully couldn't see them. With heart thumping, she jumped up and went into the bathroom to wash her face. The woman looking back at her in the mirror looked like a seventy-five-year-old, rather than a fifty-five year old. The pale face, bags beneath the eyes and stray strands of now-greying hair about her sad face were not familiar to Linda, at least not until recently. She cupped water in her hand and rinsed her parched mouth out, took a couple of slow, deep breaths and wiped her hands and face on her towel. She had to stay strong for Steve.

She went back out to the verandah and looked about again. Still no sign of them. Picking up her phone to instinctively call Grace, she sighed and put it back down again. She couldn't dump this on Grace now with Kain's chemo and her pregnancy as well. No, Grace already had enough to deal with.

Bruce. She needed the love and support of her husband now more than ever but telling him would probably only result in him saying something horrible like, *good riddance*. That would be a kick in the guts she really didn't need or could cope with. Sophie? No, probably not a good idea telling her with being there alone and dealing with her father. What if she let it slip to him? No, she couldn't risk it. Not yet anyway.

She sat on the chair in defeat. She couldn't tell *anyone* this terrifying news. News that no mother should ever have to hear or worry about. *Steve could go to jail.* He wouldn't never cope nor survive that. The thought of losing her beloved son again stabbed through her aching heart, shattering it to pieces.

CHAPTER 26

Steve slowed his pace a little more. Jenna appeared to be struggling to keep up with him, but she'd reminded him several times on their walk she didn't need any help. Her limp seemed to have worsened a little on the walk back to the cleared, accommodation area. A movement and slight rustling in the undergrowth caught his attention. "Jenna, look. An echidna!" Each native animal he'd spotted since arriving here had brought a smile to his face and some peace to his worried mind. But also worsened the longing in his heart to go back 'home'.

Jenna's face lit up. "Oh, wow! Cute little fella isn't he?" She knelt close to where the echidna poked and scratched about among fallen leaves, twigs and small bushes.

Flecks of sunlight filtered through the forest canopy, highlighting her blonde hair. As it was already mid afternoon when they set out for the walk through the bush neither bothered with a hat. Steve still wore the mask on his face, now getting more and more itchy. And of course, he got strange looks from some of the other walkers they passed along the track. That didn't bother him of course, being so used to it, and at least none of these ones had fled in terror or made nasty remarks as some used to in Karisdale when they saw his scarred face. The day he could live mask-free and have even a *half*-normal looking face just couldn't come soon enough.

He crouched down near Jenna. "He sure is. And he's not even bothered by us, just minding his own business looking for something good to eat."

"What does he like to eat?" asked Jenna.

"Mainly ants and termites, but they also like worms and larvae of beetles and moths – all that type of thing." He watched Jenna's fascinated face. Her *pretty* fascinated face, now a little flushed and damp with sweat.

She looked at Steve with smile. "I love the way you know so much about every animal and bird we've seen since we got here. I've learnt so much from you, and I don't just mean *about* you. You should write a book or do a TV doco."

She sounded serious but he laughed a little. "Nah, I wouldn't know how to do that, and I don't think I have the face for TV." He'd tried to make the last part of the sentence into a joke, but Jenna didn't even smile. In fact, the opposite. Her smile disappeared and she looked back at the echidna. Maybe she felt embarrassed for him. Maybe she agreed he had an ugly face but was too polite to say anything of the sort. *Yeah, more like it, idiot.* "Anyway, I guess we should get back. Mum'll be getting worried." He stood and instinctively held out his hand to help Jenna up. When she just looked at his hand he almost pulled it back, but to his surprise, she took hold of it and stood up with his support. The first ever time she'd allowed him to help her. His heart danced.

Jenna stood and brushed some dirt and leaf litter from her knees. "I probably shouldn't have knelt down like that in case something stung me." She walked past Steve without saying anything else.

He stood there a moment, watching her back. How he wished he could 'work her out'. She seemed so friendly and interested in him sometimes then all of a sudden she'd become aloof and distant. No way was he game to tell her how he felt about her and how he'd love to know more about her, but she just didn't seem keen to tell him anything about herself when he'd ask her simple things like what was her favourite music? She just shrugged at that one and said she liked all types.

Steve walked on and caught up with her. "Geez, dunno about you but I'm looking forward to a nice cold drink when we get back." Pathetic, he realised, but he was concerned she wasn't happy about something and thought of the first thing that might break the ice, so to speak.

"Yep, me too." She turned to him with a smile. *That* smile which sent swirls of giddiness through his heart. Maybe she wasn't upset after all.

In comfortable silence they walked back to the cottage. His mum came out on to the verandah just as they went up the several steps. Steve had slowed so Jenna could ascend the stairs ahead of him. She held the rail and dragged her affected leg up to the step her other foot was already on.

"Nice walk?" asked Linda. "See anything exciting?" She sat at the small table. A grass jug of orange cordial containing ice cubes and three glasses were on the table. "I bet you could both do with a nice cold drink." She poured each glass full.

Steve pulled out a chair for Jenna and she nodded with, "Thank you," before sitting down and expelling a long sigh. "Phew, hot out there." She removed her glasses, wiped her sweaty face with the bottom of her shirt and replaced her glasses. "Thank you, Mrs Atkinson." She drank half the large glass in one go.

"Please Jenna, call me Linda. It makes me feel too old otherwise." Linda laughed a little, but her face quickly became solemn.

Steve sat down. "Are you okay, mum? You don't look very happy." He picked up his glass and had a few sips. "Has something happened while we were away?"

Linda waved it off. "No, all good. I'm just tired. Had a good talk to both Sophie and Grace before. Your father seems to be behaving himself and even getting back into some cattle work, so that's the best news I've had for a while." She sipped her drink. "So, tell me, Jenna, how's the info for your article coming on. You must know everything there is to know about Steve by now, with what he's told you and me filling you in on his younger life during the flight down here."

'Everthing' about him? Steve cringed at that. No way could he tell her everything, especially burying the dead man at Scott's yards and the silly crush he had on Grace. Though he vowed to one day tell the police about the buried man so his family can give him a dignified funeral and have some closure. They must be worried sick.

Also, some of the gorier details of the 'jobs' forced upon him by Scott and things he'd witnessed Scott do wouldn't be mentioned. How he wished he could forget all that. "Geez mum, I hope you didn't tell her anything embarrassing about me as a kid." He laughed, more to dispel the horrific images from his brain than anything else.

Both Linda and Jenna chuckled. "Hmm," mused his mum, "I could tell her about that time you climbed a tree to put a baby bird back in its nest and as you were climbing down you got the back of your shorts caught and fell trying to unhook them, landing on the ground in just your undies. Your shorts were still hanging in the tree."

Steve laughed out loud. "You just did!"

"Thank you Mrs, umm, Linda," said Jenna with a laugh. "I can see he's always loved animals. The walk was interesting. He knows so much about every animal there is in the bush." She glanced at Steve with a shy smile. "But, yes, I do have plenty of info now, both written down, taped on my phone and in here." She tapped the side of her head. "I should be able to complete it tonight and email it so it makes the Lifestyle magazine in Sunday's paper. It might even go further afield than just the Queensland paper. I hope so, anyway." She smiled at Steve again. "I want everyone to know what a good and kind-hearted person he is and the hell he has been through."

A pang of hesitation hit Steve. "Will you let me read it before you send it?" Again, he wondered if this was a good idea after all. Part of him wanted people to know, the other part felt his life was nobody's business, but he couldn't stop it now. Jenna had put too much into it and she seemed so pleased with the opportunity to show the world what she could do. Just another thing he admired about her and the fact she wasn't letting her disability get in the way of chasing her dreams. No, it had to go ahead now. Hopefully the reactions will be positive.

"That's lovely, Jenna," said Linda. "I'm sure you can show that through the article. I have a good feeling you are the perfect person for this."

Jenna finished her drink and stood up. "It's starting to cool off now. I might go for a quick shower then get into it. Thank you again for that lovely drink." She took her empty glass and went inside.

"You're very welcome." Linda watched her go then turned to Steve. "She really is lovely. So polite and seems so caring."

Steve sighed. "Yes, she is. We've had some good talks, but it's all one sided. She never wants to talk about herself, so I hardly know anything about her, but she knows lots about me. I just wish..."

Linda placed her hand on his shoulder. "I know, love. Has she said anything at all to show she's interested? That little smile she just gave you looked like it, that's for sure! Maybe she's just so caught up in writing the article she wants to stay professional. I'm sure once it's done she'll relax more and you two can really get to know each other."

"Oh, I don't know." All the old doubts and insecurities flooded through Steve. "Look at me! Why would such a pretty lady like her be interested in me? I'm ugly. I'm overweight. Hell, I might even go to jail!"

Linda gasped. "Don't say that! Don't *ever* say any of those things again." She leaned closer to him. "You are not ugly. The surgery will help restore your face. Your *handsome* face. Okay, you might not look exactly the same as before, but that doesn't matter. It's what's in here that counts." She poked the left side of his chest. "You are one of the best human beings I have ever known, and I'm not just saying that because you're my son. You did so much good in your life and always helped anyone needing it. And as for being overweight. That can be fixed. I can tell you've lost some since you came back, so that is the least of your worries." She turned away from him, her bottom lip quivering.

"What else, mum? There's more isn't there?" Why didn't she dispel his fear of going to jail? "What aren't you telling me?" The doubts and insecurities sweeping his body changed to fear and dread. Feelings all too familiar.

Linda took a deep breath. "Detective Clements called a while ago. He just asked how things were going and said they want to catch up with you when we get back, that's all." She smiled and patted his shoulder. "Stop worrying about going to jail and think about how good it will be once your surgery is over and what good things lie ahead." She flicked her gaze briefly toward the inside of the cottage where Jenna was. "She certainly is very independent isn't she, for someone with a disability? Makes me admire her even more."

"Me too," nodded Steve. His shoulders slumped. "Oh well, I can't make her like me. I'm not even sure she knows

I like her. I don't want to tell her in case it scares her away or she laughs at me."

"Oh, I think she knows you care about her." His mum gave a little smile, not just with her lips but her eyes lit up as well.

"What do you mean? Did you say something?" His heart rate notched up with excitement. "Not sure I like that idea."

"No, not really, I just dropped a little hint here and there when we were talking out here last night while you were in the shower."

"No, mum! You shouldn't have. How did she react?"

"With a smile actually, but didn't really say anything. But you can also take that as she didn't say, or even imply, she's *not* interested. Trust me, a mother knows these things." Linda sat back in her chair and grinned.

Jenna's raised, but muffled, voice could be heard coming from her room.

Steve looked at his mother. "I wonder what's going on. She doesn't sound happy."

Linda's brow creased. "No. She must be on her phone. Hope there's no problem with getting the article out."

Jenna came out of her room with phone in hand. Her face showed anger. She stormed back out to where Steve and Linda sat, gritting her teeth and shaking her head.

Steve stood up. "Are you okay?"

"I will be," replied Jenna. She inhaled deeply. "Just my bloody annoying husband!"

Steve's heart smashed to the floor. He looked at his mother, her eyes wide and mouth agape.

Husband?

CHAPTER 27

The man turned another page of the Sunday paper, coming to the Lifestyle lift out magazine in the middle. He slid it aside, but a small photo on the front accompanying the words, 'Back From A Fate Worse Than Death', caught his eye. *No, it couldn't be.* He pulled it back toward him and opened it, flicking through pages until he found what he was looking for. He shook his head. *Bullshit! Not again!* He began to read…

On September 15th, 2018, local graziers' son and champion rodeo rider, Steve Atkinson, left his home on their sprawling cattle property northwest of Mackay, QLD, and seemingly vanished off the face of the Earth. That is, until recently when he was found living in a remote bush home about twenty kilometres from the nearby town of Karisdale. During those years police investigations and private detectives failed to find any trace of the beloved son and brother. Family and friends were left bewildered and heartbroken, believing him dead but never completely giving up hope.

Sadly, when found, ironically by his sister, Grace, who he rescued staggering injured through the bush after her fiery car crash and being stalked by wild dogs, he had absolutely no memory of his family or former life and had suffered horrific scarring to his face and head. Not even knowing his real name he went by Seth Andrews.

Even with amnesia and obviously having been through hell, his kind and caring nature shone through and he took wonderful care of Grace for a week, with no idea of the family connection. He had obviously been brought up with courtesy and chivalry. She didn't recognise him for some time, due to his scarring and increased size, but she did her best to also help him deal with his issues and fears. Initially she felt afraid of him, as he spoke gruffly and monosyllabic, but she soon realised he only wanted to help her. Grace believes if not for him she would most certainly be dead now, terrifyingly torn up and eaten by those ravenous dogs, her bones scattered and possibly never found.

The family was elated when both Steve and Grace were brought home. Grace had also been feared dead in the car crash when the hitchhiker she'd picked up was burnt beyond recognition in the driver's seat, but she'd had no idea of her 'death'. After losing her phone in the accident and having gone through some personal woes, she was happy to rest up in Steve's secluded home. It was truly a miracle for their parents, Bruce and Linda, and younger sister, Sophie, to have their family whole again.

But the mystery deepened as to where he had been all that time. Although he remembers very little of the beating that resulted in the frightening acid attack, literally melting his handsome face, he does have horrific memories of being forced to work for the well-known crime boss, James McTaggart, shot dead in his latest major crime of rustling 150 head of prime cattle. Due to McTaggart's Scottish heritage, Steve only knew him as 'Scott', nothing more. Steve also had no idea for a long time that 'Scott' not only owned the house in which Steve lived but had also got him a fake license and a utility. Steve never found out who instigated or carried out the acid attack. McTaggart has always been his main suspect, even though the thug told Steve he'd just found him that way and wanted to help him. It didn't take long for Steve to realise McTaggart was no friend, but a frightening, sadistic man with ulterior motives.

Being interrogated by police and forced to talk about the past horrors caused him fainting spells. Tests found no reason for his blackouts, so were most likely from reliving the fear forced upon him, now resulting in Post Traumatic Stress Disorder. Having had a love of nature and animals since childhood, the deeds he was forced to commit often left him sickened and he hopes to atone them one day.

Some may wonder why he didn't try to escape Scott's cruel clutches, or why he didn't ignore his outrageous and inhuman demands. He did try, many times, but witnessed the horrific and barbaric torture and fates of those who dared defy or betray the evil McTaggart. These experiences sickened him to the core and with having no idea of who he was or where he was from, he resigned himself to a life of working for that monster. A monster who had no feeling or empathy for any other living soul, except his own needs and blood-thirsty satiety.

One of the worst experiences for Steve was witnessing a man having his ears slowly sliced off because he 'didn't listen to Scott'. Then, with Scott pointing the bloodied knife and loaded pistol at him, Steve was forced to chop off one of the man's hands. He desperately tried to talk his way out of it, but the knife and pistol were then pressed against his skin. The man's agonising screams will haunt him forever. Immediately after doing the nauseating deed Steve passed out. He awoke to find several broken fingers on his left hand and a dirty boot print on that hand. Screams and moans coming from nearby bush, followed by a gunshot and silence, told him that poor man was out of his misery. Steve still has no idea who broke his fingers, but suspects it was McTaggart.

Even though McTaggart had other men working for him as well, it's been revealed that he treated Steve as his 'special' slave, spying on him and giving him the worst jobs and crimes to commit. Crimes that also included stealing, shooting livestock and beating those who upset McTaggart. Things the gentle and good-hearted Steve Atkinson would never even consider doing.

Steve has spent time in hospital recovering somewhat physically and is undergoing plastic surgery to restore his face and damaged ear as much as possible. While in hospital he longs for the peace and quiet of the bush and the wildlife he loves and in return, they show no fear of him, instinctively knowing he would never hurt them.

While back on the family property in between hospital stays, he has enjoyed horseback riding in the open paddocks and his mum's delicious cooking. Not that he lacks culinary skills himself. Grace enjoyed tasty meals cooked by him while there and I, myself, have savoured his biscuits and other delights. One of the highlights of his home coming was being greeted by his faithful blue heeler, Buddy, now old. He was hesitant at first but as soon as Steve spoke Buddy's tired eyes lit up and his tail wagged like crazy, followed by excited licks and little yaps. He knew his loving master had finally come home.

While getting to know the real Steve Atkinson, I found him to be so courteous and kind, always wanting to help me since I have a slight disability, but due to being brought up independent I often refused his help, which at times hurt his feelings. Clearly his heart is a good one, not black and cold like McTaggart's or the 'pawn' he was forced to become for those five long, lonely years.

Steve's greatest wish now is to have his face restored, so he no longer needs to avoid looking in the mirror or tear up when passersby, mainly children, run in fear of 'the ugly monster', while their parents and some other adults abuse him for just being. He also wishes to regain his memory and would dearly love to be able to forget the past five terrible years, and if possible, make up for the crimes committed. He also dearly wishes to get closer to his dad. Most of all, he just wishes he could be 'normal' again, but sadly, he has no idea what that is anymore. If anyone deserves their wishes to come true, without a doubt it is Steve Atkinson.

With trembling hands, the man closed the magazine, guzzled down what was left in his beer can and crumpled the can in his bare hand before tossing it toward the bin by the kitchen sink. It hit the floor. He stared into space for a few moments, remembering...

He opened the magazine again, quickly flicking through to the article and looked closely at Jenna's head shot beside the title. Then to her name below the picture – By Jenna

Leeson-Rowles. *So that's what she looks like up close!* He grabbed his phone from the table and took a photo of Jenna's name and picture then took photos of the article. *These will come in handy.*

And if what he told the police the other day doesn't work, there was always plan B...

CHAPTER 28

Sophie brought the Sunday paper Lifestyle magazine to her father sitting at the table eating a sandwich for lunch. "Here Dad, I really think you should read this." She placed it down beside his plate, open at the article on Steve.

He frowned. "What's it about?"

"Steve and what he's been through the past five years."

"Hmph." Looking away he took another bite of his sandwich.

"Please Dad, just read it. That won't hurt you."

Bruce sighed and put his half-eaten sandwich back on the plate. "All right. Can you get my glasses from the office?"

Sophie rushed to get her father his reading glasses.

Just as he enjoyed doing every weekend, Detective Clements relaxed on his comfortable

lounge chair, put his bare feet up on the coffee table and opened the Sunday paper.

CHAPTER 29

Steve stared at Jenna's full name after he'd read her article. He'd read it before she emailed iy and had decided to tell some of the worst details, but he still couldn't wrap his head around the fact she was married. Worse still, that she hadn't mentioned it before the unhappy phone call she'd received from her husband after they'd got back from their walk. It hadn't even occurred to him that she may be married, or at least in some sort of relationship. More fool him. Nothing seemed the same anymore and he just hadn't felt relaxed around her since. This saddened him, but he also didn't want her to know how disappointed he was, lest he felt foolish, so he either avoided her or barely spoke. He closed the magazine and sipped his tea, now lukewarm. Mid Sunday morning and the hot sun beat down on his back where he sat on the eastern side of the small verandah of their holiday cottage. The wallabies had disappeared into the nearby bush to escape the increasing heat of the morning.

"You okay, Steve?" His mum sat opposite him at the small, round table. "You looked a million miles away. Are you worrying about tomorrow?"

Steve turned his gaze to Linda. He hadn't even heard her slide open the screen door, let alone walk out toward him. "Huh? Oh, sorry, no, I was thinking about -" He looked toward the inside of the cottage then lowered his voice, "Jenna being married."

"Yes, that was a surprise and a half. But she didn't seem too happy with him so maybe they're separated. Has she said anything more to you about it?"

He shook his head. "Not a thing. Just acts like nothing is different. I don't get it." He shrugged. "Just goes to show stupid me was imagining things when I thought she might have been interested." He sighed, long and heavy and leaned back in his chair. "How could I have thought any different. I'm hard work. Too much baggage for any-one. Of course she wouldn't be interested."

His mother reached over and briefly held his forearm resting on the table. "Don't sell yourself short, love. How about we just focus on the surgery tomorrow and take it one day at a time?" Her face lit up. "This is the big thing. Soon you'll be able to look in the mirror and like what you see. Can you imagine how much better that will make you feel about yourself?"

"I suppose. Well, I can't get any uglier, that's for sure." He flung the rest of the cold tea over the wooden rail and stood. "I'm going to make a fresh cup. Want another one?"

"No, thanks. I might call Grace and see how things are going there." Linda put down her cup and picked up her phone.

With the weight of disappointment still sitting heavily on his shoulders he trudged inside and clicked on the kettle. Part of him wished Jenna could go back home now, but at the same time he knew he'd miss her. *Serve yourself right, idiot, for thinking she could like you.* He shook his head to dispel the thoughts and put a fresh teabag in his mug. He really didn't need that annoying little voice making him feel any worse than he already did.

"Is there enough water in there for two?"

That sweet and cheery voice. He spun around. Jenna stood beside him with an empty cup. His mind still so preoccupied he hadn't heard her either. "What? Yes, plenty here." He handed her the box of teabags so she could take one out.

"Are you alright, Steve? You still seem very quiet." She chuckled. "Lucky I've done the article. You've barely said a dozen words to me since I sat down to write it and send it in. There wouldn't have been much in it at this rate." She put her cup beside his on the bench, waiting for the hot water.

He could barely see her out the corner of his eye, but the discomfort of being so close to her and having her sound like she had no idea of why he'd become so quiet felt bigger and more soul crushing than anything else he'd been through. He had absolutely no idea of what to say to her and wished he didn't have to say anything at all. "Oh well, at least it's done."

"Are you sure you're happy with it?" She sounded worried.

The kettle boiled and automatically switched off. He poured water in both cups before getting milk from the small fridge. "Yes, you did a good job." Still without looking at her, he stirred his tea. The clinking noise almost deafening with the elephant in the room. "What are you plans now, Jenna?" Might as well ask her outright. As hard as it was to just come out and say what he thought, the tension of not knowing and trying to avoid the issue was getting a bit much. He had to know, one way or the other.

"Umm, not sure." She used his teaspoon to stir her tea and dropped the spoon in the nearby sink, with a *clang*. "I was hoping to stay here for a few more days, at least, and see how you are after the surgery." She sat at the indoor table and indicated for him to sit on the chair opposite. "That's if you're okay with that. I can't help feeling you don't really want me around anymore, so if that's the case I'll arrange to go home tomorrow." Her face changed from worried to sad.

Her sad look confused him. He sat down. "But isn't your *husband* missing you?" As hard as he'd tried not to emphasize the word, he couldn't help it. Damn! Now she'll know he's jealous. Jealous. It dawned on him that was his issue now. He was jealous!

"Maybe, but I don't really care if he is. We're separated. Have been for months."

The weight on Steve's shoulders and mind suddenly lightened a little at those words. "Oh." For the first time since she stood by his side for some tea he actually looked at her. Now what to say... "Sorry." *You idiot. You aren't one bit sorry!* He hoped it sounded genuine. He wanted to ask questions but didn't know what to ask without sounding like he had feelings for her.

Jenna shrugged. "Don't be. We should never have got married in the first place. It just seemed like a good idea at the time, but it wasn't long before we realised, well, I realised, it was a mistake. We'd been friends since school and just should have stayed that way."

"Are you getting a divorce?"

"You bet! In about another four months." She chuckled. "Oh well, you live and learn, don't you?"

Steve drank the last of his tea. "Why were you cranky with him on the phone the other night? Oh, sorry, none of my business."

She rolled her eyes. "I'd totally forgotten that we'd arranged for him to get the rest of his stuff from our flat this weekend. I still live there and he's been staying with friends until he found his own place, which he has now."

"Couldn't he just go get it himself?"

"No, he doesn't have a key anymore. He carried on a bit, but there isn't much of his still there and nothing that he can't do without for a bit longer anyway."

Steve bit the bullet. It was now or never. "So, you don't love him anymore?"

Jenna shrugged again. "I don't think I ever really did. Well, not in the way a wife should love her husband. He was more like a mate than anything. Mum and Dad were a bit disappointed it didn't work out. They thought he was the bees knees but they can stay friends with him. That doesn't bother me."

Steve took a deep breath, preparing to hear something good or something bad. "Is there anyone else?" Heart thumping, he held that breath...

CHAPTER 30

Linda put her phone on the veranda table. It'd been a good, long chat with Grace. Now she needed to stretch her legs. She got up and headed toward the steps. Just as she reached the bottom of the stairs her phone rang. Thinking it may be Bruce and hoping he would show some concern and send best wishes for their son's surgery tomorrow, she bounded back up the stairs and grabbed it. *No Caller Id.* Thinking it may be that stranger after Steve she put it down and let it ring out but then a message came up. Curiosity got the better of her. With trembling hands she picked it up and listened to the message.

'Mrs Atkinson, it's Detective Bill Clements here. I really need to speak to you. Call me as soon as you can, please, on -' He said the number.

He sounded cranky. She certainly didn't need any more stress right now. Best find out. With nerves firing up in her stomach, she returned his call. Luckily, she had a good memory for phone numbers.

"Hello, Mrs Atkinson. Thank you for calling me straight back."

"Yes, Detective Clements, sorry I didn't answer." No point telling him why she didn't since the police don't believe anyone *is* after Steve. "W-what can I do for you?" She looked around into the cottage. Steve and Jenna were chatting at the table. Probably best Steve doesn't hear this conversation. She got up and went down the stairs.

"It's about this article on Steve in the Sunday paper. I've just got off the phone with my boss. I gather you have seen the article?"

"Yes. Is there a problem with it?"

"Yes, a big problem."

Linda's swirling stomach turned into fierce rapids. She swallowed hard. "What's wrong with it?" Her knees weakened so she sat down on a picnic table seat beneath a nearby shady tree.

"It's totally biased. Do you know this 'Jenna' who wrote it?"

"Well, yes, she is a journalist who wanted to write a story on him. We didn't think there was anything wrong with that. Has she done anything illegal?"

"Well, no it's not illegal for a journalist to do their job."

"Then what's the problem with it?" Her edgy nerves and fear turned to defence, maternal defence. "It shows some of the hell my son has been through! Don't you think people have the right to hear the truth?"

"The *truth?* One part that annoys me is where she states his fainting spells were a result of *our* interrogation. To my knowledge he was having those turns before he was even found! Isn't that correct?"

"I think so, but the stress of the police interrogations made it worse for him. I do believe that."

"Well, we won't know that for sure. Is this journalist..." He hesitated a moment. "It sounds like she's in love with him or something, for this to be so one-sided."

If only that were true. "Detective, I can assure you she was very professional in her attitude toward Steve while spending time with him gathering the information for the article. No, there is no relationship between them. She just saw a situation and a person who needed their true story told." No need to tell him Jenna was here with them. "As his mother I think she did a wonderful job, but yes, I may be biased there too."

"Of course." He sighed heavily. "Look, millions of people have probably read the article by now, so we can't change it, but it does change the whole course of things for us."

"How?"

"Well, I'm sure you, and your family and especially Steve himself, with be pleased to know we now have to throw his case out. There is no way we could find an unbiased jury if his case went to court, which I'm sure it would have. Especially going by the information we recently received."

Linda gasped. Was she hearing and understanding him properly? "You...you mean he won't be arrested and tried for the crimes he was forced to commit?"

"Yes, that's what I mean. *BUT...* don't get over excited. He'll still have to be placed on a bond and some other things will have to be sorted out, but, no, he won't be going to trial."

Linda choked back a sob of exhilaration and relief. "He's a free man then and can stop worrying about going to jail?"

"Yes, it seems so. But we will still need to see you both once he's over this surgery, so I will stay in touch. Goodbye for now." The phone went silent.

Linda ran back up the stairs of the cottage, her shoulders and mind now a tonne lighter. "Steve? *STEVE!*" Tears streamed down her cheeks but all she could do was laugh.

"What's wrong, mum?" Steve slid the screen door open and stood before his mother.

"Sit down." She grabbed his arm and led him to a chair at verandah table. "I just got a call from Detective Clements. Remember him?"

Steve nodded. "Yes, what about him?" Jenna came out the door and stood behind him.

"He said they've had to dismiss your case because of the article. He said it was too one-sided and they'd never find an unbiased jury." She jumped up, leaned down and hugged her son tightly. More tears flowed but she didn't care. Finally, she let go. "Isn't that wonderful?"

Steve just sat there in silence, staring at her.

"It means you don't have to worry anymore about going to jail. It's not going to happen. You can concentrate on getting a life back, a happy life." She glanced at Jenna, whose face now beamed with a huge smile.

He broke into a big grin. "Wow, that's... that's unbelievable. Are you sure that's what he meant?"

"Yes! He said you'll probably be on some sort of good behaviour bond, but they'll sort that out once you're over the surgery."

She picked up her phone. "I'm calling Grace and Sophie to tell them. Oh, and your father. He'll be pleased."

"I doubt it," Steve mumbled, his happy smile now gone.

CHAPTER 31

Kain tried again to get up from the bed but dropped his head back on the pillow. Three days since taking the oral chemotherapy and the effects had now hit hard. His eyes watered, nausea stirred his gut and all energy gone.

Grace walked into the bedroom carrying a steaming mug. "Here you go. A fresh cup of peppermint and ginger tea to help settle your stomach." She placed the cup on his bedside table. "Do you want to sit up?" She sat down on the edge of the bed beside him, sympathy on her pretty face. Rubbing his forearm, she sighed. "Poor darlin'".

Kain couldn't stop a groan. "I don't really know what I want, Grace. I feel like shit! I don't think even the worst ever hangover is as bad as this." He pulled himself up to a sitting position. Grace stacked the pillows behind him. "Thanks." He leaned back a little and ran his hand through his hair then held out that hand containing quite a few strands. "It's starting to go." He knew it would most likely happen, but the reality of seeing it still shocked him. The overwhelming urge to yell, punch something, even cry, overtook him but he didn't even have the physical energy for any of that, and it wouldn't do any good anyway.

Grace handed him the mug. "Just try a few sips anyway. It might help. Then when you feel like it I'll make you a smoothie or some toast, or whatever you think you can stomach."

Kain took a few sips and put the mug back on the bedside table. "Is today Monday?" Grace nodded. His brain a foggy jumble. "I wonder if Steve's surgery is over yet?"

"Mum said she'd ring when he was out of surgery and awake. I really hope it goes well. I just can't imagine what it's like for him, after all the horrible things he's endured and now having to literally get a new face or, at least, try to recreate his old one. Even I didn't know how bad his life was in the past five years. He never told me some of those things when I was at his house." Her face lit up, brightening the room and Kain's dreary soul. He adored her gorgeous smile. "But isn't it great he won't have to go to court? Oh, Joe rang your phone before when you were asleep. He said he'll call back later."

Ah, Joe. Fun loving Joe. A mate who could always make him laugh. "How is the crazy bugger? It's only been days since I saw him but it seems forever."

Grace laughed. "Crazy, as per normal. But he was a little more subdued than usual. He's worried and looking forward to you getting back on your feet after this."

"Me too." Kain's tired eyelids closed but he forced them open again. "I think I need to sleep a bit now, sweetie."

Grace stood. "No worries, darl. I have some washing to put on and a few other things. I'll leave you to rest." She pointed to the little bell on the bedside table. "Don't forget to ring it if you need me before I come back to check on you." She leant down and kissed him warmly on the lips.

He mustered the strength to kiss her back and wished it didn't have to stop. "Can you please close the curtains? It's so glary and hurting my eyes." She closed them. Kain hoped sleep would come quickly. The doctor had said to try and sleep as much as possible through the worse side effects. Grace left the room and he tried to turn his brain onto something relaxing, like lying under a shady tree by a waterhole or riverbank.

He drifted in and out of sleep for an unknown time. His head ached and coldness swept over him, even though it was the middle of summer. He'd even needed the air conditioner on earlier. Shivering, and with the covers pulled up to his chin, he reached over and rang the little bell.

Grace rushed in the door. "What's up? Are you okay?"

"I'm cold. Can you turn off the air con, please?" His body trembled and he lay on his side drawing his knees up to try and get warmer. "I think I need a blanket or the doona on now."

"That's crazy, it's so hot today." Grace turned off the air con, wiped sweat from her forehead then placed her hand on Kain's forehead. "You feel hot. And you're sweating!"

"I can't be," mumbled Kain through chattering teeth. "I'm so cold. Grace, *please* get our doona and put over me."

Grace rushed to the wardrobe and pulled out the doona, spreading it over Kain. "Something's wrong, Kain, this isn't good." She grabbed the thermometer from the bedside table, clicked 'on' and held it to his mouth. "Let me check your temp. Remember what they said to do if you suddenly feel cold?"

Kain opened his dry lips a little, while still shivering, and closed them over the thermometer until it beeped. Grace took it out and stared at the reading. Even in the darkened room he could see the horror on her face.

His nausea worsened and he swallowed down saliva. "What is it?"

"It's forty degrees. Hell, that's not good. I'm going to call an ambulance." Grace ran out of the room.

"*Wait!*" Kain mustered the strength to shout to her. "Come back."

She rushed back into the bedroom, phone in hand. "What? We can't waste time. You need to get to the hospital."

Fear brought the nausea to a head. He leaned over the side of the bed and vomited on the floor, just missing the plastic bucket put there for that purpose, should he need it. Wiping his mouth, he looked at Grace, all blurry through his watery eyes. "But I can't go to the hospital. You know they said once my immune system is affected a hospital was the last place I should be in. I could catch anything." He swallowed down bitter, hot saliva and dropped back on the pillow. Another groan passed his lips as cold shivers shot down his spine.

"And if you stay here you'll get sicker!" Panic saturated her voice. "Kain, you *have* to go to hospital. You could *die!*" She stifled a sob and tapped on her phone.

"Right now I *feel* like dying."

CHAPTER 32

Steve opened his eyes. Dr Thebo stood by his bed, smiling. "Welcome back, Steve. Surgery is over. It went very well."

Steve tried to focus but the room blurred and his eyelids weighed heavy. He licked dry lips and tried clearing his throat, scratchy from the breathing tube while under anaesthetic. "Hey, Doc. That's good," he managed in a raspy voice. He looked about the room. "Where's Mum and Jenna?"

Doc gave a cheery laugh. "Don't worry, they're waiting outside. If you're up to it I'll call them in, then I'll come back a bit later and talk to you more about the surgery."

"Yes please." He inhaled deeply, hoping it would wake him up a bit more.

"Okay, see you in a little while." Doctor Thebo left the room.

Steve closed his tired eyes again. Images of the crazy dreams he'd just had came to his mind. All so jumbled, he wished they'd go away. *Sigh. That's my life – jumbled.* Jenna featured a lot but he couldn't string any of the bits and pieces together. She was calling out to him to help her in one dream. His father, with angry red eyes chased him. Grace tried to save him, but then she turned into a savage dog with large, drooling canines. Scott was shooting at the dogs then turned the gun toward Steve.

He shook his head, just as footsteps entered the room. Opening his eyes, the sight of Jenna and his Mum coming in, both with huge smiles, lifted his heart and brought a smile to his lips.

Linda leaned down to hug him but hesitated. "Oh, I'd better be careful with your dressing." She held his hand and kissed him lightly on his bandaged face. When she stood up and let go she wiped away a tear, though her face glowed with happiness. "Dr Thebo is very pleased with how it went." She stepped back and brought a chair closer to his bed before disappearing out the door.

"Hey, Steve," Jenna came close and touched his arm. "How are you feeling?" She laughed a little. "Apart from glad it's over of course." She pulled the chair closer and sat down, just as Linda came back with another chair and sat on the opposite side of Steve's bed.

"Ohhh, a bit groggy, but yeah, glad it's done." He reached up and touched his face, covered with surgical dressing. "I can't really feel much. Does anyone have a mirror?"

Linda opened the drawer on his bedside table and took out a mirror. "The doctor said you'd probably want to see yourself, as most patients here do, so they keep a mirror by each bed." She held it in front of his face.

Steve stared at it for a few moments, not knowing what to say. The person staring back at him totally unrecognisable, like some Egyptian mummy. "Can't wait to see what I look like once these bandages come off." He reached up and touched his head. "Doc said he would shave off the last bit of my hair. Hope he did. I want all trace of Seth Andrews gone."

"He already has gone," said his mum, touching his forearm. "You're Steve Atkinson now and for always."

"I don't really feel like him though. I just feel like…I don't know, a nobody, I suppose."

Jenna leaned closer to him. "You aren't a nobody, Steve. You a good person and a good friend to me."

Linda stood. "Excuse me, I must go find a loo." She disappeared.

Wondering if that was an excuse to leave him and Jenna alone, Steve smiled and felt a little glad. He reached out and took Jenna's hand. "I'd glad you stayed on. It means a lot to me."

She smiled. "Well, like I said when you asked me if there was anyone else in my life, you are special, and I really like being around you. Who knows what might happen down the track." A little shrug and a loving, warm smile before she let go of his hand. "As long as your mum doesn't mind, I'd like to stay here for a few more days at least. I do have to go home sometime soon for a few work commitments and, of course, stop the Ex from whinging." She rolled her eyes. "Hey, now that you are no longer going to be arrested you should be able to have your own phone."

"Yeah, hope so." It certainly would be nice to be able to ring and chat to Jenna, or whoever he wished to. He closed his eyes for a moment.

Linda walked back into the room, followed by Doctor Thebo.

"Steve?" The doctor's voice was a little louder than usual.

Steve's eyes opened. "I must've dozed off, sorry. I didn't even hear you two come in." He glanced from his mother to the doctor. "Is everything alright?"

"Perfect," replied the doctor. "I shaved the remaining bit of your hair. There are possible options for regrowth in the scarred part of your scalp but some of your damage is quite deep so I'm not confident it will work for you." He grinned. "You might have to stay bald, but I did do a skin graft on your scalp as well, so it won't look as bad as it was."

"Where did you take the skin from?" asked Steve.

"Your thigh and one buttock so you'll be a bit tender there for a little while too." He looked at Linda. "I want him to stay down in Brisbane this time so I can monitor him. Later today we'll have him transferred to the Royal. It's close by and I'll confer with colleagues there and also pop over twice a day to see him." He looked back at Steve. "You're my special project, Steve, and I want the best possible outcome for you. I read that article in the paper yesterday and like it said, if anyone deserves only good things from now on, it's you."

Those words should have comforted him, but he still had trouble believing he deserved goodness. "Will I look like my old self?"

"Not quite exactly the same, but I did the best job possible with having your old photos to study." He broke into a grin again, showing perfect white teeth. "You'll be even better looking than before! Anyway, I have another patient waiting. I'll be back in later. Call the nurse if you need anything in the meantime." He gave the thumbs up and walked out.

"That is so exciting, Steve." Jenna grabbed his hand again. "But it doesn't matter to me what you look like." She pointed to the left side of his chest. "It's what's in there that counts."

"Thanks, Jen." Steve squeezed her hand. "Oh, hope you don't mind me calling you that."

"Not at all. Call me what you like, just not late for dinner." She kept a straight face for a few seconds then had a little giggle.

Steve laughed too. "I promise not to."

Linda got her phone from her bag. "Okay, I'm going to leave you two for a bit and go ring Grace." She looked at her watch. "Too early to ring Sophie. I'll wait 'til she's on lunch, but I'll try your father again, since he wasn't interested in talking to me the other day." She walked out of his room, muttering something under her breath. No doubt to do with his father's attitude.

CHAPTER 33

Linda ended her call to Grace. How she wished she could be in two places at once, especially when it concerned her beloved children. Grace was by Kain's bedside in the hospital, worrying about in infection he'd picked up and spiking his temperature. Luckily, the doctors had assured her this was quite common in chemo patients and with the help of intravenous antibiotics he'd soon be out of there and back home. Apart from that he was doing okay, Grace had said, so that was one good thing. Linda toyed with the idea of flying home in a few days to see them all, but Grace had assured her Steve needed her more and to stay down with him as long as necessary.

Now to try ring her husband. Waves of apprehension, even bordering on foreboding, washed through her body. How crazy to be nervous about ringing her own husband, but it dawned on her this is what it had come to. Thirty-odd years of marriage and a wonderful, exciting two-year romance before that. How they'd adored each other and worked hard to create a life on their huge, successful cattle property. Having children had only enriched their love and respect for each other. Jon's death was heart-breaking of course, but not once did she feel Bruce no longer loved or cared for her. Steve's disappearance created a strain between them but that soon healed and their love strengthened once again. Grace's presumed death again caused cracks in their relationship, but luckily that didn't last long with her being found alive a week later and, amazingly, with Steve.

That should have been one of the happiest times of their lives, having two of their children miraculously back from the dead, so it seemed. But Bruce's blasé attitude toward Steve, worsening into hatred, was too much for her to bear. This was *not* the Bruce she fell in love with. How much longer could that love last? It was already dangling by a meagre thread, in her heart she knew that, but once Steve got his life back, and Kain was again in good health and, of course, welcoming twin grandchildren, Bruce would be back to his old self...*surely*.

She called him on the house phone, but no answer. That was a plus, as it meant he may not be sitting on the verandah drinking, even though it was still morning. She tried his mobile. It rang and rang. With each ring her nerves frayed that little bit more. Needing fresh air, she headed out of the building. The call went to his message bank. *Damn!* She hung up without saying anything and looked about outside, hoping for a seat beneath one of the shady trees out front of Dr Thebo's rooms. No seats but manicured lawns and some beautiful flowers growing in beds nearby seemed to calm her a little. She sat on the soft grass under one of the trees, took a deep breath and tried his number again, trying to think what she'd say if she had to leave a message this time.

"Hello...Linda."

No 'hello love', like he used to answer. He sounded annoyed or maybe tired. "H-hello Bruce. How are you?" Probably pointless asking, but she really did want to know.

"I'm alright...how are you?"

The annoyance that she may have detected seemed to lessen as he spoke, and it was nice he asked about her. Maybe there was hope yet. "Yeah, good, thanks. I-" Her mind suddenly went blank. "Umm, did you get my message the other day about Steve not having to go to court or trial now?" As hard as she tried to sound strong and confident, her voice quavered. She expected him to carry on negatively about Steve yet again.

"Yes, I heard it."

Linda waited for more, hoping he'd at least say how good that was, or why he didn't return her call that day. But nothing came. Disappointment pulled her shoulders down in a slump. Oh well, at least he didn't carry on badly. "He's had his surgery. Doctor Thebo is pleased with how it went. He'll be down here in hospital for a while though. Doctor Thebo wants to keep an eye on him. He's had skin grafts and-"

"When are you coming home?"

Annoyance back in his voice. Obviously, he wasn't interested in hearing about their son. Her nervousness shifted gear to anger. "When *our* son no longer needs me here and that could be a while! What the hell have I got to come home to, or for, Bruce?" Silence. "Well? Answer me!"

"What do you mean? This is your home." He sounded confused, even bewildered.

"You're not the man I fell in love with and married, Bruce. I'm sick of tip toeing around you, worried I'll make you angry. And the grog doesn't help. It just makes you worse. Even since we thought Grace had died you changed. Look at the way you treated Kain! Then our son came back to us and you were okay for a while then you just carried on like he's some sort of monster with a contagious disease!" Her shackles rose. "That boy deserves a decent life and a family who love and care for him! Don't try and tell me you didn't read the article because Sophie told me you did! Did you understand what *hell* he has been through? *Our son! Our boy!*" Without warning, tears burst forth. She put the phone on the grass and dropped her face into her hands, sobbing and crying out her frustrations. Footsteps and voices went past her but she didn't care enough to look up.

After a minute or so she straightened up and wiped her eyes. She picked up the phone and was about to end the call, expecting Bruce would have hung up but a noise, similar to a cough, from the phone told her otherwise. She put the phone to her ear and tried a different, calmer approach. If that didn't work, nothing would. "Bruce, I needed your love and support when we lost Jon, and when Steve disappeared and when we thought Grace had died. You were there for me those times. We got through those things together. I need that love and support now. If you can't give it to me then there's no point us staying together." Another noise from his end. Was it a sob? The line went dead.

He'd left her hanging yet again, with no idea of what he was thinking or why. She shook her head. Why was he so bloody infuriating? Right at that point she wished she was home, with a saddled horse and could just mount and take off galloping across a paddock. One of the best remedies for reducing stress and settling the mind.

She looked at her phone, wondering if she should try and call him back. No, no point. He chose to hang up on her and not once had he called her any time she has been away with Steve. It was always her calling him. Well, no more. No point bashing her head against a stone wall. From now on she would just focus on Grace, Kain and their babies, of course. She smiled, so excited about soon having two grandchildren to love and spoil. And Sophie. Dear Sophie, always seems to be stuck in the middle. She made a mental note to do something special with her after she returns home, maybe a girls' day at a health spa. Sophie deserved it.

Then Steve. She still had to pinch herself that he was really alive and back with them. She'd do everything within her power to help him get a life back...hopefully one which Jenna is a major part. Jenna, so sweet, kind and caring. They'd make such a lovely couple. Maybe more grandkids one day...

The shrill tone of her phone zapped her out of those precious thoughts and daydreams. She glanced at the screen – No Caller Id. Maybe it was Detective Clements enquiring about Steve's surgery. She swiped the screen and put it to her ear. "Hello, Linda speaking."

"She shouldn't have wrote that article." The call ended.

The ominous warning saturating those gruff words shot prickles down her spine and turned her blood to ice.

CHAPTER 34

TWO WEEKS LATER.

Grace grabbed her bag and car keys from the kitchen bench. "C'mon slow coach, let's get going. I really want to be there when Mum and Steve arrive home." She gave Kain a gentle, but playful, shove toward the door.

Kain laughed. "Okay, okay." He put his phone in one back pocket of his shorts and wallet in the other. "My first outing. Well, since that little stint in the hospital. So glad that didn't turn out worse than one night there. And glad you haven't picked up anything." He pointed to her growing stomach. "And our precious bubs. But I sure am looking forward to getting out in some fresh air, even if it means seeing your father."

Although Grace could barely contain her excitement at seeing Steve after his surgery, the niggling feelings of apprehension about how her father would react to him wouldn't leave her gut. She totally understood Kain's attitude. "Yep, I know, but hey, don't let him upset you, you don't need that. Think positive and if he does get...annoying, just go for a walk." She grabbed his arm and gave him a hug, one that was reciprocated warmly. "You've done so well, darl, and you *look* good for someone who's just had chemo, but you still need to look after *you*." She let go of the hug.

Kain kissed her. "I look and feel good because of how well you looked after me, Grace. Oops, nearly forgot." He disappeared into the bedroom and returned wearing a cap. "Have to keep the knob warm."

Grace laughed and shook her head. "You're the knob, Kain Burrows! Let's go." She followed him out the front door, locking it behind them.

"What was it Joe said I'd be?" Kain said as he got to the car. "Oh, that's right, a roll-on deodorant."

"Silly bugger," chuckled Grace, getting into the driver's side.

"And the bonus - we save on shampoo!" Kain chortled as his phone rang. He leaned forward in his seat and pulled it out of his pocket. "Speak of the devil." He answered the call from his best mate.

"Okay," said Grace. "You chat to him on the way. Oh, I might stop somewhere and get a cooked chook and some fresh salads for lunch. They probably haven't had a chance to eat much today." No doubt both her mother and brother would be feeling anxious about what they're coming home to, so food was probably the last thing on their minds. Linda had spoken to her regularly in the past two weeks, including talking about her father and his apparent apathy over the whole situation. Any normal father would be thrilled to have his son back and no longer likely to be sent to jail. Sadly, it seemed her parents may even split up.

She couldn't blame her mum, but she'd try one more time to get some sense into, and out of, her father.

She'd also talked to Steve on his new phone. He'd sounded happy and positive too. He hadn't mentioned Jenna much, only concerning the article, but her mother had spoken about her a few times, and very positively. Seems like she and Steve were getting on very well, with Steve often speaking to her on his phone, once she'd returned to Anchor Bay. Most of the conversations Grace had with Steve were about his hospital stay, and then a few more days at a resort by the beach. This time Linda had chosen to be near the beach so she could go for walks, and Steve hadn't minded. He hadn't been to a beach in the past five years, so he had no memory of it. Grace was thrilled to hear him talk about it almost like a little kid. How he was in such awe of the waves, the smell of the salt water, the feel of the sand beneath his bare feet and the overall powerfulness of the ocean. It was as if he was beginning a whole new life. In a way he was, and she couldn't have been happier for him. It was the shining light in this strange tunnel of darkness that shrouded her family, with her father in the middle of it, blocking some of that light.

After picking up the fresh food, and with Kain still chatting to Joe, Grace's excitement grew, as did her anxiety, unfortunately. Finally, Kain hung up his phone, and had a drink of water from the bottle Grace had just bought and placed between the seats. She thought he'd need it, as he'd often complained of a dry, foul-tasting mouth during the past two weeks and now with talking non-stop for half an hour or so, his mouth would be parched. But it was good to hear him happy and laughing. Joe was a great mate and lots of fun. Plus, it would've kept his mind off the possible tension that may arise at her parents' place.

Grace turned into their driveway. Sophie's red car was near the front steps. She was to pick them up from the airport. The car doors opened. Three people got out. Grace drove closer. She gasped. "Wow, Kain. Look at Steve!"

CHAPTER 35

Steve got out of Sophie's car and looked about, while taking in a deep breath of warm, country air. It felt so good both in his body and mind. The Jacaranda trees near the cattle yards bloomed rich and full, with their stunning purple flowers covering the trees and, almost in a mirror image, the ground below them. Magpies, one of his favourite birds, warbled and marched around on the lawn not far away. He watched them for a few moments, enjoying their melodic, peaceful sound. A car door closing drew his attention behind him. He spun around. Grace and Kain were out of her car and walking toward him, both sporting huge grins.

Grace opened her arms wide. "Look at you, handsome." She hugged him tight, before letting go then patted his stomach. "This is looking good too. You'll soon have six-pack abs again."

Kain stepped up, holding out his right hand. "Welcome home, mate. You look good."

The handshake was warm and genuine. "Thanks, Kain. How are you feeling? You look pretty good yourself, for what you've been through."

Kain nodded. "Yeah, I'm going okay. Can't complain." He greeted Linda and Sophie with a hug. "You two are a sight for sore eyes. It's good to be outside again."

All smiles, Sophie and Linda got the bags from the car boot. Steve was about to take his from Sophie when an excited *yip, yip* then two paws hitting his hip almost bowled him over. He grabbed Buddy on the sides of his neck and ruffled his fur. "Hey, boy, how ya goin'? Good to see you." Buddy continued yapping, licking Steve's hands and jumping up and down on his hind feet, as much as his old body would allow. Steve leaned down and kissed the furry head. Even though he didn't really remember Buddy he felt a lot of love for this dog. There was no doubt he and Buddy had had a strong bond in his previous life.

Steve looked about and up toward the verandah. No sign of his father. In one way that was good, but on the other hand no point putting off the inevitable. His mum must have read his mind as she too looked about, concern on her face.

Grace was the one to speak what they were thinking. "Where's Dad?" More to Sophie than anyone else.

Sophie shrugged. "He was here when I left. C'mon, let's go upstairs. Don't faint in shock but I actually baked a cake early this morning and I'm hungry."

Grace and Kain got the supplies out of her car and went upstairs. Steve ascended the stairs last, carrying his and Linda's bags. At the top of the steps he stopped and looked back along the driveway. Jenna had texted and said she'd be here when or just after they arrived home. She was usually so prompt but no sign of her yet. Butterflies danced and fluttered happily in his stomach at the thought of seeing her again.

He put his mum's bag by her bedroom door and took his to his room. Voices, laughter and a bit of crockery noise came from the kitchen. They were obviously getting an early lunch ready. Sitting on the edge of his bed he pulled out his phone to call Jenna, but something out the corner of his eye took his attention away from his phone – the mirror.

He put the phone on the bed and stood. He'd seen himself after the dressings came off his face and head, but it was still quite red then and had more healing to do, but he hadn't looked in a mirror in the past few days. Not that he would look much different now, but being here, at his parents' place, in his old, but still unfamiliar, room, somehow had him thinking he may look different.

Slowly he walked the several steps and stopped in front of the mirror. A tall, bald man looked back at him. One with wider, clearer eyes that were no longer puffy slits and now with a left ear that didn't look all that much different to his right one. The face staring back at him still held a quite pale, pinkish hue but the deeper, whitish scars were gone. No straggly, greying hair hung down one side of his head. Some whiskers had grown a bit, in patches, but in a little more time, when it had healed properly, he'd shave. He pulled in his belly, not quite as big as it was when Grace had found him and smiled at his reflection. For the first time in memory, he didn't hate what he saw in the mirror. Hopefully, Jenna will like it too. He held his breath, waiting for the annoying inner voice to belittle him yet again, but nothing come. Another smile at the thought, and *hope,* he'd never have it niggling him again.

He grabbed his phone and was about to call Jenna when the dogs barked at the sound of a car. Steve rushed out to the front steps. Jenna pulled up in her small white car and jumped out, a huge smile on her beautiful face. Her long blonde hair hung loose, something he'd rarely seen as she usually wore it tied back. The hot, sub-tropical sun reflected off it, giving it extra shine. He sucked in a breath at her beauty and rushed down the stairs.

"Hey, Steve. So good to see you back home."

"Hey, Jen. It's good to be back." A slight moment of awkwardness then she rushed into his outstretched arms. He held her tight and kissed the top of her head. Her hair smelt like a summer breeze when flowers are in bloom. Breathing in her beautiful, fresh scent, he kissed her head again then reluctantly pulled back. "You look beautiful today."

She smiled, reached up and gently touched his face. His new face. "You're looking great too. I can't believe how different you are." She touched his lips. "And that big smile. I've never seen that before. It really suits you." She stood on her tiptoes, kissing him lightly on the lips, sending his stomach butterflies into a warm, fuzzy frenzy. He wanted more of those lips.

"Ahem," came a voice from the top of the steps. "Lunch is ready."

Steve and Jenna grinned at each other briefly and looked around. Grace was up there, a huge smile on her face. Clearly a smile of approval.

"Coming." He took Jenna's hand and helped her up the stairs, so pleased she no longer stopped him when he wanted to help her. Entering the kitchen behind Jenna, he looked about again for Bruce, but still no sign of him.

Linda smiled and pointed to the two empty chairs and table settings. "Sit down you two."

Steve sat at the large table and noticed the place set at the opposite end to him, then glanced at his mother. "Where's..." He still couldn't call him 'dad', even though he felt his mum wished he would. "Bruce?"

"Sophie just called him. He's out on a horse but will be back shortly. We may as well start." Linda picked up the container of coleslaw Grace had bought. "All this looks great, Grace. Thank you for thinking of this. I didn't sleep much last night so not thinking too straight this morning." She looked at Sophie. "And I can't wait to have some cake for dessert."

They enjoyed the lunch of chicken and salads, making small talk and laughter. For the first time, Steve felt *almost* like he was at home with family. His stress levels had decreased with no longer fearing police prosecution and now having some semblance of a decent face again. No longer the ugly monster who frightens children. But some worry remained, mostly his father's attitude. He had no idea what more he could do to change that.

Heavy footsteps up the back stairs. Steve stopped chewing. He glanced at everyone around the table. They all looked at each other, a little nervous. He choked down that mouthful, suddenly not feeling hungry anymore. His father appeared in the doorway, tall, his face more lined than before, and with no apparent emotion showing. Steve had expected him to look angry, but he couldn't read Bruce's face at all. He took a sip of water, hoping to swallow down the unease building in his gut. Bruce stared straight at him. Steve just nodded in acknowledgement, unable to get any words out even if he'd wanted to.

"Bruce!" Linda stood up and walked to him, giving him a quick hug. He barely reciprocated, but mumbled something that sounded like, "About time you came home."

Steve looked at Kain, knowing he'd also much rather be anywhere else than in the same room as Bruce. At least, in that respect, Steve didn't feel so alone. Kain just gave Bruce a half-hearted wave and continued eating.

"Sit down, Dad." Sophie pointed to the empty place at the end of the table. "Hope you're hungry. There's plenty here." She picked up the plate of cut up chicken and placed it closer to his plate.

Bruce looked downwards. "Thanks." He walked behind Grace and Kain, patting Grace on the shoulder but ignoring Kain.

"What have you been up to, Dad?" asked Grace, placing her knife and fork on her now empty plate.

With a deep frown, Bruce shot her a defensive look. "Nothing, why?"

Steve's stomach tightened. He glanced at Jenna, who looked uncomfortable. Beneath the table he patted her thigh in reassurance. She smiled at him, then back to her food. How he wanted to stand up and demand this angry man, his father, speak in a decent way and acknowledge his family and stop being so bloody ignorant and rude. But, no doubt, that would only make him even worse and upset the others, especially his mum who certainly didn't deserve it. How grateful he was for her unwavering support and love for him. He looked at her, as she watched her husband with wariness.

"How are the cattle?" asked Linda, still not taking her eyes off Bruce.

"Yeah, good," he replied, spooning some potato salad on his plate, without so much as glancing at his wife.

"Buddy sure was excited to see Steve," continued Linda, darting her gaze around the table, then back to Bruce. A few murmurs of agreement from everyone except the one person she was directly speaking to.

It seemed like she was hinting that *he* should have also been excited to see his son, but he just started eating, without so much as a brief glimpse up from his meal let alone a response. Steve couldn't stand it anymore. Another minute here and he'd have trouble controlling his tongue and temper. Jenna had finished her meal. "Jen, do you still want to go for that horse ride we talked about before I went to Brisbane?"

Her face lit up. Probably from relief just as much as happiness. "Yes, that'd be great."

They got up from the table. "Mum, is it okay if I ride Blaze. Which one can Jenna ride?"

Linda looked confused and a little upset. "Umm, I'll come over to the yards with you and we'll see which one suits her the best." She scraped her chair back noisily, got up and followed them out the door.

Kain got up. "I might come too. I can't get enough of the fresh air and sunshine at the moment."

Steve smiled to himself, knowing that was an excuse, but he couldn't blame Kain. Grace and Sophie would be able to handle their father and maybe, with a bit of luck, get him to talk a bit and find out what the hell was going on in his mind.

Once the horses were saddled and he'd helped Jenna up onto hers, they headed off through the gate into the open paddock. A cool easterly breeze took the sting out of the sun, making the ride more pleasant, but Steve wore his hat to protect his fragile face and Jenna had pulled a cap from her bag. Not that anything could take the pleasure away from spending time with Jenna, out in the fresh air and on horseback, two places Steve felt so completely comfortable.

Nothing much had been said between the four of them at the yards, especially about his father. It was as if each knew what the others were thinking so there was no need to say anything. He'd asked his mum if she was okay, and she just nodded with a sad smile. He knew at that moment *someone* had to try and get some sense into his arrogant father, one way or another, and that *someone* will most likely have to be him.

CHAPTER 36

Linda dawdled back to the house. Kain had said he wanted to go for a walk around the place, claiming he needed exercise and didn't want to be indoors. Fair enough, considering he'd just spent two weeks in home isolation, but she knew very well he preferred to be away from Bruce. Her slow walk and increasing anxiety in her gut had her feeling the same, even if she didn't want to. He was her *husband* for goodness' sake, but these days he certainly didn't feel like it. He'd become a stranger. A brooding, angry stranger who drank far too much beer. And one she didn't want to be near, but as Grace and Sophie's mother she had to head inside and see what was happening. She'd always prided herself on being strong and able to handle anything life threw at her – and she'd been through a lot of grief – but this situation between her husband and son was almost too much.

She stopped, looked back and smiled. Steve and Jenna were riding off over one of the undulating hills, not far into the first paddock. The horses were only walking so they'd be chatting and, hopefully, laughing. It was fantastic to see Steve looking happier and it swelled her heart to see the genuine care and, dare she think it - *love* - toward him from Jenna. Such a sweet girl.

Linda trudged up the back stairs, hearing voices from the kitchen. Bruce was still there. She stopped halfway for a moment and took a deep breath, trying to think what to say to him once she got back inside.

She pushed herself up the rest of the steps, staring out to the side, deep in thought. Bruce collided with her at the top of the stairs as he rushed out the back door. She hadn't heard his footsteps. Thrown off balance, she grabbed the handrail to stop herself falling back, but her sweaty palm slipped off. She fell back. A sharp pain hit her head. Her name was shouted. A scream from the top of the stairs, or was it from her own mouth? More pain in her knee and back. "*MUM!*" The world around her tumbled and spun. She hit the concrete at the bottom of the stairs, coming to a hard, painful stop.

"Are you alright, Mum?" Sophie and Grace's worried faces were both leaning over her when she opened her eyes.

Star sparks flew around the air above her face. This was not good. She reached up and touched her head where it hurt the most, then brought her hand into view. No blood, thankfully. "Yeah, I think so." She tried to sit up. Both girls held one of her hands and placed their other hand behind her back, lifting her to a sitting position. They helped her to sit on the second bottom step. The stars kept darting about, but soon eased. "Geez, I..." She moaned a little. "I hope I haven't broken anything." Now was *not* a good time to be holed up in hospital.

"Where does it hurt the most?" asked Sophie, her voice frantic.

Grace gently squeezed down her legs. "Can you move your legs and feet okay? I think we should call an ambulance."

"No! Not yet anyway." Linda stretched out each leg in turn, moving that foot around and up and down as she did so. She stifled a groan as she stretched out the second leg. That knee hurt, but not enough to warrant medical attention. Certainly nothing like when a cow had kicked it. "Nope, all good there." She grabbed the handrail and pulled herself up. A sharp pain in her wrist. She gasped and the swirling stars returned. Swaying a little, she grabbed the rail with both hands.

Both girls took hold of her. "Easy, Mum," said Grace.

"Whoa, bit of a blood rush there," said Linda, trying to brush it off. "Can you help me upstairs, please?"

Grace and Sophie helped her back up the steps and inside. "Do you want to lie down?" said Sophie.

"No, no, I'm not that bad, thanks. Just the lounge chair will do." Linda wiped sweat from her forehead and headed to the lounge with each daughter gently holding one of her arms. As they walked she wriggled her sore wrist, out of their view, and flexed those fingers. The pain wasn't bad enough to fear a break. That had happened during a riding accident years earlier. She'd been in a cast for weeks, but this pain wasn't near as severe, so she didn't mention it.

Sophie and Grace helped her to the large, comfortable lounge chair, placing cushions behind her back and head so she could lay back a little. Grace let go and switched on the ceiling fan. A bolt of recollection hit Linda faster than the cooler air. She looked about. "Where's your father? I think he pushed me down the stairs." The pain of the fall was nothing compared to the stab to her heart at that possibility. He couldn't even bother checking she was okay.

Sophie shook her head, tears in her eyes. "No mum! He wouldn't do that, surely. I'll go look for him."

"And I'll go get a cold pack. You must have a few bruises there." Grace left the room just behind Sophie.

Both turned toward the kitchen, Sophie most likely heading out the back door. The front screen door closed and footsteps came up the hallway. Linda stared at the doorway, heart pounding against her rib cage.

Bruce appeared and stopped. He stared at her. His face worn and weary and eyes red and watery. "Are you alright?" He dropped his gaze. "I didn't mean to bump into you. I didn't even hear you walking up the steps."

He sounded sorry but couldn't seem to say the word. Linda didn't know what to think. Was it even worth talking to him about it? Part of her wanted to yell and scream at him. Tell him to wake up to himself and stop hurting those around him, but she couldn't muster the energy. She sighed and shook her head. "Why were you rushing out the door so fast?"

Grace came back with the cold pack. "Yes, Dad, why did you get up and take off as soon as I started talking about Steve? You can't hide from the fact he is your son and our brother. And Sophie is outside looking for you."

Bruce looked from his wife to his daughter, his face expressionless. "I – I don't...want to talk about him." His face reddened. "You know that, but you started harping on and it gave me the shits." He turned to go, then looked back. "I'm glad you're okay, Linda." Then he was gone, heavy footsteps through the kitchen and back screen door slamming shut behind him.

Tears burned Linda's eyes. She closed them but didn't have the strength to stop the watery sadness. He couldn't say sorry and couldn't even refer to her as 'love', like he always used to.

Grace grabbed a tissue from the box on the nearby coffee table between the lounge chairs, sat down beside her mum and handed it to her. "I'm so sorry he's like this, Mum." She put her arm around her mother.

"You're not the one who should be sorry, Grace." Linda wiped her eyes and blew her nose. Her heavy heart dragged her shoulders down in a deep sigh. "I think our marriage is over. I can't handle being around him anymore." Fresh tears burst forth. Grace held her tighter.

"Would you like a drink of water?" Grace let her go and handed her the cold pack she'd been holding. "Where do you need this the most?"

"Probably my knee," replied Linda, stretching out the leg and putting her foot on the foot stool. Her shorts were above her knee. "Might need a bit of paper towel or something first, please love."

Grace disappeared and was soon back with some paper towel, a glass of water and Linda's phone. She handed the water to her mum and placed the paper towel on her knee before positioning the cold pack on it. Glancing at the phone she then put it on the chair beside Linda. "Looks like you've a missed call. If you're okay for a bit I'll go and find the others. Don't want Dad and Kain having some sort of confrontation. They can be just as hot headed as each other these days." She rolled her eyes and headed out of the room.

Not feeling up to talking on the phone, Linda drank all the water and placed the empty glass by the tissue box. She dropped her head back against the cushions. What a day. So many ups and downs. What could and should have been a happy homecoming has ended up a horrible mess. She closed her eyes and tried to imagine Bruce, instead, welcoming both her and Steve home with warm hugs and happy smiles.

The shrill ringtone snapped her out of the wonderful daydream. She picked up her phone and checked the caller – Detective Clements. She remembered he'd said he wanted to come see them both, especially Steve, when they'd got home, and she had kept him informed of when they would be back, but surely not right now, today...*please.*

"Hello Detective." No point making small talk.

"Mrs Atkinson, how are you?"

Geez, if only you knew how bad I am right now. "Fine thanks."

"Did you and Steve make it home today?"

"Yes."

"Is now a good time to come see you both?"

"No, sorry, not good at all. Steve and Jenna have just gone for a horse ride and I'm...I'm lying down. Bit knackered after the trip back."

"Okay, how about in a couple of hours?"

She sighed. "Does it have to be today?" She *really* didn't want anything else to deal with.

"Yes, unfortunately. I do need to talk to you both. In fact, the whole family. Some new information has come to hand and it's imperative you know about it as soon as possible."

"Tell me now...please."

A few moments of silence. "Alright. It appears you may have been right about someone stalking your son."

CHAPTER 37

Steve pulled Blaze up in the shade of a single large tree, swished the flies from around his face and dismounted. Blaze immediately dropped his head to eat.

Jenna stopped her horse beside Steve. "Why are we stopping here?" She gazed around. "It's such a beautiful, clear day. Can we keep going a bit more?"

Steve took his water bottle from his saddle bag and had a big drink. He pulled a soft cloth from his shirt pocket, gently dabbed the sweat from his face and looked at Jenna. Her enthusiasm for riding and general love of horses thrilled him. "I just thought we could have a rest here in the shade for a while. All this time in and out of hospitals has turned me a bit soft, I think." He chuckled. "I can't seem to handle this heat like I used to."

"Okay." Jenna laughed. She took a smaller water bottle from the bag she had strung over her shoulder and opposite hip, and had a few sips. "Oh, I have to..." She looked a little awkward and embarrassed, "pee." She gazed about, obviously searching for a secluded spot.

Steve pointed to a bushy area over by the creek, a few hundred metres away. "That's probably the closest place to go."

"Okay, I'll be right back." She turned her horse in that direction.

"Wait a sec." Steve walked closer to her horse.

She pulled on the reins. "What's wrong?"

"Will you be right getting off and back on again? You could ring me when you're ready to mount and I'll ride over and help you."

Jenna grinned. "It's okay, I can do it. But," she quickly added, "I *do* appreciate you offering and I *do* like you helping me these days." Her face blushed a more pinkish hue than just from the heat.

"Righto, well ring me or yell out if you do decide you need help, little Miss Independent." He loved her more and more with every second he spent with her. "I'll be here waiting."

She waved, her face beaming a huge, gorgeous smile, turned and rode off toward the thicker trees.

Steve watched her go, her long hair loose beneath her cap and flying in the wind. *Race the wind.* He felt like pinching himself to make sure this wasn't all some crazy dream. A dream from which he'd soon wake and find himself back in his former home and still at the mercy of deranged Scott.

When Jenna had almost reached the trees he turned to Blaze and rubbed his sweaty neck. "Whatcha reckon, boy? She's alright, hey?" With his heart swelling with love and happiness he breathed in deep while looking about. Cattle grazed not too far away, a gentle breeze continued to blow, and the cloudless sky a deep blue. Life was good.

He had another drink from his water bottle and looked toward the trees. No sign of Jenna emerging yet. His phone rang. Grabbing it from his shirt pocket he didn't even bother looking at the caller identity, pleased to be able to go help Jenna. "Okay, Little Miss Independent, I'm on my way."

"Steve, it's me – Mum!"

She sounded upset. His bloody father! "What's up, Mum?"

"You have to come home right now!"

"What's happened? What's he done?"

"Who? No, not your father. Detective Clements just called and said they know someone is after you. He's coming over shortly to tell us what they know. You and Jenna come home straight away, *please.*"

"Okay, we'll be there shortly. Jenna's just gone over into the bush for a nature call. She'll come out any second and we'll head back. See you shortly." He ended the call and put the phone back in his pocket while scanning the tree line for Jenna returning. He expected she'd be done by now. His nerves livened up, stirring a pot of dread in his gut. He'd give her another minute or so.

Stuff it! He got back into the saddle and headed toward the trees at a fast walk. Just in case she wasn't ready he didn't want to embarrass or upset her, but something pushed him to give Blaze a slight kick with his heels and into a canter.

Steve wasn't far off the trees when Jenna's horse came trotting out of the bush toward him, riderless and the reins dangling on the ground. He spurred Blaze on faster until he reached the nervous horse. Jumping off Blaze he grabbed the loose reins and led both horses toward the trees. "*JENNA!*" He shouted as loud as he could. "Are you okay?" No answer or sound except a few birds chirping in the trees and he and the horses walking through the grass. "*JENNA!*" Nothing. Dread and fear coursed through his veins.

Quickly he tethered both horses to a bush and ran through the trees to the creek, calling her name over and over. The calm, slow running creek looked so innocent and peaceful. Maybe she'd fallen into the water. He tried to recall if she'd ever mentioned that she could swim...or not. Scouring both sides of the bank he ran downstream a little, calling her name until his throat itched and voice became hoarse.

Steve turned and ran back upstream, past where he'd arrived at the creek, searching and calling, but no reply from or sign of Jenna. The creek wasn't deep which could be to her advantage if she'd fallen in. He waded into the water and was about to dive under when he realised he shouldn't get his face and head saturated. *Shit!* What to do?

He backtracked out of the water, called again and again, while turning 360 degrees. Still nothing. His heart dropped but anger rose, melding with the fear engulfing him. There was only one explanation and that terrified him – she'd been abducted by whoever was after him. God knows how he took her or even how the psycho found her, but that wasn't important now. He had to find her! No way in hell was he going to lose the best thing that had ever happened to him.

What should he do now? He could gallop home and get the police on to it, but that will lose valuable time and give the abductor a chance to get further away. No, then again, it's him they want, so surely he wouldn't go too far with Jenna. Call his mother? But what could she do, besides worry more?

He turned to go back to Blaze and search more of the immediate area when something red caught his eye on the other side of the creek. Jenna's bag! He ran upstream thirty metres or so to a shallower spot the cattle use to cross, raced through the water, splashing it up including on his face, and back to the bag hanging on a low stub of a broken branch. A freshly broken branch lay on the ground nearby. Quite thick, he didn't think Jenna would have been physically able to snap it off. Clearly the bag was put there for him to discover. He grabbed the bag and looked inside, not sure what he hoped to find, but seeing her phone still in it was not good. She wouldn't be able to call him. Her water bottle was gone. While grabbing her phone he also noticed her epi pen still there. Hoping like hell she won't need that he ran back across the creek with her bag.

Before he reached Blaze her phone *pinged.* He stopped and pulled it out of the bag, not expecting it to possibly be her, but hope was all he had at that moment. As he read the message ice water gushed through his veins – *'G'day*

Seth. Yes I have ur girlfriend. u want to c her again come meet me at ur fav place. No cops or ur both dead.' Around him, everything spun. His gut somersaulted and erupted. He leaned over, losing his lunch and the water he'd just drank.

He straightened up, wiped his mouth and looked toward the opposite side of the creek. The area was semi cleared with more bush on the other side of a nearby fence line. He knew that other side was part of this property but had no idea how far the road was away. There must be a gate of some sorts. He'd heard no vehicle so how did the abductor take Jenna? On horseback? Or was this bloke who took Jenna just through there and watching him? Was that how he knew when to send the text? Had he seen Steve get the bag? But if that were the case and Jenna was with him why didn't she call out? Maybe she couldn't. That thought was too horrifying. So many questions, but he had no time to contemplate the answers.

Running to the horses, he threw Jenna's bag over his shoulders the way she wore it and untied her horse. He wrapped the reins around its neck, tying them beneath and with a loud, *"HAAH"*, slapped it on the rump. The chestnut took off cantering back toward the homestead.

He mounted Blaze, just as his phone rang. Once in the saddle he fished it out of his pocket. His mum again. *Oh shit.* What to tell her? He had to think quick. "Mum!" He knew she'd tell the cop and he couldn't risk that. What the *hell* should he tell her? His mind raced with a million thoughts. None of them good.

"Steve, where are you? Are you both alright? I thought you'd be back by now." Worry mixed with relief in her voice.

"Yeah...Mum I can't talk right now." He tried to calm his voice to a more casual tone. "I'll call you back. And don't worry." He hung up, but his mother wasn't stupid. She'd know something was wrong...very wrong, but he'd deal with that once he'd got Jenna back safely. Putting the phone back in his pocked he turned Blaze around and urged him into a canter over to the cattle crossing, splashing through the water and up the other side. His phone rang again, but he ignored it. Pulling up beside where the bag was, Steve searched the ground for any sort of tracks. No sign of anything except a few tufts of grass lying over here and there. Cattle could do that as well. *Damn!*

He galloped the fifty-odd metres to the fence line. Which way to go? He recalled the message – *'fav place'*. There was only one place he could think of fitting that - his old home in the bush. This bloke must be the one who shot him, so he would know where that was. He yanked the left rein, kicking Blaze into a gallop along the fence in the direction of his former home. He leaned lower in the saddle and let Blaze have his head. "Hang on, Jenna, I'm coming."

CHAPTER 38

Linda hung up her phone after leaving a message for Steve. Hopefully he didn't answer because they were cantering back but her gut and heart weren't so confident. She tried Jenna's number, but same thing – straight to message bank. She got up from the lounge and limped to the kitchen. The cold pack had helped her knee, but any pain from the fall paled in comparison to this new and terrifying worry. Bruises will heal, but going by the previous phone calls, text and the drawing delivered to Steve in the hospital and now Detective Clements ominous words, this stalker was out to kill her beloved son, and maybe poor Jenna too.

Sophie came in the back door. "Are you right, Mum? You should be resting that knee." She frowned as she got closer to Linda. "What's wrong? You look more worried than usual." Quickly, she pulled out a dining chair. "Here, sit down."

Linda shook her head. "I don't think I can, love. Where's your father?"

"In the shed, fixing an old pump. Why?"

"Just wondered." She took a deep breath trying to calm her rattled nerves. "What about Grace and Kain? Can you go find them and bring them here, please." She then sat on the chair. "Thanks Soph."

"Okay." Sophie spun around and headed out the back door.

"Wait, Soph!"

Sophie appeared back in the doorway, her forehead creased even deeper than before.

"Just Grace and Kain, don't bother your father right now." Sophie nodded and disappeared. Linda could just imagine Bruce's reaction and it sickened her, so best leave him out of this. He'd be happier with that anyway. The hopelessness of his attitude and what it had done to their relationship ripped at her heart. It hurt like hell. Placing her hands over her chest she breathed in deep, while blinking back tears. She couldn't let herself fall apart now. No way - she had to remain strong, for *all* of them. She tried Steve's phone again, but still no response. *Where are you?!*

Linda got up and went out to the back steps, hoping to see Steve and Jenna back at the yards, or, better still, walking toward the house, smiling and happy. She looked in different directions, but no sign of them or their horses. Sophie, Grace and Kain rushed toward the house from one of the flowering jacaranda trees. Grace held one hand beneath her growing belly while holding Kain's hand with the other. Sophie strode several paces ahead of them. All three looked worried.

Just as they were almost to the house a horse neighing caught Linda's attention. *Thank God. They're back.* She ran down the stairs, trying to ignore the pain in her knee and not to bend her sore wrist.

"What's going on, Mum?" Grace grabbed her mother's arm. "What are you looking for or at?"

Linda headed toward the yards. "I need to see if that's Steve and Jenna back. I heard a horse." Muffled voices behind then both daughters caught up with her.

"Mum, tell us what the heck is going on," pleaded Grace. "Something has obviously happened since I was upstairs with you earlier."

Linda stopped and looked from Grace to Sophie, then behind them. "Where's Kain?"

"He's really tired so he's gone up to my old room for a rest," replied Grace. "Well?"

As hard as she tried, Linda couldn't hold back the tears any longer. A loud sob wracked her body, followed by another. *Keep it together.* She took a deep breath and exhaled through her mouth. "Detective Clements rang before and said they now know that someone *is* trying to kill Steve. He's coming over to talk to us about it. He wants Steve here, and," another sob, "so do I. I'm scared of losing him again." A wail escaped her lips before she collapsed against Sophie's shoulder, no longer able to control more tears." She heard gasps and sobs while arms encircled her.

A louder neigh. Linda broke the embrace and wiped her eyes. Through some blurriness she could see the riderless horse on the other side of the yards. "There's one of the horses." She rushed through a wooden gate and into the yards. Sophie and Grace followed. Coming out the bottom side of the yards, Linda held her hand out to the horse.

"Easy, boy." The puffing, sweaty horse let her walk right up to him. She grabbed the reins, scanned the direction from which it had come, and undid the knot beneath the neck before leading the horse into the yards. "Something is very wrong." She handed the reins to Sophie and climbed up two rails of the yard fence, hanging on to the top rail and gritting her teeth at her pain. She gazed over the paddocks and horizon as much as she could see. No sign of them. Her stomach rolled and mouth soured. She spat saliva on to the ground, then climbed down.

"I'll go and take off his saddle and bridle," said Sophie, walking away with the horse.

Linda just nodded, barely able to muster the mental strength to speak. A car horn beeped near the house.

"Looks like the police are here," said Grace. "C'mon mum, let's go see what they say." She put her arm around Linda's waist and they walked out of the yards toward the house.

Detective Clements met them halfway. "Hello, Mrs Atkinson. And...Grace, isn't it?"

"Yes," replied Grace. "Hello, Detective. What's going on?"

"I need to sit down." Linda pushed on to the house, sat on the back steps and dropped her head into her hands for a moment.

Clements looked about. "Is Steve back yet?"

Grace ascended the stairs. "I'll get you a drink, Mum. Would you like a cold water, Detective?"

"Ah, no thanks, Grace. Just had one in the car."

"No, Steve isn't here and I don't know where he is, or Jenna." Linda's lips and chin quivered. She sucked in her lips tightly for a few seconds to stop it, then continued. "I have tried and tried to call both of them, but neither are answering. Jenna's horse just came home by itself, with the reins tied under his neck, so it wasn't like she would've fallen off. And Steve is a top rider, he would never just fall off a horse. Something bad has happened, I can feel it." She brought one hand to her mouth to stop more quivering.

Grace came back with two cold glasses of water, handed one to Linda and the other to Sophie who'd just arrived back from letting the horse go.

"Okay," said Clements. "Let's just stay calm and take this one step at a time. Have any of you noticed anyone hanging about your gate or out on the road? Any strange phone calls?"

"Easy for you to say 'stay calm'!" Snapped Linda. "Do you have children, Detective?"

"Yes. Yes, I do." He dropped his gaze for a moment. "Sorry, I shouldn't be so clinical about it." Gazing about he suddenly looked uncomfortable. "And I'm sorry we didn't take this threat seriously when you first told us your suspicions."

"If anything happens to either of them…" Linda's voice trailed off. Her body tensed. She wanted to say more but realised it would be pointless.

"What were you told?" asked Grace. "And who told you?"

"It was anonymous, but we think it came from one of the other blokes in Mctaggart's lot, who we arrested. We followed it up, including talking to the nurse who received the box with the chilling drawing in it, and brought it into Steve's room. She described the man, but going by her description, he's not known to us, so that makes it a bit harder to find him."

Linda gasped. "I bet he was the one who shot Steve at his old house that day."

Clements nodded. "Possibly. So, where did Steve and Jenna go on the horses?"

"Just out into the paddocks. Probably to one of the creeks or dams," said Linda.

"Are there any roads into this property other than the main driveway?" Clements took a pen and small notebook from his pocket, flipped it open and began to write. "Even tracks. Something that would allow a vehicle in?"

"No, not really," replied Linda, thinking hard. "There are some gates into the neighbours over the back and a few rough tracks. Steve rode a horse that way to his old house."

"What about if Grace and I jump in the ute and go looking in the paddocks?" said Sophie.

Linda stood. "Good idea, I'll come. Grace, you should stay." She glanced at her daughter's belly. "It'll be a bit bumpy going through the paddocks. It might be too rough for these precious bubs."

"Okay," agreed Grace. "I'll keep a watch out here in case they come home from a different way. And I'd better check on Kain." She turned and went upstairs.

"What's going on here?" Bruce appeared from around the back of the house, wiping his blackened hands on a rag and, as usual, wearing a scowl on his face.

Linda's shoulders slumped, tightening her chest. Now she'd have to tell him. "Steve and Jenna are missing. Jenna's horse came back without her. Detective Clements now knows someone is out to kill S- our son."

Bruce laughed a little and shook his head. "They're not missing."

"Bruce what do you mean?" Linda strode toward him a few metres then stopped, her heart galloping. "What do you know? Where are they?"

"Calm down." He rolled his eyes and frowned at her, lips upturned as if he thought she was an idiot. "A bloke rang me an hour or so ago and said he was an old friend of Steve's, well, he said Seth, anyway he asked if he was here and said he wanted to catch up with him. I'd seen them go up the paddock on the horses, so I told this bloke where and explained where there was a track from the road to a gate into that area, so he said he'd find them. Said he had a surprise for...Steve."

"Did he say his name? Or have Caller ID?" asked Clements.

Bruce shrugged. "No, neither."

"What the hell have you done, Bruce?!" Linda's ears pounded from blood and adrenaline speeding through her body. "You bastard! You've handed our son over to a killer!" She rushed up to him, fists raised, wanting to lash out, hurt him like he'd been hurting her and Steve since he returned.

Everything around her blurred and spun then went black as *"MUM!"* echoed through her head.

CHAPTER 39

Steve arrived at the last gate into the National Park. At least this time he was more familiar with the route. Last time he rode Blaze back to his former home he'd been guided by hilly and mountainous landmarks, gut instinct and sheer hope. This time, he'd have torn barbed wire from posts with his bare hands if need be.

He dismounted and opened the gate, quickly leading the puffing and sweaty Blaze through before closing the wire gate. "Sorry boy, but we have to keep going, and fast!" Just as he was about to jump back into the saddle, Jenna's phone pinged. He pulled it from her bag, still strung diagonally across his chest, and read the message. *'Hurry Steve, your old place. He's getting impatient. I'm sc'* This time it was from Jenna, and she was frightened. *'nearly there',* he texted back, got on Blaze and took off, but the National Park was bushy and rugged in places. He was almost thrown off a couple of times as Blaze stumbled on rocks. Dodging and weaving around bushes and trees, ducking low under some branches, Steve also had to watch for steep banks near the creeks and waterways. With the wet season just cranking up the creeks were not yet full, luckily. Swimming Blaze would have only slowed him down.

In what seemed like forever, he finally arrived the back way to his former home. Letting Blaze drink at the small creek behind the house, he then rode through the open back gate straight into the yard, the grass even longer than last time, and toward the front of the house. A dirty, dark coloured SUV vehicle sat outside his closed front gate He yanked the reins. Blaze tossed his head upwards and stopped. Steve listened out. No sound except a few birds and both his and Blaze's heavy breathing. He held his breath but still no other unusual sounds.

Heart thumping, he wasn't sure what to do next. He wanted to call out to Jenna, but sitting here on Blaze made him an easy target for this maniac. Looking about, he searched for any sign of them. Nothing. *Shit!* He got off Blaze, who dropped his head to eat, and walked toward the vehicle, all the while alert and looking about. Mouth drying to sourness, his legs and knees weakened, and his gut tightened.

He peered in the open driver side window. Surprisingly, the keys hung in the ignition. Steve walked around the back of the car and looked through the tinted glass. Totally empty. This didn't make sense. He glanced up at the front door of the house, half expecting to see it open, but it was closed. Just as he turned away from the car something on the passenger seat drew his attention. He opened the door and grabbed Jenna's blue cap from the seat. It was the one she'd bought as a souvenir from their stay down near Brisbane.

He stuffed it into her bag and ran to get the house key from the post beneath the back end of the house. Racing up the stairs two at a time, he wasn't confident they were inside but had to check. Opening the door, he was again, hit by the musty, closed-up stuffiness. Gut instinct told him the house was empty, but he ran from room to room to make sure. No sign anyone had even been here.

Back out on the verandah he looked about, hoping to see *something* from this slightly higher point. A thin waft of white smoke rose above the trees in the same direction as last time, and, seemingly, in the same place. It had to be them. Running back inside he opened a kitchen drawer, pleased to find the cutlery still there. He rummaged around and found his favourite knife, a small, pointy and very sharp knife he'd often used in the kitchen. Dropping it into Jenna's bag he hurried out of the house and down the steps. He wished his pistol was still here but the police had taken it. A gunshot rang out from the direction of the smoke, echoing among the trees. He raced to Blaze, threw the loose reins over his head onto his neck and mounted, yanking him around toward the back gate. Once through the back gate he heeled Blaze on in the direction of the smoke, hoping like hell he wasn't too late.

CHAPTER 40

Linda opened her eyes to the glaring mid-afternoon sun. "Grace! What happened?"

Grace knelt before her, worry etched on her face. "You fainted, Mum. Here, let me help you." She took her mother's hand, slipped her other hand under Linda's shoulder and helped her up to a sitting position.

"Whoah. Things are spinning a bit." She rubbed the side of her pounding head. "Did I hit my head?" She looked about. "Where's your father? The last thing I remember is being angry with him. Where's Sophie and the detective?"

"Hang on, Mum, slow down." Grace handed her a glass of water. "I don't think you hit your head. Dad has taken Sophie and the cop out into the paddocks to see if they can find Steve and Jenna, mainly to the area he told that bloke he might find Steve."

"Help me up, please love." She took hold of Grace's hand and got to her feet. "Thanks." Looking past the yards, she hoped to see them returning, and more so, hoped to see Steve and Jenna riding back on Blaze. No sign of any of them. Bleak heaviness washed over her body. "How long ago did they go?" She scanned again, this time shielding her eyes from the sun with one hand, hoping a better look would have more success.

"Not that long ago. Just after you fainted."

Linda headed toward the steps. Her body swayed as if her legs were rubber. "Ohh, still a bit woozy." She grabbed the handrail just as Grace got to her and took hold of her upper arm. "I'll just sit here for a bit." She handed Grace the empty glass and sat down on the steps. The last moments before she blacked out came back to her, stirring up her heart rate. "That's right! Bruce admitted to telling the stalker where to find Steve. How could he do that!" She sucked in a tight breath. "Oh, of course, quite easily since he hates Steve so much." The same anger she felt for him before returned with a vengeance. "This is the final straw, Grace." She fought back tears. "If we lose Steve again I'll *never* forgive him!"

"Mum, we don't know for sure the person who rang Dad was the stalker."

"*Don't* defend him! Of course it had to be."

"I'll just go check on Kain. Back soon." Grace went past her mother on the steps and disappeared into the house.

Linda got up and walked away from the house again to have a clearer view past the water tanks and into the paddocks. To one side she saw the horses grazing in their smaller paddock. Perhaps she should go saddle one up and do her own searching - be better than just sitting around here. She headed toward the tack shed by the yards. Her legs still weak and wobbly, but she'd be fine once on the horse. Just as she was about to enter the tack room, Grace called out to her.

She turned to see Grace rushing in her direction. Good news? Linda strode back toward Grace. "What's happened? Have they found them?" Hope was all she had at this point.

"No, but they're on their way back, along the road. Sophie just called. No sign of Steve or Jenna." Grace sighed and looked worried. "I'm sorry, mum. I just tried to ring Steve again, but straight to message bank. But he could just be out of range."

The farm utility came roaring along the driveway, around to the back of the house, stopping just metres from Linda and Grace. Bruce jumped out the driver's side while Clements and Sophie got out the passenger side.

"Well?" Linda rushed closer to Clements, avoiding looking at her husband. "What did you find out?"

Grimness on Clements's face told her enough. "It appears there was a vehicle parked near one of the road-side gates. We couldn't find any other evidence, but the tracks were fresh in the long grass."

"So, they *have* been taken?" Linda wanted to shout and scream but somehow managed to hold in the worst of her anger. "But what about Blaze?"

Sophie shook her head sadly. "No sign of him either, but we saw horse tracks in the mud going across the creek, but we lost them a little further along, in the grass. They were heading west."

"West?" Linda sparked up. "I bet they're at Steve's old place. We should go there!"

"It's worth a try. I'll call for backup. What's the exact address?" Clements pulled out his phone and looked at Linda.

Panic almost froze her to the spot. "I'm not sure, I didn't take any notice of the name of the road."

"I'll check back with the station." Clements tapped his phone screen and walked away before starting to talk. His words weren't clear but his tone was urgent.

Bruce came close to Linda. "I'm sorry..."

"Don't waste your breath!" She pushed him aside and went over to Clements, waiting for him to finish his calls.

"Right, done! We'll go to his old house. I've called for backup and Pol Air will also be there soon to search from the sky."

"I'm coming with." Linda said. "Just let me grab my phone from upstairs."

"I'll come too," offered Bruce.

Linda stopped midway up the stairs and looked back at him, feeling nothing but disgust and contempt. "Don't bother, Bruce. If you want to do something worthwhile for once, keep searching the paddocks. Oh, and pray! Pray our son is okay. Because if he's not..." She gritted her teeth, holding back the scathing words she would much rather say.

CHAPTER 41

Steve pulled Blaze up some fifty metres from the fire. Hopefully, he wouldn't be seen, at least until he had time to assess the situation. Smoke continued rising. Jenna and a man were sitting on a log a few metres back from the fire. The man's deep voice could be heard, but his words unclear. He may not have heard the horse approaching. Jenna sat with her back toward Steve giving him no idea of her condition. Relief at seeing her still alive, at least, soon gave way to anger and worry. How could he get her safely?

He gently wiped the sweat from his forehead and stuffed the now dirty, damp cloth back into his shirt pocket. Getting off Blaze and hoping the horse had no reason to neigh, he led him several metres back to a thicket of bushes and tied him behind it. Heart hammering against his rib cage and belly agitating like his gran's old washing machine, Steve walked toward the fire and Jenna, glancing down at each step to ensure he didn't trip or dislodge something that may make even the slightest noise. Quite a few bushes and trees stood between him and them. Birds sung and flitted around in the treetops above him. Sticky bush flies danced about his face. One got between his lips. A short, sharp exhale blew it away. A mosquito, or some bug, bit his arm, but that was the least of his worries.

Sneaking closer, he ducked down a little, hoping to decrease his chance of being seen. A stick snapped beneath his boot. Steve froze, held his breath and hoped the man couldn't hear his heart pounding. The man looked around, straight in Steve's direction. Jenna also turned around. Her face pale, and red around her eyes showed she may have been crying. She didn't appear to have any injuries, thank goodness. The man stood up. Steve felt for the knife in Jenna's bag, gripping its handle. He swallowed bitter saliva and willed the man to walk toward him, prepared to jump out and grab him by surprise. He didn't look very tall, but his muscular arms and shoulders in his dirty, red tee shirt showed he'd be strong. But Steve was also strong and had the height advantage.

The man walked several steps in Steve's direction, stopped, lifted the front of his black hat a little higher and looked about. "*SETH*! Is that you?" His strong voice echoed through the bush.

Hearing that name struck Steve like a lightning bolt. The man's hands were empty, while Steve held a sharp knife in one of his. He stood upright and charged toward the man, pulling the knife out of the bag and raising it above his head, ready to drive it in deep.

The man jumped back. Jenna screamed Steve's name. Steve had almost reached him when he pulled a pistol from his hip area and pointed it at Steve. "Stop right there, Seth!"

Steve froze to the spot. He glanced at Jenna, visibly shaken and crying.

"Drop the knife!" The man took a few steps toward Steve, firmly holding the pistol out in front of him.

His nerves at breaking point and a million thoughts and scenarios rushing through his brain, Steve dropped the knife and tried to stay calm, for Jenna's sake. "What the hell do you want from me? Who are you?"

The man's serious face broke out in a grin, revealing stained, uneven teeth. "I can't believe you don't know who I am." He laughed out loud. "But you'll soon find out."

Steve looked at Jenna, desperately wanting to run to her, but knew that was too risky. "Are you okay, Jen. Has he hurt you?"

She shook her head. "No, not really. He's asked me lots of questions about you and-"

"Shut up!" The man turned toward Jenna. "You just keep your little mouth shut!"

Steve looked down at the knife and made a dive for it. A shot rang out. Dirt and grass flew up near his foot. He stood straight up, his short sharp breaths in time with his heart rate.

"Step back from the knife, Seth, or next one won't miss-" His gaze darted toward Jenna. "Her."

Steve stepped back and raised both hands in the air. "Look, you've got me here now. Just let Jenna go."

The man casually strolled over and picked up the knife. "Nice knife. Might come in handy later on." He put it through the belt of his jeans, stepped back a little and looked at Jenna. "Move over that way." He pointed in the direction of Steve's right. Jenna walked several metres and stopped, her face pale and eyes wide. "Go a bit closer to him." He nodded toward Steve.

Jenna moved closer to Steve, her bottom lip quivering. "Why are you doing this?"

"Never mind why." A smirk lit up his face. "Say goodbye to your boyfriend here. You'll never see his pretty face again." He laughed out loud again. "Good joke, hey, considering what he looks like." He looked at Steve. "Shame you had to spoil things and get your handsome face all melted and ugly."

"It was *you*?" Steve mustered every ounce of restraint he could not to lash out at this deranged human before him. "*You* burnt my face with acid!"

The man laughed again, evil and cold. "Yep. I did a bloody good job, didn't I? Oh, and how's your arm now?"

Steve frowned a moment before realising what he meant. "You shot me that day at my old house, too."

"Yep, sure did. And will do it again, only this time you won't be so lucky."

Jenna sobbed. "Please don't hurt him. What can we do for you?"

"You can get the hell out of here," snarled the man.

"What do you mean?" Jenna looked confused. "Both of us?"

"Ha! Not likely. Just you. Now *go!*" He pointed in the direction of Steve's house.

"Do as he says, Jen," said Steve, taking her bag off his shoulder and holding it out. "Here's your bag with your water and epi pen. Blaze is just over there. Ride him back to my old place." He wanted to add, *and take the car that's there and get help,* but hoped she'd realise to do that anyway.

Just as Jenna was about to take her bag from Steve, the man sprung forward and grabbed it. "Not so fast. Let me see what's in there." With one hand he upended the contents on the ground. A plastic bottle half full of water, her epi pen, phone and a few other bits and pieces fell out. The man swooped up her phone. "You're not taking this." He dropped it on the ground, grabbed a nearby large rock and smashed it to pieces.

She gasped in horror. "Why did you do that?"

Steve reached out to her, just touching her arm. "Don't worry about it, Jen, just go." Then in a whisper. "I'll see you soon." Her sad, frightened eyes looked at him with love, stabbing his heart. This was all his fault she was here in danger. *Yeah, arsehole, all you do is hurt people.* That annoying inner voice couldn't have returned at a worse time. "Go now, Jen." He gave her arm gentle push.

She limped toward the thicket where Blaze was tied. Her disability seemed worse. Before going around the thicket she turned and looked back for a moment, wiping her eyes. Then she was gone. Seconds later Blaze's footsteps could be heard then faded. At least she should be safe.

"Right," said the man. "Just you and me now. Give me your phone."

Knowing he had no service here anyway, Steve pulled his phone from his pocket and threw it over closer to the man, still holding the rock in his hand. He brought it down hard on Steve's phone, shattering the screen, before stomping his booted heel on it and kicking it to the side.

"Why don't you just shoot me here and now and get this over and done with?" Steve hated the thought of dying now that he had Jenna in his life. Six months or more ago he wouldn't have cared. But challenging the man might bluff him, or at least make him say why he hated Steve so much.

"No, no, no." The man grinned. "What I've got planned for you will be a lot more fun than that. *Then* I'll shoot you." He patted Steve's knife on his belt. "Better still, I'll just cut your balls off and tie you to a meat ants' nest." He laughed. "Wonder if they'll eat you before the dingoes find you." Another sick, evil laugh, this one more exaggerated.

Steve wanted to vomit, wanted to yell and lash into the man, but he was powerless against a pistol held by a madman unafraid to use it.

"Let's go." The man flicked the pistol and his head, indicating the opposite direction in which Jenna went. "And don't try anything stupid, or I'll go get her *after* I've dealt with you."

"Where we going?" Steve knew the national park well and hoped like hell that gave him some advantage.

"Oh, just a pretty little spot through the bush, with a nice waterfall. *MOVE!*" He jumped behind Steve and poked him hard in the back with the pistol. "Faster! It'll be dark soon."

CHAPTER 42

Linda opened the door before the detective's car had even stopped, and was out and peering into the vehicle parked outside Steve's former home before Clements had turned off the ignition. "I bet this car belongs to the killer."

"Don't touch it!" Clements was quickly beside her. "We'll get the prints off it. Backup will be here any minute." He looked at his watch. "Pol Air shouldn't be too far off now, too."

Linda glanced up and gasped. "The door is open. They must be inside." She rushed towards the steps.

Clements grabbed her arm. "You stay here. I'll go up and check."

Linda yanked her arm out of his grasp. "No, I'm coming!"

Sophie took hold of her mother's arm. "Mum, let him do his job."

Clements nodded at Sophie and pulled out his gun. "You two get back in my car, in the back seat and lay low."

Linda sighed, and for the hundredth time that day, fought back tears. When will this nightmare be over? Her legs weak and body tired, she let Sophie help her back to the car. They got in the back seat and watched the stairs.

Sophie gently rubbed her mum's thigh. "It'll be okay, mum. I'm sure they'll be alright."

Linda looked at her daughter. "I know you're trying to make me feel better, love, but we both know things are bad and-" a sob stopped her voice. She breathed in deep, trying to calm her racing heart. "And they might not be alright." She wiped her sweaty palms on her shorts. "Oh, why is he taking so long?" She leaned forward, trying to see right up to the door.

"He's only just gone in. He'll have to check every room. I'm scared too, mum." Sophie took hold of Linda's hand and squeezed it.

"Here he comes." Linda pulled her hand from Sophie's and jumped out of the car. "Well?"

Clements hurried down the stairs, putting his gun back in its holster. "No sign of them even having been in there."

Linda ran around the bottom side of the house, unsure of what she expected to find. She stopped. "Come here. Look, fresh horse poop. Steve *must* have been here." She looked about. "*STE-EVE.*" No answer, except for her echo through the trees. She pulled out her phone and tried his number again, but still no response. *Damn!*

Sophie and Clements were immediately beside her. "The back gate is open," said Sophie. "He must have went that way."

"Are there brumbies in this national park?" Clements put his hands on his hips and gazed about. "Could this be from wild horses?"

"I've never heard of brumbies being in this area," replied Linda. "It has to be Blaze."

"Look!" said Sophie, pointing toward the bush.

Linda and the detective looked in that direction.

"Blaze! And Jenna!" Linda ran out through the back gate and met Jenna only metres from the house yard fence. The other two were right behind her.

"Where's Steve?" Linda grabbed the cheek strap of the bridle. "Jenna, are you alright?"

Jenna's messy hair hung about her shoulders, sweat dripped from her red face, her lips and eyes puffy and swollen. "Not really, I've been-" She slumped forward. "Help me off."

Detective Clements caught her as she toppled toward the ground, carried her into the house yard and lay her gently on the grass. "Jenna, what happened to you?"

Jenna lifted one hand a little. "Tung." Her hand fell back down, and her breathing rate increased.

"What does she mean?" Clements looked from Linda to Sophie. "Is there something wrong with her tongue?"

Linda dropped to her knees and leaned closer to Jenna's face. "I think she means 'stung'. It certainly looks like it. She's allergic." She shook Jenna's shoulder. "Jenna, where is your epipen?"

Jenna moaned and tried opening her swollen lips, but only something indecipherable came out. She lifted her hand again, pointed the way she'd ridden and grunted.

"Jenna, did you drop it when you were riding back here?" Linda said in a raised voice, as Jenna seemed to be drifting in and out of consciousness. "Is it in your bag? Did you lose your bag?"

Jenna gave a slight nod.

"Okay, we'll find it." Linda jumped up. "Come on you two, let's look for her bag where she came riding from. It's red."

Sophie had already run out the back gate and was frantically looking around on the ground. The three of them searched. Sophie went deeper into the bush. Pretty soon, "Got it!" rang out and she was quickly back with Jenna's bag.

Linda grabbed the bag, ran to and knelt beside Jenna and took out the epipen. "Quick, Sophie, lift her shorts leg up higher." Within seconds a click of the epipen and it was done. Linda sighed in relief and held Jenna's hand. "Jenna, love, you'll be okay now." She looked in Jenna's bag. "No phone in here."

"I've called an ambulance and backup is almost here. When she comes to she might be able to tell us where Steve is," said Clements, walking back toward Linda.

Linda was now sitting on the ground beside Jenna. Her knee too sore to remain kneeling or crouching, and she hadn't even heard Clements on his phone, but that didn't surprise her, since her heartbeat pounded in her head and ears. She looked up at him, too mentally exhausted to say much. "Thanks. I sure hope so."

Jenna slowly opened her eyes. The swelling was beginning to subside. She looked about and tried to lift her head, but let it drop back on the grass. "Steve?"

"Yes, where is he, Jenna?" Linda's breath caught in her throat, awaiting the answer. "And where's your phone?"

Jenna's brow creased deep, as if deep in thought. She shook her head. Tears ran out of the corners of her eyes, down her temples and into her hair. "Man smashed our phones...and took Steve."

With a stab of pain, Linda's heart dropped to her stomach. Her worst fears had come true. "What man? Who is he?" Her heart palpitated uncontrollably, threatening to explode inside her chest.

Sophie knelt closer. "Was Steve okay when you last saw him?"

Jenna nodded.

"Do you know where he took Steve?" Linda blinked back tears yet again and tried to swallow them down. "What was he planning to do?" Her voice now a whisper and just as shaky as her hands.

Jenna closed her eyes a moment as more tears trickled down her temples. "Torture then...kill him."

CHAPTER 43

Steve clasped his hands behind his head, as ordered. He'd been walking in front of this madman for at least half a kilometre. The man had tried to talk to him, goading and teasing him, but, as difficult as it was, he knew it was best to remain calm and not to give in to him so he answered questions monosyllabic. The sinking sun glowed orange in the western sky. He didn't want to be out here after dark with this maniac, so he needed to think fast. Overhead a chopper whirred toward them. He looked up but couldn't see it for the treetops.

"Stop!" demanded the man, poking him yet again in the back with the pistol.

Steve clenched his hands together. *One more time, arsehole...* His mouth dry and gut rung out, he'd had enough. "I need a drink."

"You'll be right. Turn around."

Steve turned toward the man. The helicopter thrummed closer. He glanced up, then back at the man, whose red, sweaty face now showed worry, not a good thing in his deranged state of mind.

"I told you *no police!*" He looked to one side. "Get down here under this thick bush. Crouch down and keep your hands on your head!"

"I never told anyone, especially the cops." Steve moved slowly toward the bush. His darker coloured clothes probably difficult to spot from the air but the man's red shirt should be visible...he hoped. He crouched down beneath the thicker bush, but looked around for a stick or anything he could use as a weapon. He spotted a suitable stick to his left, and some rocks of various sizes. The man was looking toward the sky. Steve reached for the stick while keeping his eyes on the man. A crack rang out and the stick flew a little way into the air. Steve yanked his hand back and put it behind his head again, his heart banging. This man was fast with his gun. Too bloody fast.

"Don't even think about trying anything like that again, Seth." He laughed. "They haven't seen us. It's gone."

The helicopter noise lessened. Steve's shoulders sunk in defeat. He had no hope against a gun. Even if the pilot did spot them he wouldn't be able to land close by and if they tried using a loud hailer he'd have a bullet through his heart or head long before they'd find him. "It probably wasn't even the cops. Could've been anyone." Part of him wished it was the police, the other part hoped not as that would enrage the man even more. He just hoped and prayed Jenna made it safely back and was okay. If he gets out of this alive, he vowed to spend his life making it up to her. *Yeah, if she ever forgives you.* No! He banished that horrible thought. If she didn't, he'd shoot himself dead.

"Get up. Let's keep going. The waterfall isn't far now. I can hear it." Agitation in the man's voice increased, almost to a panic. He'd be even more unpredictable now.

Steve tried to stand up, but one boot slipped on loose stones. He stumbled and fell forward with a grunt, face hitting a patch of grass. He lay still, arms by his side, hoping the man would think he'd been knocked out. He had no idea where this would go, but with nothing to lose, anything was worth a try.

A hard kick to his thigh. "Get up, Seth. Don't bullshit me."

Steve's heart thumped against the earth. He slowly lifted his head. "What happened?"

"You fell over. That's not like you. Now, *get up!*" Another kick, this time to the ribs.

Air gushed from Steve's lungs. He jumped to his feet and back from the man. "Don't *ever* do that again!" He could tear this mongrel's head from his body if he could just get his hands on him. After five years of hell following the beating and acid attack, he would enjoy ripping apart this pathetic excuse for a human being.

"Ha! Like you're in any position to tell *me* what to do." The man gave a smug grin and waved the pistol around. "Now, get moving again."

Steve placed his hands behind his head again and headed toward the waterfall. He could hear it but knew the way there anyway. Surely that could be to some advantage. Before the waterfall there was a cliff, usually hidden by bushes and undergrowth, and only flowed with water after big rains. If he could get the man close enough to that cliff... He walked faster. Time and daylight were running out.

The ground became rockier, a sure sign the cliff was close. The waterfall roared a mere fifty metres away. Steve's thirst increased. The sound of the rushing water triggered his bladder. "I need a pee." He stopped and turned toward the man, who just stood there staring at him. With a flick of his head he indicated toward the cliff. "Can you go over there a bit so I can piss in peace?"

"I'll watch."

Steve hadn't expected that reply. "Do you think I have a weapon in my jeans?" If only...

"Yeah, I do, but probably not the sort you mean!" He grinned.

Steve didn't even want to contemplate the undertone of that. He turned his back to the man, undid his button and zip and relieved himself. At least he could think a little clearer without a full bladder niggling at him. When done, he did up his fly and turned back toward the man, who now had his back to Steve and was also peeing. The waterfall roared loud in the stillness of the late afternoon.

It was now or never. Steve lunged forward, tackling the man to the rocky ground. The pistol fired but Steve felt no physical pain, so it hadn't hit him, thankfully. The man let out a grunt and lay still. Steve sat astride his inert body several seconds then got to his feet, bending down and turning the man over. Bright red blood stained the ground beneath him and his clothes. His eyes were closed while the pistol remained in his right hand.

Steve reached for the pistol, but the man's hand jerked up, firing the gun. The bullet whizzed past Steve's head. He ducked and tried again to grab it. Another shot, and familiar searing pain tore into his upper arm. He jumped back and grabbed his arm, trying to stem the blood. "You bastard! What the hell do you want from me?"

The man pulled himself up to his feet, still pointing the pistol toward Steve. His hand now shaky and eyes watering, he looked down briefly at the blood on his stomach and thigh area, his fly hanging open, revealing more blood. A chilling scream flew from his lips. Birds scattered from nearby trees. "You shot me!" His reddened face screwed up then paled to a strange calm look. "You shouldn't have done that, Seth."

Steve thought of Jenna and hoped she knew how much he adored her, and his family as well, but not Bruce. He could go to hell. Any second now he himself will probably be blasted to hell as well. "Now we're even, but I didn't shoot you. Why the hell do you want me dead? Before you kill me at least have the bloody decency to tell me who you are and why you hate me so much."

More sweat dripped from the man's pale face. His eyelids half closed for a moment. He didn't look well. Sitting down on a large rock nearby, he kept the pistol pointed toward Steve. "Righto, you want to know?"

Steve nodded, with absolutely no idea of what he was about to hear. "Of course I do."

"Well, I'll tell you a little story." He licked his cracked lips and swallowed, his brow creased, and he sniffled. "Once upon a time, I was in love with someone. We had a good life." A faraway look of reminiscence shrouded his face for several seconds before it hardened to hatred. "But then *you* came along."

Steve frowned. "How could I have taken your woman." From what Grace and his mum had told him he'd broken up with his long-time girlfriend shortly before he disappeared and had nothing to do with any lady thereafter, until he found Grace, that is.

"It wasn't a woman." His eyes teared up.

Steve was totally confused. "What the hell are you talking about? Or *who*?"

"My James...or you knew him as Scott."

"What the hell..." Confusion changed to bewilderment. "What do you mean? What has Scott got to do with all this?"

"Me and him were together. But when he met you he fancied you. You were tall, good looking and he couldn't stop talking about you. I saw the way he'd look at you too."

"Bullshit! This is *bullshit*! I'm not gay and I didn't know he was either. You're lying!" Steve's stomach rolled and churned at the thought. "So you beat the crap out of me and scarred my face just so he wouldn't look at me anymore?"

"Yep, pretty much. But only, it didn't really work. He still fancied you. He was going to take you away with him." His eyes narrowed to slits and nostrils flared. "But you shot him! That day at the cattle yards? I read that it could've been your bullet that killed my James." He let out a wretched sob and got shakily to his feet, still pointing the gun at Steve. The bloodied patch on his clothing had spread. "Now, I have to kill you. That's only fair, isn't it?"

The thudding pulse of the chopper increased again, signalling its return. It *has* to be the cops, although at this point all seemed lost. Steve took several steps backwards, still clutching the throbbing wound on his arm. "There's nothing fair about any of this." He gritted his teeth. "What's your name?"

A noise further over in the bushes caught his attention. He glanced over. Several uniformed police stood by a large tree trunk with another man, maybe Detective Clements. All had their guns drawn. Relief flooded through his body, but he couldn't have the man know. He returned his gaze to him and took another step back, still hoping to coax the man closer to the cliff, now only several metres behind him.

The helicopter now a vibrating machine gun rumble almost directly above them. The man looked up. "You aren't taking me!" He raised his arm and fired into the air.

"*STOP! POLICE!*" The officers charged toward Steve and the man. "Drop the gun!"

The man glanced around, then dived for Steve, grabbing him around the waist. The weight and force of his stocky body, propelled by fear and panic, threw Steve off balance. He flew backwards, crashing to the ground, the man on top of him. He managed to push the man off and tried to stand, but the man was fast. He grabbed Steve around the legs, dragging him down again. Steve kicked out, struggling to get the man off him. Dirt, leaves and grass hit his face. Blood smudged everywhere. He tried again to stand.

The chopper pulsated overhead. Rotor wind blew gravel and leaves around, stinging Steve's fragile face. Bushes and tree branches thrashed about.

"Police! Get up!" A shot fired.

Steve was almost to his feet when his back foot slid downwards, behind him. He reached out to grab a branch, but it snapped off. He tried again, grasping another branch, but the man's booted foot shot up and rammed him in the groin, reeling him backwards, falling, crashing. Pain exploded in his head. Everything went black...a calm, peaceful black.

CHAPTER 44

Linda stood by Steve's hospital bed. He lay there, pale and motionless with tubes everywhere. One machine slowly beeped while another heaved in and out providing air to his lungs. With eyes closed he seemed at peace. Peace well deserved after all the horrors he'd endured. Not bothering to wipe the tears sliding down her cheeks, she reached over and stroked the side of his face, now scratched and bruised from his terrifying ordeal. "I love you, son. You can't leave us now."

Sophie and Grace stood on the other side of his bed, with Grace holding Steve's hand. Both crying, the love for their brother strong. "This should never have happened," sobbed Grace. "He deserved so much better."

Sophie put her arm around her sister in comfort and looked around with red, glistening eyes. "I can't believe Dad isn't here." She shook her head. "I really thought that deep down, he still loved Steve, even if he didn't show it." She sobbed loud and wiped her eyes with the already damp tissue she'd been holding.

Kain walked into the room, stood near Grace, and placed his arm around her waist. She let go of Steve's hand, turned and fell against his chest, crying into his shoulder. He held her tight with both arms and kissed her head while her body convulsed with loud sobs.

Linda lost it, letting go more tears. She couldn't be bothered trying to stay strong any longer. In the four days since Steve was rescued and brought to hospital she'd barely left his side, sleeping in the not-so-comfortable chair by his bed. After numerous initial tests, the doctors had concluded that his head injury was too severe for a positive prognosis. With no sign of brain activity, her precious son was put on life support. The only comfort was the news the man who attacked him had died from blood loss before he reached the hospital. Bruce hadn't been in to see Steve or comfort her, but she didn't care anymore. If he couldn't be there for his son in life, he didn't deserve to be there for him in death either.

Two male doctors walked in, both with grim expressions. "Are you ready?" asked the older one in a low, sad voice.

Linda looked at them then back to Steve. This was it. Time to say goodbye. "No! Not yet, *please.*" She leaned down and kissed Steve's forehead. "I love you, Steve." Her tears dripped on his face. She remained bent over, her face close to his but her view blurred by tears, desperately searching for any sign of life. "Please open your eyes. Even just move your eyelids. Come on, you can do it. Prove them wrong." After a short time waiting for a response that didn't happen, she stood upright, wiped her eyes and turned to the doctors. "Surely there must be more tests you can do. What about another scan? The last one was two days ago. Things might have changed since then. He's strong. He-" A fresh flood of tears suffocated her words.

Sophie walked around the bed and embraced her. "Mum, they've done all the tests they can. He's not coming back to us this time." She sobbed and hugged her mother tight for a few moments.

"Wait!" Jenna rushed in, with the help of her walking stick. "I know I said earlier I couldn't be here when..." Her chin quivered. "B-but I changed my mind. I want to see him again."

Linda hugged Jenna briefly and stepped aside. "Sure, love, here sit down." Linda moved the chair closer to the bed and turned to the doctors. "Can you please give us a bit more time. Let Jenna say her goodbyes."

The older doctor nodded. "Okay. We'll be back soon." Silently, they left the room.

In the hallway, staff walked and talked. Buzzers went off at the nearby nurses' station. A phone rang. A siren wailed out on the street. For everyone else life went on as usual, but not for the Atkinson family. Life would never be the same. Linda wondered if she'd ever feel like smiling again. Could she muster the strength to organise and cope with his funeral? She doubted it. Glancing from Grace to Sophie she was grateful for her two beautiful, strong daughters. They, and the twins Grace carried, were the only ones who'd get her through this terrible time.

A movement at the door caught her peripheral vision. She turned to see Bruce standing there. Her bottom jaw dropped. He took a step inside the room and stopped. His hair uncombed and greyer than ever, his hagged face unshaven, eyes bloodshot. Was he drunk? Surely not! Linda's stomach agitated as she glanced about the room. All eyes except Jenna's were on Bruce, a look of shock or surprise on their faces. The air suddenly thickened with tension and suspense. The machines the only noise. She held her breath, just as she imagined the others were doing.

Finally, someone spoke. "Dad!" Sophie walked to Bruce and hugged him around the waist, briefly laying her head against chest. "I'm... *we* are glad you came." She let go of him and stepped back beside Grace and Kain.

Linda had no idea what to say. She had no strength left for what she felt like doing -shouting at him, taking out her sadness and anger. If only he hadn't told that monster where he could find Steve. If only he hadn't been so horrible to Steve and to her. So many 'If onlys' swirled in her exhausted brain.

After more awkward silence, she stepped aside but avoided his eyes. "Do you want to say goodbye to your son? I assume you know they're turning off his machines today." Her words as shaky as her whole body. Fearing collapse, she sat back on another chair in the corner of the room.

Bruce took another step closer to Steve's bed. Hands by his sides and shirt unironed, he stared at his son.

Linda watched this once tall, proud man standing here now looking fragile and broken, shoulders slumped. A tiny piece of her ached to go to him, hug and console him, and have his strong arms around her, but she remained transfixed to the chair, wondering what he would do or say, if anything. Nobody spoke a word. Jenna remained sitting by Steve's bedside, holding his hand up to her face, her head bowed.

Bruce's downturned, tightly closed lips opened slightly. His chin trembled. A large tear slid down his cheek. He didn't bother wiping it away. Another tear followed. His Adam's Apple moved as he swallowed hard, the noise echoing around the small room.

Linda's heart thumped and her mouth dried to bitterness. She wished he'd say something, *anything.*

Bruce turned to Linda, large wet tracks down both cheeks, his chin still quivering. There seemed to be pleading in his eyes, or was she just wishful thinking? For the first time in ages she saw no anger there, only a deep sadness. She stood up, hanging on the sides of the chair.

His mouth opened a little. "Linda, I-", croaked out in a hoarse whisper. "I'm so sorry." He shook his head, clenched his lips shut again and looked at Grace and Sophie. "To you all, I am so bloody sorry." He put his face in his hands and crumpled, dropping to the floor in a sad, sobbing heap.

Jenna looked around and gasped. Grace and Sophie rushed to him, crouching down, each put a hand on his back. Linda stepped closer, unsure what to do. This was definitely not how she expected him to be. She hadn't seen him like this since Jon died, but even then he hadn't turned to the bottle. Unlike many other times of late, she couldn't smell stale beer so maybe he was actually sober. A spark of hope sped through her aching heart.

"Here, let me." Kain took over from Grace, aiding Sophie help her father to his feet.

Bruce nodded once to Kain. "Thankyou." He wiped his eyes with his hand and glanced in turn to Grace and Sophie, then keeping his gaze on Linda. "Can yous ever forgive me? Especially you, Linda." He took a step toward her, now standing so close she could feel his warm breath. "I don't know why I've been such a bastard. You didn't deserve it." He turned and looked at Steve. "And neither did Steve." His lips and chin quivered again. "I don't want to lose him again."

Jenna got up. "Here, you can sit here."

"Yes," said Linda, "Please sit down and tell him how you feel." *Even though it's too late now.*

Bruce looked at Jenna's vacated chair then to Steve. "I...I don't know if I can. I don't deserve to be here... I can't be here." He spun around and rushed out of the room.

Linda hurried out to the hallway. "Bruce, *WAIT!*" But taking long strides, he was already some distance away. He didn't stop or turn back.

Bewildered, Linda returned to the room. Jenna had sat back down by Steve and was now speaking quite firmly to him. "Steve, you need to come back to us. I have never met such a wonderful, caring man as you. I want to grow old with you. I want to learn all you know about the bush and its animals. I want to laugh with you, cry, *everything!* I love you! You just can't go." She took a deep breath and sniffled. "You saved my life! You saved me from that madman!" She squeezed his hand hard. "Don't you dare leave us!"

The two doctors returned.

A slight noise escaped Steve's throat and his lips moved a little around the breathing tube. Linda sprang forward.

"Did you all hear that?" She touched his shoulder and leaned forward. "Steve, can you hear me?"

His eyelids fluttered and slowly opened but closed again. No, it wasn't her imagination. Grace, Kain and Sophie crowded in closer on the opposite side of the bed amidst gasps and several short squeals of laughter.

Jenna sucked in a sharp breath. "He just squeezed my hand!" She leaned closer to his face. "Steve, if you can hear me, squeeze my hand again, and blink." His hand clenched around hers and his eyes fluttered open then closed again.

Laughing and crying, Linda turned to the doctors. "He's waking up!"

They rushed over. "Let us look." Steve opened his eyes and glanced between the faces. The older doctor looked at the machines, then at Steve. "Steve, can you see and hear me? Blink if you can." Steve blinked. The doctor shook his head, his face now sporting a huge grin. "That's incredible."

"Should we take out the breathing tube?" asked the younger doctor.

"Yes, please. Can you?" Linda couldn't hold back her own happy grin, and looking around, neither could anyone else in the room.

"Yes, we sure can," replied the older doctor. "If you all can just stand back a moment. But I must add, if he has trouble breathing we'll have to quickly reinsert it."

"I'll go find dad." Sophie disappeared out of the room.

Linda stood away from the bed, her arms around Jenna to her left and Grace on the right. Kain held Grace's hand. Linda held her breath, afraid to so much as blink lest she miss a moment of this amazing turn of events. This *wasn't* goodbye. Steve would be okay. Her heart swelled with love and happiness as she inhaled deeply with relief.

One doctor kept an eye on the machines while the other gently pulled the white tube from Steve's throat. He took in a breath and coughed.

Linda's breath caught and her heart beat sped up. "Is he alright?"

"Drink," said Steve with a raspy voice. He looked to his bedside table but there was no water cup or jug.

"I'll get some," said the younger doctor and left the room.

Linda rushed forward, eyes brimming over again. She took his hand. "You've come back to us. Do you feel okay?"

"I think so." Steve nodded and smiled. "Jenna?"

Jenna came to his bedside. "Hey, you. Don't you ever scare us like that again." She leaned down and kissed his cheek.

A nurse returned with some water and helped Steve up to a semi sitting position to have a few sips. She put the cup on his bedside table and rearranged his two pillows so he could remain in that position.

Steve smiled at Grace, Kain and Linda but held out his hand to Jenna. She took hold of it. "Jen, I heard you before saying that I saved you. Or did I dream that?"

She removed her glasses, wiped her eyes and put her glasses back on. "Yes, you did. It wasn't a dream."

He shook his head. "But it was you who saved me."

She frowned, looking confused. "What do you mean? I didn't save you. I rode off on Blaze. I left you." She burst into tears.

Linda put her arms around Jenna's shoulders. "It's okay, love. You were forced to. It's all over now."

Steve continued. "I mean, if I hadn't met you I'd still be a..." He shrugged then grimaced. "A mess. And if you hadn't written that article I would probably be in jail now."

"Are you in pain?" asked the older doctor. "Your upper arm has a gunshot wound and you have several broken ribs, a head injury plus some bad bruising on your shoulder and hip. You're very lucky not to have more injuries. You fell quite a way down that cliff."

Steve frowned and stared at the ceiling. His eyes closed for several seconds then reopened. "I remember now, though it seems like ages ago. That bloke tried to kill me. Did they catch him?"

"He's dead," replied Linda. "Good riddance. And it was four days ago. You've been in a coma."

"Did they say his name? I didn't know him."

"Yeah, John Allen or Alan Johns...something like that," replied Linda.

Steve looked at Grace and Kain. "Are you two alright? And how much longer 'till we meet your little ones? And when are you going to make an honest woman of my sister, Kain?"

"Mate, as soon as she'll let me," said Kain with a grin while rubbing Grace's belly. "Soon after these two get here.

We've already started making some plans, but wanted to wait for you." He kissed Grace on the cheek.

"Hey Grace, don't forget the promise you made to me when we were kids that you'd call your son, 'Steven'."

Grace laughed, then gasped. "When we were kids?" With eyes wide, she looked at her mother.

"Do you remember that?" Linda laughed, unable to believe what she'd just heard.

"Yep." Steve nodded. "I remember that and lots of other things. My first horse, Cisco. He was grey. The day I fell off him and broke my wrist." He chuckled, then coughed again.

Jenna handed him a drink of water. "Wow, you have your memory back." She put the cup back.

Steve looked about. "Where's that annoying Soapie?"

Linda laughed again, a huge boulder now gone from her shoulders. "Soapie? You haven't called her that since you were about fifteen."

"I'm right here, 'Weavin' Steven'." Sophie rushed over from the doorway, leaned down and hugged him, then stood back. "Someone else is here to see you too." She took Bruce by the elbow and encouraged him over to the bedside. He was hesitant, looking nervous, even frightened maybe.

Again, tears slid down his cheeks. "Hello, son. Welcome back." He slowly held out his trembling right hand.

Steve looked at him and frowned briefly, then smiled. "Hello, Dad." He let go of Jenna's hand and took hold of his father's.

SIX MONTHS LATER

Linda pushed the double pram back and forth, as she stood inside the beautifully decorated marquee set up beside their house. The twins, Jonathon Kain and Amelia Grace, slept soundly amidst all the fuss going on around them.

"Are they okay, Mum?" asked Grace walking over to Linda. She leaned into the pram and gently stroked each one's cheek in turn. "Thanks so much for watching them. We couldn't do this without your love and support." She looked around at caterers putting the finishing touches to the stunningly set up tables while Joe and another friend pottered about in the bar area, looking neat in their dark blue vests, jeans and white shirts. Joe's hearty laugh bobbing his brown curls about and he was the perfect choice as one of the barmen. "Everything has worked out so well, hasn't it, Mum? After all the bad things that have happened."

Linda hugged her daughter. "Sure has. And you look absolutely gorgeous – as I knew you would and it's so good that Kain is still going well with his health. Where's Sophie?"

"She's upstairs getting the last of her hair and makeup done. I'm glad the rain cleared up for today."

"Yes, me too, but even rain couldn't dampen my spirits today." Linda smiled. "Life has a strange way of turning around, doesn't it, love?"

"Sure does. Eight or nine months ago I never would've thought we'd be here like this today. How's dad been? Is he excited for today? He didn't say much when I got here earlier."

"Good," replied Linda, still rocking the pram. "No, he's been a bit quiet the past couple of days, but I think it's more reflection than anything."

"Has he had a drink yet since Steve almost died?"

"Nope, not a one. That I know of anyway." Linda took one hand off the pram handle and crossed two fingers. "He says he doesn't feel like it at all, even on really hot afternoons."

"It's so good that he and Steve have been getting on like a father and son *should*. Steve has been a lot happier these days too. He really is back to his old self. The shaved head really suits him, and his face looks good, considering how bad it was. You can barely tell one of his brows is a tattoo." Grace shuddered. "Oh, I remember what I fright I got when I first saw him after he rescued me from those wild dogs in the bush."

"Let's not even think about those horrible times. Today is a day for celebrating and smiling."

"You're right," replied Grace. "I'll go see how Sophie is going. Getting close to starting time. The men had better hurry up."

Linda watched her daughter walk away then looked down at these two precious babies. Life couldn't be any better than it was today. A hand on her shoulder startled her. She turned to find Bruce right there. "Oh! I didn't hear you sneaking up on me." She leaned up a little and kissed him, looking handsome in his suit and tie, hair neat and eyes bright and happy. The man she fell in love with.

"I'm sorry, I didn't mean to give you a fright, love." He kissed her forehead. "It all looks good, doesn't it? But not as beautiful as you look today." He looked deep into her eyes. "I'm so glad you forgave me for all the hell I put you through. And Steve." He sighed. "I'm going to miss him when he moves out." He shook his head. "I don't know what the heck I was thinking all that time. I don't even know why I hated him so much or what I blamed him for. I think I just hated myself. But at least the counselling helped me and, best of all, helped *us.*" He wrapped his strong arms around her in a warm hug. "I still can't believe I nearly lost you, Linda."

With their hearts beating in unison, she enjoyed their private moment together, so grateful things had worked out well. It took a long time, with some shaky times, but slowly they got their relationship and love back on track. Cars began pulling up. She pulled back from Bruce. "Here come the guests." She gave him a playful punch on the shoulder. "Probably your job to go greet them."

He grinned and saluted her. "No problem, I can do that." He winked at her with a cheeky smile she hadn't seen since they were young and walked out of the marquee.

Steve got out of the car by the marquee and looked around. His father stood over a bit, talking and laughing with the couple who'd just alighted from another vehicle. Kain and the other groomsman got out. Steve was glad they decided against wearing suits in this hot weather. Cool, white shirts and dark blue jeans worked well. More cars drove in.

Kain slapped him on the shoulder. "I don't know about you, Steve, but I reckon we scrub up pretty well. Can't wait to see the ladies, though."

The other groomsman walked to Steve and held out his right hand. "Good on you, mate."

Steve shook the hand. "Thanks Doctor Tim. So glad you're here."

"For the hundredth time, just call me 'Tim'." He laughed. "You're about to become my bother-in-law...and I'm pleased. I've never seen my little sister so happy."

"I can't remember ever being this happy either. I don't think anything could top today. I love Jenna so much." His chest twinged from his heart swelling with excitement and love. Butterflies danced in his stomach, but a wonderful, happy dance.

He recalled the day, two months earlier, when he'd proposed to Jenna – they'd been out riding, just ambling along, talking about anything and everything. Steve had suggested they head over to the creek and have a cooling swim. Jenna had eagerly agreed. Once they'd reached the trees, Steve stopped Blaze and got off, tied him to a branch before helping Jenna off her horse. He'd made her promise to keep her eyes closed as he guided her over further, closer to the water's edge. When she'd opened her eyes she let out a little squeal of delight at the sight before her. Linda had helped him set up a picnic rug with all the trimmings, including a bottle of champagne and two glasses. While Jenna was still in awe he pulled the little box from his pocket, dropped to one knee and proposed. Without hesitating, she'd said *YES*. He'd stood up, swooped her up in his arms, swung her around and laughed as tears flooded his eyes. When he's set her back down, she was also crying tears of happiness. That day, they'd enjoyed their first love making, and had drifted off on the rug, blissfully comfortable in each other's arms.

It'd been the most amazing day as today would be. The thought of loving and cherishing her for the rest of his life, was something he'd never dreamed possible for a long time. They hadn't found their own home yet but were content to live here until they found something suitable. He enjoyed working on the property again. He'd been hesitant at first, fearing he and Bruce would clash too much, but to his surprise they'd got along just fine, with virtually no disagreements. A few appointments with a psychologist had also helped him come to terms with his past and present life. He'd remembered leaving home, shattered after his long-time girlfriend had broken off their relationship, and fed up with his father's constant negative attitude toward him, but beautiful Jenna had erased all that hurt. So far, he'd compensated the farmer whose horses he'd been forced to shoot for Scott, part monetarily and partly by breaking in some horses for him. He'd told the police about the man buried by the stockyards. Jimmy had backed up that the horse had killed him, and they were too frightened of Scott to tell anyone. It hurt deep in his heart that he'd lost his beloved former home in the bush, but realised he was still the luckiest man alive.

"C'mon, mate, let's get up there. Here she comes." Kain took hold of Steve's elbow and headed to the area in front of many white chairs decorated with large cream-coloured ribbons and bows, set out in the shade of the shed. "Nervous?"

Steve laughed. "Nope. Let's go. But I'm looking forward to seeing you as a groom very soon."

"Me too, mate," replied Kain, walking beside Steve. "If you hadn't beat us to announcing your engagement it'd be Grace and me tying the knot today instead of two months' time." He chuckled. "At least she has got a proper engagement ring now."

"We could've had a double wedding."

"Nah, mate. You and Jenna deserve to have your own special day."

The three men of the bridal party stood side by side in front of the celebrant. Steve glanced back and almost lost his breath at the sight of pure beauty. Jenna rode up on Blaze, from the other side of the shed. Her hair done up with Babies Breath flowers, and wearing a lacey, cream dress. When she'd almost reached the gathering of seated guests, her parents went to her. Her mum held Blaze's reins while her dad helped her off. The guests got to their feet. Grace and Sophie, gorgeous in their royal blue dresses, walked over and stood in front of Jenna.

Jenna's father led Blaze to the shed where he tied him for the ceremony, then hurried back to his daughter, already holding out her hand to take his arm. Soft music began to play. Steve wiped a tear from each eye, his cheeks now hurting from the smile he couldn't erase even if he wanted to.

Jenna smiled all the way up to him and giggled when she reached him. "I'm nervous", she whispered. "Are you."

"No," said Steve, taking her hands in his. "Just really happy."

The female celebrant welcomed everyone and went through her words. Once Jenna and Steve had said their own, short but loving, vows, the celebrant said with a huge smile, "I now pronounce you husband and wife." She looked at Steve. "You may now kiss your bride."

He leaned down to kiss Jenna, but she stopped him by placing her finger on his lips. "Not just yet," she said softly. "I have something to tell you."

Steve frowned, glanced around at the guests and back to her. "What?"

She took his right hand and placed it on her belly. "We're going to have a baby."

Steve's shoulders jerked up and his body stiffened as his eyebrows shot skywards. "A... *A BABY*!?"

The crowed oohed and ahhed, followed by joyous clapping and cheering.

"Yes," continued Jenna. "I'm pregnant."

Steve *whooped* with delight, grabbed her around the waist and picked her up in a massive bear hug, laughing as he did so, but momentarily lost for words, so gave her the biggest kiss he could. "I love you, Jen."

"I love you too." Another big squeezy hug and more tears of joy.

The guests milled around, each embracing the newlyweds on both their marriage and the wonderful baby news. Once everyone had settled down, Bruce and Linda ambled over to Steve and Jenna.

Linda hugged both. "I am so thrilled for you two, and I can't believe another grandbaby is on the way." She wiped her damp eyes.

"Me too," said Bruce, stepping up and slapping Steve on the back then hugging Jenna. "Welcome to the family, Jenna." He pulled an envelope out of his shirt pocket. "Steve, your mother and I have something for you both." Bruce handed him the envelope. "It's our wedding gift to you."

Again, Steve frowned, glanced at his mum then to his father, and to Jenna, who looked as confused as he felt.

"Well, come on, open it," urged Linda, her beaming grin almost splitting her face.

Steve ripped open the envelope, unfolded the piece of paper and read it. His eyes widened and chest tingled. He reread it, before looking back at his parents, both smiling excitedly. "I...I don't know what to say. How...?"

"It took some wrangling," said his mum, "and a bit of rigmarole and some frustration when we didn't think it was going to happen, but at last we got the good news two weeks ago."

"And it's been bloody hard keeping it from you," chipped in his dad.

Steve's hand trembled, shaking the paper it held. "I can't believe it." The words choked past the lump in his throat. "Is it really true?"

Linda laughed. "You bet! You now have your old home back. It's yours and no one will ever take it from you again."

ACKNOWLEDGEMENTS

This novel took me just over seven long years to complete and publish, due to my life being cruelly interrupted by breast cancer in late 2017 and all the associated surgeries and treatments. Some have left me with long term physical and cognitive side effects, so getting my foggy brain back into writing mode hasn't been easy. Firstly, I must thank friends and readers who have patiently waited for this sequel to "Secrets, Lies & Grace". If it hadn't been for you supporting and encouraging me I may have never got it finished. Many times I did think I would never complete it so the moment I wrote that last sentence I 'Yahooed & Yippeed', jumped around, laughed and cried with momentous relief and absolute pride in myself. My amazing and supportive daughter, Ayla, was here at the time and was equally proud and joyous.

I must thank the lovely Christine Shirley for her painstaking and thorough job of proofreading. I had gone over and over it, but she picked up the things I missed, finding more than I expected she would.

Thank you to the talented Willsin Rowe for his amazing cover design. I gave him a basic idea of what I wanted and he nailed it first go. Love it.

A huge Thank you to fellow local author, Selena, who shared her range of knowledge of the Indi Publishing world and helped this old girl learn some of the finer points of self-publishing. You can find out more about her and her books at www.srsilcox.com

Thank you to my wonderful friend, Dannielle, owner of 'The Book Boutique' in Bundaberg, who not only stocks my books, but has loved each of them and has helped and encouraged me along this journey. Her bookstore/coffee shop is a treasure trove of new and second hand books, gift lines, vinyl records and comfy chairs in quiet areas to relax. Check out her shop's Facebook page for different artistic events she often holds there.

Lastly, thank you to my beautiful family and friends for your continued love and support.

AUTHOR BIO

Julie McCullough enjoys life on her small farm at Rosedale, Qld, where she endeavours to be as self-sufficient as possible. She has two house cows, lots of chooks, three ducks, two cats and a dog plus numerous fruit trees and a huge vegie garden.

Writing has been her passion since high school, and she has had non-fiction articles and short stories published as well as novels, this one being her fourth. She loves to write Aussie Rural Suspense fiction, tapping into some of her own past experiences of life on the land.

You can find out more about Julie and her books or contact her through her website www.juliemccullough author.com